Gregory Benford is a professor of physics at the University of California, Irvine, a Woodrow Wilson Fellow and a fellow at Cambridge University, and an advisor to the US Department of Energy, NASA and the White House Council on Space Policy. Dr Benford is also one of the most honoured authors in science fiction. His many novels, including the classic *Timescape*, have won two Nebula Awards, the John W. Campbell Award and the United Nations Medal in Literature.

Find out more about Gregory Benford and other Orbit authors by registering for the free monthly newsletter at www.orbitbooks.co.uk

D1225863

By Gregory Benford

FOUNDATION'S FEAR
COSM
THE MARTIAN RACE
EATER
ARTIFACT

By Gregory Benford and Arthur C. Clarke

AGAINST THE FALL OF NIGHT/
BEYOND THE FALL OF NIGHT

By Gregory Benford and David Brin

HEART OF THE COMET

ARTIFACT

GREGORY BENFORD

orbit

www.orbitbooks.co.uk

An *Orbit* book

First published in Great Britain by Orbit 2001
Reprinted 2002 (twice)

Copyright © 2001 by Gregory Benford

A CIP catalogue record for this book
is available from the British Library.

ISBN 1 84149 062 8

Printed and bound in Great Britain
by Mackays of Chatham plc, Chatham, Kent

Orbit
An imprint of
Time Warner Books UK
Brettenham House
Lancaster Place
London WC2E 7EN

The past isn't dead.
It isn't even past.

—WILLIAM FAULKNER

ARTIFACT

PROLOGUE
Greece
[ca. 1425 B.C.]

They buried the great King as twilight streaked the west crimson.

Inside the tomb the holy men were placing the oiled and waxed body. The procession paused. A hawk spiraled overhead, hovered, then plunged toward prey. The village below was a disorderly brown jumble. People stood in its streets, watching the zigzag of torches scale the hillside.

Inside, the ritual party was enclosing in the tomb walls the severely fashioned stone. It was a miraculous thing—humming, giving an unceasing, eerie glow through the amber ornament. The abode of a god or a demon beast.

Some in the procession said it should be kept, worshiped, not buried with the King. But the King had commanded this placing in the tomb. To protect his people from the fevered, blotchy death, he had said.

A hollow shout. Commotion from the tomb. Men came running from beneath the high lintel, their eyes white, mouths gaping.

"Death from the stone!" one of them shouted.

Ragged screams.

"Close it!" a high priest called loudly near the entrance.

Heavy wooden doors swung inward.

"No! My son is in there!"

"No time!" the high priest yelled. "Those the thing struck down, leave them."

"My son, you can't!"

"Seal it! Now!"

The massive doors banged shut. Priests slammed home the thick iron bars. Then the teams above began to fill in the long entrance hall with sand, as planned—but now they shoveled frantically, driven by black fear.

The high priest stumbled down the hillside, wild-eyed, shouting to the milling throng: "The men were easing the concealing slab into place when it happened. They hurried, mortared in the slab. But some . . ." He gasped. "It is for the best. They are all gone from us now. The people are safe. As our King willed."

The laboring teams above filled the entranceway frantically, tipping reservoirs of sand into the deeply cut passage. Soon it would seem like an ordinary hill, the tomb concealed.

"No! Please! I beg you, open it for but a moment. I will bring out—"

A tired wisdom filled the priest's lined face. "The thing has gone back to the underworld, where the King found it. We must leave it that way. It will harm men no more."

PART
ONE

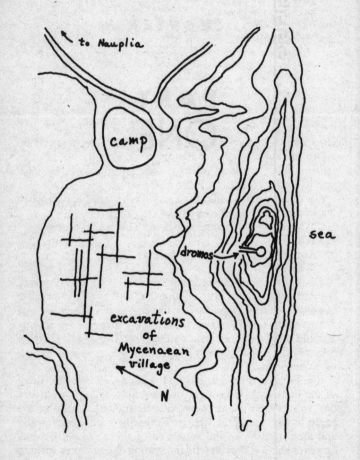

CHAPTER
One

Deep inside the tomb they barely heard the snarl of an approaching vehicle.

"That'll be Kontos," George said, putting down his calipers.

"It doesn't sound like his car." Claire carefully punched her computer inventory on HOLD.

"Who else would come out here? That union moron?"

"Possibly."

"Come on, I'll bet you it's Kontos."

"Wait a sec."

Claire shut down the inventory program. She was checking the last catalog numbers of potsherds against the printout manifest, a tedious job. The computerized field inventory was a marvel, neatly organizing six months of archeological data. It could be hypertexted and correlated with a single keystroke. Scarcely the size of a water glass, it carried six months' worth of archeological data.

She brushed off her hands and walked out under the lintel of the huge stone doorway, into the midmorning sun. Every day was slightly cooler now and she thought fondly of the green bowers along the Charles River, the silent glassy water and crisp red brick. She was tired of the colors of Greece, however sharp and exotic. Inland, young cypress trees speared the pale sky. The heat haze of summer was gone and she could make out distant dry canyons that sloped toward the Aegean. Empty stream beds carved bone-white curves down the spine of each canyon, shimmering like discarded snake skins.

High above, a hawk lazed on thermals rising from the sea. Shading her eyes against the glare, she pondered how irrelevant the narrow valley would look from up there—tawny hills crisp from the drying winds, a gray grid of the Greek-American excavation, brown rutted paths worn by the digging crews, all bordering a sweep of steel-blue sea. Or perhaps the hawk glided above such signs with indifference, much as when the stone walls sheltered a living, vibrant race. Man's strivings would seem like mere background noise from up there, compared to the squeak and rustle of prey.

The hawk banked and began a descending gyre, intent on essentials.

She started down the rocky path. A jeep braked noisily to a stop several hundred meters away, where the dirt road met the work camp. A plume of tan dust enveloped it.

"So he's got a dapper little jeep now," she said.

"Very fashion conscious, is the Colonel."

As they descended she heard quick, agitated talking. From his tone she identified Doctor Alexandros Kontos, the Greek co-director of the dig, well before she could recognize him standing beside the jeep. He was speaking rapidly and angrily to the "camp man"—a weathered brown figure who stood and took the abuse without blinking.

Kontos did not glance up at Claire and George as they wound their way down the hill among the few remaining tents of the camp, and approached the jeep. Claire could not follow all the colloquialisms and rapid-fire slang that tumbled out of Kontos, but it was clear that he blamed the camp man for the absence of the manual laborers. His target merely shrugged, explaining that the men were either involved in the spreading political meetings and demonstrations, or afraid to work for Americans out of fear of disapproval by their friends, or both.

Kontos slapped his hand on the jeep in exasperation. "Get them back!" he shouted in Greek. Then he saw Claire and his manner abruptly changed.

"Ah! The lovely Claire. I hope the absence of these ignorant peasants has not perturbed you."

"Not at all. We didn't have a great deal of work left when—"

"Excellent. Great things happen in Athens and I will not have time for this site now. It is well you be on your way."

"What things?" George asked.

Kontos' face altered as he turned to George, the strong jaw jutting out more. "Nothing you would approve, that I am sure."

George grinned wryly. "Try me."

"The divisive times, they are finished. The center parties, they come over to our side."

"What'll you end up with? A one-party state?"

"True socialism."

"And the other parties?"

"In time they follow."

Kontos was wearing a smartly tailored Army uniform that showed off his thick biceps and bulging chest very well. His hat, with freshly shined braid, adorned a full head of gleaming black hair. The long, somewhat sallow face was saved from thinness by the interruption of a bushy moustache. His tan almost concealed the fine webbing of lines at the eyes that gave away his age—mid-forties, Claire guessed—better than anything else.

George said blandly, "No doubt."

"This is why I must break off my stay here with you." He turned to Claire and his face brightened again. "It will be a sad thing to be parting. Very sad."

Claire said, "But there's still work to finish!"

"I will get the laborers back. This lizard"—he jerked a thumb at the camp man—"will stop lying in the sun. He will go to the village, round them in."

"There's chemical analysis, some soil studies, on-site metallurgy—"

"*Ohi, ohi.*" He shook his head violently. "That we do in Athens."

"Who will? I know—Ministry lab techs. But they haven't visited the site, they don't know everything to do." Claire defiantly put her hands on her hips.

"You will write instructions."

"There are always idiosyncratic features, samples that have to be treated differently. There's no replacement for being—"

"Your Greek is excellent," Kontos said smoothly in Greek, smiling. "They will understand."

George put in, "Come on, Alex, soil analysis is in the schedule, you can look it up."

"A secondary consideration now, this schedule."

"It was agreed!" Claire said. "We have nearly a month left."

"*Ohi!*" Kontos narrowed his heavy-lidded eyes—the expression, Claire saw, that had produced the crescent lines that fanned back from his eyes almost to his ears. In English he said sharply, "These are not treaties or contracts, these schedules. They can be withdrawn."

Claire began, "The soil sampling is—"

"I never like that sort of thing, me. Seldom it yields anything in digs of this sort."

George began, "Well, so much *you* know. There's plenty here you don't—"

"I fail to understand, Alexandros." Claire overrode George's rising tone, trying to keep the discussion within bounds. It always helped to call him by his full name, for one thing; Greeks were funny that way. "Why the speed?"

Kontos leaned against the jeep, and noticed the camp man again. He waved a hand of dismissal. "We are trying to, you say, pedal softly this kind of thing."

"*What* sort of thing? Archeology?"

"No no. Co-operative endeavors."

George said sourly, "Uh huh. So the Ministry is putting the same hustle on the French down in Crete and those Germans up north?"

Kontos looked stonily at George. "Not precisely."

Claire said, "So this policy, this soft-pedaling, it's especially with Americans."

"I did not say that."

George said hotly, "It's what you mean."

"The Ministry has sent a *tilegraphima*, a cable, to Boston University—"

"What!" Claire stepped back.

"It asks, to terminate quick as possible this dig."

George said sarcastically, "Gee, I wonder who asked the Ministry to do that."

Kontos reddened—but not with embarrassment, Claire saw—with anger. "Decisions are made collectively!"

"Uh huh. Who decided you'd come back in a jeep?" George asked.

"I was issued it. I am an Army officer, I am entitled."

George drawled, "Interesting, how they're making all the Ministry staff Major This and Cap'n That."

"Our society, we mobilize. The depression your country and the others, the Japanese, the British, brought on—we respond to that."

Kontos stood rigidly erect, moving his body consciously to confront George—arms slightly forward of the chest, chin up to offset George's two inch advantage in height. Claire decided to step in and deflect the two men, who were now staring fixedly at each other with growing hostility. She said brightly, "George, get back to closing up the tomb, would you? I hate leaving it open like that, nobody around."

George looked at her blankly, still wrapped in his tit-for-tat with Kontos. "Close. . .up?"

"Yes, right. I want to show the Colonel some of that pottery."

George said nothing. In the strained silence a bird suddenly burst into full-throated song from a nearby oleander bush. Claire lowered one eyebrow in what she hoped was a clear signal to George. He saw it, and swallowed.

"I think we're gettin' the bum's rush here," he said bitterly. He stalked off, occasionally glancing back over his shoulder at the two of them.

Kontos murmured urbanely, his composure returned, "That one, he has a hot head."

"You weren't the soul of reason yourself."

He sighed heavily. "I am subject to pressures. You understand, you speak our language, that must bring some knowledge of the way we think. Come." He gestured and they walked into camp. "This cable, it is necessary to—how is it? In diplomacy, they say—to send a signal."

"To whom? You could tell *us* right here."

"To the people who rule you, though you may not know it, Claire."

"Boston University doesn't precisely 'rule' me, Alexandros."

"*Ohi, ohi.* Your government. The men behind it. And those

who act for you at the International Monetary Fund. They oppress unfavored nations like ours."

"One little joint expedition—"

"It will be felt. Diplomacy is subtle, my dear."

As subtle as you? Claire thought derisively. But kept her face impassive.

They reached the pottery sorting tent. He held the flap for her with a formal, sweeping gesture. They ducked into its yellowish aura of collecting warmth. "Iced tea?" Claire offered, opening their tiny refrigerator.

He nodded. "I hope you see this was not policy I made."

"You had a hand in it."

He shrugged. "I assure you, I mean nothing bad to you."

"Sure," Claire said sarcastically before she could catch herself. George had pretty well proved that approach didn't work.

"I did not! Not to such a fine, lovely woman? Impossible, for a man, for a Greek."

"All those who are not Greeks are barbarians?" Claire asked lightly, pouring the tea and sitting at a sorting table. Bits of pottery were arrayed according to size, curvature, glaze and other properties on the tabletop grid. Automatically her eyes strayed over the pieces, searching for connections, fragments that might meet. The past was a jigsaw puzzle and you never had all the pieces.

Kontos smiled broadly, liking this shift in the conversation. "Me, I do not think like Aristotle. My foreign colleagues are very close to me." He demonstrated by touching his chest.

"Not so close you would go to bat for us with the Ministry?"

He smiled, puzzled. "Go to bat for. . .?"

"Support us."

He spread his hands expressively. "One mere man cannot do the impossible. We are civilized."

"Then why don't we start being civilized, by sticking to our agreement."

Kontos sighed theatrically and sipped his tea. "You appreciate, mine is only one voice. Still. . .I might be able to do something."

"Good."

"Only, you understand, because of our personal relation.

You are a charming woman and I have very much enjoyed working with you on this site. Indeed, the abrasions from such as George and the other Americans—they are not like you. They cannot see out of their little boxes, do not see the world as it is becoming."

"There is some truth to that," Claire said politely. Her years of experience in the Mediterranean had prepared her for the steady leftward drift in Greece. The American press now had prepared her for Greece's hardening stance. The economic slide of the late 1990s had been worse along the eastern Mediterranean. Robotization in Europe had sent Greek laborers home, where they became a disgruntled irritant, calling for stronger measures. The centrist parties had little to offer them. Gripped in another chronic financial crisis, the US-backed International Monetary Fund was not likely to bail out any Greek government. There was little support from northern Europe, which had yet to stop its slow, lazy slide that began in the late 1970s. The only northern Mediterranean power which was doing well was Turkey, still on bad terms with its ostensible NATO ally, Greece. With a bemused fatalism Claire had watched the Greeks form coalition governments and juggle parties; she cared little for conventional politics, and Kontos's news was only confirmation of what she had long expected.

"You have been the solitary good spot in this summer. You are a lady, a true scientist, and it has been delightful."

Claire never felt quite at ease fielding bald-faced compliments. "Ah, thank you, but—"

"Our friendship, it is the only element I shall miss if the site is closed this week."

"This *week?*"

"*Ne.* Of course. That is what I say to the camp man."

"Impossible."

"Necessary, however. There are forces in our government who would like to create an incident, with this as a pretext."

To Claire's look of disbelief he nodded slowly, sadly. "It is so."

"This is an internationally agreed-upon expedition, we have all the papers, we have every right to—"

"You are also unpopular with the surrounding villages."

"Who says? Why?"

"You are Americans."

"I was in Nauplia just the other day. The shop people were just as friendly as ever."

"Oh, they, yes. They depend on your money."

"Alexandros! You're not seriously suggesting that the villagers share the ah, exaggerations. of that bunch in Athens? They don't—"

"You do not know the *souls* of these people, Claire. They are enraged at what years of deprivation have—"

"I don't believe it."

He said quietly, "Your laborers have left, *ohi?*"

"And who instigated that?"

"Local unrest, the workers . . ."

"If there were the slightest element of truth to this, *your* duty would be to protect the site."

Kontos brightened. "So it is. I post a guard here. You will return to Athens."

"But my work is here!"

"You can supervise the laboratory people in Athens. George can remain here to complete what is necessary."

"I don't like that arrangement. We've *got* to finish, there is the excavation behind the tomb walls—"

"I offer this as a friend. Not as negotiator," Kontos said mildly, folding his hands before him on the table. "To get the Ministry to approve even this, I will have to pull ropes with the correct people."

"Pull strings?"

"Whatever the phrase."

Kontos had clout, yes. He had made his international reputation on the expedition which dove for the Elgin marbles. The famous set in the British Museum was actually the second shipment by Lord Elgin; the first had gone down at sea. Kontos and several of his countrymen had mustered money and experts to recover the priceless, striking stoneworks. They were now the highlight of the Athens Museum. Whatever Kontos said was now law in the small world of Greek archeology.

"Listen, Alexandros—"

"No, do not talk this way." He stood and walked around the table, and stopped beside one of Claire's partially assembled bowls. He glanced only a moment at the shards, though she knew he had done his doctoral work on just such routine work. That was far behind him now. She caught a faint aroma of him, a heavy musk.

"Look, I've found—"

"So much business, no no," he said, smiling broadly.

Claire's eyes narrowed. *If he interrupts me one more time I'll scream*, she promised herself.

"I do not want our dealings to be so, so formal, Claire. We are special friends, we can work out this." He put his hand on her shoulder. "Colleagues, of course. But more than colleagues."

Claire sat still, not sure she understood him.

He continued suavely, carefully, "It will cost me influence and time, you know, to do this."

"I certainly appreciate anything you can—"

"I hoped you might come to Athens, where we can grow to know each other better."

"I think we already know enough."

He began to knead her shoulder. "Claire, these matters, they require time."

"*What* matters?" She looked up sharply. He was speaking from over her shoulder, making it awkward to confront him. *Perfect*, she thought. Much easier for her to bow her head and shyly go along with him.

"Between us—"

"Between us there is nothing more than professional courtesy!" Claire said sharply. She jerked away from his still-kneading hand and stood up quickly, backing away from him.

"I do not think that," he said serenely, "and neither do you."

"So now you know what I think? 'Little unsophisticated American, doesn't know her own mind, needs a sure hand, some quiet instruction in the delicate arts?' " She snorted.

But he still stepped forward, using the imposing bulk of his shoulders beneath the crisp uniform, his hands waving slowly to dispel this sarcastic torrent, a coolly condescending smile playing artfully at the edges of his lips.

She grimaced and said loudly, "Maybe she just needs a little Old World *cock*?"

This had the desired effect. He halted, mouth twitching in a spasm of offended irritation. "That is. . .insulting."

"Damn right!"

"Your understanding is—"

"I understand perfectly."

"You are quite. . .American."

"Do you know what you just tried to do?"

"I think so. I am not so sure you know."

She said sternly, "You're willing to give us more time if I'll come to Athens, set up there"—her eyes widened—"I'll bet you have a little hotel room reserved already, don't you? Something near the Ministry, out of the way? An easy walk during a long lunch hour? Or suitable for a stopover, on the way home to the wife in the evening?"

He stiffened.

"I'm right, aren't I?"

"You are a child."

"Maybe, by your definitions," she said quickly, feeling the wind go out of her sails. Had she mistaken the situation? No . . .but already, despite herself, she was replaying her reaction, seeing it as too harsh, too offensive.

"I offered a compromise, a bargain between scholars. I cannot help it if my own feelings become mixed in."

"You'll have to separate them," she said coolly.

He spread his hands in a Mediterranean gesture of acceptance. "I cannot divide myself beneath the knife."

"Well, it's no deal, got it?"

"You do not—"

"I'm not going to become your little poopsie just to wring a few more weeks out of this dig."

His face flushed. "You cold bitch!"

"Cold, huh? Ever think it might be your technique?"

His face congested with rage. She felt suddenly the compressed force of the man, and saw she had gone too far.

He stepped forward, fists clenched.

She cringed back for an instant, then impulsively stepped to the assembly table and picked up a pot. It was nearly complete, carefully glued. She held it up precariously in one hand.

"Come closer and I'll drop it."

"You . . ." He swore in Greek.

Kontos was still an archeologist, even though he had spent most of this dig playing politics in Athens. His early professional days, spent laboriously piecing together shards, still meant something to him.

Or so she hoped.

A long moment passed. Then something changed in his eyes.

"Take your hand away from the heritage of my country," he said stiffly.

"Heritage?" She restrained a laugh. The man's moods were incredible.

"You are here with our consent."

"True enough."

"And I will not tolerate your. . .insults."

He spat into the dust.

"Alexandros—"

He jerked the tent flap aside and left without looking back.

CHAPTER
Two

Just before noon they found something odd.

Claire was busy, trying to tie up a thousand straggling ends. She did not notice George Schmitt trotting up the dusty path until he called, "Hey! I got the slab out."

She looked up, brown eyes wide with disbelief. "*Out?* You were supposed to check the mortar, period."

"I did. It's only a couple inches deep. So's the slab."

She shook her head and stepped outside the tin-roofed sorting shed. "You were supposed to see if the center slab was different, right? Not pry it away from the wall."

"Yeah, but it was easier than we thought."

"With that piece missing, the whole damned dome could collapse."

He grinned, blond hair glinting in the slanted sun of crisp morning. "I've got the hole braced real well. Crowbars, steel and wood. No big deal, anyway—the slab's only five centimeters thick."

Claire grimaced. "Come on," she said tensely.

I should've known better than to let him do it alone, she thought. It would be a miracle if his brace held, considering the lintel support he had put up several months back. The local workmen had to start over from scratch on that one. If only the damned Greeks weren't off on this strike, she'd never have let George touch such a tricky job.

Kontos was deliberately keeping the men away now, she was sure of it. He had returned to Athens in a foul mood,

all measures in meters

frontal view -- cross section
at time of discovery (see initial report)

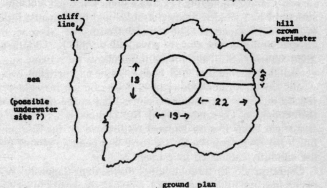

ground plan

and was probably pulling the strings in the labor unions of the nearby towns.

But strikes came so often now they had gotten used to working around them. This strike was a protest, saying the archeologists ought to hire more workers, rather than put the present laborers on overtime when it was needed. A curious kind of solidarity; usually people simply asked for more money.

They went along the worn path around the hillside, scuffing up dust. A lone cypress tree held out against the odds, a freak green richness amid the rough scrub. Claire liked the fresh scent of it, and habit made her glance up toward the distant hills where files of trees cut the horizon. Until the fall rains came the countryside would not truly begin to recover from the searing summer just past. A welcome breeze stirred the dust from her steps. It carried a whisper of waves from the other side of the hill, where the cliff dropped to the Aegean.

The area seemed deserted now, with most of their expedition gone home. She missed the supportive sense of community, with its loose-knit organization of surveyor, cataloger, field technician, foreman and other jobs. Now the khaki tents were empty, the collected fruits of the summer's labors awaiting their journey to Athens.

Their base work camp was only five minutes' walk from the entrance to the tomb. As they climbed they gained a view of the excavated ancient village which had taken most of the season's labor. Though the exposed stone walls and collapsed structures had yielded many potsherds and implements, little of it was distinctive. Their understanding of Mycenaean Greece would not be greatly advanced by this hot, conflict-filled summer. Still, the *tholos* tomb above the village suggested that the region had been significant, perhaps even wealthy, with a ruler worthy of elaborate burial. It might yet reward these last explorations, carried out at the nub end of the expedition. Or so she hoped. She had taken a semester's sabbatical from Boston University to close up the site and finish her own projects. So far there had been no payoff for her carefully calculated investment of time.

Claire strode in through the excavated passageway, between massive limestone blocks, a few steps ahead of George despite his advantage in height. She moved with efficient, bunched energy, her smart tan jumper going *snick snick* as her legs scissored. At twenty-eight, she had been on seven major digs in Greece and Turkey, which had brought a sinewy heft to her thighs.

The long unroofed corridor rose to each side, knifing into the hill to meet the great rectangular entrance. They went from sunlight to sharp shadow as they passed under the huge lintel, their footfalls echoing back at them in false welcome from the beehive tomb.

Claire stopped amid a clutter of tools. "That frame is pathetic." She picked her way forward. "God, what a rat's nest."

"It'll hold," George said defiantly. He slapped the timbers. The slab swung, creaking in a double-ply rope cradle. She saw he had done the simplest job possible, not bothering with a side brace. The important part was the framing of the hole left in the wall, though. That seemed okay. He had used standard steel struts, wedged in to carry the weight. She bent to inspect the slab.

Three concentric circles had been chiseled in the outer face. This was what had intrigued her about it in the first place. There were scratches near the edges—probably insignificant, she judged. She ducked around to see the other side. Gray mortar clung feebly to the edges, crumbling to the touch. The back face was blank, uninteresting.

"Too bad," she said.

"Yeah." George brought a hand lamp and crouched beside her. "Point is, look inside."

She turned awkwardly in the cramped space against the wall and peered into the large hole. An amber-colored cone gleamed dully, pointed straight out at her. It was mounted somehow on black rock.

She sucked in her breath. "What. . .?"

"A beauty, huh? Here we thought the slab might be carved on both faces, but who'd think they'd *bury* something behind it?"

"Mycenaean burials didn't use the walls for—" she started, and then shut her mouth. So much for the conventional wisdom.

"Look how symmetrical it is," George said lovingly. "Perfect. Only, a perfect *what*?"

"I never saw anything similar."

"Ornamental, that's for sure."

"No hole in it that I can see, so you couldn't wear it on a necklace."

"Check. Too long, anyway—must be ten centimeters at least. Wonder how it's stuck on?"

"Looks like it's imbedded." He leaned forward, reached between the steel struts and touched the rock beyond. "Yeah, see? It's been tapered at the base, to fit into the dark limestone."

"A fairly rare material. Funny, concealing it."

"You'd think they'd show it off. I'm sure glad I didn't hit that cone when I jammed the steel in there."

Claire thought, *I suppose that's his way of saying he realizes how lucky he was.* All alone, struggling with weights he couldn't handle, sticking supports in blind. She shook her head.

George caught her. He said roughly, "Shine the spot over here."

He squeezed himself into the narrow space between the hanging slab and the hole it had left. The added yellow-tinged light showed that the black rock did not fill the opening. It stopped five centimeters short on one side, and left a slightly larger gap on the other. There was no gap at top or bottom.

Claire said, "Looks like these top and bottom blocks are as thin as the first one."

"Look at the side ones, though. Half a meter thick, easy."

"To carry the weight down around this thin part," Claire said. She rubbed the black surface. It was bumpy, perhaps simply roughed out by a stonemason with the same quick efficiency devoted to paving stones. "Large chisel marks," she said to herself.

"Yeah, you'd expect anybody making an art object would do finer work. This looks messy."

"Get the light pipe, would you? Let's look behind this thing."

He backed out of the narrow space, dragging the lamp. In the dimness Claire thought she saw a golden glimmering in the cone, reflecting specks. Impurities, perhaps. George muttered behind her, casting shadows that made the flecks ripple, wax and wane.

Probably amber, she thought. Fine work, over 3500 years old. Her years of training had not erased the sense of wonder she felt at such thoughts.

The cone was about as long as her hand, tapering smoothly to a rounded point. As she touched the rock, spreading her hand across it, a slight uneasiness came over her, a prickly feeling, and she withdrew.

"Here," George said, handing her the light pipe. She was his superior in the expedition. Though the archeologists usually made no great fuss about pecking order, now that the big names had cleared out Claire had right of first inspection.

That had never happened before, and she felt a small quiver of anticipation. Thank God Kontos was back in Athens.

She inserted the thin, flexible plastic tube in the right hand gap around the black limestone. The pipe carried a shaft of light down its core, illuminating a small patch at the tip. The image returned in a thin coaxial layer.

George clicked off the tomb lamps. Claire slipped a helmet on, swung its goggles into place, and saw a faint rough surface. She poked the tube to the side. "Raw dirt and pebbles. Original hillside."

George squatted beside her and fed the tube forward. She maneuvered it gingerly, using a guiding rod with articulating joints.

"It closes off about ten centimeters to the right. No, wait—there's a little hole. Looks like water erosion."

"Can you get around behind this black limestone?"

"Trying. Got to—damn!—work this around. . . ."

In the gloom the two crouched figures were ghostlike. Radiance escaping the light pipe cast huge shadows reeling up the curved walls to stretch and lose themselves in the inky blackness of the dome.

"There. Poked it through. Now. . .if. . .I can turn . . ." Her clipped, precise voice echoed from the arched stone, giving it a ringing, almost metallic edge. "The rock ends. Can't see any markings from this perspective. It's flat on the back."

"Anything behind it?"

"Open space."

"How big?"

"I'm getting no reflection."

"Couple feet long, then, at least."

"Probably more water hollowing. Here, have a look."

When George had the helmet on he jockeyed the light pipe around and whistled to himself. "This is a pretty sizable block. Can't see that it connects to anything else."

He studied it a moment longer and then pulled off the helmet. Claire returned his grin. "Decidedly odd, Watson," she said.

"It's a good find, isn't it?"

"No Mycenaean tomb has a false wall like this. Or that amber ornament. A first. A real first."

CHAPTER
Three

The Greek laborers didn't turn up the next day, though.

This would have been a serious problem if it had happened in the middle of the excavation. With the expedition shutting down now, it became only a nuisance. No one had expected any more important finds, or else Director Hampton would have stayed on, getting one of the postdocs to fly back to Boston University and take over his lectures for a few weeks as the semester began.

Claire had stayed principally to finish her own analysis of pottery found at the site. As the senior remaining American, she had to work with the Greeks to finish inventory, handle the shipping and seal up the tomb to prevent vandalism.

She and George were the only staff left in camp qualified to work the dig. Originally, Kontos was to supervise this last phase, but since late June he had spent most of his time in Athens. His absence now left the Americans alone, except for a woman from the village who did the cooking and the camp man.

Claire grudgingly admitted that George's original framing in the tomb was probably structurally sound. Still, they reinforced his frame in the hole and studied the slab he had extracted from the tomb wall.

It was unremarkable except for the concentric circle markings—the only design like it on the entire interior of the tomb. There were also chips around the edges and the mortar was

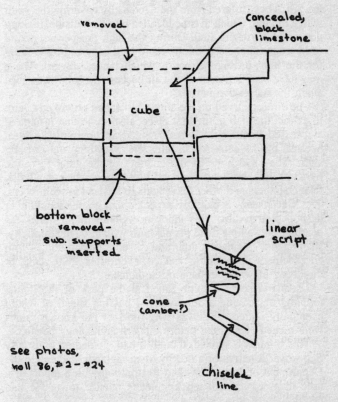

removed

Concealed, black limestone

cube

bottom block removed - sub. supports inserted

linear script

cone (amber?)

chiseled line

see photos, roll 86, #2 - #24

partially gone. George proposed that these marks represented half-hearted efforts by looters to extract the slab. During the first thousand years after the burial the mortar should have been tough enough to discourage casual efforts.

Mycenaean tombs were austere, a product of a people who had never known opulence. They echoed the Cretan fashion of a deep circular pit cut into the slope of a hillside. Modern archeologists termed them *tholos* tombs, from the ancient Greek word for round.

The Mycenaeans made them by lining the pit with stone blocks, building to a high corbelled vault that projected above the hill. They differed from the Cretans by covering the vault with a mound, which in time blended into the hillside, making the tombs harder to find. During the high prosperous period of Mycenaean society, tombs could be discovered by looking for the long passage, *dromos*, which lanced inward. These may have been left open to the air because the tomb was used again for successive burials.

The circles carved on the single block had provoked Claire to extract the slab in the first place, suspecting that it marked a recessed burial site. It had seemed an unpromising idea, because the Mycenaeans usually left everything out in plain sight. They had none of the cunning of the great Egyptian pyramid builders, who arranged blind approaches, deadfalls, fake chambers and other deceptions to mislead grave robbers. The Mycenaeans apparently expected that no one would ever despoil their tombs. This innocence Claire found rather endearing. These long dead people built with a tough simplicity, shaping and calculating their arched subterranean domes with an exactness that seldom yielded, even after 3500 years, to the decay of water seepage or earthquake.

Usually a beehive tomb failed at the peak of the dome, toppling in, leaving a hole which a passing shepherd would eventually notice. This was why most of the known tombs were picked clean long before modern archeology began.

This tomb was typical, though it had yielded an unusually rich trove. A native of a nearby town, Salandi, had called the Department of Antiquities and Restoration with a report of a hole in a seaside hill ten kilometers outside town. He had heard about it in a cafe.

Grave robbers had gotten there long before. Beehive tombs were used only for royalty, and their descendants knew it; few had survived intact. Here the thieves had broken open urns and boxes, scattering most of the contents. There was no gold left, no crystal vases, nothing readily profitable.

Tourists remembered best such valuables as the famous gold mask of Agamemnon, mistakenly identified by Schlie-

mann when he took it from the Grave Circle at the Mycenaean Palace. It was glorious, beautiful, and told much about
the royal life of the times. Archeologists, though, are equally
interested in artifacts which show ordinary life, and in these
the site was a good find. The dutiful servants of the dead had
included tools, sealstones, daggers, bronze shortswords, uten-
sils, stoneware, mirrors, combs, sandals—everything the dead
King would need to set up housekeeping in the afterlife.

The King himself was a jumbled sprawl of bleached bones,
probably cast aside when the robbers tore apart his decayed
shroud for the attached jewels. The bones were divided
equally between the laboratory teams at Athens and Boston
University, where they awaited further study. There were several sets of bones found, all at the same level. This could
mean the Mycenaeans used the tomb for several generations,
or that several were buried at once, or even that shepherds
died here after the cave-in.

Small items—pottery, minor jewelry, amethyst beads—
were found buried under the heaps of infallen rock and dirt.
The looters had apparently not bothered to dig to get everything possible. Streaks of black soot on the walls spoke of
centuries of use as a shelter from storms, probably by shepherds. Weathering gradually widened the hole in the dome,
letting in the slow gathering of dust. The plumes of soot
started several feet above the original floor, mute evidence
that the fires had been laid on the accumulated debris of centuries.

As usual, Kontos had whisked the prettiest or most striking
artifacts off to Athens. He had given the Boston University
expedition little time to study the best items, and rebuffed
attempts to see them during the cleaning and analysis in the
Athens laboratories.

Last year the Marxist Greek government had demanded
that digs no longer be run as before, through the American
School of Classical Studies. Kontos became co-director, with
veto power. Friction with Kontos over that and other issues
had made the camp tense from early summer on.

"That's why I want to get a good look at everything, *fast*,"
Claire said to George the next day.

"Just because of Kontos? I know he's hard to take, but

we've got something special here. Have to be careful, or—"

"Or we'll run out of time."

"Once Kontos sees this, he'll for sure let us stay on the whole month."

Claire had not told George about being pawed in the pottery tent. Kontos had left smoldering, which did not bode well. "Our permit has been withdrawn, remember?"

"Just a formality."

"Ha! We've got a week, period. Kontos will stick by the book, you can bet on that."

"You're exaggerating. Okay, he didn't get along with us. But he's a real scientist, for Chrissakes—"

"And a colonel in their hotshot new Interior Guard."

"So? The government's handing out titles and ranks right and left. Comic relief politicians."

"Listen, I'm in charge here." Claire stood up, scowling. She remembered that having your opponent seated, looking up at you, was a useful maneuver. A yellow glow diffused through the tent, highlighting the dust on the boxes of potsherds that surrounded them. "Let's pull out the top and bottom slabs. *Now.*"

George shrugged. Claire felt momentary elation, but kept it from flickering across her face.

"It'll be easier if we wait for the damned laborers to come back," he said sourly.

"*If* they come back. They're hot for politics these days, not grunt labor."

"Anything in this morning's paper?"

"Same old rantings. Japan and Brazil have cut into the Greek shipping trade again. Athens is claiming an international financial conspiracy." Claire dutifully kept track of international matters, but she had no strong leanings. The effort of keeping her professional life going was quite enough, thank you.

"Any US news?"

"That referendum in California went through—they're going to divide it into two states."

"Crazy! And we think the Greeks are feisty." George rolled his eyes.

"You should've seen the look the store owner gave me when I went in to buy a paper."

"Hey, good-looking single woman in a small town, I'm not surprised."

She shook her head, exasperated, ignoring the compliment, as usual. "It wasn't that kind of look. He was hostile."

"Huh. Still, I'd like some extra hands to brace up that wall, it's—"

"*I'll* help you. Come on."

They removed the bottom block first. It was the least dangerous, since it clearly was not supporting any significant weight. They worked it back from the wall, exposing the foot of the black rock, and saw a single straight line carved at the base.

"Funny," George said. "Not much of a design."

"Maybe it's just a marker. 'This end down.' "

"Could be. Not every mark has to mean much." He crouched to study it. "There's some light-colored dust caught in the pits of the chisel marks."

"Perhaps that's old paint. Leave it for the chem analysis."

"Yeah. What next?"

George plainly wanted responsibility to fall on her. Very well, then: "Let's remove the top block."

"How? The whole wall might give way."

She pursed her lips. "Frame around the cube. Then pull the top block out on a tackle and cradle rig."

George sighed. "If we'd wait until we got more help, it would for sure be safer."

"And later. Maybe too late. Let's go."

When the top block came away, swinging easily in its web of ropes and chains, they both gasped.

"That's linear script!" George cried.

"On *stone*." Claire stared at the three freshly exposed lines of symbols. The letters were made by striking straight cuts into the stone. "No one has ever found any writing except on clay."

"Look at the chiseling. How it catches the light."

Claire ducked under the swaying block and brought the lamp closer. "More of the light-colored dust down in the pit of the grooves. Clay-based, perhaps. It still has a wet, shiny look."

She stepped back. With the top block gone the full size of the black limestone cube struck them. It was more than a meter high. A musty smell drifted out from the opening, carrying the reek of old, damp earth, open to the air for the first time in millennia. Claire wrinkled her nose. She would always associate that heavy, cloying scent with a grave she had helped open in Messenia. After two thousand years the body still had some stringy, dried fragments attached to the bones. Contact with the moist air brought forth a rank odor that drove her from the site, retching. Afterward she burned her clothes.

Here it was not nearly so bad. The stench was simply organic matter in the soil, breathing out. There was no body wedged behind the blocks, she reminded herself. In a while the musty stench would drift away.

"That—that script."

"Linear B. You know it, don't you?"

Claire frowned. "Yes, but . . ."

No one had ever seen Linear B written on anything but clay tablets used for accounting. The Aegean Bronze Age had not advanced beyond the simple business-recording skills developed earlier by Syria and Mesopotamia. Scribes throughout the Peloponnesus kept track of transactions, probably for taxation, on unbaked clay slabs. There were lists of ladles, boiling pans, bathtubs, tables of inlaid ivory, ebony footstools, servants, arms, chariots, a myriad of details. Carefully stored on shelves in the archive room of palaces, they were accidentally fired to hardness by the arson that pulled down Mycenaean civilization. Phoenixlike, the tablets came forth from the flames to bring that lost world back to life.

Claire remembered the tablets, the ragged way men had struck quick angular patterns to total up grain, cows, jugs of wine. To find such symbols used here, on stone, in a tomb, was remarkable. She should be thrilled. But something . . .

"It's not Linear B," she exclaimed.

George turned to her with disbelief. "What? I haven't studied it much, but I can recognize some elements."

"Look again. There are similarities, but that could be from a difference in techniques, stone versus clay."

"But everybody around here used Linear B."

"True enough." She touched fingers to her lips, thinking,

and then noticed that she had caked them with dust. She shivered, spat, shook herself. "Uh!"

"Yeah, kinda close in here, isn't it?"

"Take some photos, will you? I—I want to go look up a reference."

She hurried from the tomb, out along the *dromos*, seventy yards long. She breathed deeply, sucking in the sweetness of distant juniper. Along the path to camp there was the welcome sight of thick bushes like holly, but with swollen acorns sporting enormous cups. She reminded herself to look up the name of the plant sometime. For the moment, though, she had something else to find.

Within ten minutes she had it. "Well, you were half right," she called as she came striding back under the huge lintel and into the echoing chamber.

George fired his flash for one more photo and looked at her. "Which half?"

"It's linear, of course. But not B. It's A."

He froze. "Can't be."

"It is. I've matched eight symbols." She held out a reference book. "Check them yourself."

"*Can't* be." He took the volume and held the transcribed pictures of clay tablets up to the light. She watched, faintly bemused, as his blond head swung back and forth from the book to the block's letters. "Well. . .I see what you mean. But how did it get *here?*"

Claire stepped under a hanging lamp and reached up to rub the chiseled marks. As her hand swept across them her arm shivered slightly, her nostrils caught the thick, musty scent, and she drew back.

"Brought from Crete, perhaps," she said softly. "Or, more likely, a Cretan laborer did the carving." Linear A was a transcription of the Minoan language, or Eteocretan.

"Just our luck. Linear B was deciphered back in the '50s, right? How long until somebody'll do the job for Linear A?"

She shook her head, still gazing up at the enigmatic lines. *They would have to get an analysis done on that clay or paint or whatever*, she thought. "Probably never."

"There are new computer techniques, methods of—"

"You need a referent. Something to make a correspondence with." Claire dredged up the memories from lectures a decade old. How Alice Kober showed there were alterations in the syllabic endings of words in Linear B, proving that it was an inflected tongue. How a British architect cross-correlated vowels, and when fresh tablets turned up at Pylos, they confirmed his predictions. Linear B was Greek. The Greeks had taken over the Semitic syllabary, attached vowel sounds to those signs, and so invented consonant signs. Thus was born the first full alphabet, a true written language. Only, was it? Or did the Minoans do the trick first, with Linear A? No one knew. "We haven't got any such information about Linear A. Nobody knows what Minoan sounded like."

"Maybe this'll give us something to go on." George jacked up the camera tripod, bringing it level with the in-scription.

"This is the only stone inscription in Linear A," Claire mused, watching him snap close-ups.

"Looks kinda like a cover for a sarcophagus." George was sweating and dust settled on his face, unnoticed. His jeans and work shirt had long since been paled by the fine grime.

"Ummm. But with an amber decoration? And the Myce-naeans used rock-cut graves, but not sarcophagi. Even if they did, and we've missed them all until now—why stick the cover behind a wall?"

George grinned. "Hiding it?"

"From whom? The dead king?"

"True enough. Squirrel it away, then mark up the wall outside? Doesn't make sense."

"We've got to make measurements, tests. Particularly of that shiny stuff in the chisel strokes."

"Nothing special about the rock itself. Plain old black limestone."

Claire started clearing the area, making room for equip-ment. "Perhaps. There's a ruined country house near Vaphio, only a few halfwalls of limestone still standing. Shepherds kept their sheep in a passageway there for a few thousand years, and the wool rubbing the stones made the limestone shine like marble. There were local stories that said it was the last wall of a grand marble palace. The Harvard team that worked the site spent a year figuring that one out."

"You figure we should do a metal analysis?"

"Damn right. I want to know what's in those grooves."

"Colonel Doctor Kontos isn't going to give you much time to dot i's and cross t's," he chided. "He'll have that in a crate and off to Athens inside a week, easy. With his name stamped all over it."

Claire frowned. "Do you hear something?"

"Huh? No. Look, no doubt about it, Kontos will take over the dig himself. He's bucking to be General Director of Antiquities and Restoration."

"Kontos was a good scientist," she pondered. "Okay, he has a weakness for strutting around in that uniform, but—"

"The man's a maniac!"

"He's just a patriot. These last few months he's gotten carried away. And I can see his arguments, too. He's simply sticking up for his country."

George drawled sarcastically, "Tom Paine in a toga, huh?"

"I'm sure when I tell him about this find he'll give us added time to figure this out."

George raised his eyebrows. "Hey, sounds like that jeep again."

She whirled. "Oh no! He *can't* be back today."

"Here's your chance to try sweet reason on the Colonel."

George's sarcasm would set Kontos off. She had to keep the two of them apart.

"Stay here, keep working."

"I wouldn't miss this for—"

"No! In fact, close the wooden door. Diplomacy isn't your strong suit. I don't want him up here."

George chuckled. "Think you can handle him?"

"Of course," she said uncertainly.

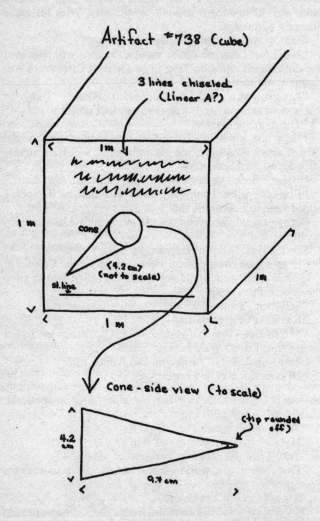

Artifact #738 (cube)

3 lines chiseled
(Linear A?)

1 m

cone

(4.2 cm?)
(not to scale)

st. line

1 m

1 m

1 m

Cone - side view (to scale)

4.2 cm

9.7 cm

(tip rounded off)

CHAPTER
Four

She found Kontos ordering workmen about. They were loading crates onto a gray Nissan truck.

"What's going on?" she demanded.

"I am taking our equipment. Also the remaining artifacts."

"What? We have weeks—"

"No. I spoke to others, we are agreeing—you are not allowed the full time." He turned to her and smiled without humor. Then he pointedly turned and marched toward the pottery tent.

Claire hurried to catch up. "How long?"

"I have got for you two weeks."

"Two—"

"Maximum."

Kontos slapped the tent flap aside and strode through into the heavy warmth. He found pottery already boxed by Claire and marked it for the men, quick swipes with a flow pen. He moved down the aisles with deliberate speed, still smiling, obviously enjoying making her tag along like a supplicant. Claire gritted her teeth.

"You can't do that!"

"My government does it, not me."

"You'll damage relations between us, you'll—"

"There are in this world other scholars. Other sources for your precious money."

"It's not that! We've found—"

"Soon maybe we will have aid from other quarters, to help

the Grecian people to save their own history." He savored
the words as he worked, archly brisk and efficient.

"Alexandros, there must be a way to work this out."

He paused, his pen in the air. "Oh? So you think?"

"We need time. We found something—"

"Begging will not change matters."

"There are important aspects—"

"We Greeks will do it."

"Call Hampton. He'll—"

"Of no use. This is between you and me."

"Us?"

He stepped toward her, his smile a fraction warmer. "We
had a misunderstanding, perhaps."

Puzzled, she began, "If you mean that, I would hope that
a scholar of your standing—"

He reached out and seized her upper arm, stepping closer.
"Matters are not too late, however."

His other hand came up and fondled her breast. It was so
unexpected she froze for an instant, not quite believing this
could happen this way, so abruptly. She gasped with shock,
smelling the raw, sour musk of him as he pressed close, en-
veloping her.

"You—no!"

She twisted against him. His large hands held her arms
pinned and he spoke directly into her face. "We had a misunderstanding. It can be changed."

"No!"

"You are not giving a chance."

"No, not like this."

She wrenched away, slamming painfully against a table.
Potsherds shattered on the ground.

"How then?" he asked blankly.

"Never!"

He curled his lips. "I tried with you a second time. I should
not have bothered."

"Goddamn right." She wiped her brow of sweat, panting,
feeling dirty and flushed.

"We are not children, you and I."

"Well, I'm not."

His jaw muscles bunched. "Very well. I understand. Even
if you do not." He squared his shoulders and looked around,

his uniform drawn tight across his chest. "This site, you will clear it as before. Within one week from today."

"*One* week?"

"That is official."

"Son of a bitch."

"Understand?"

"You bet."

"I expect well organized sample boxes."

"Sure."

"You give a complete catalog, copies of notes."

"You bet."

"All delivered into my hands."

"I'll do as well as I can do."

He smiled sternly. "That may not be enough."

"It damned well will be," she said defiantly.

"We shall see."

George gaped in disbelief. "You said *what?*"

"Okay, maybe I got angry."

"*Maybe?* 'Diplomacy's not your strong suit,' you said."

"He insulted me! His hand—!"

"He felt the need to supplement his command of English?"

She bristled. "You're all alike."

"Only in the dark. But look—he's really going to hold us to this one week deadline?"

She nodded sadly. "I'm afraid so."

"Good grief."

"If I hadn't gotten so mad . . ."

"Hey, look, don't you go thinking that way. That oily creep comes on to you, uses his position—you did the right thing."

She smiled. "I loved the look on his face. He's not used to his pets biting his hand."

Claire had watched Kontos's jeep roar away, angrily expelling a roiling cone of tan dust, and had then trotted up the hill to the tomb.

George paced near the entrance, head down. "We're not gonna get much done. Not nearly enough."

"If this were an ordinary dig, next year we could . . ." She stopped and studied the dessicated, windy sky. A murmur of distant surf came on a passing breeze. She said with new certainty, "There's not going to be a next year."

George looked doubtful. "Hey, this was just an incident. And he's only one guy."

"We can't count on that."

George scuffed at a stone, hooked his hands into the hip pockets of his jeans. "It'll take a big bite out of the week just to break camp."

"You'll have the men back. Kontos didn't stop for anything on his way out, except to harangue the camp man about that."

"So? That artifact in there, it's going to take months—"

"Not for a prelim survey. You can work around behind it, see if there's anything else. Sift the soil back there, look for trace elements."

"So what? If Kontos seals off this site, won't let us come back, *he*'ll have the good stuff. Lab workups, time to sniff around for other artifacts—"

"Except for one thing. He doesn't know it's here."

George stared at her. "Huh? You didn't tell him?"

"I never got the chance. He was masterfully working the conversation around to where he could make his play, Mr. Macho taking charge. I couldn't get a word in."

"Aha."

"Part of my diplomacy. I thought I could wheedle him around to giving us more time, once he knew we had something important."

"Huh. It might've worked."

"Yes." She sighed. "But I didn't get to try it."

"The camp man knows something. He'll tell the laborers. It'll get back to Kontos."

"Yes, but he only knows that we found *some*thing, not what."

"Good point. I can take him aside, tell him to keep it away from the men, say the Colonel Doctor doesn't want word of this leaking out."

"No, just the opposite. Tell the camp man the Colonel wants work to go fast here, because we're shutting down."

"Right. Everybody'll assume Kontos knows about it."

"That might buy a few days. . . ." Claire stared moodily

off at the sharp ridgeline. "I hate to hand the whole damn thing over to him next week, though."

"Yeah, he'll get the easy, important stuff for free from his lab lackeys."

"With Americans on the Most Despised list, nobody's going to speak up for us in Athens. The mood he's in—"

"Right. He'll publish it himself."

"Unless we do something." Claire suddenly turned and strode down the stone corridor that led to the tomb.

"Like what?"

"Get some special gear. Do some quick work. Maybe bring some pressure to bear through BU."

George called after her, "How?"

"I'm going back to Boston. I'll take photos, my field log—and be back in two days."

"And leave me with all this to handle?" he asked with a sinking voice.

"Yes. Let the laborers break camp. You—just keep digging."

PART
TWO

CHAPTER
One

John Bishop felt unnatural carrying an umbrella. Bostonians had told him this was the first solid, respectable rain storm of what would be a long season, so he had bought a hefty defense that ejected itself from his palm with alarming energy. The bulk of it seemed unnecessary for the light gray drizzle that filmed the air, giving the brick apartments of Commonwealth Avenue a surrealistic glaze. He turned right at Mass Ave and wrinkled his nose at the heavy odor of fries, cheeseburgers and day-old grease that drifted across the cracked pavement. Students clustered inside the string of fast eateries.

He swerved his attention to the college women along Beacon Street bound for BU. They lugged heavy briefcases, as did he. It was a habit he had begun as an undergraduate at Rice University, unconsciously equating the physical effort with productive labor. A long-legged woman, her jeans tucked into high black boots, caught his attention.

He had always liked tall women, their inherent regal sway. He was a shade shy of six feet, but had dated women fully four inches closer to heaven than himself. A friend had once prodded him with the accusation that this was not in fact a natural preference, but a strategy, based on the widely assumed Truth that tall women have few suitors, and thus are easier to handle. It was almost plausible, John realized, since he was rather ordinary-looking, with unremarkable brown hair and blue-gray eyes. Presumably his athletic ability, which had peaked in high school and steadily decayed, would have counted for something if he had devoted himself to more social games, instead of lone jogging and the occasional weekend neighborhood football scrimmage. But no, the friend's indictment was off target; he simply liked them tall, as long as they didn't slump down in a forlorn effort to appear shorter. It seemed obvious to him that no woman looked good trying to be something she wasn't.

The commuter rush on Storrow Drive rose in full cry, blatting its impatience to begin the day as he crossed over it on the Harvard Bridge—so named, he thought wryly, because it speared directly into the middle of MIT. The bridge was a low ugly thing, spanning the Charles with Spartan economy. A rowing team bowed and surged under it, carving a precise wake in the filmed water: John recalled reading in an introductory pamphlet that "persons falling accidentally into the Charles are well advised to update their tetanus shots." The rowers' wake dissolved in a sudden, gusty downpour. They gave up and veered for the MIT boathouse. John hunched, pulling the umbrella closer, and reflected that it had probably been a bad idea to sell his car when he left Berkeley. Passing cars sprayed him liberally for his disloyalty to their kind, as he jogged the rest of the way.

The concrete-gray phalanx of MIT was stark, un-ivied and imposing. On the older buildings, black-trimmed windows drew the eye upward. The main building rewarded this vertical urge with a crowning, austere dome copied from an ancient Roman mode. Each slab cornice laconically proclaimed self-evident principles, unconsciously assuming that science was not a mere set of rules but the artful work of living men. The names Aristotle, Newton, Darwin were chiseled in large block letters and in lesser size, the Maxwells and Boyles and Lobachevskis who birthed the equations, found the elements or unraveled the riddles. A haughty advertisement; we produce the men, they produce the laws. (Though in fact no 'Tech graduate appeared in the list.) Nearby, stones mounted above great, fluted columns crowned the MASSACHVSETTS INSTITVTE OF TECHNOLOGY, giving the impression of a secular temple of high tech. In World War II anti-aircraft batteries, though in short supply at the war fronts, had been spared to ring the campus.

Shaking his umbrella, he clumped into the heavy warmth of the Pratt Building. He particularly liked the insouciance of the students here. Near his office there was a religious flyer pinned to a bulletin board, the leading title solemnly proclaiming, THERE ARE THINGS MAN WAS NOT MEANT TO KNOW. Across the columns of type below was scrawled, *Yeah? Name one!* John liked that: put up or shut up. It was refreshing, after the politely attentive, boring students he had taught while earning his doctorate at Rice University.

He left his raincoat to drip on an ancient wooden coatrack and opened his window slightly. He liked to work with the gusty spattering of rain for background, a random chorus testifying that ample, tumultuous life went on even as he burrowed into his equations.

He looked up from some calculations when the quick rapping came at his door. "It's open!" The woman strode in three steps, looked around, frowned at him.

"Doctor Sprangle said I should see someone in the Metallurgy group. I'm Claire Anderson."

She stuck out a hand and John Bishop came around his desk to shake it. He accomplished this maneuver, nearly toppling an already full wastebasket, without taking his eyes from her face. Her appearance had struck him like a physical blow. She was not a beautiful woman, but the angular set of her face captivated him. Her chin's severe sharpness was blunted at the last moment by a mitigating roundness, somewhat red from the chill, and the V of it drew his attention up, across the planes of her cheeks to their meeting with delicate high ridges, ramparts that defended the glittering blue eyes. And, yes, she was tall.

She took in his office in a sweeping glance, lingering only over his cluttered desk; her ample lips crooked into a faintly derisive curve. "I'm from Archeology, over at BU." Her handshake was firm and businesslike. "Mind if I smoke?"

"No," he lied.

She turned, her red skirt swirling, and sat on the ample oak window ledge. "I'm trying to get some help, expert help. Watkins is the man in your group who usually handles the metallurgy problems that are out of the ordinary, I'm told."

"Yes?" John had found years before that a simple agree-

ment carrying a questioning lilt invariably extracted more information, without admitting anything.

"Well, I've got one. I need somebody to bring that equipment of Watkins' to Greece, help me use it, and take responsibility for getting it back to him when I'm done."

"Watkins is in—"

"China, I know. On sabbatical." She puffed energetically
on her cigarette, generating half an inch of ash, and tapped a
foot rapidly on the worn maple flooring. He wrinkled his nose
at the smoke.

"Ah. . .I may not be the best person to—"

"Look, it's a simple job. I just want somebody who understands metallurgy. You don't have to know the archeological end, I can handle that."

"Still, I—"

"MIT requires that a staff member go along with the gear,
I know that, too. So I'm willing to pay all your expenses.
Our National Endowment grant will cover it. Look, it's a free
trip to Greece! But you've got to go *now*." She underlined
this with another deep drag on her cigarette. She expelled a
huge blue cloud and tapped the ash out his half-opened window.

"Well, well." John was filled with conflicting impulses,
and covered this by offering her an ash tray.

"No thanks," she said, and smiled wryly. "This one isn't
filled yet."

"Greece? What part?"

"Peloponnesian peninsula, near Mycenae."

"Uh, I see."

"Never been there?"

"No. I always wanted to."

"Mycenae is the ruins of an ancient palace. It was once
the center of what we call the Mycenaean culture. Possibly
an offshoot of the Minoans, who traded all over the eastern
Mediterranean. But the Mycenaeans got big and prosperous,
and there are signs that they became the dominant power in
the region, even bigger than the Cretans, by about 1400 B.C."

"Ah hah." He leaned on his desk and cupped a hand
around his chin, pretending to be lost in thought, trying to be
as casual as possible about tracing the outlines of her legs
under the skirt.

"Anyway, our dig is about forty kilometers from Mycenae, down on the coast of the Gulf of Argos. It's—"

"On the ocean? How's the diving there?"

She blinked, taken aback. "I don't know."

"The water's still warm this time of year, I guess?"

"Oh yes. You. . .dive?"

He nodded enthusiastically. "I learned down in Texas. Not much to see round there, but it was sure a lot of fun."

She said cordially, "I'm sure there are excellent spots near the site. We're right on the coast. Matthews at Brown did archeological diving off Spetsae, an island near us."

His furtive inspection of her body outline stopped and he liked the result. She was slender as a fish, yet with a ripening swelling at the hips that promised a lush wilderness. Women who interested him struck him this way; as unknown territory, rich and forgiving, complex as a continent.

"Sounds nice," was all he could manage to say.

She flicked her cigarette out the window, into a brimming puddle. "The only condition is, you have to leave tomorrow."

"*Tomorrow?*" This jolted him out of his reverie. "Can't—"

"I'll explain it on the plane. I've already got reservations. Here." She fished in her purse and held out an American Airlines ticket.

"You don't waste time," he said appreciatively.

"No, I don't. Never have." She stood up. "Can you come?"

"Well—" His mind spun among myriad details, lofted above them, descended. "Yes. I'm on the research staff, so I don't have teaching to worry about."

She smiled. "That's what I figured. I saw that on the directory. You were the first non-faculty member listed. Regular faculty would have classes. So I figured the next most senior was the best bet."

He grinned. "Well, ma'am, I guess I'm lucky you didn't notice that postdocs are listed by room number alone."

"Oh." Again the full lips curled in a self-mocking curve.

"Say, isn't the political situation pretty rocky over there?"

The gathering, slow motion world depression had unleashed a lot of smoldering resentments.

She shrugged casually. "It has its ups and downs. We'll

take only a few days, remember." She started toward the door.

"But wait—what should I bring? And Watkins' equipment, I'll have to . . ."

"To what? Just pack it. Put it through as your luggage."

He hesitated. Then, to cover his confusion, he boomed out, "No problem. You're right."

She eyed him. "Good. By the way, travel light. It's still fairly warm in Greece. Oh, and here."

She tossed him a packet. "Medicine?" he asked, peering at the polysyllabic label.

"It's that new microbio stuff. Take one a day. It lives in your gut and eats whatever microbe causes dysentery."

"Oh?" John looked doubtful. He didn't like the idea of tinkering with his body. Even when he had been injured in sports he resisted the pills offered him.

"No other side effects, don't worry," Claire said with distant amusement. "Put your faith in science."

"I thought the whole point of science was that you didn't have to merely have faith," John said sarcastically.

Claire chuckled. "Picky, picky. But do take them."

"Okay."

"See you at the gate. Be early."

"Will do," he said with what he hoped was crisp confidence. He opened his mouth to say something more, but she was gone, without even a goodbye. He leaned back against his desk again, puffed out his cheeks, and blew. The office now had the stale flat stink of smoke, a smell he hated. A small price to pay, though, for moments with such a delicious woman. She had riveted him from the first, making his breath catch. That hadn't happened in years, not since Ann. A heady, jolting moment like this had to be pursued. Minor aspects— his own plans, her annoying smoke—must be brushed aside.

He would have to tell Sprangle he was taking a quick vacation. Luckily, he had nothing crucial looming in the next few weeks. He hadn't been in Boston long enough to stack up obligations. He did have to hunt up the Watkins stuff, though, and bone up on it.

He collected his papers from the desk. The scribbled symbols seemed like something he had written weeks before.

"Things happen fast up north," he muttered to himself.

CHAPTER

Two

He didn't get the full story until they were driving from Athens to the site. The flight to Paris had been packed; the dollar was high again and tourists were spilling into France, even long after the usual season. He had to pay a hefty extra charge to get all the equipment aboard. Claire had been unable to get seats together.

On the Paris-Athens leg Claire had slept, but he sat up reading about Watkins' equipment. Now John blinked sleepily at the improbably bright and orange-tinted day and tried to assimilate the scenery flashing past as Claire kept up a rapid-fire summary of the tangled events so far. She digressed frequently, piling on nuances and technical jargon without pity, assuming he knew far more than he did.

"We'd been having troubles with Kontos all summer, everything from political discussions to disagreements over how to organize the collection boxes, so I guess it's not surprising that—oh, see there? That island with a hump back in the bay? That's Salamis. Themistocles broke the Persian fleet there, burned them to the water line, and saved Athens."

The outskirts of Athens seemed an unending line of cement works. Farther on, gray cement shells of two-story houses stood like bared bones of a mechanical monster. Some ground floors were inhabited, sporting antennas and flowers, while the skeletal promise of future affluence hung overhead. They sped westward, the glittering bay to the south, and crossed over the canal at Corinth. She parked beside it and they ate triangles of honey and nuts, while John walked halfway through and peered down at the geometrically exact slice cut through solid rock. "When the Germans retreated, back in World War II, they jammed the canal with trains, trucks, anything they had."

"Nice guys. How long did it take to clear?"

"Years. It was merely the latest in two thousand years of grudges against outsiders."

"Including Americans?"

She sighed as a tug drew a freighter into the mouth of the canal, over a kilometer away. "It's beginning to look that way. Let's go."

She had been the same way at the Athens airport, speedily fetching the rental car while he stacked the eight carrying cases of Watkins' equipment, their luggage, and his diving gear. It filled the trunk and the back seat. He hoped he would have time to go over Watkins' instruction manual again before she demanded the first run of tests.

They turned south from Corinth, running down the coast. The Peloponnesian peninsula is a four-fingered hand grasping south into the Mediterranean. They sped down the easternmost finger, along roads that narrowed and whitened beneath the October sun. They slowed behind a cart piled high with fat, cloudy green grapes. Claire cursed under her breath and passed it, narrowly slipping by before an ancient truck descended on them, hooting its horn.

"Lord God A'mighty!"

She laughed. "I thought people only swore like that in movies."

"It was a prayer. Slow down, ma'am. This thing's been there over three thousand years, a few minutes aren't going to make any difference."

"Afraid not. Kontos was so mad, he might close us down early. He may know I went back to Boston."

"How?"

"He called Hampton, the US co-director, at BU, even before I left Greece. I don't know what bullshit Kontos fed Hampton, but when I went in to see him, he was polite, proper, and frosty. No, sorry, special help?—nossir. Not at this time of the school year. He gave me a lecture on resources. Fretted about my extra trip back. He went tut-tut about the early shutdown, said I must have done something to *offend* Dr. Kontos, he couldn't *imagine* what it could have been, but didn't I think perhaps we could simply let matters *lie*, just withdraw when the Ministry wished? All very solemn with much profound puffing on a pipe, a sad hound-dog expression, the works.''

"What'd you say?"

"I told him I'd think it over and come back the next day to see him again." She smirked, turning the car sharply around curves as they wound up into a series of rolling, tawny hills.

"Today?"

"Right-o. He could remove my control over funds if he wanted. So I went out and bought our tickets through the BU office, charged our grant's account, and drew a big travel advance besides."

"He's still waiting for you to show up?"

"Yes." She laughed. "See, I gained one day on him. So then I went over to MIT, to recruit a warm body from Watkins' minions."

"And here I thought it was my charm."

"I decided to overlook your missing limbs and birth defects. When Hampton told me he wouldn't release any of our own people who knew metals, I knew it was—"

"Time to git."

"Right again. I only hope Hampton didn't call Kontos back after I showed up. I don't want him to know I left. Even— damn!" She snapped her fingers, meanwhile swerving around a donkey. "I should've called in sick from the Boston airport, said I had the flu, put off the appointment for a few days. That would've delayed old Hampton."

"Oh, what a web we weave, when first—"

"Sho' 'nuff, honey," she said in a credible Southern accent.

He countered in a clipped, arch tone, "High moral standahds are the foundation of ouah society."

"What was that?"

"A Kennedy accent."

"Glad you told me. I thought you'd suddenly developed tongue cancer."

"Where's yours from?"

"My what?"

"That accent."

"I don't have an accent."

"Ha. I thought maybe English."

"I grew up on Marlborough Street."

"That's the original Snob Hill accent?"

She grinned and looked at him.

"No matter how fascinating I am," he said soberly, "don't take your eyes off the road. Not at this speed."

"The Kennedys speak what my father called Englosh. That's the English of people who came from where they eat goulash. He died believing that Irish stew was a bastard form of goulash."

"Quaint."

The road reared and twisted over folded ridges, and then they were coming down again, the Aegean gleaming in the distance. The site was in a hilly area that sloped down to the sea, reachable only by rough sandy roads. They worked their way south on a rocky track, the Ford bouncing roughly at the speeds Claire habitually used. They rounded a curve and John sighed in surprise. An olive wood stretched through a narrow valley, gleaming like the surface of a river, and flowing like one, too—the wind tossing the branches so that green brimmed into silver rushes, like foam on a tossing current, and breezes swept down the valley like great surges of a storm. "Beautiful," he said.

"Yes. I love Greece. It's my favorite place to dig."

"Where else have you, uh, dug?"

"Iraq. Egypt. Turkey. Every summer since high school."

"You really like it."

"Of course." She glanced at him with surprise. "A lot better than sitting in a lab all year."

He said quietly, "Aren't you taking a chance with your career, playing fast and loose with travel funds, flaunting it in the face of Hampton?"

She pursed her lips and said nothing for a long moment. "Maybe so. But I'm damned if I'll let him push me around."

"Kontos?"

"Kontos and Hampton and—well—" She grimaced and shot him another glance. "Men."

CHAPTER
Three

George met their car before the dust of its arrival had settled. To John the camp was the scruffy cluster of tents Claire had described, with laborers in blue jeans and sweaty T-shirts loading crates onto nearby pickup trucks. Ignoring George for a moment, he swept a long look down the valley, picking out the pits of the dig. They were, of course, simply bare holes along a staked-out rectangular grid, with mounds of worked stones sorted into piles nearby. The place seemed remarkably ordinary, to yield secrets of millennia past.

He searched the tawny slopes to the left and found the tomb entrance, a stone-walled passage that lanced into the hillside. Now this was something else entirely. Even at this distance its stately bulk promised not merely a way into a hole in the ground, but the entrance to an unfathomed world long past.

He sniffed, catching on the crisp breeze a welcome, salty tang from the sea. He remembered how, as a boy on a trip to Atlanta with his mother, he had been impressed with buildings that were positively ancient, well over a century old.

George studied John quizzically as they were introduced, but then was swept along in Claire's story of events at Boston University. George's sour expression told quite clearly what he thought of departmental politics and Professor Hampton.

"Damn typical," was his verdict.

"If Hampton calls him back, we may have only a day or two before Kontos comes steaming in here," Claire said.

"We can't work miracles." George gestured at the gang

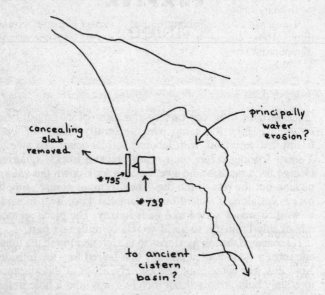

prelim sketch — Schmitt

concealing
slab
removed

principally
water
erosion?

#795

#738

to ancient
cistern
basin?

of men who were packing up the camp. "Plenty more to do here."

"He can't very well stop you from packing," John said.

"No, he'll speed it up," Claire said. "*And* stick to us like glue. So that we can't moonlight any research."

"When he sees me here—"

"That's an idea, yes. We actually *will* moonlight it. Work in the tomb at night, after the men have gone home."

"Why?" John asked.

"If Kontos has a snoop among them, he'll see nothing unusual."

"Is archeology always like this?"

George and Claire looked at each other. "No," Claire said despairingly. "This situation has gotten 'way out of hand. Sometimes I . . ." Her voice trailed off and then she visibly rallied herself. "Forget it. We're not going to be pushed around by a pig in a tailored uniform."

George sighed. "The trip didn't take any starch out of you, huh?"

She turned to him. "No, quite the reverse. Any problem with that?"

He stepped back, holding up both hands, palms out, chuckling. "Hey, no contest. I was kinda counting on some of your famous diplomacy, is all."

"What for?"

"Well . . ." He hooked his hands in his hip pockets and inspected the dust. "I was hoping this thing between you and Kontos would blow over. Then we could maybe get some more time here. Just a little easing off—"

"Impossible. Kontos won't budge."

"We need the time. I've found more stuff. I got around behind that slab, had a look."

Claire's momentum suddenly dissolved. "You did? What's there?"

"Lots. Come on."

They had to unlock and pull back the iron gate at the *dromos* entrance. George kept it closed while the laborers were nearby. The bulky wooden door that sealed the tomb itself was open. To John, entering was a sudden transit from a sun-baked valley where birds chirruped and wheeled, into a gloomy world of cool, sepulchral silence. The corbelled vault was topped by a wooden plug to keep rain out and prevent further cave-ins, but it did not mar the sense of converging, encasing mass overhead, a brooding weight of history.

When Claire saw George's new framing and support beams she ran an eye over the entire structure before venturing under it. "Rube Goldberg again. Looks like a bridge put together by somebody who'd lost the instructions."

"Aw, crap. It works, doesn't it? I got a lot of support under those ones higher up. See how I got that whole quadrant interlocked?"

"All by yourself?"

George shook his head. "Had to use two men. I draped sheets—see?—to cover the hole and other stuff. Told them the framing was to make sure the place didn't cave in while we're gone this winter."

The sheets were still in place. Claire stepped through the steel and wooden structure and slipped a rope free.

On the right side George had slipped a block forward, leaving enough room to wriggle through. Claire picked up a flashlight and pointed it into the hole.

John came forward gingerly, careful of the framework. To him the black slab looked ordinary enough, except for the chiseling at the top. The amber cone was lovely, he had to admit. Claire had waxed almost lyrical about it in the car, one of the few deviations he had seen from her crisp practicality.

"Not much room in here," she called.

"No kidding," George said. "I been leaning halfway through, scraping the soil, for two days."

He looked it. John had wondered why the man's coveralls were uniformly filthy, from neck to boots.

Claire grunted. "Find much?"

"Not a damn thing."

"How far down?"

"I took off half a meter."

"Safe to go in, then?"

"Sure."

John watched her wriggle through the opening. A muffled "Huh!" came back. He expected George to follow, but after a moment she called, "John. Come on."

He bent himself through the narrow passage and stiffly maneuvered onto the chilly, hard dirt beyond. Her flashlight lit the center of the irregular chamber but something black dominated the opposite wall. Neither said anything. It was a long moment before John realized that the unyielding inky spot was a hole. He wriggled forward a few feet. A rotten, salty smell drifted up from the opening. *A grave?* he guessed. Then a distant rushing gurgle echoed faintly. The wash of sea against stone.

"What is this? Part of the tomb?"

Claire's eyes caught the yellow of the flashlight beam as she played it around the walls. "No, I think it's natural. Look up there."

Above them for about ten feet was a gray-brown layer of hardened mud. At about chest level it met a layer of harder stuff—sandstone, John guessed. The rock spread around the entire cavity and down the throat of the hole. It stopped just short of the tomb blocks.

"They probably dug in until they hit this sandstone," Claire said. "So they stopped and built the tomb smack up against it. But there must've been mud where we are."

"They dug the mud out?"

"No. . .no, this is an erosion feature. George—" She leaned to call to him and found his head sticking through the passage.

"You're wondering what's down that pit, right?" He smiled. "I dunno. I threw a rope in and slid down maybe ten feet. No signs of work on the walls. Looks to me like you said, water wear."

John peered down it. "From the sea?"

"Not likely," George said. "It's hundreds of feet down to the ocean. No tide could force up in here."

Claire pointed up at the impacted mud. "The water came through from there. Seepage."

"Come on," George countered, "to take out that much stone—"

"Soft limestone in the cliff, remember—the waves are eating it up. This sandstone—" She reached out and rubbed. It crumbled into grains. "Greece gets a lot of rainfall—a lot more than you'd think, for a dry climate. Everything sits on limestone. Over the millennia the down-drip has carved out giant cisterns. The land is honeycombed with them. Their rainfall doesn't stay in the topsoil, it settles into stone bowls and makes agriculture difficult. That's what happened here."

"Maybe the builders knew that," George said quietly.

"Not likely. Look, it's been 3500 years. When the tomb was built, this soft vein may not have gone much farther down than here."

"They used the underground springs at Mycenae, right? Built the city walls out to reach a crack in the rock. Then they drove a tunnel down twenty meters or so, just to reach a dependable water supply."

Claire said with a little too obvious effort at patience, "They lived downslope from here, hundreds of meters away. This wouldn't carry enough water for a town. And a connection through a tomb—come *on*."

John said, "So you believe they just used it as a handy place to stick—that."

His gesture brought their attention to the slab. It was a cube, the back half resting on a flagstone block. Its rear face had no inscription, no decoration of any kind. There was a splotch of yellowish matter at the center of the back, covering a few square feet.

John stood awkwardly, bending to avoid the inward-curving walls, acutely aware of the yawning hole a few steps away. He put out a finger toward the lumpy thing. "I wonder what this is?"

"Don't touch it!" Claire's cry was loud in the close space. John flinched back.

"Why the hell not?" he asked irritably.

"There might be marks, even fingerprints," Claire said rapidly but in a lower tone.

"This looks like pebbles, dirt, Lord knows what. Nothing special."

"We don't know what's 'special' until we analyze it," she said primly.

George had wormed his way in and stood beside them. There was barely enough room without venturing too close to the edge immediately behind them. Without being obvious about it, John nudged into the sandstone for reassurance.

"Encrustation, looks like to me," George said. He aimed his own flashlight at the yellowish mass. "I already dusted it over, checked for fingerprints and so on. Nothing. Stuff looks sulfur-rich, maybe. Give it a sniff."

Claire bent and smelled it. "Salty."

"Sure. Salt water moisture's been blowing up against it so long, not surprising you'd get this. This side of the cube is caked with salt—see?"

The flashlight showed crystals glittering in the rough surface, bringing a gray pallor to the stone.

Claire nodded. "You're probably right. I can clean it off and check for anything beneath."

George sighed, his surprise exhibit exhausted. "I thought I'd really turned up something when I first crawled through. You know, a secret vault the looters hadn't gotten into, something like that."

"There's still the pit to look down, isn't there?" John volunteered.

"Yeah. I'll have a look, but I think it's just a natural cistern that's run into the ocean."

His jaw locked tight, John crouched by the hole. The sides were worn smooth and shimmered with moisture. Not an inviting surface for handholds. There were black streaks down the sides, leading the eye steeply down toward the sea. To him it looked burnished by fire, but he reminded himself that water can carry stains down from higher layers and discolor older strata. Maybe that had happened here. Anyway, that wasn't his area. None of this was, he reminded himself sheepishly. And here he had been poking around and asking questions, keeping up a pose of competence among these people, who really did know what they were doing. . . .

He got to his feet. The other two were talking about something he couldn't follow. He was at least a step from the edge but he could not turn away from it, knowing that the lip lay there in the dimness at his feet, waiting, if he should slip or if somebody fell against him. No, no, forget it. Something about the atmosphere of this place, it was a grave after all, a damp clammy smell in here, this part never had a chance to dry out like the main tomb, not as though teams of archeologists had swarmed over it, brought all their twentieth-centuryness along, this was the real smell of antiquity. He wiped his brow and made himself breathe regularly. The flashlight beams swept lazily upward, where clefts and recesses swallowed the light, forming a mottled darkness that seemed to gather at his temples, thickening the air, bringing the pungent salty smell reeking into his nostrils in the tight airless space—

"It's, uh, getting close in here."

Claire peered at him in the dim reflected radiance of the walls. His face felt flushed. Did it show?

"I want to get set up outside," he said brusquely. "Help me with the cases, George?"

CHAPTER
Four

John backed the 'scope away from the Linear A lines. "It's metal all right, down in those grooves."

"Chisel marks," Claire countered automatically. "Silver? It looks like silver."

"See for yourself, ma'am." He bowed and swept his arms toward the imposing tripod-mounted microscope. About its sleek black barrel were grouped a disc of lenses and pencil-beam illuminators. She crooked her face to the eyepiece.

"What am I seeing?"

"Some corrosion products, I'd say. Oxides. Not very much corrosion, though—lucky."

"Those greenish specks, are they bronze?"

"Maybe. Silver-copper alloy would look that way, too."

"Those reddish veins?"

"Rust."

"What's the underlying metal?"

"That's a little hard to tell right now. There could be several. The metal with the highest electrode potential is the first to corrode. That usually protects the other metals from attack, until the first is used up. Say, if you've got iron and silver and steel here—"

"This was the late *bronze* age."

"Oh. Just for example, the iron would go first. That'd give you a rust covering, but the silver—"

"I can *see* something shiny."

"Sure, because there's not much oxidation far back in the groove—I mean, chisel mark."

Claire leaned back from the eyepiece and studied the amber cone itself. "I wonder why—hey!"

"What?"

"In the amber—there was a flash of blue light."

"Some internal reflection, I guess."

"No, it was *bright*."

He had seen something like that earlier. "Some mica in the amber. It catches the lamplight just right, acting like a prism—"

"But it was so *bright*," she persisted.

"Gloomy hole like this, your eyes are sensitive."

"Ummm. Well, let's get the analysis done on the chiseling. The amber can wait."

He tried to remember more of Caley's *Analysis of Ancient Metals*. A lot of it was just informed common sense, but some of the oxidation chemistry was complicated. He remembered reading as a boy about Sherlock Holmes's writing a monograph on over a hundred different kinds of cigarette ash, and how to identify them. It had seemed bizarre then; now, compared to this, he wondered. Maybe some more equipment would help. There was additional gear in the third case, too. . . .

"Can't you study the metal content back in there? This is important."

He shrugged. "I'll have to make a boring."

She pulled away from the eyepiece. "No. Not on the script."

"I understand you don't want damage. But I think I can drill a millimeter-deep hole and cut through that film of trace impurities."

Or he could if he had enough time to read the manual. It was beautifully explicit; Watkins had written for well-meaning idiots who had to be prevented from damaging samples in the field and still get some useful results. People like him, in other words. But surely even as meticulous a scientist as Watkins had not planned on his level of ignorance.

She asked doubtfully, "What technique will you use?"

"Well, x-ray fluorescence is out," he said cautiously. "It requires too much area. Then there's electron microprobe ex-

amination. That's great, and there's one in the cases, but it
samples such a small region—a few microns across—that it
won't tell you anything about average composition." He eyed
her as he said this, and it all seemed to be going over okay.
"I'd say, neutron activation analysis. I have a small source
and it does no permanent damage."

It was also the only one whose instructions he could fully
understand. Until the late 1990s, neutron activation had been
a technique available only if you had a nuclear reactor handy,
for a neutron source. Watkins had helped develop a field-
portable kit, with a manual simple enough for archeologists
unacquainted with the new method. The kit was nothing but
"black boxes," components you wired up. The source shot
neutrons in and back came gamma rays. A tiny computer gave
a spectrum of the gammas. From the height of those peaks
and their location in the energy spectrum he should be able
to figure out what metals were present.

Or that's the way it looked from the manual, which he had
read diligently on the airplane instead of sleeping. He was
paying for that now; he yawned. His only hope lay in reduc-
ing the steps to mechanical acts, plug X1 into X3 sort of stuff.
He knew a little electronics and could use that for cover.

"Ummm . . ." She pondered. He admired the deft way she
placed a forefinger on her cheek, pursing her lips slightly,
making them fuller. She shifted her hip and the movement
seemed to lighten her, miraculously thinning her thighs beneath the khaki jumper, drawing the acute angle up to the
pedestal of her hips.

"Okay. Do it."

"Uh . . ." His attention swerved back. "Now?"

"Sure." She put her hands on her hips. "We've got only
days, maybe hours left. I'll help."

He nodded. His jet-lagged sleep last night had left him
dulled, with that faint air of watching everything from behind
a thick pane of dirty glass. He would have liked George's
help, too—like most academics, he expected that men who
worked with their hands more would have a broader knowledge of things electrical and mechanical. But George said he
knew nothing about metallurgical analysis or electronics, that
working with planks and shovels and braces was his line.

Anyway, they needed him out in the camp, diverting the laborers who were finishing up.

They unpacked and assembled in the musty, cool tomb, the clanking of metal reverberating back from the curved walls, giving each sound a stretched presence. He took his time, hoping he would recover some alertness, afraid of making errors. It was difficult maneuvering the equipment among the various stone blocks which hung in rope frames. John bumped into one of them and asked, mostly as a ruse for a break, "What's this from?"

Claire looked up from a case inventory. "That's the original block in front of the amber cone. See how it's marked?"

"Religious symbol?"

"We don't think so. There were bronze pieces mounted into the walls, too—or we think so, because they were buried when we found them."

He contemplated the stone, touched it gingerly. "Okay?"

She smiled. "Of course. Sorry I barked at you yesterday."

" 'S fine. How come they were buried?"

"The bronzes? Torn down by looters. Or else by later burial parties."

He frowned, slightly shocked. "They defiled the graves of their own ancestors?"

She smiled again. "This was a different culture, John. Apparently they gave the dead presents—tools and weapons and food and clothing, to help them on their passage. But once the flesh had decayed away, they thought that transition was complete. The dead didn't need the funerary gifts anymore. Most of these tombs were family burial sites. When a new burial party came, they tossed old skeletons aside to make room for the new arrival. We found ones scattered all over the tomb, at different levels."

"So the gifts, they were left out, where the dead could. . . use them?" He found the subject a little unsettling.

"Yes, or in boxes."

"Then how come they hid things?"

"They didn't. The looters apparently had no trouble finding what they wanted. Unless it was buried under the dirt left here by some burial parties."

He was puzzled. "Then why did they hide that?" He

pointed at the cube, still standing in its recess behind the massive corbelled blocks.

"I don't know."

"And why chisel on it, decorate it, when nobody's going to see it?"

Claire stared at the black limestone and said slowly, "That's one of the points that has been bothering me, also."

He ran a hand over the block hanging in its cradle, liking the rough coolness of it, feeling the small nicks on the unexposed sides where a long-dead craftsman had struck flakes from it to shape the surprisingly accurate angles and edges. "Some kind of design outside, saying something. . .but nobody buried behind this block, just a cube with chiseling on it. And that decoration, that cone. Funny . . ." He stooped to examine the face more closely. A long moment passed while Claire unfastened a bundle of cables and placed them on a blanket they had spread. He insisted on a systematic arrangement of the parts before they started assembly.

"How do you date the levels?" he asked.

"What?" She was concentrating and in the clatter of equipment missed his question.

"The different burials, how—"

"Oh yes, with pottery analysis. We know the styles, how they evolved. And if there's wood we can date it with Carbon 14."

"Right." He rubbed his hand over the edges of the block. "This crumbly stuff?"

"Mortar."

"And these marks here?"

"I don't know. Someone chipped away the outer mortar. There are those near the edge, too."

"Look like scratches, not chiseling."

"Yes, I think so."

"Fella used a knife or something."

"Ummmm?" She did not look up from her work.

"You'd think if anybody was doing a serious job, they'd use the right tools."

"Remember, people got rushed and did a sloppy job even in antiquity."

"On graves? Well, maybe so. So much for the good old days. Still, a knife . . ." He examined the apparently random marrings with a flashlight. "Maybe the guy used one of those ceremonial knives left in here."

"Looters usually bring their own tools."

"A knife's not good for this kind of work." He stood up. "Any way to date when that cube there was put behind the wall?"

"George found some signs it was quite late. We do know from some small jewelry in the topmost level that someone important—or rich, or both—was the last burial."

"End of the family line, umm? So this slab and the cube behind it, they might have been put in here with him."

"Or her."

"Sure. Or her." He rubbed his jaw.

"It might even have been a king."

"Yeah? Do tell." Distracted, he scuffed a toe in the hard-packed earth.

"They had elaborate ceremonies. At some sites there is minor, ambiguous evidence that the servants of the king were buried with him. It's a controversial issue."

This jolted him out of his reverie. "Really? What savages."

Offended, she said briskly, "A different culture. They were building these beautiful corbelled domes when your and my ancestors were chasing mastodons."

"I thought mastodons died out about ten thousand years ago." He grinned; this was one of the few facts he remembered from ninth grade science.

She smiled despite herself. "I can see I'll have to watch every word. But if you have Indian ancestors I could still be right."

"Every southerner has a little Indian blood in him."

"Mastodons were hunted up until a few thousand years ago by American Indians. But to get back to my point—Look at that triangle over the lintel. See? It relieved the weight of the rock above and carried it down, around the door. Advanced engineering. And they mounted a facade outside, painted stonework, beautifully carved."

"You think they might've buried some servants with this guy, this king?"

"Well. . .perhaps."

He leaned back and pondered the worn stones, trying to

put himself into that time, to see them freshly painted and decorated, witness to pomp and ritual. "Lord God A'mighty—think of that. Trapped in here."

"They filled in the *dromos* with sand after the last burial. Covered the whole hillside, too, from the signs we can find. Unusual. They knew they weren't going to bury anyone else in here again. This king, or whoever, must have been pretty special. A hero, a great law giver, a conqueror. Agamemnon we know about because of Homer, but this king could have been just as important."

"Uh huh. And his servants. Caught in here, no light—and if you did set fire to something, so you could see, it'd eat up your oxygen. Bet they didn't know that, though. Light up some of the clothing if you could, that would be easy. Did they have candles back then?"

"Doubtful. None would have survived this long, anyway. They probably used oil lamps."

He stood and gazed around the cluttered mud floor, peered up into the gloomy heights of sloped stone. "I wonder. . . wonder what it was like. Caught in here, you know there's only so much time . . ."

"Drugged, too."

"What?"

"They might well have drugged the servants, or got them drunk."

"Sure, good and drunk. Makes sense, once you accept the general idea. But how blotto can anybody get, knowing what's coming?"

Claire turned back to her work. "Speculation is fun, but this is urgent, and—"

"But you've got something to explain, too," he said forcefully. "Those markings."

"Looters."

"*Maybe* looters. It sure seems to me any looter worth his salt would finish chipping away at that mortar, see what was behind the block. The *only* marked stone in the whole tomb."

"Sure, sure, anything *might* have happened—"

"That's the puzzle." He whirled to the block and traced its circular design once more, all his fatigue burned away.

"Suppose a servant wakes up. Drunk. Knows where he is,

knows he hasn't got much time. He'd try to tunnel out, don't you think?"

"Perhaps. That *dromos* was filled with sand. He would have to burrow upward ten, fifteen feet—"

"Through fresh sand? Most of it would slide right on in, once the door was open."

"This was a sealed tomb. They would have to move several blocks out of the doorway, then dig upward."

He spread his hands expansively. "Wouldn't you at least *try?*"

"Well, yes. But I don't have the holy idea of ritual sacrifice drilled into me. They did."

He held up his hand, palm up, a mock-serious look on his face. "Pardon me, you're absolutely right, distant culture and all that sophisticated, broad-minded stuff. Bumpkins like me fail to take that into account, right?"

She smiled guardedly. "You said it, not me."

"Still, if we drop the looters theory for a minute, we conclude that *some*body tried to get out."

"Okay. Go ahead."

He gave an exaggerated bow, but when he stood up he again ran his hands over the random lines cut along the outer edges of the block. With the flashlight he traced out where a point had gouged deeper, skidded away, and come back to the job again, a little off to the side. "Sloppy work. Were there any marks like this around the entrance?"

"I'd have to consult my notebooks. Rowland did that early part of the dig. But—no, I don't think so."

"Good. Then the problem is, if somebody wants to get out, why's he chip away at this block?"

"To get to the cistern passageway we found."

"But you and George said that seepage hole wasn't there when they built the tomb. Otherwise they'd never have built so close to it."

"Well. . .maybe."

"Come on, follow the premise. The servants, poor people trapped in total blackness, they know they haven't got long. So why did they try to remove this block?"

"The cistern . . ."

He slapped the rock decisively. "They *wanted* something. And what's behind the block? Nothing"—he jabbed a finger—"except that cube."

CHAPTER
Five

That night Claire made another important discovery. John had come back to the tomb after a quick supper, planning to put in a perfunctory hour of work before collapsing into luxuriant sleep. Claire helped him where she could, but he persuaded her to leave him to his electronics. She took a roll of photographs of the space behind the artifact and then moved restlessly around the tomb.

"C'mon, Claire, find someplace to perch," John said irritably.

"You know, we haven't moved the cube yet."

"It's too heavy."

"Not with you and George helping. I'd like to look on the left side of it, see if there's a marking."

"Good idea," John said with relief.

She took an hour to arrange padded levers around the cube. The men pushed slowly on them, grunting, and managed to slide the cube sideways by the width of a hand.

"No markings," Claire said with disappointment, shining her flashlight into the gap. "Simply dust—no, wait."

She extracted the thing after another half hour of photographing and measuring. It was a square ivory sheet, thin and barely five centimeters on a side. The surface showed faint markings, dulled by time.

"Looks like someone carved the lines, then—see these reddish flakes?—painted over them to enhance the effect," Claire said.

ivory rectangle found beside cube

details are faint

some paint flakes adhered

George agreed. The ivory square had been standing edge-on in the dust. "It must've been glued onto the cube's side, and fallen off," George said.

"A decoration? What's it show?" John asked.

Claire carefully cradled it on a clean plastic sample field. "Not much. It's so *faint*. Nothing like a design—too irregular."

"Maybe it's too far gone," John said. Despite himself he yawned.

"I'll clean it tomorrow, try to enhance the contrast," Claire said. "Even if we can't extract the markings better, this is still an important find."

"How come?"

"Ivory was rare in Mycenae. The fact that it was used as a decoration of this artifact means whoever was buried here was very important."

"A king?"

"Probably."

"And the cube was important, too," George added.

John asked sleepily, "Then why'd they hide it?"

*   *   *

George was helping John move some blocks the next morning when a jeep's growing *rrrrrrr* caught their attention.

George's head turned abruptly. He grimaced. "Oh damn! We should've stuck to the plan and had you work through last night."

"Look, I was worn down to a nub. There's too—" John watched George trot out the entrance of the tomb. "Oh—that's him, huh?"

"Yeah. You stay put." George waved him back into the shadows. "I'll go down and explain that you're a tourist friend of Claire's."

"You'll bring him up here?"

"No, no, you don't—never mind." George trotted away.

John kept working on the metal analysis. He had finished boring into the side of the cube. It had been a tricky process, the tiny drill whirring like a trapped bee inside the stone. He noted with pride that the hole was clean and professional-looking.

Now he had to triple-check the black boxes. They took up a lot of space in the cramped zone around the cube. He had gotten George to move the heavy stone blocks out of the way, which gave him time to cover his own unfamiliarity with the circuit layout. The connections looked okay now, though. He turned on the instruments and was rewarded with a satisfying, unalarming hum. It would need a while to warm up properly.

He read the manual again and waited. After a while curiosity overcame caution. What the hell, he had been tiptoeing his way through this procedure for hours; he needed a break. He swung the big wooden door shut over the entrance and left the site.

As he walked down the switchback path to the camp he saw a powerfully built man talking to George. The man made quick, impatient gestures at the laborers who were loading the trucks. They weren't agreeing very much. The man's words rolled out loudly and John could tell the laborers were listening to him while trying to seem at work, heads turned at angles to eavesdrop.

He threaded his way among the last erect tents, wondering if he should walk into an argument. He was on shaky ground here in the first place, out of his field—

Claire suddenly appeared from inside the pottery-sorting area. Perspiration beaded her lip. Had she been waiting for him?

"Wait—before you talk to Kontos," she said tensely.

"Well, if you'd just as soon I didn't—"

"No, *listen*. He hasn't seen me yet and I want to stay out of his way. I don't think he saw you come down from the site. Pretend you've just returned from a walk by the ocean."

"What? You're getting—"

"Then say we're going away this afternoon, going to see Mycenae."

"I'm not following you."

"You can't work in the tomb with him around. And I don't want to be forced to tell that—that—to tell Kontos anything before I have to."

"My, you truly are agitated." He patted her shoulder. "Didn't know he still bothered you so much."

"It's—it's not just him. I haven't told him about the cube."

"So?"

"And I'm not going to."

"Ah." His eyebrows arched like caterpillars.

"Look, you don't know how it was, I've got good reason."

"How long do you think before he—"

"Enough time to satisfy our curiosity, at least. Kontos would grab it all for himself, believe me."

"Well, still now—"

She said impatiently, "Skip the advice, okay? Just skip it. Now go talk to him. But you know nothing, remember?"

"How could I forget? It's true." He smiled and ambled on.

Doctor Alexandros Kontos reminded John of a good football player—sizable, muscular, yet not heavy, with a bunched energy restrained by calculating intelligence.

John was comfortably large enough that sheer size did not impress him in another man. He had played quarterback in high school, and gotten by on his speed rather than mass. He passed accurately, ran moderately well, had made All City in his senior year, but by then dozens of heavy linesmen had hit him with everything they had and a part of his mind could not forget the experience. Shifting sideways, looking downfield for a receiver, you can't be already bracing for the 250-pound animal about to slam you into the mud. If you do flinch, the pass will go wrong. Until you let go of the ball you must carry the absolute conviction that you are immortal, untouchable. When John felt that slipping from him he knew he'd never be worth a damn anymore, and quit playing.

Kontos bristled with flinty, assured aggression. He would have made a good quarterback.

John was on guard as he approached. Deceiving Kontos would take craft; he hoped Claire didn't intend to keep it up for long.

George introduced them. Kontos instantly made his face impassive, giving nothing away, as he shook John's hand. "I fear you come just as everything is ending."

"Aw, it doesn't matter. I wanted to see the countryside, mostly, not just old bones."

Kontos, to his credit, smiled at the mild jab. "We Greeks have more 'bones' than anyone. After you have had your fill of our beautiful landscapes, perhaps you will look in at the Museum in Athens. It is worthwhile even for the purely pleasure seeker. There is more to our country than sun and wine and beaches, you know." The well-oiled voice carried just the right balance of cordiality and insinuation. All the while the eyes were glancing at his clothes, hands, face, filling in a mental picture.

"Well, I'll surely do that. Just wanted to see Claire a little, while I was here."

"You have been here long enough to visit elsewhere in the Peloponnese?"

"No. . .just dropped in," John said, taking advantage of the Southerner's slow drawl to think. "I figured I'd let Claire show me around."

"Oh?" Polite interest.

"We were just leaving for Mycenae."

"Very good. A marvelous place, one of our most ancient." He pronounced it "auncient," gazing around. "She is . . ."

"Getting dressed."

"I see. And after you leave here?"

"I thought maybe I'd go south, do some diving."

"Very good. The Cycladic islands, then?"

"I reckon so."

Kontos visibly lost interest in probing and turned to George. "Perhaps you should plan on a vacation as well, eh?"

"What do you mean?" George said evenly.

"On your return journey to the United States, you could stop somewhere. There is perhaps some money left in the account for the group."

"Is that your idea of a bribe?"

To John's surprise, Kontos took no offense at this. The man simply pulled his lips leftward, sardonically. "An unfortunate word. You say, before Mr. Bishop appeared, that you wished to remain a while longer. I just am pointing out that you could spend such days in a better, a more relaxing place."

"Come off it," George said sourly. "I don't want any vacation. I want to get this job done."

"It will be finished in due time." Kontos's voice turned suddenly cold. "Meanwhile, you. Will. Leave."

"Now just—"

"No! I want you—all of you—gone. In two days."

"That's crazy," George said.

"I am fearing the situation warrants it."

"What situation?"

Kontos shrugged. "I try, but who can guarantee the good will of these laborers? They might do anything, in reaction to the current actions of your government."

"These guys? Come off it."

"What you think, it does not matter. You will follow the orders of the host co-chairman."

"I don't like your explanation. I think it's phony."

"I do not *at all* have to explain you why. But I am polite now. You can do equally?"

George bit his lip.

Kontos put his hands on his hips. "You do understand?"

"Yeah. But that's two days clear, right? I don't want to have anything slow up the work."

Kontos smiled, his moustache gleaming in a shaft of sunlight. "You may work, of course—as long as the packing is complete in time. And I will return to check the materials, the cataloging for the Museum, everything. I personally."

George said grimly, "Great."

CHAPTER
Six

As they drove toward Nauplia, John said to Claire, "I thought we were going to that ruined city, Mycenae."

She smiled. "That was the first plausible thing I could think of. There'll be plenty of time for ruins later."

"No Mycenae?"

"I thought you wanted diving. Notice that your gear is still in the trunk?"

"You told me to leave it there. You said it might get stolen otherwise."

She glanced sidewise at him, her cheeks dimpling with a grin. "I had plans."

"Which are?"

"You'll see."

He chuckled; she wasn't as subtle as she thought. They joined the main road that wound up the coast of the Gulf of Argolis. Claire provided commentary with the effortless welling-up that bespoke a lifelong fascination. Her hair streamed behind in the breeze and her eyes danced.

Here the Mediterranean was rimmed by sandy inlets that had provided ideal anchorage for the ships of antiquity. To the north, rugged mountains descended into lesser eminences, framing the plain of Argos with rocky hills. This was the stony stage for the great myths of Perseus, founder of Mycenae, for the labors of Heracles, for the Trojan war launched from here. From these innumerable sandy coves had come the "thousand ships" drawn by Helen's beauty and the lure of

Troy's wealth. Agamemnon led them forth in myriad small boats, to return years later, full of victory—and be slaughtered by his wife, assisted by her lover. The land lay drenched in blood from a million battles, betrayals, sacrifices. Its soil was thin and iron-poor, two facts that led the first dwellers here to exploit the sea, and to make remarkably beautiful pottery of pure yellow or light red clay. These were their trademarks: daring seamanship aboard slim, shallow-bottomed craft that bore the beautiful jugs, carrying rich oils or dark, astringent wines—a people known from Asia Minor to Crete to Egypt.

They swept into Nauplia at Claire's customary speed, scattering some dozing, dirty goats.

"Why do they have their hind legs tied to the foreleg on one side?" he asked as their dust wake obscured the scrambling herd.

"That stops them from climbing into the hills. They can't step high enough. It's simpler than building fences."

He nodded. His mathematician's eye appreciated a solution both sensible and elegant.

The lamb at lunch was rich and well marbled with fat. Cafes lined the street alongside the classic quay, sporting gaudy displays of touristy books and trinkets. John had white fish, cooked and eaten whole in lightly spiced oil. The pungent dip of yogurt and garlic made him gasp.

"Local culture," she said, laughing.

"Like those postcards?" He pointed.

Atop the rack of standard cards was a set of cartoon figures, resembling the stark scenes of classical Greek vase painting. Heracles was performing the fourth of the labors imposed on him by Eurystheus the King—bringing a huge captured boar before the King and his women. A fair copy in reds and blacks on a rose background, so typical that one might miss the modern additions of swollen genitalia and lascivious stares.

"Oh, those," Claire said disdainfully.

"Local pornography?"

"Simple bad taste. Some tourists will buy anything. Particularly Americans."

"Your Bostonian reserve is showing."

"Not at all. Something done badly has no excuse."

"What about the real thing?"

"Pornography? I like food, but not somebody saying, 'When I eat peas, I take three or four and mash them between my teeth, then spread them over the roof of my mouth, getting them even, making them all gooey, and—' See?"

He laughed. "You win."

After lunch they strolled along the quay, John lugging his diving gear from the car. Somewhat to his surprise there was a diving shop with tanks. He rented a pair, checked them with his own regulator, and went out to the commercial boats. There were dozens in port, mostly fishing craft with nets. The state of the Greek economy was apparent at a glance: men idling alongside their boats, some tending to the perennial jobs of painting, cleaning, repairing, but most wearing the sour look of boredom.

He studied a small fortified island offshore while Claire spoke to the captain of a red fiberglass motorboat. The gray stonework commanded the harbor with a high square tower and semi-circular fort. "Imposing," he said to Claire.

She broke off negotiations. "The Venetians built that, when they held Greece. They could close off the harbor by stretching a half-mile chain out to it. When Greek independence came along, the government used the island as the home of their executioner."

"Charming place."

"Concensus politics isn't a habit in the Mediterranean," she said lightly. "Get your diving gear. I've bargained this fellow down as far as I can without rending my garments."

"Do go on, then. I have to stay within budget, remember."

She made a face. "You'll have to work harder than that."

"Effortlessly, ma'am."

The red motorboat cut a white V across the azure flatness of the Gulf. The peninsula of Hermionis, where their dig perched on a cliff, served as breakwater for the Gulf, deflecting the mild-mannered waves of the Mediterranean. Each time Claire gave the pilot directions the swarthy man bit down on his perpetual cigarette and twisted the wheel abruptly, even if no course correction was required. "Macho Hellenic tradition," Claire remarked.

"They don't like taking orders from a woman?"

"Who does?" Claire eyed him wryly.

"Ummm," he said noncommitally.

"But they'll take the money," she said.

They headed southeast, past barren knobs of islands, salt spray wetting Claire's white blouse. She shucked it casually, revealing a swimsuit underneath. John suited up in the stern, admiring her covertly. She was slim and proportioned with what he thought could, in artistic circles, be termed admirable restraint.

When they slowed beside a ragged, stony beach he peered overboard, looking for rocks or seaweed, some sign of good diving spots. "Would you like fish tonight?"

"I don't care," she said. "That's not what we're after."

"Oh?" He was not surprised.

"Recognize that?" She pointed at the cliffs nearby.

"No."

"Our dig is just out of sight around that hill."

"And you want me to . . ."

"Correct."

He slid over into the warm salt clasp. Visibility was excellent. He swam downward to a muddy bottom. There were large fish nestled in among patches of sea plants, and a surprising number of strange-shaped, barnacled protrusions littered the floor. Pieces of old shipwrecks, he guessed. All that remained of millennia of disaster and pillage and brave, bloody venture.

The serene schools of fish seemed to have no fear of him, no experience. He felt almost guilty at how easy it was to spear three large ivory-skinned ones. He took them up to the boat and Claire called, "See any signs of it?"

"Nope."

"Try nearer shore."

"Sho' 'nuff." He suppressed his irritation at her single-mindedness, and dove again.

Mud gave way to sandy bottom as he swam shoreward. Weed clung to outcroppings of rock. A rusted shaft like a truck axle kept his attention for a moment as he tried to figure out how it could have gotten here, and then he resumed his slow, systematic search. He felt natural and free like this, slipping easily through water that was like a bath compared to most of the dives he had known. Squeezing his breath through a narrow tube did not seem constricting, somehow, compared with the chest-tightening sensation of being in close confines, like the other day in the tiny opening inside the tomb wall. Under water things were different—he could move freely, flying and swooping in shafts of brimming golden sunlight. Most people were afraid of being underwater, but he had been a swimmer since he was two years old, flailing about in the Gulf of Mexico, associating the ocean with vacations and freedom and timeless fun. If he'd had to learn in a swimming pool like the gloomy, chlorinated, joyless one at MIT—

There. Two parallel ridges of rock.

He had come upon them at an angle. They stood a few feet above the sandy bottom, bracketing a jumble of rocks. He followed the ridges away from shore. They went straight, parallel as train tracks and somewhat narrower. He followed them away from shore for over fifty meters before they disappeared under an expanse of mud.

He doubled back. The rocks filling the middle of the tracks were fairly large but did not look unusual to his untrained eye. He picked up one and carried it in his burlap fish bag.

A school of gray motes flashed into silver and then back to gray, hovering in rigid ranks a safe distance away, studying him carefully. They kept an exact spacing between themselves and then, as he approached again, dissolved instantly, to reform again at the edge of his vision. Their hovering precision was a marvel. In such ordinary things mathematics seemed most casually elegant, he thought. How did nature specify the fishes' spacing against the tugging currents, what measure told them when he came too near? That was what drew him to mathematics. Not because it was rarefied, but because it probed to the subtle, deeper reality. People said that mathematicians were unworldly, and yammered on about how Einstein couldn't make correct change. Nonsense. Einstein just didn't give a damn. It was the subtle, the beautiful that concerned him.

He swam toward the shadow of the cliff. The ridges were still straight and now they began to rise up from the sandy floor, stubs of rock jutting obliquely, perhaps betraying the angle of the local strata.

He glanced up. Still at least twenty feet under. He swam

into the cliff's shadow. Details were muted here and weeds clung to every crevice, green and scarlet and cinnamon, waving at him drowsily, obscuring the ruined contours of the stone tube.

The angle of the two small ridges steepened as it neared the bulging rock of the cliff wall. Erosion was worse here, probably because of wave action. Behind the regular burbling rush of his exhaled bubbles he heard the low mutter of turbulence overhead. He lost sight of the blurred ridges in the gloom. By now he was under an overhang and the rippling refracted light played tricks of perception. The shadows were deeper there, higher up the worn rock. He swam upward, into darkness.

A cave. A water-formed passageway knifing up into the cliff. He remembered standing in the cramped little stone pocket, a foot from the edge. There had been the distant swish of water. So this channel went all the way up.

John unhooked his flashlight and clicked it on. The cave walls were smooth and unremarkable in its yellowish splash radiance. He ventured a few feet farther. The steepening continued. Claire said that seepage from above had slowly opened this weak seam, in the 3500 years since the Mycenaeans sealed their king's tomb. Interesting, he supposed, for geologists.

Something brushed his shoulder and he whirled, heart thumping. A strand of seaweed. The wave surge here was weak but he went rigid each time a current forced him farther up the cave, bracing with one hand to prevent being taken farther in.

His tank clanged on an upthrusting of mossy stone. The flashlight showed nothing more than a smooth bore ahead, snaking upward and away. Inky cold currents flowed across his chest. He decided he had reconnoitered enough, thank you.

Claire jumped when he broke surface next to the boat. "My God! You were gone so long—what happened?"

"I found a seep hole."

The pilot helped him wallow aboard. He shrugged off the tank straps.

"You're certain?"

"Sure. I know what you're thinking—that it was a tunnel, dug by the tomb builders."

"Uh, yes."

"Well, they were sure gluttons for work if they did. It continues out into the sea bed, maybe a hundred yards or so. Only a couple feet wide. Looks like a collapsed tube. Then it runs into mud."

"Oh. Too narrow for a man to dig."

"You're pretty desperate for a big find, aren't you?"

She looked affronted, dark eyebrows descending. "I'm following up every possibility. Archeology—"

"I know, you said before—the science of endless details."

"There was always the chance—"

"Look," he said impatiently, "that seep hole was worn through 'way back. It runs out into the gulf. The sea bed's just gradually washed most of it away and—"

"Yes, you're undoubtedly right. There's a subterranean stream tube that emerges offshore at Anabalos, too, I remember. There must be many—what's that?"

"Sample from the caved-in rock."

"Oh." She seemed mollified by the gift of a slimy, wet stone. She handled it gingerly.

"I'll try roses next time."

She laughed. "You are an *odd* man. And—I do thank you. For doing this."

"I couldn't very well let that Kontos browbeat you all day."

She nodded. "I hate him," she said matter-of-factly.

When they docked there was a band playing on the quay.

"Quite a reception," John said, studying the crowds in the twilight. Clouds scudded overhead.

"It's not for us, I assure you," Claire said lightly. "See those signs?"

"Politics?"

"Yes. Let's see—National Socialist Labor Party."

"That's the one Kontos is so fired up about?"

She nodded. A loudspeaker boomed down the quay, impossibly loud. On a platform a man obscured by the crowd called out a singsong phrase in a giant's voice and the crowd answered, their ragged chorus a faintly comic echo of him.

He shouted a few sentences and again the people answered, stronger this time. This went on for several minutes, with the man becoming more excitable. In white-washed cafes lining the quay old men sipped beer and watched, blank-faced. John noticed that the crowd was mostly young people wearing denims. He heard the word "America" used in sentences that rose in inflection, ending with a shout. Each time some men in the crowd waved their fists. They seemed to function as cheerleaders.

"What's it about?"

"The Elgin marbles, air bases, the price of olives."

Several men nearby had heard the English. They turned and stared.

"Let's eat," John said. He shifted his diving belt over his shoulder.

"Greeks don't have dinner this early."

"What? I can't hear in this—"

"I want to find out what he's leading up to."

The chanting stopped. They were over a hundred meters from the platform. The quay was filling with men in baggy work clothes. Several Army officers appeared on the platform, waving to the crowd. One of them began to speak.

The deep tones rolled down the quay, reflecting from the stucco buildings, distorted. The crowd shouted in agreement. Their voices were hoarse, angry. John noticed the men still looking at them, nudging others nearby, talking.

"At least let's get a drink."

"What? Something about national unity."

One of the men smirked at his friends and ran his gaze slowly up and down Claire's body. John caught his eye and the man jutted out his jaw defiantly.

"I need some supper."

"Too many political parties, he says."

Now half a dozen people were watching them, not paying attention to the speaker at all. There was a set to their faces John did not like.

"Come on." He picked up his diving gear, grunting.

"No, I want—".

"Come *on*." He took her elbow and steered her away. One of the men started after them. John glared back at him and Claire, watching, understood instantly.

They walked rapidly away. The man slowed, stopped, and finally contented himself with an obscene gesture.

Claire said, "That junior-grade Hitler can steam them up."

"I'll say. Funny, I didn't see that stuff on the travel posters."

"I've never seen people so stirred. That man, he was truly *angry* at us."

"The justifiable rage of the oppressed, y'know," John said, doing an imitation of Kontos's accent.

Claire laughed. "This cafe's open—let's stop. You can put down that diving stuff."

John set down the air tank with a groan of relief. His sandy hair was mussed and he itched all over from the salt still on his skin. Still, it had been exhilarating, exotic. Much like Claire herself, he mused, as they ordered wine with retsina in it. She was thoroughly, unconsciously Bostonian. He watched her as she gestured at the fish he'd speared, asking in a quick flow of Greek that they be cooked as the main dish. The waiter did not seem to find this unusual. She studied the menu and asked the waiter questions without glancing at the man, at ease, not even making a gesture toward letting John handle matters. He liked that. It was one thing to be instantly attracted to a woman, and another to like her independence, the way she took no notice of what he thought of her, one way or the other. She was indeed a modern woman—not aggressive, yet not submissive. A self-possessed apartness, a lack of cling. A far remove from the southern girls he had dated and bedded and became bored with.

Her lips pursed in a businesslike, introspective way as she pondered a choice, running a forefinger down the edge of the menu, oblivious to the languidly sensual undercurrent in the gesture. Yes, that was what held his attention: her reserve. The promise of depths you could not guess merely by seeing her in a swimsuit.

"Was it one of your boyhood hobbies?"

"Um?"

"Diving."

"Oh. No, the only hobby I had as a teenager was amateur gynecology."

She laughed lightly and gave him a guarded look. "With those serene-looking southern girls?"

"Under the crinoline they're not so different," he said loyally.

"Ummm."

More of the cautious look. He decided not to tell her about his short postgraduate stint at Berkeley, and the mixed reviews he gave California women. Generalizations were hopeless anyway. He had had some disastrous affairs and some of the good-but-doomed variety, and doubtless so had she. From the relentless specifics of each one it was hard to refine any comforting lessons. Even worse, it was hard to say anything intelligent.

He asked brightly, "What did you order for us?"

"A side dish of calamari. That's squid. Could you understand any of my Greek?"

He shook his head. "I'm bilingual in English and calculus."

"You'll pick it up if you pay attention."

"I'm about as improved as I'm gonna get."

"I'd have thought you would at least learn Spanish or something, down there in . . ."

"Georgia."

"Oh yes. I keep thinking it's close to Miami, and with all the Cubans there . . ." She picked up a bread stick and bit it off with a satisfied crunch. "Didn't something happen in Georgia in the Civil war?"

He drawled, "You refer to the War of Seccession, ma'am?"

"Good Lord, I've never heard that."

"A term of my father's."

"Sheridan's March, that's it."

"You mean Sherman's March."

"Yes. He won a great battle outside Atlanta, wasn't it?"

"Burned a lot of houses and crops, if that's what you mean," he said sharply.

She raised her eyebrows. "My. You still *feel* it, don't you?"

He managed a smile. "Losers don't forget as fast as winners."

"I suppose that's true. No one ever talks about it in Boston. My great-grandfather bought his way out of military service, I believe."

"Yes, just a li'l interruption between Independence and Kennedy."

"I wonder if that's what's happening here," Claire murmured softly. "Civil war."

"That rally, you mean?" He gazed back toward the floodlit quay, where the loudspeaker was silent at last.

"There was a lot of jargon I couldn't understand, but he seemed to be calling for getting rid of some of the 'obstructionist' political factions."

"Uh oh."

"Yes. And that man who—who—"

"Gave us the finger, that's the technical term."

"Well, I've *never* seen such public impoliteness in Greece."

"Why, then?"

"The economy is flat on its back. It's always tempting to blame a foreign scapegoat."

"Good ol' us."

"I'm afraid so. Kontos may be right about many political things, though. He used to be such a *good* archeologist."

"Well, right or wrong, he's still an SOB."

"It's not that we're blameless."

He grinned wearily. "Who is?"

The waiter arrived with wine. John poured. He was much more interested in Claire than in politics. Best to steer conversation to lighter areas.

"Y'know," he began, "maybe the more you travel, the more things look the same. Greece reminds me of Mexico a lot. Same tinny music on the radio, same bare-bones style, electric light bulbs with no shades, same—awk!"

She giggled. "The dread retsina strikes again!"

CHAPTER
Seven

When they returned to the site Kontos and his men had just arrived. He shone his flashlight into their front seat.

"Where did you go?" he demanded.

John said, "Around, looking at things."

"The site officer at Mycenae saw no one matching your description."

Claire said calmly, opening her door, "We went into Nauplia. When John saw the water, he wanted to get in some diving. By the time we were through, it was too late to reach Mycenae."

"I do not think it is wise to go anywhere you are not expected," Kontos said.

John said, "What's 'expected' mean?"

"I called the site officer to see that you were given a special tour."

"Very kind of you," John said. They picked their way along the shadowy path to the camp.

"Perhaps you saw my speech in Nauplia?"

Claire blurted, "That was *you?*"

"I am a party official as well. A show of a united front was needed, Army plus the people. I went with my brother officers of the town." He smiled warmly, remembering. "A great evening for our country. I told them of the excitement in Athens."

"You certainly got them lathered up," Claire said coolly.

Kontos said confidently, "You are unaccustomed to see a

country united? Come, have a glass of tea." He led them to a table outside a nearby tent. Four Greek Army enlisted men accompanied them.

"Who're they?" Claire asked.

"Assistants," Kontos said casually. "I need help in the difficult business of forging political connections with the countryside." He pointed out two sedans on the road below. "I am hoping that I can contribute at the Ministry of Culture, to mobilize our society."

While he fussed with a small kerosine stove and a pot, Claire described the hostile glares they'd received.

"What can you expect? You are obvious and foreign. They are poor, they are angry. The major exports of the fields here are oranges, apricots—principally to the Ukrainians and Russians. Yet they too are poor, now. They cut back their buying."

"So?"

"It may be this would not happen, if we could form a united front against the sources of capital."

"Uh huh." John shrugged and changed the subject. "I couldn't recognize your voice, distorted over the loudspeakers. What was that about the Elgin marbles?"

"They are beautiful sculptures from our Acropolis. In Athens are the ones I saved."

"Oh. I didn't stop in Athens."

"To see the others, you must go to London for that. The British, they take them in 1803, before our independence from the Turks. We demand having them back. Otherwise, we break diplomatic relations with the British."

"Isn't it a little late?" she asked. "After all, the English took care of them while the rest of the Acropolis was falling apart."

"They are ours."

Claire said, "The Turks vandalized the Parthenon, the Venetians shelled it, and the British saved marbles from it. Don't they deserve some credit?"

"The marbles, they are a useful symbol for us, for the party. Against foreign oppression. If we Greeks stand together, demand our birthright, we will be heard."

"Sure will," John observed over the sweet coffee. "You weren't doing much to calm them down."

"They are tired of your factories here, taking their labor and sending the profits to the USA."

"Where should the profits go?"

"To our government. To our people."

"Those two aren't necessarily the same."

"Soon they will be. *Soon*."

"You want the profits, why didn't you build the factories yourselves?"

"Today, we would. But the banks have all the money. The banks *you* control."

"I sure don't," John said to lighten the mood, glancing at Claire. She was staying out of the conversation.

"I understand," Kontos said. "You are a victim as well. You devoted your life to a technical area, yes? Only to find when you have to live in the real world that it is not the technical men who rule, eh?"

"Who does?"

"The banks, of course."

"Come on."

"Your films, your television, they do not show it, the truth. But we know. In your country the munitions makers ride in their limousines and prepare their wars, while the workers cannot afford new shoes."

"Back where I come from, not wearing shoes is fun. I used to do it all summer."

Kontos pursed his lips and stared gravely at John. "I do not joke, you know. That crowd tonight, they were angry at your country's arrogance."

"Let 'em buy back any factories we've got over here."

"What? Buy what is on our own soil?"

"Easier to steal it, huh?"

Kontos slammed his fist to the table. "Our people have paid many times that. With their sweat!"

Claire said mildly, "What were you saying in Nauplia about obstructionists?"

"That there should be none. That we must have a single-party state."

"Eliminate the opposition, you mean?" John asked. "How?"

"We must dissolve our parliament for the duration of the present difficulties."

John waved a hand in dismissal. "I thought this was the birthplace of democracy."

Kontos smiled coldly. "We will be just like the USA. Only we will be more honest."

"We've got two parties."

"No you do not. You have only the party of the banks, of the money men, and they divide it into two pieces for your voting."

"Look," John said earnestly, waving his hand again, "I know you people are having hard times, but all this rabble-rousing—"

Without warning Kontos grabbed John's hand and slammed it to the tabletop. "You will not dismiss that 'rabble' if they have men to speak for them!"

John was shocked at the sudden flaring anger. He wrenched his shoulder around and struggled, muscles bulging. Kontos pressed the hand flatter on the table, as if the two men were in the terminal stage of an arm-wrestling contest. He leaned across the table and smiled silently, watching the American grunt with effort. "Try harder," he said, panting.

John made a sudden surge, lifting his arm a foot off the table. The arm held there, both men gasping. Slowly Kontos forced it back down, pressing it to the rough wood. John could not get free. "Dammit, let go!"

"Of course," Kontos said blandly, releasing him. "I was showing how it feels to be powerless. You see?" Again the cold smile.

"What the hell—"

"An illustration, Mr. Bishop, of the mood of my country."

John bunched his fists. "I'd like to give you—"

"Yes?"

Claire broke in, taking John's arm. "Back off, both of you. This is stupid."

John looked at her, uncertain. "I'm not going to let—"

"Forget him. Believe me, he's not worth it."

"I'm not afraid of any—"

"John, please! Come away." She tugged at his sleeve.

"Well . . ." He took a step back and Kontos did too. "Damn fine hospitality you got here, Kontos," John called.

The other man gave an ironic salute, still smiling.

*   *   *

Even hours later, John couldn't leave the subject alone. It galled him further that he had had to sneak up to the tomb at night.

"I still say I'd rather have popped the bastard."

"And get us thrown out of the country, of course."

"So what? Better than—"

"You're here as *my* guest, *I'm* paying the way, so you do as—"

"Dammit, woman, that man's not going to let you stay much longer anyway." Irritated, John went back to peering at his oscilloscope traces. They'd had this out twice before, and he knew where it led—to his finally having to admit to himself that he'd been intimidated. That at the crucial moment he had known that his own anger was no match for the fury in Kontos. So that when he hesitated, Claire's words had come through to him and his mind, ever agile, had interpreted her to say, *Don't jeopardize anything*. So he had backed down.

A rational decision, probably. But he didn't like the reasons.

"Actually," Claire said soothingly, "I thought it was a marvelous tactic you were following, getting him onto politics right away. Before he had a chance to ask about your diving."

He nodded, jotting down numbers. "Sure, brilliant. Got my face pushed in."

They were gathered around the instruments, a single lamp throwing sharp shadows onto the cube face before them. They had gotten up an hour before, just past midnight. It had been silent in the camp and they had slipped away easily, up the hillside. Claire had one of the two keys to the Yale lock. The door was made of fresh wood and creaked awfully when they opened it.

Claire wanted to be sure his measurements were done by morning, in case they never got back in here again. As he worked on the long routines of analysis and triple-checking each step, she boxed the cube in with standard crating materials, working around him.

When George had swung it out yesterday, suspended on his system of ropes and straps, they had all been impressed by its bulk. Claire had measured it again and again, surprised that its proportions—94.6 centimeters on each side, with scarcely five millimeters of error anywhere—were so exact. Now it lay on its packing bed, its squat mass relieved only by the delicate amber cone on the forward face.

"I hope they can't hear that hammer down at the camp," John said.

"The door absorbs most of it. . .I think."

"I don't like this sneaking around."

"Stick with it just a little longer. I don't want Kontos knowing anything about this piece until I have a chance to think it over and see your results."

"He'll see it back in Athens in a week or so, as soon as they start unpacking."

"Maybe not. I think he's going to be too busy with his politics."

"Wishful thinking. Anybody who opens that crate, or reads the manifest carefully—"

"It's not on the catalog yet."

"How come?"

"I'm leaving it for last."

"Boy, you've got this figured down to the second."

"All summer Kontos has been making insulting remarks, leering, trying to arrange little tête-á-têtes with me. Plus handing me the dullest, least promising jobs. I'm getting mine back." She drove a nail in with such fierceness that John started.

"Hey, easy."

"Oh. Sorry. Any results?"

"Too many, that's the problem." He pointed at the curve on the Tracor oscilloscope face, a yellow line interrupted by narrow spikes. "Dozens of little emission peaks. Every damn element in the book."

"Metals?"

"Plenty. Copper, tin, zinc, indium—"

"An alloy?"

"If it is, it's pretty damned sophisticated."

"They knew a good deal of metallurgy. Remember, in the *Odyssey*, how Homer describes Odysseus and his men getting the giant Cyclops drunk? Then they blind him so they can escape. Homer said the hot olive stick going into Cyclops's eye sizzled the way a piece of iron does when a blacksmith plunges it into cold water."

"Uh, nice image," John said queasily.

"But see, it means a smithy cooling iron in water to harden it was a familiar experience for Homer."

John said nothing, not wanting to admit that he'd never read any Homer. In the sciences there wasn't time to read a lot, and scientific prose was so condensed that your reading speed slowed through the years. He could remember reading two or three books in an afternoon during rainy days in Georgia; now he spent a week on a respectable-sized novel.

"Alloys, okay," he said. "But inside *rock?*"

Claire had finished all but the cover of the crate. "So it must be metal-rich stone. Dark limestone can come from sea bed deposits, laid down by river runoff."

"I dunno. There are signs of melting. You get a characteristic dendritic pattern if cast alloys cool off, when different components solidify out preferentially."

"Come now. That can't be *cast*, not down in the chisel marks."

"Um. I suppose not."

"What more can you tell me, from all this data?"

He punched in a storage command. "Nothing. I've got it all on disk. We'll have to analyze it back at MIT."

"Good. Now help me with this crate lid."

He saw she had secured the slab in a cross-lacing to protect against shock. "Yes, against jolts and dolts, both," she said. "You'd be amazed how some of these—"

"You hear something?"

They froze. Silence.

"Come on," she whispered.

They struggled the heavy wooden lid into place. The amber horn was well cushioned; John checked it one last time. The flecks deep inside it were orange motes that in the wan lamplight seemed to float, airy and light. Sparkles of ruby and gold seemed to be lit not by his lamp, but by some momentary inner glow. The radiance came only fitfully, like a spreading warmth within. John moved slightly and lost the right viewing angle; now the cone appeared dulled, passive. A beautiful effect.

"It's damn pretty, all right."

"Um."

"Bet they'll put it on exhibit right away."

"Probably."

"Kontos'll be fit to be tied when he sees it."

"Too bad I can't be there. I'd like to see the look on his face."

"He'll raise a stink."

"Let him. He'll know he can't claim discovery himself."

"True. But he'll have the artifact to show off."

"And I'll share credit with the National Museum in Athens," Claire said primly, tightening down the wood screws. "I'd have had to in any case. But this way he doesn't get to elbow me aside." She grunted, turning the big screwdriver with both hands.

"Here, let me do that." He still disliked seeing a woman struggle with a tool while a man stood around. "So everybody'll get equal credit, right? Kontos won't be able to toot his own horn."

"Even having our names on a paper together is too much contact for me. I—"

The entrance door swung open, creaking.

Kontos stood framed by the massive stones, eyes bright and glittering with excitement, his face creased by an amused sneer. Several enlisted men crowded behind him.

"A little party?"

CHAPTER
Eight

The gray Greek Army sedan swerved around a slow truck, tires howling, throwing Claire and John violently across the back seat.

"Dammit, watch out!" John shouted. The soldier sitting on his right watched him steadily, menacingly. The sedan's driver tromped down on the gas and they surged forward.

Colonel Kontos turned from his position beside the driver and regarded John coldly. "You are afraid?"

"Stupidity always scares me," John said.

Kontos bridled, his lips drawn back into a thin, bloodless, vindictive line. "It is not too late to take you to headquarters. A few days in the cells."

They rocketed along the expressway, heading southeast toward the Athens airport. To the right the island of Salamis shone like a rough marble in the jeweled setting of the sea. Salamis, where the Greeks destroyed the intruders. Though he had seen it only a few days before, it seemed like a long time had passed.

"You'd have to tell our embassy," Claire said.

"So I would. But I could have you transferred from one holding prison to another every twelve hours. Very hard to find such people."

"Typical," John spat out.

Kontos ignored the comment. "Also, your ambassador has much else to concern him. We have formally announced plans to withdraw from NATO this morning."

Claire said, "Gorgeously dumb."

"You think we would remain in an alliance with your—"

"Never mind us, what about the Turks?"

"We can deal with them," Kontos said stiffly.

Claire sighed. "The same old grudge match, going all the way back to Agamemnon."

"*You* speak of international cooperation?" Kontos laughed harshly. "Concealing your results, carrying out excavations without consent of the director—"

"Dr. Hampton approved! He gave me the go-ahead before he left."

"*I* became resident director the instant he left. And I am the senior director because I am Greek. You had to get—"

"The hell I did. Ask *you* for approval, when the first thing you'd do is invite me back to your tent to discuss the matter?"

Kontos said blandly, "I am sure I do not know what you are meaning." He glanced at John. "But I do know what to do with those who violate the international standards. You are leaving Greece—forever, I am sure."

Claire paled. "You can't magnify a thing like this into—"

"A wise woman holds her tongue. You merely prove how little of a woman you are."

"Hold on," John said. "This is personal enough without—"

"Shut up," Kontos said viciously, "or I will bloody your face again."

John gritted his teeth and was about to say something when the car shot across two lanes, throwing him against Claire. The soldier on his right held onto the door handle for support. The car shot into the turnoff for the airport. He was glad of the interruption. Getting into another shouting match with Kontos would get him the same result as last time; Kontos was for damn sure right about that.

They skidded to a halt outside the international terminal, an anonymous steel and glass box. Two soldiers standing guard at the main entrance snapped to attention, hoisting submachine guns. John helped Claire out. A second sedan pulled up immediately behind them, disgorging George and the baggage for all three of them. John walked over to find his carry-on bag and diving equipment.

"Your ticket," Kontos snapped. John stooped, rolling his diving bag onto his shoulder, and said, "What for? I'm going down into the islands."

Kontos took tickets from Claire and George and turned to confront John. "I have changed my mind. I do not believe you had nothing to do with this. Therefore, I declare you *non grata*."

"You can't do that, I don't care *who* you are. That's a diplomatic function and you're just some tin-hat Army jerk-off."

Midway through the sentence he saw Kontos nod slightly to someone behind him, but it was too late. Hands gripped his arms. He might have shaken off the soldier behind him but he was carrying the luggage.

Kontos expertly backhanded him across the face. John spun away, wrestling with the unseen opponent behind him. Kontos hit him again—a sharp crack, this time square on the nose.

Pain snapped the world into sharp focus. He felt blood running freely. He said nothing; that would just give Kontos some slimy satisfaction.

A babble of excited Greek. Kontos was saying something— a grating, insinuating voice, for the benefit of his own men.

He blinked. Claire came swimming up from the too-bright surroundings, Claire holding a handkerchief. It swelled, a white cloud, and engulfed his face. He pulled away but the hands still held him. Claire was cursing in Greek, too, and Kontos was answering her. She gave up with the handkerchief, turned to shout at Kontos. The soldiers grinned. Slap the American man around, that was good, foreign policy in action. Hit him again, yes. Bloody him, that was even better. He could see they all ached to do the same thing.

They all stared at Claire and John saw the look come into their eyes. Even better to slap around an American woman. Yes, a pleasure. He could see them wanting it, their eyes jerking from Kontos to Claire, sweat gleaming on their faces, waiting for Kontos to do it.

"That's okay, Claire," he said, voice croaking. "Leave off."

She turned. "He can't—it's an outrage that—"

"Leave it!"

Kontos blinked. He smirked at John and waved a hand in

dismissal. "I cannot allow this uniform to be dishonored. I would expect even you to understand that." Another casual wave. "Escort these three into the terminal."

Hands pushed him forward. He nearly stumbled, dropped his carry-on, and picked it up, half expecting a kick from behind. *Not as bad as last time*, he thought. *Maybe I'm getting used to it*.

Kontos had thrown a first-class fit after he'd discovered them. The framing structure was still in place, so he saw instantly that some blocks had been moved, that they'd found something and not informed him. John had expected him to open the crate instantly, but Kontos gave it little attention, preferring to slap the framing bars and kick some of John's half-packed equipment, ranting loudly in Greek. John shoved Kontos off the equipment and the soldiers grabbed him. He'd thrown one of them down but the others pinned him to the wall. Kontos slugged him in the stomach and then in the mouth. John's lip opened and the red spattered his shirt. Kontos stopped then and went back to shouting.

Claire had tried to explain, to put the best gloss on it, but Kontos wasn't having any. When Kontos calmed down enough to think he fixed on one idea—throwing George and Claire out of the country. He didn't buy the explanation that John was merely helping Claire out, doing odd jobs because she asked him to help speed things up, that Claire was only trying to get everything done under Kontos's own deadline. But Kontos couldn't prove John was guilty of anything, so he contented himself with ordering John off the site.

Kontos wasn't a man to negotiate with—not when he had armed men to back him up. John packed up the MIT gear while Claire got her bags together. Kontos wouldn't let Claire even go back into the tomb, and halfway to the airport she realized she had left several of her notebooks there.

Kontos had them marched down to the waiting sedans and they drove off, leaving the camp for Kontos to close down. He called ahead and used his rank to get them seats on the first morning flight. Claire and George were booked on American Airlines, Athens to Paris to Boston. John was to fly to Crete.

George fetched some paper towels and stopped John's nosebleed as they waited beside the jammed counter. People stared. There were a lot of Army uniforms around, but they weren't paying much attention. Instead, knots of men talked excitedly to each other.

Claire said appropriate things, mixing sympathy with a virulent anger. Kontos was at the American Airlines counter, loudly demanding an extra ticket for John. The counter was mobbed with hundreds, many of them wide-eyed, desperate, raising a loud babble of questions and protests. Kontos's uniform got him attention from the clerks.

George hadn't done or said much. He seemed intimidated by the soldiers, watching them, jumping to do whatever they communicated with gestures and pointing and clipped orders. They made him go out and carry all the bags in, and then lift them up for checking on the weighing counter. Kontos snapped his fingers at George to hurry, enjoying it.

John kept his two bags. He didn't want anybody throwing around his diving equipment, and he didn't trust the soldiers to not somehow steal the bags even after they'd been checked on the flight.

Kontos came back with three tickets. "You leave in an hour. I will have the soldiers stand outside the departure waiting room. Do not come back into the terminal."

"Why so suddenly formal, Colonel?" Claire mocked. "Wouldn't you like to hit me as well?"

So she caught it, too, he thought.

"Do not insult this uniform," Kontos said stiffly.

Maybe he thinks he's over-reached, John thought. *Even politically influential types can't get away with everything.*

"Oh, I wasn't insulting the uniform. I was insulting the little man hiding inside."

Kontos glared. "Do not push me." The voice was dead level and strangely calm.

John recognized the signs of a barely restrained fury. Kontos was doing what was smart but the man didn't like it. *Break this up.*

"What's happened?" he asked, edging between the two of them. "Why are those Army men meeting over there?" He pointed to a dozen or more, all talking at once.

Kontos said slowly, "The Parliament, it is dissolved. Our party declares a special circumstance."

"Special. . .?" While Kontos was looking at him, John surreptitiously waved to Claire to be quiet.

"We cannot reach an appropriate compromise with some of the reactionary elements, so we are suspending the normal political processes until we can, ah, create solidarity through all our society." The words came out like a press release.

"Uh huh."

"So—I return to Athens immediately. Great events are happening. I not waste my time on *you*." Kontos snorted, pivoting with military polish on one heel, and stalked off.

Claire sighed. "And to think that man used to be a good archeologist."

"So? People aren't consistent. Hitler was a vegetarian."

She peered blearily at him and he saw with a shock that she was close to tears. The tough veneer was only so deep and no more. He put his arm around her. "Come on. We'll wait for our flight. Maybe rustle up a little breakfast."

He nodded to George and they walked slowly through the passport control, numbly watching a sleepy clerk stamp the pages without looking at them. They were coming down from the tension now, worn out by the shouting, the forced packing, the long ride through darkness and dawn. Kontos had prodded and tongue-lashed them at every delay, robbing them of their dignity as scientists, confusing Claire so that she left work behind, using his position to humiliate them.

He said gently to Claire, "No point in getting into a political fracas here. Could be it's good we're getting out."

She sniffed and nodded. "Probably a lot of people wanted to be on this flight."

"Be good to be back home, after all this."

"Yes."

They were silent in the waiting room. George went out to fetch coffee and some curious triangles of nuts and sesame seeds held together by honey. John devoured two and felt better. Claire ate looking down at the floor. He knew what she was thinking, but there was nothing he could say to dispel those demons.

She was going back in defeat. Kontos would make a big thing out of this, feed lurid stories to Hampton at BU, damage her reputation. He might very well be able to get her banned forever from Greek archeological work, her specialty.

He sat back, wishing he had something to read. Well, he did, at the bottom of his carry-on bag. Somehow he didn't have the energy to dig out a book. He closed his eyes, wishing for sleep. Maybe on the plane. No, definitely on the plane.

Claire shook his arm. "Wake up," she said. "I need a coin."

"Aren't the johns free here?" He fished in his pockets.

"No, it's for a phone call."

"To who?"

"To whom, you mean. Olympic Airways."

"Purist." He gave her a heavy handful of coins. "Why?"

"Praxis."

"What?"

"Watch."

PART
THREE

CHAPTER
One

Claire scribbled the flight numbers and departure time on the back of her ticket envelope. She bit the end of the pencil, fretting, and hung up the telephone.

It was going to be a tight squeeze. She had spent too much time moodily slumped on a chair, rehearsing what she'd say to Hampton at BU, how she would describe what happened, how to put the best face on what was, no matter how she tried, a total defeat. Too much time not thinking, while the minutes until departure slipped by. The classical Greeks spoke of the proper balance between thought, *theoria*, and action, *praxis*. But she had been doing neither.

So she had fretted some more, getting nowhere, eyes roving the jammed waiting room—and abruptly the large Olympic Airways route map on the nearby wall had jumped into prominence. She had stared at it in disbelief, thinking suddenly of the small ivory square, of its markings, wishing she had even a sketch of it to compare. And suddenly she had known that she had to follow this idea. She could not give up now.

The rest had been easy. She needed a way to stay in Greece. There was only one possible method.

She chewed the pencil some more and decided. A man puffing energetically on a cigarette caught her eye, smiled. She glared back. He looked affronted.

As she walked back to where George and John were sitting a monotonous voice announced their flight. John was reflectively feeling his nose and puffed-up cheeks.

"Come on, let's get in line," she said, scooping up her own light bag, thinking furiously.

"Let the others load first," George said wearily. "It'll be a long flight."

"Come *on*."

"Okay, okay." George got up. John eyed Claire speculatively.

"No, wait," she said suddenly. The departure lounge was jammed and people were already pushing at the line. She whispered, "George, listen. When I give you a nod, play sick."

"What for?"

John shot a look at her. "Just do it," she said. "We can't talk here."

George grumbled and got in line. They inched forward. Claire would have told them her idea, but there were too many ears nearby.

A sleepy clerk collected boarding passes. Claire turned and saw two of Kontos's men watching her from beyond the glass partition. They didn't seem very interested but they were still there.

George in front, they walked out onto the open runway. The big jet waited about a hundred meters away. The brisk, salty air was liberating after the stale cigarette reek inside. Claire waited until the last possible moment, until there were a dozen passengers behind them. George put his foot on the portable stairway and turned back toward her. She nodded.

George dropped his bag and clutched his right side, sagging to his knees. He groaned believably.

"Oh, he's had another!" Claire squealed. "George! Is it the same as before?"

"Ye. . .yes," he wheezed. "Only. . .worse."

Passengers were stacking up behind them. An American Airline officer shoved his way through and kneeled beside George, who grimaced and moaned.

"He's had this before," Claire explained. "We hoped we could get him back to Boston but—"

"What's he got?" the officer asked rapidly.

"Well, that's the thing you see, we don't really *know*, only it hurts him something awful." Claire babbled on into the officer's ear while George breathed noisily. "George, you *can't* go, that's what I told you back at the hotel, you just have to see a doctor *here*, no matter how much you want to get back to Dr. Oberman you have to go to someone *now*, isn't that right?" She looked beseechingly at the airline officer.

The man bit his lip and said, "Well, I suppose. . .I'll call an ambulance and—"

"No no," Claire said rapidly, "no ambulance. I know how they run the price up in these places. You just tell us where the first aid station is here, okay?"

The officer shook his head. "Lady, he can't move, and our policy is—"

"Sure, sure I can," George said. He heaved himself up, grasping the railing of the stairway. "See?" He took a step.

"Don't you fake with me," Claire said, "you are in *no condition* to—"

"Oh, all right," George said. "Where's first aid?"

The officer looked back at the terminal. "You're sure you can walk?"

"Yeah," George said. "Just lead us to the first aid station. My, uh, she's right, I'd better not go on this flight."

"Give our seats to somebody else," Claire said.

The jam behind them now blocked any view of the waiting rooms, so Claire could not see if the soldiers were still there. They crossed the tarmac, George moving so quickly that the airline officer had to work to keep up, explaining airline policy on cancelled reservations and the difficulty of getting another flight right away. As she had guessed, the officer took them through the door with AIRLINE PERSONNEL ONLY stenciled on it. In the office beyond she glanced rapidly around. No soldiers.

"Could you take us around to one of your carts?" she asked.

They did. Airlines were careful to avoid involvement in medical problems of their passengers, preferring to shuttle any difficulties to a first aid station in the terminal and forget them. The cart carried them down a narrow alley and across the main street outside. Another airline officer had joined them, carefully explaining that they could not guarantee that the luggage would not go on to Paris, since the flight had to take off immediately. Claire nodded, keeping her eyes straight ahead. She remembered from somewhere that people were more conscious of you if you were looking their way, so she affected indifference to the knots of uniformed men in the street.

In the antiseptic-smelling first aid station George faked a number of contradictory symptoms. The lone doctor tuttutted over him, poking and peering. John and Claire insisted on staying with him. While a nurse was away with a sample bottle, George chuckled and said, "I played that pretty well, huh?"

Claire answered, "Perfect. Listen, we're not clear of them. I called Olympic Airways. I got reservations for two of us on a flight leaving in fifty-five minutes for Crete. Those were the last two seats on the plane. George, you've got a reservation for the next flight out after that."

"Ah," John said. "That way we won't all three be seen together."

"I hadn't thought of that, but you're right. Good."

"Hey, what's this *for*?" George combed his hair with his fingers, frowning. "I've gone along okay, sure, but what the hell are you—"

"We don't have to take treatment like this. I'm not leaving Greece until I get justice." She looked fiercely at the two men. "For *all* of us."

John had said nothing. He began slowly. "Well, I'm not fond of having the bejeesus beat out of me, but Claire—what're we gonna *do*?"

"I'll. . .I want to go back to the site. Get those notes of mine. I noticed something just now, in the waiting room. Remember the ivory decoration? The scratches on it might be a map."

"Yeah, sure, we talked about that possibility," George said.

"I didn't take it seriously because there are no known maps from the Mycenaean age. But looking at the Olympic Airways map, I saw that I had been unconsciously assuming that if it *was* some crude depiction of Mycenae, then the big land mass had to be at the top, to the north. But that's just a convention we use today—north is up. From what I remember of the ivory piece, if you turn it upside down, the biggest area vaguely resembles a part of Greece. Not the mainland, no— Crete. The large mass is the Crete coastline, and the smaller object above is an island. Maybe Santorini or Milos."

"Um," George said noncommitally.

"But I need my notes to really make a case."

John asked, "You figure a scholarly paper is worth all that much?"

"Yes, I do. But mostly I want to get back at Kontos some way. I'll send a telegram from Crete. Professor Hampton must be told of what has happened. I'm sure Kontos will be filling his ear full of—"

"You could've told Hampton when we landed in Boston," John said mildly.

Her eyes flashed. "Yes, and with empty hands, without any results, with nothing to show—"

"Now, I was only commenting. Me, I'm willing to go to Crete, if that's what you want. I'm on vacation, you remember."

"Yeah," George added with fresh energy. "Kontos hasn't taken any official action against us. Yet. I mean, if we can stay away from him and his storm troopers, we're okay."

Claire subsided. She saw that something of the mischievous schoolboy had been aroused in George, something she could play upon. To him this could be a lark, a bit of cops and robbers, better than returning to a Bostonian winter and the university routine. Very well, then.

"Good. George, you stay here, recover in about an hour, and walk across the street to the domestic air terminal. It's the one to the left. Here—" she handed him a wad of bills. "Use this to buy your ticket. When you land at Crete, come into the main square in Heraklion. We'll meet you there."

"Okay."

"By that time I'll have had time to telephone Hampton. He can intervene with Kontos. I want permission to go back to the site, see that things are sealed up professionally, and get my notes."

"Hampton could make Kontos send them to Boston."

Her eyes flashed. "And keep whatever he likes? I don't want him pawing through my things!"

John said wonderingly, "You think Kontos won't look for us? Word will get back to him and—"

"Are you willing to take that risk?"

A long silence. John avoided her eyes. He was remembering the beatings, she knew. She hated to use that, to refer to it even obliquely, but she didn't have any time.

He stiffened slightly. "I suppose so, yes."

"All right then," she said cheerily. "I'll go across first."

"Why not together?" John asked.

"They'll look for a group. And I can talk my way out better, knowing Greek."

John didn't like that very much, but he agreed to follow in ten minutes. She left the medical aid station. She thought wryly that it wasn't hard to look like a weary, anxious traveler, because that was exactly how she felt. When she was halfway across the street two jeeps came barreling toward her, horns honking. She jumped out of the way. They zoomed past, three men in each, ignoring her. They turned, tires howling, and blocked the international terminal entrance. The soldiers bounded out and checked their swiveled heavy machine guns. Claire had put down her bags to watch. Soldiers came over to the new arrivals and bombarded them with questions. Claire picked up her bags and noticed that nearly everyone within sight had melted away, leaving the street nearly deserted, and she was conspicuous. She hurried for the domestic terminal.

It was quiet inside. During a crisis in the capital, no one seemed interested in flying to the provinces. Speaking Greek, she got their two tickets and checked them onto the flight. No one paid her the slightest extra attention. She turned away from the counter and a soldier came abruptly out of nowhere and stood directly in her way.

"Where are you going, Madam?" he asked formally in Greek.

He was thin but wiry and his dark eyes shifted rapidly over her face, assessing. She held her breath and thought irrationally of running. But where? "I. . .Crete."

"You have a ticket on this flight?"

"Yes. I am on holiday and—"

"Then I would consider it a great favor if you would take this." He held out a letter. "Please, I ask you, drop it in the post at the airport. It will be delivered in Heraklion within a day."

Relief was like a weight lifted from her. "But—but why not post it here?"

The dark eyes studied her, looked to the left, slid uneasily back. "I am afraid that mail from Athens will not reach Heraklion quickly. There are...political divisions. This letter, it is to my relatives, people who may not be in . . ."

"In favor?"

"Please, it is all I can do, I will pay you for the trouble if you—"

"No no, of course I'll take it. But do you really think—"

Apparently he did, because the man poured out a rich stream of thanks before bolting away, as if afraid to be seen talking to a foreigner.

When John arrived a few minutes later she was still turning it over in her mind. John reported that there was a line of soldiers at the international terminal now, checking carefully anyone who entered. The monorail from Athens wasn't running due to a labor strike, and bunches of people arrived in overloaded buses, only to be slowed at the entrance. "Typical," he said. "Heavy weapons, as if somebody's going to escape by attacking the airport."

"Don't look concerned and no one will notice you. We're just tourists, remember?"

"With this kind of security, somebody'll catch on to us."

"Not necessarily. Outside Athens, people are more relaxed."

"Like in Nauplia?"

"Okay, my optimistic streak is showing."

"All this, just to get those notes?"

"They represent months of work. I can't do my part of the project without them. And on Crete perhaps I can find some connection to that ivory map. Archeology is mostly a process of making associations between objects, and every discovery opens up possible resonances with things we already have. Sometimes, simply wandering through a museum or a site can open your eyes."

He sighed.

She was quiet for a moment, second thoughts beginning to surface. But it was too late now. *Praxis*.

She put a reassuring hand on his shoulder. "I'm sure a call to Hampton will straighten this out." She grinned, even though she didn't believe a word of it.

CHAPTER

Two

John settled back contentedly. A short order of garlic-laden souvlaki, a full plate of oily moussaka and a bottle of tart red wine had all conspired to smooth out the world, filming it with a pleasant and benign glaze. He sat in piercing autumn sunlight, blades of it cutting crisp and clean through the olive branches. So *this* was the fabled air of Greece. He toasted it with more Metaxa brandy. His fatigue had retreated, but he felt it biding its time, ready to smother him with sleep if he challenged it.

Claire came out of the hotel across the small park, looked both ways—always a good idea in the bee-swarm traffic of Heraklion—and strode toward him. Her lean, focused body had an ample sway, an unconscious lushness of gait transcending mechanical necessity and mocking the severe cut of her red blouse and gray slacks. The inevitable lounging men, out of work and unshaven, followed her trajectory like rotating radars.

"You have fans."

"What? Oh, them. It's always like that."

"Occupational hazard of working in the Mediterranean?"

"You don't know much about Boston Irish, do you?"

He smiled. "Any luck?"

"I got two rooms. And called Boston."

He sat up. She was vexed.

"I got through right away, using the new satellite link through Cairo." She sipped her brandy.

"And?"

She said reluctantly, "Hampton. . .wasn't cooperative. He hadn't heard from Kontos, thank God, but he brushed off what I told him. He said if I had irritated Kontos he was sure he, Hampton, could straighten it out."

"Didn't you say that—"

Her eyebrows flared upward. "I couldn't tell him *every*-thing. Use your head! I don't want Kontos hearing that I think that artifact is important."

"Or that you want to go back for your notes in person."

"Of course not. I described Kontos bringing in his Army goons, and roughing you up, and confiscating a lot of our notes—okay, a shading of the truth, I'll admit—and expelling us from the country without any official authority. Hampton went tsk-tsk and told me there was a lot of political unrest and to leave everything to his great big capable hands." She made a face.

"He'll call Kontos right away."

"Perhaps not. I said I was calling from Paris, that I wanted a few days of holiday. I asked him to hold any action until I could describe what happened in detail, in Boston. Hampton likes to write long, thoughtful letters and circulate them widely—'getting a forum,' he calls it. That's how he wants to deal with this, I think."

"Maybe that's the best course."

"No, it's just a way to sweep it—*me*—under the rug. Hampton and Kontos will Old-Boy-Network this until I find myself working some Syrian mud village dig while they carry on the Mycenaean sites."

He said carefully, "Well. . .maybe you shouldn't place too much weight on those notes."

"Nonsense. Remember, part of it is that data of yours I was going to incorporate into my records. If I'd had time to copy it and get it back to you, you'd have it."

"Well, still . . ."

"After those spectral lines you found? Some kind of alloy, or an unusual stone at least. Plus the fact that it's unique, a funerary relic nobody's seen before. Who knows what it means, being hidden like that? Next year we can dig down on that ledge behind it, explore the water cistern, maybe find things they threw down it"—her eyes flashed—"and I want to be there!"

He took a deep breath. *Here goes.* "What I meant was, my results are preliminary and could be. . .wrong."

She blinked. "Why? You were careful, I watched you."

"Yes, but. . .well, it's not my area."

"Ancient metallurgy has its tricks, certainly, but you—"

"My point is, I'm not a metallurgist."

She looked blank. "What?"

"I never saw equipment like that before in my life."

"What *are* you, then?"

"A mathematician."

She stared in disbelief.

"I. . .I'm working on a new mathematical model of impurities in metals, applications of group theory."

"Your office . . ."

"They had space so they stuck me in there. I talk to some of the metallurgy people, but otherwise—"

"You lied to me!"

"Not exactly. I never said I was any good at this stuff, you'll remember."

"I thought you were—were—"

"I know, and I do apologize. I thought it was going to be a lark, you know, sort of a vacation."

"So for the free trip you—!" She slammed her brandy glass to the table. It broke. She didn't notice.

"Not really. Mostly it was you."

"Me?"

"I was attracted to you from the first second." He hung his head. "I know that sounds stupid. I—I just let my glands run away with me, I guess."

To his surprise, she subsided. "So you decided to simply . . .fake it?"

"Yes. I got the equipment easy enough. Signed out for it. Ransacked the library for reference books. Read 'em on the plane."

"All that . . ." She gazed at him as if he were a stranger. "For me?"

In the *For me?* he saw a momentary chink in her dazzling armor. Unremittingly competitive and self-confident in her professional life, did she harbor doubts about her womanly qualities? He would have to do something about that. Somehow.

He said sheepishly, "I did as best I could. I know a little electronics, built some stereo components once, but. . .I can't be sure the work is accurate. I know you're disappointed, but I want you to know that, well"—he looked directly into her eyes—"I'm not. It was worth the experience."

"Hell," she said irritably, "you could've just asked me for a date."

"I didn't want to let you slip by. I just acted, well, straight from the heart."

"Some cold, analytical mathematician you are."

"I should've admitted it when I got to the site, saw what a job it was, more than I expected. But then you'd have had nobody at all to help you. If I hadn't been such a poltroon—"

"Pol-what?"

"Poltroon. Coward."

She softened visibly. "No, that's not. . .you worked *hard*. I couldn't have gotten what I did without . . ."

"I'm sorry. But I'd still do it again. It's been worth it."

She blinked rapidly, suddenly discovered the spilled brandy and began sopping it up with her napkin, not looking at him. After a moment she laughed unevenly and gave him a crooked smile. "You know, I've felt. . .different. . .about you, too."

He gazed at her wonderingly. "Why, that's—"

A certain reserve came back into her face and she licked her lips. "Maybe it's because we have a lot in common. You realize, don't you, that we're both sneaky, lying bastards."

He didn't like hearing women talk that way, but he had to agree.

George brought bad news.

His flight had been delayed by general hubbub. More troops had arrived at Athens airport and were screening all passengers. They checked even those on domestic flights inbound from other parts of Greece. He had gotten through because the officers were paying more attention to incoming passengers, probably because of fears of a counter-move in Athens by opponents of the takeover. George had witnessed several arrests.

All this implied that returning through Athens was a poor bet. Yet Claire persisted—she had to return to the tomb, retrieve her notes.

They could try to charter a private plane. But the airports were more closely watched—George had seen more police arriving at the Heraklion airport as he collected his luggage.

That left the sea. The best and most inexpensive way would be to cruise gradually northward on the regular tourist ships. And, since Kontos could trace them to Crete from the airline passenger list, they had better get quickly clear of Heraklion. This was not immediately possible. The government had kept the tourist trade running well, because it was now a chief source of hard currency. The schedules for northbound ships were filled. By bribing a booking agent Claire managed to get three seats on a ship leaving for Santorini the next morning. There was one seat available that afternoon.

They would be less conspicuous if they separated. George wanted to take the single, rather than wait. Claire and John would follow the next morning, meeting George at the Atlantean Hotel.

Meanwhile the smart policy was to look as ordinary and touristy as possible. Police patrols were moving through the streets, asking for IDs, but not bothering obvious foreigners. George left to catch his ship, grinning, enjoying the intrigue.

John tried to look relaxed. He was uneasy about the clumps of police and Army uniforms at every major intersection. Suppose Kontos found out they hadn't left the country? There was certainly some charge the man could dream up. In the current climate, it might stick.

They strolled through the open market, resisting the blandishments of traders. Claire bought some saffron—a wildly eccentric indulgence, he thought, since she had only the clothes on her back, some underwear, two paperbacks and a few toilet articles.

She led him through narrow streets of blaring cars and hawking vendors, into the vaulted quiet of the Museum. "Browse around," she said. "The frescoes are upstairs. I'll go get some cash on my American Express card and pick up some necessities. And cable American Airlines, asking them to store our baggage in Boston."

John deliberately concentrated, shutting out the dusty, un-

ruly world outside. He liked the clean, skillful lines of the
stone vases and urns, some with jeweled handles. Most of
the elegant gemwork and gold necklaces reminded him of the
Mycenaean artistry Claire had shown him at the site, so he
was not surprised to learn from the museum booklet that
cross-cultural currents ran through the great eras of Cretan
civilization.

The first era ended with an earthquake, but the Cretans
rebuilt, leading to their golden age that lasted 250 years. A
label beneath an exquisite gold pendant described the end as
"engulfment in tidal waves and earthquake." Two bees
curled toward each other, forming the arcs of the pendant as
they stored honey in a comb. Or perhaps they were mating.
The tiny granulation glowed with inner life and purpose, and
he felt suddenly the reality of this past—the millions of struggling, loving people who had built, hoped and died, the pulse
of their times now an invisible presence, their only sign these
elegant oddments. He often thought of the past as a crude,
raw time, but here the deft craft of the ancients was a mute,
forceful statement. He wandered among the artifacts, the carbonized relics of wood and wheat and furniture from the
fallen great palaces, breathing in a sense of the long arc of
history.

"Looks like a Californian fashion, doesn't it?"

Claire's voice at his shoulder startled him. He had been
studying a Snake Goddess statue, arms outstretched, snakes
crawling over her arms and round her body, even up into her
tall tiara. A tight bodice left the breasts bare above a long
flounced skirt and apron.

"Some themes are eternal," he said.

"Their cults kept snakes in clay tubes—see those?—and
fed them milk." When he looked puzzled she added, "They
may have used them in worship, but I think snakes were medical technology. Their bites could be used for some ail-
ments."

She led him through rooms of pottery. "Fired clay outlasts
everything."

"Even modern materials?"

"Certainly. Our toilet bowls will still be usable ten thousand years from now. Oh, look."

In the blue fresco a bull charged at a flying gallop, head

down. A woman in a codpiece and high boots gripped its horns. A brown, jeweled man was halfway along its back, grasping the bull, flipping heels over head. A woman had landed on her feet just behind the charging hooves, arms poised from her flip. The three stages of the "leap of death." The composition vibrated with energy.

"They really did this," Claire added. "It was a sport."

"No religious connection?"

"Well, these events might be what started the myth of Theseus, who was sent here from Athens with other young men and women to be sacrificed to the Minotaur. We don't know a lot about Cretan religion."

"And we think it's a big deal to dodge one of these with a cape."

She smiled. "Don't be so hard on the matadors. Everybody shaves the odds if they can. Some excavations found bull skulls with the horns sawn down, dulling them."

"Ranchers do that if they're keeping a bull indoors a lot, y'know. Keeps them from gouging the walls, or people, or the cows."

"Really? How do you know?"

"Farming's in the DNA of Georgians."

"Um. I wonder if the excavators know that about keeping bulls."

"They must. I mean, that's what the Minotaur was."

"No, it was half man, half bull. The god Poseidon gave a bull to the king of Crete, Minos, to sacrifice. Instead, Minos kept it, and his wife fell in love with it."

"You're right, it was like California."

She looked askance at him. "No, Poseidon made her do it."

"I've heard that one before."

A sigh. "She had a child by the bull—the Minotaur. Minos shut it up in a labyrinth. Later on, after Minos's son was killed by the Athenians in a war, Minos demanded that they send him a sacrifice of young people, as tribute. He fed them to the Minotaur."

"Nice fellow. That's where Theseus comes in?"

"Correct. He was one of the sacrifices. Only he went armed and killed the Minotaur. He found his way back out because he had unwound a thread to mark the way."

"How'd he kill the Minotaur?"

"We don't know. He'd already practiced—the legend says he had already slaughtered the fire-breathing bull of Marathon."

"Two bulls? And where was the labyrinth?"

"I'll show you."

Knossos was a short taxi ride out of town, away from the ever-present police uniforms. On the way out they were stopped at an Army checkpoint.

"What if they want our passports?" John asked. "The hotel's got them."

"Then that's what we say."

The officer peered in, saw they were tourists and waved them on. "See?" Claire said. "Things are more relaxed away from Athens." She pointed at a donkey which browsed beside a tumbledown wall in the shade of an ilex, ignoring the buzzing flies around it.

"Then what's the roadblock for?"

"Political. Cretans aren't going to like this one-party business."

"Let's get going to Santorini, then. Stay away from this."

"I booked us on tomorrow's ship at eight A.M."

In the open sprawl of Knossos, though, John began to regret having to leave so soon. The walls of dazzling white and veined blocks of gypsum cast an ivory aura over the excavated ruins, framing the frescoes with a luminous radiance. There was a feeling of openness to the ruined palace with its ample rooms giving onto courtyards and squares, an hospitable welcoming in the scent of oleander and pine that blew down from the low hills. Lizards scuttled among the brilliant white blocks and vultures patrolled above, circling and crying sweetly in the high sharp air.

"Hard to believe this was a labyrinth."

"Oh, this is merely the unearthed part. The original palace had fifteen hundred rooms."

"That's why historians think the Greeks based the legend on it?"

"Well, it was certainly the most complicated building a Greek had ever seen. And Minos is the dynastic term for the line of priest kings of Knossos."

"And he kept a man-eating, fire-breathing bull around the house for laughs."

"It's a legend after all, not a newspaper story."

"This labyrinth was the palace itself?"

"Presumably. They cut tombs into the rock, but nothing very big. Something like the Mycenaean ones."

They climbed up spacious stairs supported by thick pillars of gaudy scarlet. Even inside there was a fresh, luxurious air. The inhabitants, she told him, were only four and a half feet tall.

"The Mycenaeans took over there?"

"After the second burning of this palace, yes."

"But I thought the Athenians were the big Greek power."

"Oh no, Athens was a backwater at this time. Plato, Pericles—they came a thousand years after all this."

"But Crete fought battles with the Athenians, and it was Theseus who killed the Minotaur."

"Well, you've got to remember that history is written by the survivors. The whole Minotaur business might have involved Mycenaeans, not Athenians at all. The Athenians simply expropriated the existing legends."

"Boy, no wonder Henry Ford said history was bunk."

She bridled. "What does it matter? Some nameless hero from the region around Mycenae came here. Perhaps he was a great bull-leaping athlete. Or perhaps he slew fearsome beasts. It became a big story back home, got passed on and amplified. Homer used it."

"So Homer is just a bunch of tall tales."

Primly: "In a manner of speaking."

They walked among the stairways and toppled columns, John reflecting on the silent stones. Claire fidgeted.

"Say, are those police over there looking at us?"

Claire whirled, "What? Where?"

He chuckled. "Well, they were, a minute ago. You're not as calm as you make out."

She gave him a guarded look. "Okay, I'm jumpy, too. Let's get back to town."

He returned to the museum in late afternoon, drawn by its atmosphere. Even the museum tickets were unusual, bearing line drawings of ancient scholars or statesmen, and quotations

from great works of antiquity. Inside, the glass cases laid bare
the silent eons. He felt as never before the yawning abyss of
things lost, great deeds forgotten, people gone to dust.

In a case of its own a black steatite bull's head gazed out
at him across the millennia. Its glossy seashell nostrils flared
angrily and eyes of rock crystal and jasper regarded him om-
inously. The descriptive card said, *Rhyton from the Knossos
Palace. The hair is skillfully rendered by incision. Styles and
tools used suggest an origin shortly before the final catastrophe. There is evidence in Homer that ceremonial bulls had
their horns gilded. The horns of this work have not been
found, but were probably of gilded wood like those of the
famous rhyton of similar type found in the royal tombs of
Mycenae.*

The malevolent stony gaze seemed to follow him as he
moved, studying the craftsmanship. The recently added
wooden horns were artfully curved and painted a luminous
gold. They gleamed in the cool light of the Museum, and he
imagined running toward them in the smell of dust, heart
pounding, as cries of the crowd rose around him, hooves
thumping, the great beast lunging for his belly, horns lowered
and glinting in the clear sunlight, death hot in the eyes, as his
arms tensed to reach out, to grab and lift and fly free above
the brutal devouring rush.

He admired it for a long time, chewing absently at his
lower lip, thinking that it reminded him of something, but he
could not remember what.

CHAPTER
Three

As the *Attika* pulled out of Heraklion harbor Claire pointed out a scrawled message painted by spray can on the gray concrete bulwarks of the dock: YANKEE GO HOME.

"No cliché like an old cliché," John murmured.

"They mean it, though."

"Yeah. I thought that guy at the hotel this morning was going to throw our filthy exploitative money right back in our faces."

"He was rather rude, wasn't he?"

"Is that why you fed him that guff about going to get our rental car?"

She nodded. "If the police come checking, they'll waste time running down all the rental agencies first."

"Thought so. Anyway, I don't take signs like that personally." He lounged lazily against the railing, the soft wind ruffling his hair, musing at the passing fishing boats. "They don't apply to me."

"Why not?"

He deepened his drawl. "Ah'm not a Yankee."

She laughed despite herself. He went to such lengths to separate himself from her New England heritage, yet with a mocking sense of himself. As if he knew he came from a culture that was fading, still wrapped in its past. Perhaps that same sense let him relax so easily; she envied him that. Last night she had chattered on about what had happened, what they might do, letting her own anxieties out in a torrent of ifs and supposes and maybes. He had listened attentively but contributed little, almost as though he was humoring her. She had gotten them into this on impulse, and now had second thoughts. John didn't seem to mind that. He simply took in all the possibilities she fretted over and nodded, as if he was calculating somewhere, but not needing to talk about it. A strange man.

The Greek sun came cutting through morning mist, the same sharp radiance that had lit antiquity, proving anew its ability to light, to warm, to make everything known. They went inside to get some sweet coffee and a honeyed roll. The ship was packed with Germans, all talking excitedly and waving newspapers. He asked her if she understood what they were saying.

She studied the Greek newspaper headlines. "There's a new state censorship law. That one says they're printing only releases from the government for now. Umm. . .Borders are closed to everybody except tourists. Controls on movement of currency and capital."

"The usual. Banks closed?"

"Yes. I'm glad I got my money yesterday."

"What are the Germans saying about it?"

"I don't speak German."

"You, the language whiz?"

"I'm not really that good. I can read German for archeological purposes, that's all. Except for Greek, I simply spend the month before I go to a country boning up on vocabulary. I learn the present tense of a few verbs—to be, to get, things like that. Then I spend an evening speaking with someone who knows the language, a day or so before leaving. There's no big trick to it. I decided to stop at a reading knowledge of German when I discovered that the word for maiden took a neuter article—*Das Mädchen*."

"So?"

"Only by getting married could I get a feminine article, *Die Frau*. That told me enough about the German mentality."

"My, my."

She had told this to a number of men, but none of them had simply leaned back, hands behind neck, and yawned, as did John. The others—earnest, quick-witted Cambridge types—had instantly professed understanding and support.

Having passed this litmus test, however, they had all eventually dropped away or turned her off in some fashion. She had never been certain whether the reason for this lay in her or in them, but in time she had come to distrust men who immediately endorsed her position, and seemed to be looking to her for clues about which posture they should strike to win her approval. John's indifference—or was it?—left her unsettled.

Two hours later they watched the red crescent arms of Santorini rear slowly from the sea to embrace the *Attika*. Layers of gray ash, ruddy lava and pumice streaked the high cliffs. Claire leaned on the railing and let the impossible liquid blues seep into her.

Across the turquoise shimmer came a fishing boat with rough planking and a big-bellied white sail, its prow raking in a pure proud curve above its rippling image in the bay. Its captain shouted orders in a harsh, penetrating bark as old as seafaring.

They slipped near the stubby protrusion of the Great Kameni at the center of the bay. A faint sulphurous tang prickled her nostrils. Pitch black lava boulders tumbled down to the water's edge, obdurate and threatening, their angular faces undulled by the rub of waves.

"That's the volcano?" John asked.

"Yes, the active one. The last big eruption was in 1956. Half the population left after that."

"How do they live here?" He surveyed the bleak, rocky land high above the bay.

She pointed. "Those layers of pumice are good fertilizer. See those ramps down into the sea? They load freighters with the stuff."

He turned back to the receding low profile of the Great Kameni. "That doesn't look like much of a volcano. What's the size of the open hole?"

"We can motorboat over later and see. But if you mean the caldera of the whole volcano—this is it."

"No, I mean—" Then he understood. "This *bay* is the caldera?"

She nodded. "The explosion of 1426 B.C. blew half the island away. The date comes from tree rings of bristlecone

pines in California. They showed reduced growth that year.
Santorini's dust made it a chilly summer all over the planet."

"All this. . .clean to smithereens?"

"The ancient name for the whole island meant 'round.' The
eruption took half the island. Now it's crescent-shaped."

"My God, it's five or six miles across, easy."

"It must have been like a hydrogen bomb."

"That's why I wanted to come here. Remember the ivory
square?"

"Oh yes. You figure it's a map."

"If we were looking at it upside down the whole time, then
the big land mass at the bottom represents Crete. Santorini is
the only major island to the north, so the round blob halfway
up the square probably represents this island."

"The distances don't seem right, from what I remember."

"They aren't—but the ancients had no accurate way of
measuring, remember, other than sailing time, which depends
on the prevailing winds. There were other marks up to the
left, too, that may correspond to other islands; the location is
about right. The important point is, the Santorini mark is
nearly round."

"I see." John gazed wonderingly at the vast azure bowl.
"Before the volcano blew this away."

"Now see why I'm determined to piece this together? This
connects to the legend of Atlantis, to the myth-making days
of earliest Greece, to *everything*."

John nodded, studying the map of Santorini he'd bought.
"Hell of a note," he said with respect.

They moored near the base of the cliffs. The Germans
pushed into a tight jam at the disembarking station, grimly
determined to be among the first into the small boats that
ferried them ashore. Claire had seen the pattern before and
stayed on deck until the last boat. They ambled along the
quay and up to the donkey station. The animals were remarkably quick at propelling them up the zigzagging cobble-
stone path, the guides shouting and administering slaps. As
their straps landed a cloud of dust rose from the beasts' matted coats. John automatically dug his heels into his donkey,
passing the shrieking Germans and earning a reproachful
glare from a guide.

Phira, a clustered town of striking blues and whites,

crowned the cliff. Trinket shops lined the snaking streets. Terraces and courtyards had been designed to deflect the perpetual gusty winds into narrow alleys and smother them. Long, belled strands of blue convolvulus looped down walls, uniting neighborhoods. Scarlet geraniums poked from unlikely pockets in the walls.

Claire always thought of this island as the embodiment of the Greek spirit. Limestone houses lay their courtyards bare to the piercing sunlight, open but unyielding. Each domed and ribbed building added to the challenge that Phira hurled at Great Kameni across the shimmering bay. Humans had again returned to the lava island and impudently lived on the old battleground where Vulcan had won before and would doubtless win again. The Greeks always came back, beaten down but undiminished, to make a beautiful upthrusting testament that sparkled in the eternal sun glare.

The Atlantean Hotel was blocky and balconied, so close to the cliff edge that it seemed to lean forward, tantalizing the abyss with its audacity. Claire and John dumped their bags in the foyer and she negotiated for their rooms. Yes, there were a few left. (Clerks always implied that one should be happy to get anything.) No, none with a view. (Unless you wished to pay more. . .?) Well, if only for a day, perhaps they could find something. (It was off season and they were probably empty.) The clerk sniffed when she asked to see the rooms first.

They were scrupulously clean and the view from the iron-railed balcony was superb. While the clerk pointed out sights to John in his room she ducked down the hallway toward the EXIT sign. There was a back stairway. She returned and gushed over the view, too, hamming up the tourist role. John, poker-faced, gave the man a tip. Claire handed him their passports and asked for them back soon, so they could use them to cash travelers checks in the shops. The man nodded curtly and left. He had seemed surprised that an American man and woman traveling together would not sleep together.

"Not the friendliest character, is he?"

"I wonder if the tourist season has worn them out. Usually the Greeks are wonderful hosts. I love this country, but in the last few years . . ." She shook her head.

"Why didn't you ask him about George?"

She sat on a bed of crisp starched sheets. "I don't want to associate the three of us in his mind. If Kontos has a bulletin out on us, or whatever you call it, we'll be described as a party of three."

He smiled knowingly. She knew he hoped she had split them off from George for romantic purposes, and with a demure smile encouraged the belief without saying anything more. John was attractive, yes, but she had other things on her mind. Still, it was best to distract John, not let him worry about the seriousness of their situation. She had no clear idea of how she could return to the tomb, but she was determined to keep the men from simply skipping out, back to the States. Cold-blooded, perhaps, but she was in this now, and damned if she would give up.

"And you spoke only English to that clerk just now, to look touristy—"

A knock at the door. "Passports, I guess," John said, and answered. George stood there, looking drawn.

"You made it!" Claire embraced him, surprised at her own excitement.

"Yeah. Your reg'lar bargain basement James Bond." He grinned and shook John's hand.

"Did you have any trouble?"

George shook his head. "Not a bit. Took the ship, checked in here, saw all the sights. Got us reservations on tomorrow's tour ship headed north."

Claire nodded. "Great. Kontos won't follow a zigzag like this."

"Seems reasonable," John said. This settled, he stretched and yawned. Claire studied him. He seemed genuinely unconcerned, radiating a lazy self-assurance.

"I'm hungry," he said. "Let's eat."

They idled in the restaurant after lunch, logy with green peppers and spiced sausage, squid, fried zucchini, rice with pine nuts and two bottles of a fierce local red wine named, appropriately, Lava. A pair of American girls came in and sat near the door. Beyond noticing the usual uniform of scruffy jeans and nondescript blouse, Claire paid them no attention until one suddenly fell sideways out of her chair, hitting the floor with a heavy smack. The restaurant owner hurried over, brought a napkin dipped in water, pressed it to the fallen girl's throat.

"Hey, don't make such a big deal out of it," her companion said. "I mean, y'know, it's her own fault. I keep telling her, hey, don't take a big hit before you get some breakfast in you." She looked around the room for support, fixed on Claire. "Right? Geez."

They watched as the fallen girl regained consciousness, mumbled something and, helped by the restaurant owner, crawled back into her chair. Coffee appeared and the girl downed it in a gulp.

"I'm starting to feel a little more sympatico with our hotel clerk," John said dryly.

"More fuel for the likes of Kontos," Claire said. "Flouting the local mores only turns the Greeks toward a political creed that echoes their Mediterranean Catholic values—paternalistic, central, dogmatic."

"So in hard times it's easier for them to opt for the Marxist-style authoritarian bamboozle—gimme dat ole time religion?" John asked.

"I'm afraid so. Kontos doesn't look much like Thomas Jefferson."

"C'mon, you two," George said. "You're depressing me."

They ambled out into the slanted light of afternoon. At the edge of town a balcony hung over the cliff, mute testimony to the eruption and slides of 1956. Claire breathed deeply of the crisp, tangy air. Hermes, god of wayfarers, was with them.

They took the meandering cliffside path back toward the hotel. John admired the sweeping view and said, "So this was Atlantis, huh?"

Claire could hardly let this pass. "No, that's Sunday supplement archeology. Crete was Atlantis. The Egyptians got confused somehow. They told the Greeks a thousand years later that a great island civilization was destroyed by explosion and sank beneath the waves. Well, Crete got all the dust and ash from here dumped on it, and suffered earthquakes, too—that was the origin of the legend. But Santorini did the job, not a mountain in Crete."

John asked, "But Crete is a hundred miles from here."

George waved an arm at the bay. "Wonder how many hydrogen bombs it would take to do this?"

John replied, "I calculated it. Half a dozen of the big hundred-megaton ones." He turned to Claire. "If it happened all at once. But you said the palace at Knossos burned down twice."

"Santorini exploded twice, too," Claire said. "There were a steady series of small eruptions in between, and the second big one finished them off. It was the largest catastrophe in history."

And, she thought, *in an odd kind of payment, it left a beautiful island*. The other Cycladic islands were part of the limestone range that sloped down through the Peloponnese, yielding sea-facing valleys, which in turn led the ancients to voyage south to Crete. Geology sped history. Santorini was something freshly thrust into that world, a volcanic intrusion.

She turned to walk down a steep slope to the Atlantean. She searched out her room, counting up floors and identifying it by her balcony's filigreed wrought iron railing. Tomorrow was time enough to visit the museum, search for some connections to the ivory map. For now she was tired from the strain of the last days. She needed to relax, forget things, lounge in the sunset and doze until it was time for another walk, some shopping, a dinner of the miraculous seafood—

A man in a black suit walked out onto her balcony.

He looked out at the view. Claire stopped, looking for cover. There was none.

"Turn around!" she cried. The two men halted, stared at her. "Back down the path!"

John's eyes widened as he looked beyond her. He turned and George followed.

She said, "George, walk out ahead. Make it look like we're not together."

George hurried ahead. John asked, "Don't police wear uniforms?"

"Not always. There are new security branches that don't."

It seemed forever before they regained the top of the hill and descended beyond view of the hotel. She peeked back from behind a bone-dry bush. Her balcony was bare. Well, if the man had recognized them it was finished; they had no place to hide.

"It could have been the hotel manager or something," George volunteered.

"We can't bet on that," John said.

"If they're looking for us, Phira is too damn small to get lost in," George said.

Claire said decisively, "It's better than standing in the open. Come on."

At the first new path they turned inland. *It was bizarre*, she thought, *hiking through lovely countryside, discussing how to elude the police. Surreal.* They increased their pace, warily studying every native who came within even distant view.

"Look," John said. "I picked up our passports when we left for lunch. George has his already. We can just go to the airport, wait for the first plane—"

"Naw," George put in. "That airport's a dinky little thing. We'd stand out, the police'd grab us right away. Besides, I don't think there's another tour ship till ours."

"And they'll have that covered," Claire added.

John said, "Then let's take the *Attika* back to Crete."

Claire shook her head. "They'll watch that, too."

"We're trapped," George said.

John thought for a moment. "Not if we can rent a boat."

"To sail ourselves?" George asked. "I can't."

"Me either," Claire said.

"I can do it, I think. At least get to the next island," John added.

"This is a dangerous season for sailing," Claire said, remembering reading that somewhere, a history of Aegean commerce or something. "Unreliable winds, the *meltemi* I think they're called."

John said sarcastically, "OK, that leaves swimming."

"I was merely considering all possibilities," Claire said stiffly.

"Where can we get a boat?" George asked.

"Not here in Phira," John said. "A cop could stand on the pier and see us coming down those steps for fifteen minutes."

"All right," Claire said. "We have to go across the island." They had circled around and were re-entering the white-washed streets of Phira. "I'll find a cab."

"Wait a minute," John said. "Suppose we get to the next island. Then what?"

"Let's go back to Crete, hop a flight to Egypt," George said.

"And end up with nothing to show for all this running around?" Claire said scornfully.

"All right then," John said firmly. "There's only one way—by sea. Back to the Peloponnese."

Claire thought. "And then?"

"Out of Greece. They'll grab us at any airport, any commercial ship, certainly at a train station. We have to sail out."

They all stopped, looking at each other.

"Look," George said, "this is getting out of hand."

"You got any better idea?" John asked irritably.

Another silence. Then: "No."

"I don't want to alarm you gentlemen, but I have one requirement more. I want my notes."

"The ones in your bags?" John asked.

"Correct."

"We can't go back to the *hotel*," George said.

"I'm not leaving my research notes here."

"Hey, this is getting—"

"I know, out of hand," Claire said. "All right, you two stay here. I'll do it."

John said slowly, "Now, hold on. I'll help you."

"Good! Let's find a phone."

"You've got an idea?" John seemed surprised.

"Certainly." She started toward an open air restaurant.

Both men ordered beer in the bar while she called the hotel. The clerk answered. "Hello, this is Miss Anderson, the American? In Room 308? Well, I ordered a taxi to pick us up there in, um, well, right now."

"Yes?" The clerk sounded interested.

"To take us to that town north of here? Oia?"

"Yes?"

"Well, we're going to be late. We met some friends here at the Delphi Hotel and we're having drinks and I don't think we'll have time to go to Oia today. So could you tell the taxi man that please, when he comes?"

"Of course, yes."

Claire thanked him and gushed a little more. As she rattled on she heard him whisper in Greek, "Yes, them." She smiled, finished and hung up.

They approached the hotel cautiously, down a winding back pathway between brilliant white houses. "This is too risky," George said.

"Stay here, then," John said brusquely. "If we don't come back, try the airport."

Claire watched the two men eye each other. George saw he was being challenged. Still, he shook his head. "I just don't think this is a good idea."

"Fine," John said. "Stay here."

"No, wait," Claire said. "George, wait until we get around to the back. See that terrace on the left?—I'll wave to you from there. Then call the hotel and keep the clerk on the line. That'll be some kind of diversion."

George leaped at this. "Hey, sure."

It didn't take long. She and John reached the back entrance to the hotel easily, encountering only an old woman who tried to sell them a necklace of obsidian beads. There was no one in the first floor corridor.

"I'll go up first," John said.

"No, I don't want to stay down here."

"I didn't say you should." He looked at her quizzically. "I think they'll pay more attention if they see you first, is all."

Claire followed him, breathing more rapidly than the steep, winding stairway explained. The hotel held a prickly silence, the air heavy with the oily smell of lunch long past. She brought the heels of her sensible walking shoes down gently, listening for footsteps from the side corridors as they passed.

She heard a distant irritated voice. The clerk, talking to George.

The hallway leading to their rooms was empty. John signaled to her. They each went to their rooms and opened the doors. Nothing. No sign of disturbance. For an instant Claire was sure it was a stupid mistake, that the man on the balcony was innocuous. She hesitated while she thrust a blouse into her bag, thought of calling to John, and then she saw the cigarette butt in the ash tray. The brand was ENOE, and it had been economically smoked down to the barest brown nub. No hotel manager would leave such glaring evidence of intrusion.

In seconds they had their bags and George's. They hastened down again, flushed with success.

When they circled around to George he had already arranged a taxi. She was jumpy, looking in all directions, and John forcefully opened the door of the cab and ushered her in. They set off for the eastern shore of the island, urging the driver to hurry.

The small village of Perissa had a short quay of weathered concrete and rock. A single shack stood at the entrance, and the man there responded drowsily to her questions, getting slowly to his feet.

Was there a man who could take them on a long cruise, several days, to the islands, perhaps north? The dock attendant was unsure. Perhaps the boat near the end, did you see? It was for fishing but the owner lived aboard; it could be that he would do such a thing. But the boat, it was only so big, not for so many people. Not for Americans, who were used to living with the best, yes?

She assured him they were interested anyway. The man promptly sat down and resumed reading his newspaper. The headlines bore gaudy accusations against the USA.

They walked along the quay, where a fishing boat lay with nets strung high, airing in the sun. This was a working vessel, its name, *Skorpio*, half obscured by discoloration. Rusty winches and a hoist needed oil. It lay stern on to blue and yellow diagonals painted on the concrete.

John pointed to them. "If they use standard harbor markings, those mean this area's reserved for visiting boats. Must be a fisherman from another island."

Claire said, "There aren't any significant islands south of us. He must be heading north from here, then."

"Good. Before we go aboard, let's plan. We've got cash—show him some. I want to get under way fast."

"He'll need supplies, though."

"We can help him bring them aboard."

"The police won't know we came here. We have a little time."

"No we don't. If they come back from the Delphi and check our rooms, they'll see our luggage gone. One phone call to that dock man back there and we're finished."

"Oh." She scowled. It was all going so fast. What had

started as an adventure, a thumbing of her nose at Kontos, was deepening, never giving her time to rethink. She remembered assuming light-heartedly, only a day ago, that surely if they were caught, the police would simply send them out of the country. But now there were new laws and restrictions in Athens and she hadn't had a chance to read a newspaper, to consider what that meant. Could they be charged with something serious? Kontos knew they were still in the country, he had alerted the police. What would he do if they were brought in to him?

Claire had thought they'd gotten away with something. Now she saw that things were only beginning.

CHAPTER
Four

After midnight you got a feeling for the different densities, even the different colors of darkness.

John stood on the narrow fantail of the *Skorpio* and felt the murmuring darkness of the living sea around them. Beyond, a few hundred yards away, the looming lamp-black mass of the cliff swallowed the sea's mutter and gave back a faintly tinny echo of waves and slapping surf. Above, thick clouds made a clotted inky silence. Beneath this blanket a faint luminous ivory-yellow line of foam marked where waves creamed hollowly among the fallen boulders of the thin, ash-gray storm beach.

They would land a little to the right, where a path wandered down to the grainy sand. He had studied it yesterday afternoon through the captain's binoculars, trying to remember exactly where everything was at the camp site on the other side of the hill. It had been odd to ride at anchor only a few hundred yards away from the site, but secure in the knowledge that no one ever paid any attention to the sea around the hill. Or so they thought.

By the time they had reached the coast of the Peloponnese the captain, a Mr. Ankaros, had begun demanding more money. The ship's radio had carried static-spattered news of more government measures. Foreign nationals were asked politely but firmly to leave within two weeks. Exceptions were allowed, but the intention was clear. The regime formally ratified its exit from NATO, denouncing the alliance's policies as restrictive and warlike. Currency restrictions were tightened further. On the international front, there was another border dispute inside ever-shaky Russia, and the United States had begun operation of its High Orbit Laboratory.

Claire had convinced Mr. Ankaros that they were merely down and out tourists who wanted a touch of the *true* Greece, a few days of something unusual, a taste of how the real people lived. John wasn't sure that Mr. Ankaros bought her earnest explanations, but the man did take the money they gave him, and had even agreed to sail them around the Peloponnesian peninsula and on to Italy. They had made a convincing show of swimming in the Gulf of Argos yesterday afternoon, and he and George had gone ashore for a little hiking at the island of Spetsae. Claire had insisted on devoting at least a full day to tourism, to establish in Mr. Ankaros's mind the impression of a bunch of mildly eccentric travelers, taking in the crisp air and sun of late fall.

They had carefully urged him further up into the Gulf, eyeing the cathedral-like cliffs until they agreed that they were beneath the tomb site. Then it was a matter of eating the food Mr. Ankaros prepared—fish caught during the day, vegetables bought at Spetsae—along with three bottles of wine.

John burped suddenly, loudly, and hoped the sleeping Mr. Ankaros didn't catch the sound. The fisherman had begun to sing before the second bottle was done. The three of them had seen to it that the captain got much more of the strong red than they did, and stayed up late with them. Necessary, yes, but John didn't like to go off in a small skiff with a head even slightly dulled. They had all slept three hours, fully dressed, and had then silently gathered on the aft deck. John and George slept on the deck anyway, atop the fore and aft hatches, because there was only room for two below. Mr. Ankaros had his own V-berth forward, and Claire was given the privacy of the aft cabin bunk.

They had barely managed to abide the cramped, smelly boat for the three days it had taken them to get here. The thought of another three days, if not more, to reach Italy was not appetizing. John was glad of this opportunity to get ashore and do something, to start bringing an end to this whole affair.

It had started out as a lark, but three days at sea with the others had cured him of that. George threw up the entire first

day and for the next two either lay on the deck or complained.
Claire had endured stoically, after being violently sick for the
first hour out from Santorini. When they had said they
couldn't sail, they meant it. They didn't know the mast from
the mainsail. And three days on even as mild a sea as the
Aegean had convinced both of them that they never, never
wanted to learn.

George murmured at his elbow, "How come we're waiting?"

"To let the wind shift more toward the bow. I want it to
carry our noise away from where he's sleeping."

That was true, but he also wanted to get the feel of the
night, see if the weather was turning. It would be just fine if
they found a choppy, high sea when they came back to the
beach, stranding them. Operating at night was always risky,
and doing it with minimum noise was worse. He already regretted going along with Claire's insistence that they not tell
Mr. Ankaros anything. True, he had not been able to think
up a plausible reason for their going ashore at night. But as
he felt the swelling power of the dark sea the consequences
of failure were more real, the risks far larger than their calm,
rational discussions ever admitted. His sunny boating weekends off Galveston were ludicrously skimpy preparation for
this.

John sighed. He shook off the effects of food and wine and
gaffed the skiff closer. Claire was a slightly darker shadow
behind George. "You two get in first. I'll hold it."

They moved cautiously and managed not to thump noisily
against the wood. John got in and pushed off with one motion.
He fumbled for an oar and backed them off, memorizing the
configuration of *Skorpio*'s running lights for later. George
found the other oar and they paddled away, not risking the
oar locks.

It seemed to take a long laboring time to reach shore, navigating by the mutter of whitecaps on rocks. The purple sea
shielded the foaming ivory wave line. A vagrant wave caught
them amidships, wrenching the boat, and John thought for an
instant they were going to go over. But the bow came around
and abruptly they were skidding down a curling slope, dim
luminescence springing in their wake. A black wedge rose to
port and their keel bit in.

"Out!" John leaped into the surprisingly warm water and pulled the bow forward, using the ebbing momentum of the wave. The others splashed beside him, tugging. On the next wave's surge they hauled it up onto fist-sized pebbles. John secured it fore and aft with ropes tied to rocks. By the time he was finished George had their equipment in hand and had scouted the shoreline. They quickly found the barely visible path.

They worked their way up without speaking, except for whispered warnings: "Hole up here." George's flashlight snapped on, only long enough to navigate. "Watch these rocks." Their main fear was of starting a slide of the loose stones.

They crouched at the brow of the hill and peered over. A few bare bulbs cast yellow shadows across the camp. Nothing moved.

"Looks like they just left it," George said.

"Kontos hasn't had time to get back and finish up," Claire whispered.

"Maybe," John said. "I'll bet his men are still here. The site's not secured from vandalism."

Claire's voice rose in pitch with alarm. "Do you think there'll be a guard awake?"

"Probably. They're military men, not scientists."

"What'll we do?" Plainly the thought of a guard hadn't entered her calculations.

John said, "Work our way along the back of the hill. Come over the crown, just above the *dromos*. But watch out, don't kick rocks down."

The sea lay leaden below them as they picked their way across steep, eroded gullies. John glanced at his watch. Only fifteen minutes since they left the *Skorpio*. It seemed like an hour, easy.

Going down was tedious. The dim glow from the camp helped, and from this fresh angle he was sure no one stood or walked among the tents.

They reached the broad path and ducked eagerly into the *dromos*. The big wooden door was padlocked.

"At least they thought to do that," Claire said, producing her key.

The bulky door creaked and popped, sounding impossibly

loud. Inside, they pulled it to before clicking on the ship's lamp George carried. He swung it around.

"They haven't touched a thing!" Claire said excitedly. The long blue shadows distorted John's memory, but everything seemed in place, even George's concealing sheets draped at the wall.

She rushed over to the stacks of equipment and crates. "My notes and samples are in this one. Damn Kontos for not letting me back in here. Help me."

George pried open a small crate with a hammer and screwdriver. John threaded his way among the jumble. Somehow, things were changed. In the pale lamplight the inward-curving walls seemed menacing, like hands cupped to keep him prisoner. He thought again about being trapped in here, drugged or drunk, knowing there was a hopeless heavy bank of sand beyond the huge door even if you could cut through it, air getting stale and thick with oily smoke—

"That's them!" Claire said, pawing several notebooks free. "Here, let me take a few of those. . . ."

She bundled it all together and stood up. All three beamed at each other.

Something jogged John's memory. "The cube—it's gone."

"What?" Claire spun around. The space where the crate had been was bare. "So he's taken it back to Athens, first thing."

"Funny, only that one item," George muttered reflectively. "You'd figure, put all the stuff on one truck, save extra trips." He looked around the tomb.

"Let's go," John said.

"Sure, just a sec. . . ." George walked over to the block and tackle rig. He fingered the sheets. "These don't look the way I left them. I didn't pin them back to the wood this way." He jerked one edge loose. "Hey, bring that lamp closer, will you?"

He peered through the open hole. "Hey! It's inside here."

They crowded in. The cube's crate sat beyond the wall, in the flat area.

"Now why'd Kontos do that?" John asked.

Claire pursed her lips. "To keep it out of the inventory for the expedition."

"So?"

"That way he can come back here in a year or so, 'find' it and claim the discovery for himself."

"Use the fact that you kept quiet about it, you mean," John said.

Claire gave him a sharp look. "Yes, I suppose so. Kontos probably noticed that it was listed under 'miscellaneous' on the inventory."

George said, "Kontos hasn't unpacked it. Prob'ly doesn't know what it is."

John said, "I'll bet he's hijacked everything under 'miscellaneous,' come to that."

Claire put her hands on her hips and her eyes flashed over the tomb. "I don't doubt it for a moment. Damn!"

George said, "So Kontos sends out some men, they don't know anything, he tells them to clear out everything on the floor of the tomb but not bother the draped stuff near the wall. Then next year . . ."

"Smart man," John said.

Claire said savagely, "Not smart enough. If this crate turns up in Athens, he can't hide it. His colleagues will see it."

George said, "So?"

John saw what she meant. "We haven't got the time."

She whirled to confront him. "Kontos obviously did it with George's pulley system. It'll take—what—ten minutes?"

"Even if we moved it back among the other crates, there's nothing to guarantee that Kontos wouldn't intercept it, stop—"

"Oh, crap! Come on, George." She fumbled with the ropes, exasperated.

George began, "Well, I don't know if—"

"Aren't *either* of you going to help? Okay, I'll do it myself. Just get out—"

"Here now." John, resigned, pulled a block and tackle into position. "Let's make it quick."

George saw immediately how Kontos had suspended the crate—there were eyelit screw hooks mounted along four edges. "He must've swung it in through the hole, using one of the wooden ramps. There, that one'll work. We'll just reverse the process."

As they arranged the elaborate web of ropes John glanced at his watch. Another fifteen minutes gone. Plenty of time until dawn. The tide was still going out, so the boat wouldn't be catching any wave action.

"I'll crawl through and thread the ropes through the hooks." George said. John positioned the ramp and handed through the ropes. Despite the weight of the artifact, the time-honored mechanical principles should make it a fast job.

"Okay!" George called. "Start lifting the front two hooks like I showed you." Claire released the safeties and John steadied the ropes. The crate tilted back and up. John slid the ramp under it. By pulling forward they could drag it along the ramp. John took the command rope and pulled.

"That's it," George called. "A little more."

John and Claire both strained at the main ropes. The crate wobbled slightly.

"The rope's snagging on something," George said. "Keep the tension on, I'll see what it is."

George kneeled beside the crate and fumbled with the rope. "Some rocks, must've been scraped up by—"

Suddenly the crate shifted sideways. The taut ropes tilted it farther back. In an awful slow motion it rolled backwards, surprising George, coming down on his left leg, rocking brutally to the side. It crashed against the rock wall.

George screamed. The crate lurched. Wood popped. It was still reared back, and now it rolled.

The crate went end over end, backwards, and slid into the open hole beyond.

John heard it smash once, twice, wood splintering. The lamp had sprawled aside and to John it seemed that light danced in a frenzy around the walls, raking across slick stone, seeming to come from everywhere. Loud boomings like cannon shots. A rattling, as though something fell far below. A humming, drawing down into nothing. A distant splash. Then silence.

CHAPTER
Five

Claire turned the lamp fully on George's bared right leg. "Look, it's turning darker." She gingerly ran fingers along the trembling calf muscle. Her heart thumped loudly in her ears. "I think perhaps it's merely a sprain, but . . ."

"Looks like. . .a break. . .to me," George wheezed.

Claire nodded. "Did you feel anything snap?"

"I dunno. . .maybe. It was on me only a second but *man* it hurt."

John asked, "How bad is the pain now?"

George moved the leg experimentally. "Ah! H-hurts, but nothing. . .real sharp."

Claire took his ankle and gave it a slight pull. "How is that?"

"Not bad. I mean, no change."

Claire said, "That could mean there's no major fracture. Perhaps a hairline. And a massive amount of broken blood vessels and muscle damage."

"It was rolling when it came onto me."

"Lucky you didn't get carried down with it," John said.

"Yeah . . ." George gazed forlornly up at them. "We really screwed this one, huh?"

"I . . ." Claire hesitated. "I don't know what went wrong. Perhaps I kept pulling on the rope too much or something."

"We both did," John said.

She went on, "Whatever, I don't care. It was my idea and I take the responsibility."

"I. . .guess it's down there, huh? Must be pretty smashed up."

"It sounded terrible," Claire admitted. "I heard breaking wood."

"I'll look." John slowly, gingerly moved to the edge of the hole and shone the lamp down it. "There are some boards caught in a crevice far down. Some long scrape marks on the wall."

"I don't think I want to see," Claire said, feeling sick. A priceless piece of the past, ruined because of her own game-playing. It was like bitterly cold water dashed in her face, the realization that she had been self-centered, unprofessional, heedless, smug, careless—

"Long gone now," John said, and handed the lamp back to Claire. He started to turn around and then gazed down the dark tube, frowning. Then he shook his head. "It must be a hundred yards down to sea level, but—"

"That's not important now," Claire said. "We have to get George to a hospital."

George blinked. "Hey, no. I mean, we're nearly home free, right? I don't want to go to any Greek hospital and have them throw my ass in jail."

John said firmly, "You need help."

"Look, I'm not that bad off. I say we get the hell out of here."

John said, "You can't walk."

"Who says? Help me up."

Claire steadied George as John pulled him carefully up to lean on a shoulder. George turned ashen but held on.

"See? I can take a step, even."

"Now, don't—"

George lurched forward and landed unsteadily on his left foot. "There. See?"

"Is there very much pain?" Claire asked.

"Not. . .not really. That calf muscle sure is sore, though."

"Maybe it's only a muscle bruise and a minor fracture," John said reluctantly. "That's still nothing to be casual about."

Claire thought quickly. "Look," she said, "we can take him to Nauplia. Once we're back on the ship it's a short trip. They can probably take care of him within an hour or two, if it's nothing major. Then we can sail out again."

John said, "All right. We'll have to be careful to—"

"Listen!" Claire whispered.

A distant creaking.

"The door!" Claire abruptly stooped and clicked off the lamp. Total darkness descended.

The sheets were pulled back from the opening, she remembered. Anyone could see directly in. She inched forward feeling for the edges of stone. There. Now, if she remembered correctly—

A rough surface, then smooth, cold metal. Up above somewhere would be the cloth. She reached—

A man's voice. The door was swinging open. A faint glow from a flashlight showed her she was groping the wrong way. She snatched the nearest sheet and yanked it down, over the hole.

She crouched, looking toward the sound of creaking and a swelling bass mutter of male voices.

A thump. That would be the door banging fully open.

Light playing on the sheets.

A slurred voice said in Greek, "See? Nothing."

"Could have been."

A thud. "You forgot to lock it, I tell you."

"I remember right. I closed the door, didn't I?"

"Hurrying down to supper, soon as the Colonel went, you forgot."

The yellowish glow faded.

"You heard that sound just now."

"The waves, a big one, that's all."

Creaking, a bang—the door closing.

A moment of complete silence. She listened intently. When John sighed behind her it seemed startlingly loud. "So much for cops and robbers."

She switched on the lamp. The cramped area leaped into vivid reality. "What?"

"They heard the crate."

George said unsteadily, "Yeah, it sure was loud enough. Musta carried through that door. That boom, what was it?"

"The artifact, turning into gravel," John said sourly.

Claire bit her lip. He was almost certainly right. All because she had wanted to play one last card, trump Kontos on the final move. John's face held little sympathy.

"That was fast, pulling down the sheet," John said. "Not that it does any good. We'll have to bang on the door now, try to attract their attention."

She blinked. "Why?"

"Because they've locked us in."

He was right. Mortifyingly, infuriatingly right. She and John pressed against the bulky wooden slats. The door caught up against the Yale lock and hasp. She could feel it solidly take hold, letting the door move a mere centimeter.

She sagged against the wall and sat down. So she was going to have to surrender to them, go through all the awful questions and sneers and accusations she had imagined and tortured herself with these last few days. Kontos, and probably men far worse than Kontos. The regime would play up the whole incident, getting mileage out of foreigners sneaking around, conniving, trying to steal the Greek birthright.

She felt tired. The worst of it was, she was now responsible for George's leg. It had been going so well, despite the awful three days on the *Skorpio*, and now suddenly this exciting maneuver had turned to injury and loss. If only, if only . . .

"There's got to be *some*thing we can do," she said without real hope. "I have the key right here. If there's some way to—"

"I checked. The bolt and fittings are on the outside."

She sighed. "If we took some of the tools and worked around the frame . . ."

"Without making enough noise to draw the guards back?"

She thought, gazing up at the thick timbers, and finally nodded. "Probably you're right. But it's a chance. All we have."

John walked over to George, who sat holding the lamp for them. "Let me take it a minute." He stepped through the hole. George lay staring at the ceiling, blinking, numbed.

Claire struggled with her storm of emotions, at the same time feeling a chilling weakness seep through her. She could talk John into prying at the framing, but it would be slow and noisy. There was no way to extract the large nails without brute force. She shivered. Six days ago she had been working here, ready to go home, riding high, carrying a fat pouch of research results and looking forward to Boston again. Now look at her. She shivered again.

John stepped back into the tomb. "Claire? Come help me with these ropes. There may be another way out."

CHAPTER
Six

He felt the first dizzying sensation as he gripped the rope. The workman's gloves helped grasp it, and he had a loop-trap hold with his tennis shoes, but still he felt uneasy.

It was not the descending bore of the eroded tube that bothered him, fitfully lit by the lamp Claire held beside him. Perspective narrowed the passageway, but he could see it neck and twist, getting tighter, about fifteen feet below.

He grimaced and put the thoughts away. He wouldn't do anything risky, just have a look. In that moment after he passed the lamp back, he had seen a blue glow far down the hole. It must be the glow of early dawn, filtered through sea water, refracted upward. Such dim rays would be absorbed easily, so seeing them from the top of the hole must mean there was very little water at the bottom. When he had gone diving, the entrance seemed at least a dozen feet below the surface, probably more. Was there much variation with the tides? He seemed to remember that Mediterranean tides were small.

Seemed. Might. Maybe.

It was all guesswork. The only way to check it was to go and look, and if the required dive looked clear, he would do it.

"If there's any question, come right back up," Claire said anxiously.

"Yes ma'am," John said with a lightness he did not feel.

"Where are you carrying the key?"

He patted his vest pocket, buttoned, and started downward again. He fished George's pocket flashlight from the other vest pocket and switched it on. Its beam was feeble compared with the lamp.

Claire read his thoughts. "You don't suppose you could. . .?"

"No, I can't manage that lamp. I'd sure as hell like to."

He knew he was talking to delay going down there. Abruptly he realized that he had not decided whether he wanted to do this, not really. The idea had come to him and he had talked it over and then they were arranging the ropes and now here he was, without really thinking it through.

At first Claire had said no, she didn't want any more risks, not after what had happened. So he had persisted, partly because the idea intrigued him, but mostly because he could look daring even in the face of all that had happened. Like most men who live quiet, reflective lives, the tang of action carried an exotic zest they seldom knew.

What had she called it? Yes, praxis. He had even mentioned his mountain climbing experience, though in fact he had only taken a weekend course, and done a little scrambling up the rough hills of Texas. So he had been taken aback when her face changed from a rigid, distant skepticism to a hedged curiosity, and then guarded acceptance. His own damned mouth had run away with him. And now the same impulse, to look good in her eyes, was making him cinch the rope around his waist again, checking it for the nth time, but unable to look at her and say he didn't think this was such a great idea after all, ma'am.

Claire said, "I've been in the grottoes along the Amalfi coast. The light there was a lot brighter than this."

"It looked stronger before. Probably cloud cover moving in."

"Yes, that might be it."

More stalling. Well, the hell with it. "You be on the other end of that block and tackle, okay? Three jerks means I want to come up."

She nodded, half opened her mouth, but said nothing. He leaned over and kissed her. Her lips went rigid for a moment, then softened, then pressed warmly back.

"Umm. I'll be back for more."

He waved to George, who was peering through from the tomb, and swung over the side.

The first fifteen feet were easy. He played out the rope and slowed himself with his feet, watching the glistening walls rise past him, still lit by the lamp. The rock exuded a salty, fetid odor.

At the first turn he got a purchase on the wall and worked his way to the right. The shaft squeezed down, but not badly. He twisted and got through, though he could feel his heart accelerate as he brushed against the smooth, wet stone.

Past the turn, the glow from the lamp above showed only streaks of yellow down the shaft. He had left the flashlight on in his vest pocket, and its diffuse radiance helped.

Here two smashed boards were caught in a crevice, pieces from one of the crate's corners. Deep gouges in the wall led his eyes downward. His vision had adjusted and he could make out below another neck, then a branching into several side vents. The shaft was leveling off somewhat, and a large stone formed a platform. On it were more boards and some packing material. Some boards were still fastened together by nails, others were thrown back into a side passage that dropped away to the left.

He jerked once on the line and Claire fed out more footage. The rope above scraped on the turn in the neck. He watched it, but the dampness let the rope glide smoothly. It was a thick rope, he told himself, not likely to wear away quickly. He told himself again. Then he dropped toward the stone.

"Ledge here!" he called, so Claire would not be alarmed when his weight went off the line. He sat down on the slimy, cold rock, not trusting the footing. The main chimney dropped away at a slant under the rock, which looked to be dripstone. He got out the flash and crawled over clammy slickness to the side passage. A harsh, almost acrid smell filled the hole that dropped away steeply. A few boards had been flung that way, but his guess was the crate had gone the more direct route, below. He clicked off the flash.

Was that a blue glow down the side passage? He waited for the afterimage on his retinas to fade. Yes, that was real, no figment.

But faint. Too faint, he was sure, to see from above.

On the other hand, maybe this side passage was the way

out. He clicked on the flash again. This side hole was not as slick and gray as the chimney. The rock was brownish, and rough edges blocked his view.

A hint of warmth brushed his face. A breeze from this side passage? Hard to tell. What was that sour tang in the air, like something burning? The senses played tricks down here.

He crawled back over the brow of the stone ledge. There were no loose rocks, consistent with the subterranean cistern theory. Everything had been swept clean by millennia of seepage, carving an underground streamway. Certainly this wasn't man-made; he had seen no handiwork, or any artifacts that had fallen in.

At the edge he studied the steep drop of the main shaft. A dozen feet below it twisted and angled left. He killed the flash and waited for the yellowish afterimage to go. "Still looking!" he called.

"Okay!" Claire's high, echoing cry came from a long way off.

There, below—light. Definitely a pale ivory luminescence. Reflected off the damp walls.

He listened for sounds of wave action. Nothing. Absolute, dead silence.

But was this faint light stronger than the one he'd seen down the side channel? Even though there were apparently two ways down, they might not be negotiable.

Best to choose the brightest. It was either closer, or bigger, or both.

He grimaced. Comparing two fuzzy patches of blue, trying to decide. He squinted. Hard to tell. He coughed from the dampness.

The hell with it. This one looked good enough, and he hadn't liked the looks of that side way. Too many tight angles. Squeezing into there, when a comparatively wide shaft was open here—no, this one was best.

"Stepping off!"

He eased over the edge and hung. *Like bait on the end of a line*, he thought. Claire let off the ratchet on the rope—he could feel the jerk—and he coasted down.

The turn was closer than he thought. He had to squirm through. Slime eased his way. It reeked, something like dead kelp.

His foot caught on something. His breath rasped. He felt around for a way through and suddenly the full force of it came on him—wedged in between two slabs of pressing rock, turned at an impossible angle, chilled, hands aching as they clenched tight, in damp darkness with only a slender rope connecting him to the world of light and air—

No, drop that. He had to keep moving.

He squirmed farther down. His right foot found more obstruction, but the left slipped and dangled in space. He wormed over that way. There was room for maneuver, but the cloying near-total darkness made it seem as if the rock walls pressed in, their weight and mass blocking all escape.

He found a way and slid down chilly rock. The rope brought him up short, then eased him down a gentle slope.

He thought of Claire laboring above. Was she strong enough for this, even with the pulleys giving mechanical advantage?

More gray stone buttresses glided by. Clammy, clinging air. It was like descending a shaft of a Gothic cathedral.

A brightening below. He descended, peering. Light suffused the pit of the passage. The rock leveled off here and John cautiously lowered himself down to it. Thirty yards downslope, a dimly radiant azure pool filled the passage, beyond a pebble beach. Inky shapes of boulders lined the slope. Long gouges in the sand and splinters of wood marked the passage of the crate. He picked his way forward in the gloom, feet crunching on pebbles.

Water, gently lapping. How deep? He could swim down a short way, assess the situation.

"I'm OK!" he called through cupped hands.

A ringing, indecipherable answer.

He unhitched the rope. Arms ached and tingled, shoulders knotted painfully.

He stepped into the pool. After the chilly stone it was warm, reassuring. He waded down the steep slope, panting to store up oxygen, and then dove.

The gurgle of submersion seemed loud. He struggled downward toward flickering shafts of dull light. Lumpy stone masses moved past with unnerving slowness.

He fought down the throat of rock, feeling a tightness in

his chest that must mean he had little air left. Should he turn around? No, it looked so close, so easy—

He swam frantically now, the burning coming up into his throat, the mad desire to open lungs and suck in. Something tan-colored below caught his eye. And suddenly the light was brighter, the rock mouth opened and he was out, free. Shimmering mirrors danced above. He opened his mouth, releasing bubbles, kicking upward. He broke the surface with a rough gasp.

It was not yet full dawn. The eastern sky was turning from red to yellow as he watched. How long to get ashore, up the hill? He looked for a quick way onto the sharp rock cliff, and remembered the thing below.

He dove, and yes, there it was—the crate. One side ripped clean off, edges smashed, but otherwise intact. The side he could see was the back. That meant the front, with the Linear A and the cone, was still protected by the packing.

He gulped air and swam to the right, looking for a hand-hold.

CHAPTER
Seven

The sudden rattling at the door startled her. She was standing beside the open hole, ready to respond to any call or yanking on the rope. But there had been no signal for at least ten minutes now.

George whispered, "Damn! Here, help me back in there."

"Those men?" Her throat tightened.

"Must be," George said.

Claire plunged into the tomb and reached for George. More rattling, a clank.

Creaking. She seized George's arm. Dim sunlight. The door swung open.

"Presto!"

She gaped at John, framed in the doorway. "You—you—"

"Damn. . .right," he gasped. He staggered in and pulled the door closed.

"What did you find, how did—"

"It's getting light fast out there. We've got to move."

"Well, I—" Flustered, she looked around, spotted her things, snatched them up.

George had gotten himself erect, leaning on the scaffolding.

"Let me hold onto your shoulder, I can limp," he said.

"Man, that was *fast*."

John nodded, out of wind. "I didn't spot anybody in camp."

"You get your breath, I'll pick up here," Claire said, beginning to unfasten the rope arrangement they had made.

149

"No time. Doesn't matter anyway," John puffed.

"We can disguise—"

"Come off it," he said sharply. "The crate's gone, lying in twenty feet of water. They'll damn sure know we were here."

"I. . .I suppose you're right."

"Let's go," John said, taking George's weight on his shoulder. "Up and over, the way we came. Got to get out of sight fast. George, I'll count so we keep the same pace."

The camp was bare when she glanced at it. As she scrambled up the hillside, clutching at clumps of brush and oleander, she felt sure there would be shouts behind, running footsteps, a rifle shot.

She reached the top and plunged over, then looked back. The two men came lurching behind her, grunting, and still the camp slept below. Incredible, after all her dark thoughts, to be released from that tomb, carrying her notebooks, into a bright reddening dawn, with the *Skorpio* lying at anchor below. The world was impossibly sharp, precise.

John and George stopped below the brow, panting. She grabbed John's collar and kissed him, saying nothing. A look of surprise crossed his face, he grimaced, and then studied the hillside, estimating the best path back to their boat. "Come on."

They were rowing out to *Skorpio* before she remembered what he had said. "You—you saw the crate?" she gasped. George was braced in the stern and she had to grunt to keep up her side of the paddling.

"Huh? Sure did. Looks pretty good, considering." He scanned the hillside behind them.

"That thing on the tail of *Skorpio*, what is it?"

"What? Oh, some kind of hoist. Used for trawling and bringing in loaded nets."

"How much can it lift?"

"I don't—oh, oh no—I get what you're thinking."

"We can't just leave it down there."

"With the whole goddamn Greek army on our tails?"

"If they look now, they'll simply see a fishing boat at work."

"Forget it."

George said, "Hey, look, don't you think we've had enough—"

Claire wheezed between strokes, "Damn it, I'm not going . . .to let a unique artifact. . .get destroyed on the sea bottom."

John said slowly, "You may be right about the guards. I locked the door again, so there's no obvious sign we were there. But I can't operate that hoist, and we damn sure can't do it without Mr. Ankaros knowing it."

"We'll tell him we woke up early, went out boating, saw something underwater that we want to salvage."

John snorted. "Likely story."

"A lot more believable than the truth!"

"And George's leg?"

"He slipped getting into the boat."

George groaned. "Oh no."

John looked sternly at the set of Claire's mouth. He was tired, she saw, the energy of his triumphant return dissipated. Perhaps it was too much to ask of him, adding one more to a pile of debts she had built up.

George's leg was bad, but it would heal. A month or two and he would probably be all right. All things considered, they had come through pretty well. Luck helped. Dumb luck, sure, but who was choosey?

They were silent as they worked toward *Skorpio*, panting.

"I don't believe this," George drawled.

But then an amused, resigned expression came into John's face. He smiled. "I do," he said.

PART
FOUR

CHAPTER
One

John Bishop belted up his coat outside the Pratt Building, squinting into yellow sunlight glaring on thin snow. Cambridge did not deign to clear snow from its sidewalks, but an army of students had trampled it into slush already. A late afternoon chill promised a freeze tonight.

He sniffed, nostrils flaring. Storm coming again, he decided, using the automatic system of weather prediction every Tech inhabitant learned. A sweet tang in the air meant the wind blew from a nearby candy factory to the south, promising warm breezes and fewer thick-bellied clouds. A stink from Lever Brothers in the northwest threatened dark days and another wedge of moisture from Canada.

Exams were just finishing up. John had helped with the grading in the introductory mathematical physics courses, and felt a restless fatigue. Passing judgment on an endless stream of mechanics and calculus problems numbs the mind while demanding that it still remain alert for the slight error, sometimes a mere jot of notation, that signals where a harried student had gone astray. Professors everywhere deplored examinations as an archaic technique, a fossil that recalled little red schoolhouses and memorizing the capitals of all the states. Regular progress and daily diligence mattered more, they felt, not an hour spent compressing months of learning onto a few sheets of paper. Far better to stress homework, classroom participation and the professor's judgment. Regrettably, the large size of classes, and the requirements of society itself for pseudo-objective standards kept the exam structure firmly in place.

None of these sentiments kept the professorial from devising examinations which caused sleepless cram sessions, caffeine addiction and despair. Old exam problems congested the files of fraternities and dorms; there were dossiers on each professor's predilections. This constituted a challenge to each instructor, to find problems which would furrow any student's brow while still being defensible as straightforward, clear, illustrating a central topic thoroughly explored in class. The ultimate quest was for problems which could trick the unwary into a blunder at a predictable point, allowing the grader to check these crucial turns quickly, assign demerits for failure, and move on.

John adjusted his scarf—still a foreign garment he continually misplaced—and watched the fatigued faces leaving the building. There was a certain satisfaction in having taken part in this ancient academic ritual, for the first time from the vantage point of a judge. Tonight the movie houses and gaming rooms would be jammed, he knew, in search of distraction. Surely several thousand dazed and tired young men and women were a sign of a job well done.

Well, enough musing. He was late for his appointment. He merged with this stream of dull-eyed, scruffy students and headed away from the Charles River down Mass Ave. His office was in the Center for Materials Science and Engineering, tucked into a confused assembly of buildings named for the fortunes which begat them—Sloan, Guggenheim, Pierce, Bush, Eastman, names which honored science, school and self. He could have worked his way through these labyrinthine corridors lined with display cases of geological specimens, arcane instruments, interactive experiments, pictures of great scientists. He preferred walking outdoors past the time-honored red brick buildings and across Vassar Street, to the unimpressive gray concrete and sheet metal of newer laboratories. Here in a bay of Building 42 he had arranged to examine the artifact.

The bare cold floors and unceremonious entranceway were virtually empty. The solid state stress-test facility had moved to roomier, updated facilities over on Albany. Materials Science still held title to this bay, though, since in the university as in foreign affairs, territory once held is never surrendered without a struggle or a deal. John had wangled permission to use it, and the privilege of using experimental equipment which came available. Since few archeologists carried out year-round digs, the diagnostic gear was usually free in winter, and he had brought most of it here. He stood, hands in coat pockets, and watched as a powered pulley inched along its track in the ceiling, its *rrrrrrrttt* echoing from the naked walls. A moment passed before he realized that the men at the far end of the room were those he had seen this morning at the truck which brought the artifact from the docks, and therefore the object suspended below the track was the tarp-shrouded crate itself.

It seemed smaller in this expanse. He had no doubt the thing didn't weigh too much for the thick steel cables, but something bothered him. That was it—the angle. The crate was not hanging straight down. He held up a finger vertically and sighted on the cable. It made about a ten degree angle. He frowned and then shrugged. Probably *something off center in the T-clasp at the apex*, he thought, *or a misalignment at the joint. Still, it seemed that the workmen should have gotten it right; this was a valuable piece.*

Claire had gotten the artifact repacked in Italy. A man pulled the tarp away. The pale wood seemed oddly fresh as it settled to the concrete floor, air freight stickers garish against the knotted pine. The men nodded toward him and began opening the crate with crowbars.

"Where's the mount?" Claire's voice called to them from behind him. He turned, realizing that it hadn't been him they had nodded to.

"We'll bring it over soon's this's done," the foreman answered.

She wore a navy blue business suit, the stylish dressed-for-success look, over a frilly pink blouse. Severe exterior, feminine peekaboo beneath. He liked it.

"Lord, they took forty forevers to get here," Claire said to him, never taking her eyes off the laboring men. "Crawled through every back alley from Logan."

"Do they know how to handle it?" He watched the men stripping away the packing material. One dropped a crowbar and it rang jarringly.

"It's pretty rugged, you know—it survived that horrible fall. Except for occasionally moving it around, we'll be doing delicate work here. I'll handle that."

"Alone?"

She smiled enigmatically. "As near to it as I can get."

"You called Watkins in China?"

"Yes. Watkins grumped a while and then gave me carte blanche to use the equipment, so long as it doesn't leave the sacred ground of MIT."

"And Sprangle? He's department head, he could keep you from using the expensive gear if he thought you might mess it up."

"He passed the buck to Watkins."

"Bravo. How'd you do it?"

The enigmatic smile again. She knew she could be charming when she wanted, he could tell that, but the curiously guarded way she used this ability puzzled him. Other women would squander it, he had seen that often enough. Claire kept a cool exterior, perhaps realizing that the melting of such a facade was more interesting to men than mere continual warmth.

"I did have to make one concession," she admitted.

"To Sprangle?"

"Yes. It seems he is an archeology buff. He wants to be kept up on my results. I think he sees it as an opportunity to push his group's capability."

"Maybe drum up a little more support from his dean?"

"I think you read the tea leaves correctly." Her eyes had never left the uncrating. Now she stepped closer.

"Anything wrong?"

Heavy padding had fallen away, revealing the golden cone. "I don't. . .no, nothing. The cone, it. . .reminds me of something."

"Of what? Some tests?"

"No, something I've seen. . . ." She shrugged. "It'll come back later."

They circled the laboring men. The artifact stood bare now. It had been a great surprise to him how little the fall down the shaft and plunge into the sea had done. The crate had been demolished, of course, the back half stripped away entirely. They had a sweaty, aggravating time of it, getting the thing aboard. He had dived repeatedly, attaching three cables to the sides of the remaining crate, not truly sure the rig would hold together. It did, though, and they secured it on deck. Claire went over the exposed stone carefully and found miraculously little damage: a few scrapes and gouges at unimportant points, and the accumulated hard mud at the rear scraped off.

John asked, "What're you going to look into first?"

"Better resolution of the metal content. Materials analysis. X-ray that cone, too."

"What about that ivory piece?"

"The rectangle?" She sighed. "Kontos has it. I packed it separately."

"Too bad."

"I have plenty of photos."

The men finished and stepped back to admire their work. "Okay, Miz Anderson?" Claire nodded and thanked them.

The artifact seemed small here, its deep black drinking up the light. At the back, where the hard soil had been, John saw a small hole. It was filled with some tan-colored matter. He bent closer. "What's that?"

Claire looked puzzled. She crouched, reached out gingerly and touched the hole. "It was still covered with a tough clay or something when the Italians packed it up. That must have worn away in transit. This. . .ummm."

"What is it?"

She leaned closer. "A plug of some kind, I think. George and I were careful not to remove the soil on the back, afraid we might damage something underneath. Odd, isn't it—a little hole, no more than a centimeter across, filled with some hard material." She tapped it with a fingernail.

"What do the Mycenaean experts at BU think about this?"

Claire stood abruptly, glancing at the men who were putting away their tools. "Let's celebrate," she said vigorously. "Ever been to the Ritz?"

"Nope. Is there one in Boston?"

She made a face of mock shock. "Some things are eternal. The Ritz-Carlton will be here when all we know has vanished into dust."

*　　*　　*

Her Alfa Romeo buzzed angrily across the Charles River and plunged without hesitation into the sluggish stream of early evening traffic. She took it down Boylston Street, avoiding delays by the simple maneuver of changing two lanes at a time where possible. Horns blared in their wake. They passed the Prudential Center's blank majesty at a good clip, slowing only when she caught sight of a policeman on an incongruous bay horse. They idled beside the public library.

"Did Hampton give you a hard time when—"

"I hate that new wing of the library. Did you know an elderly woman went into one of the side corridors in there, thinking it led to the restrooms, and got caught? She didn't have the strength to push the door open, that's how badly engineered it is."

"How long was she in there?"

"They figure two weeks."

"You mean—"

"Right. She died. Of dehydration, the coroner said."

The fountain in Copley Square flung joyous crystalline tribute into the sharp air, ignored by the earnest gloomy mumble of traffic. Two huge golden lions guarded the entrance to the Copley Plaza Hotel. Claire peered hopefully at parked cars, visibly willing them to turn on their headlights in announcement of an opening space. The brown stone spires of Trinity Church were moist, reflecting the swarm of headlights, and the side of the Hancock Tower gave watery echo to this image a block away.

She finally sought refuge in the underground lot beneath the Commons. Getting out, John said, "There's a ticket on your windshield."

"Oh." She pulled at it. It stayed attached to the wiper by a string. "Look at that," she said with mild admiration. "They have a little loop on it, so it doesn't blow away when you start up. Good idea." As they left the lot she carefully placed the ticket in a public trash bucket, and laughed at the look he gave her.

It had begun to rain and the Commons was emptying. Droplets drifted, threatening to turn into ice, making big luminous globes hang in the air around the street lights. Traffic was hushed, as if a long distance away. The same traffic policeman came clip-clopping toward them, his well-muscled bay alert. The man's yellow slicker reflected the roiling lights of the city, but the two of them seemed to John like an island of stability among it all.

"Late at night," Claire murmured, "when there's no one out, you can imagine Emerson and Thoreau walking through here in their top hats, arguing poetry."

They crossed Arlington Street and up the steps into the Ritz. Strangely, it didn't look ritzy to John. The public rooms and bar were Yankee with a touch of the China trade, mixing lacquered desks and rose carpeting with lithographs of old Newbury Street. No filigree or flourish, no chrome or cut glass. The fireplace roared with crisp yellow life, and they got seats nearby on a camelback sofa. While they waited for their Tanquery martinis she pointed out the antique wing chairs and cranberry carpeting, describing how the hotel employed one staffer full time to touch up the gold paint on the furniture. "And now that you're convinced this is an awful citadel of privilege, I'll remind you that the labor leader, Cesar Chavez, stayed here when he came to town to stir up proletarian passions."

He smiled wanly. She had an airy, girlish joy when she showed him things Bostonian, and the serious professional woman dropped away. They had seen a good deal of each other in the few days since returning, and he had detected a shift in her moods here on her home turf. As yet he could not quite sort the signals she was giving him. At moments she would abruptly tighten up, become much more the proper Boston lady, and then, moments later, she would be open again. Maybe it was the continuing worries she had?

"Do you suppose Colonel Professor Kontos will stay here, then? Proletarian though he is?"

She sighed. "Ah, you're getting used to my dodges, are you?"

"Not that they aren't likable."

She recrossed her legs, frowning. He admired the sensible shoes, which did nothing to reduce the agreeable swell of calf beneath nylon. He waited her out, speculating on the odds that she did not wear those awful panty hose, but instead went in for the real thing, complete with garter belt. Probability about point one percent, he guessed. As usual. Odd, how some male fantasy objects persisted long after their practical use vanished. Even in Boston—

"I might as well come straight out with it. I didn't tell Hampton about the artifact."

Despite his surprise he only raised his eyebrows. He was beginning to get the knack of underplaying, in response to her.

"He had me up on the carpet yesterday, and again this morning."

"No kiss on the cheek for the heroine's return?" He signaled the waiter for another round of martinis. The waiter indicated that they were already being made. He realized Claire was undoubtedly a regular here. The fire snapped energetically and he turned to present a larger cross section for its radiation. Even the Ritz had drafts.

"Kontos sent a long letter detailing my crimes."

"And Hampton buys it."

"Of course!" She snorted. "Why wouldn't he?"

"Hampton gave you the Dutch uncle talk about being polite to the host country representatives and so forth. Then you argued."

"Something like that." Drinks arrived and she took a healthy pull.

"So you elected to minimize damage by skipping over the matter of the missing artifact."

"Right. Those customs forms, they'll be addressed to the department at BU. But they'll come to me first, because I wrote my name over the address. So Hampton won't know right away that we flew anything back with us."

"He still thinks we went docilely along? That we didn't slip off to Crete and all the rest?"

"I saw the Kontos letter. It deals only with events up until we left Athens. Or were supposed to."

"But he knows we were down in the islands."

"All he saw on Santorini was a dragnet in operation. He knows we didn't leave on that flight, and we were on Santorini, but he doesn't know what we did after that."

"The artifact—he'll miss it."

"But he can't claim we took it. He hid it, remember. If it's not at the Museum in Athens, how is he going to account for our having it?" He eyed her. There was something here, something she hadn't mentioned. She was fidgeting.

"Eventually he'll find a way to nail us. So? You'll have the artifact to study for a while, tucked away at MIT."

She shook her head, gazing into the fire, distant and distracted. He watched the yellow light flicker across the planes of her face, never fully banishing the shadows from it.

"You don't understand this field. What I did, it—it was *crazy*. I stole a priceless artifact!"

"You were mighty provoked."

"That's no excuse! I simply got so—so wound up that I forgot entirely about my professional standards, about ethics, about respect for the *past*."

"What about respect for other people? Kontos wasn't showing a lot of that."

Her expression had been shifting, ranging between chagrin and agitated puzzlement at her own actions. Now it subsided into an abstracted sadness. She still stared into the popping fire, eyes a distant dusky blue. "No, I understand what you're saying—I *felt* those things, certainly. That's why I acted as I did. But now sanity has returned and I see no way out."

"Out of what?"

"Eventually facing the music."

"What'll happen?"

"I'll be finished in Grecian archeology. Probably in the whole field."

"No chance of tenure?"

"Of course not."

"You'll have other avenues."

"Today I'm a chicken. Tomorrow I'll be feathers."

"It doesn't have to be right away, does it?"

"Not necessarily. I do want to study the artifact some more, do some library work on it, try to find connections to other digs."

"Fine. We'll hang onto it. Unless Sprangle runs into Hampton and spills the story over a lunch or something, you'll be safe."

Her gaze slid away from him. "Well . . ."

"Come on." He leaned forward into the pressing glow of the fire, gesturing, trying to cheer her up. He liked her buoyancy and spark; it hurt him to see her down like this. "Sic transit gloria mundi-wise, you're not doing all that damn badly."

She smiled grimly. "Hampton's holding a review panel about this. He's raising the issue of my continuing on at BU as an assistant professor."

Deflated, he sat back. "Oh." So it was worse than he'd thought.

"And he wants to call you as a witness. He got your name from Kontos."

Silence for a moment, broken only by the snapping of the fire. John finished his drink and wished for more. "Well, I'll follow the story up to the Athens airport. Then I'll say we flew to Italy."

"Well . . ."

"Okay, look—it's not ethical to lie. But maybe we'll find a way to answer and still not give anything away."

"Ummm."

"What about George?"

"The pressure's on me, not him. Anyway, he's scooted for Columbia. He was supposed to go there for a year of detailed artifact work, starting January. When we got back, he saw this storm brewing and left early."

"Brave fellow."

"Look, it's not his fight. He wasn't responsible for the dig. I was."

He leaned toward her again, trying to lift her spirits. "With enough practice, what the hell—we can get around 'em."

Her mood did not change. "I wonder."

"Sure we can. We'll just have to think over our approach, is all."

"Think fast."

"What do you mean?"

"The review panel is tomorrow."

He sat back, puffing out his cheeks. "Oh."

CHAPTER
Two

When John came into Building 42 the next morning he found a team of technicians working around the artifact. Their leader was Abe Sprangle, a ruddy, balding man whom John knew fairly well from the metallurgy group. He had brought a dextrous expertise and good-natured executive skills to the department, when MIT recruited him from Denmark a decade earlier. Sprangle had already lifted the artifact onto a working pedestal. It could be rotated slowly, bringing to bear the snouts of several detectors arrayed around it.

John said, "Already started?"

Sprangle beamed happily. "I wanted to get some preliminary data. It's a very exciting object, do you think?"

"Sho' nuff." John could not resist occasionally throwing in a conspicuous Southernism. He vaguely sensed that this was a way of distancing himself from the pervasive, smug certainties of Northern culture, of which Boston still considered itself the apex. "I had one devil of a time with it. There's a good chance all my measurements were wrong—I'm no pro. So beware. That's an x-ray sampler, isn't it?" John pointed at a large set of portable cabinets linked together, all leading to a barrel projection.

"Yes, but there is something wrong with it. We have had it set up an hour now, to make x-ray fluorescence measurements. But there comes noise in the thing, some glitch."

"You're trying to get a reading from that little hole I bored? I thought it was too small."

"Not for really good equipment, I think. Mind, I'm just an interested amateur at archeology, but I do know my diagnostics. Couldn't prove it today, though. See that big reading Fred's getting there?"

He pointed at a needle which showed a steady x-ray count, occasionally jumping up or down a bit. A lanky technician looked up ruefully from a tangle of cables at the base of the device. "A glitch, fer sure," Fred declared.

John tried to look knowledgeable. He stooped to see where the barrel of the detector was pointing. The artifact was facing away from them, and the barrel focused on the rear of it, near the center. "What are you trying to find?" he asked.

"We discover what metals are in the rock. That boring you made, we can use that for depth studies."

"And this noise?"

"Just some electronics screwup. Fred'll find it."

Fred shook his head. "Nothing in the connections, anything like that." He sighed. "This was up and running fine before, when we first plugged it in. Maybe something in the power source . . ." He opened a cabinet and began studying its myriad connectors.

John said, "The idea is, you put the barrel right up against the rock and give it a burst of x-rays. Then you turn off the x-rays and look to see if the metal atoms in the rock emit radiation of their own—right?"

"Yes, yes," Sprangle muttered, distracted. "But we have not turned on the source yet. So there is no fluorescence to detect. Yet our meter, it hops around."

"Well, good luck." He wanted to get a better look at the front, but the apparatus left little room. He wormed in next to the artifact's pedestal, hemmed in by equipment, slightly uncomfortable in the presence of so much machinery whose function he did not understand.

It was all fairly straightforward stuff, he knew, easily understandable once someone carefully explained it. He did know a fair amount of physics, had minored in it at Rice. But to him physics at its best was an ideal world of clean solutions, strings of deduction, mathematical chains. Like most mathematicians he was a Platonist, a believer that the world was an imperfect expression of an underlying crystalline order, a mathematical plan—though if challenged, he would have automatically rejected any such label, knowing it was considered rather simplistic. His instincts, though, were another matter.

He bent and inspected the artifact. In the bright lighting its every detail seemed more significant, a swarm of clues. The spotlights in the tomb had cast shadows over one face while illuminating another, and now, seeing it fresh, the stark incongruity of the amber cone was more striking. He placed a hand on the rotating platform and pushed, meeting heavy resistance, turning the block slightly to have a better look.

"Hey? What'd you do?" Fred called out.

John heard Sprangle answer, "Nothing. I was checking calibrations—"

Fred said, "Well, somethin' cut the noise."

Sprangle said, "John, did you step on the cabling or something?"

He stood up. "No, I don't think—Wait a minute. I rotated the sample some."

"You did? Well, that should not matter. Fred, look at those AMP units."

"Okay. I think maybe—"

"Abe, Fred, watch the scope a minute," John said quickly. He gingerly pushed on the platform, bringing the cone revolving back to where it had been before.

Fred called, "The noise is back."

"John, what'd you do?"

"I rotated the artifact back the way it was before."

Sprangle came around to where John crouched. "See?" John nudged the pedestal a bit.

"Noise is droppin' off," Fred declared.

Sprangle muttered, "Getting a signal without...damn! The thing's radioactive."

"I never thought to check for that," John said.

"Well, certainly—who would? Fred, there is a hot spot on that back face. Those are real x-rays we're seeing, by God, from the sample itself."

They grouped around the barrel detector and swung the pedestal slowly back and forth. The inertia of the block required a steady, powerful push. John began to sweat. "There!" Fred called. "Maximum intensity."

"It points at that plug on the rear of the cube," Sprangle

said. "There must be some pitchblende in there."

John asked, "Pitch what?"

"A black, lustrous mineral, an oxide. Contains uranium or radium. A common natural x-ray emitter."

"There's some in that plug?"

"Probably. They might've used it as a coloring agent."

The two men stood up, Sprangle grunting, face flushed. John noticed the man's paunch, well concealed by a cardigan, had bulged more with even this minor exertion. The man wheezed, "I suppose Claire will find that fascinating, but it brings bad luck to us."

"Why?"

"We'll have to be sure that pitchblende doesn't foul up our measurements. It's putting out x-rays at a hundred, maybe a thousand counts per second more than our fluorescence will."

"Just revolve the pedestal. The block itself will shield your detector."

Sprangle brightened. "Of course. It's solid rock, there'll be plenty of shielding." He called to Fred, "Watch the noise while we spin it. Give me the integrated counts."

The two men rotated the block slowly while Fred called out numbers. The count rate dropped by over three hundred as they reached ninety degrees, which was the center of the adjacent face. It stayed low until the front face came into view. Then the rate began to climb as they pushed farther.

"Something wrong here," Sprangle said. "The counts, they should keep dropping off."

"Here, swing it back some," John said. "Careful, careful— there." The x-ray detector was peering straight along the front edge of the artifact, level with the center, so that it looked directly at the amber cone. "How's the count, Fred?"

"Not much."

"So?" Sprangle asked.

"There's no pitchblende in the amber, then. The barrel's pointing straight at it, and we don't get much. Let's swing around now and look directly down the axis of the cone."

They positioned the block. "Lotta counts," Fred called. "As high as from the other side."

"Then the source, it is inside the cube," Sprangle said, panting slightly. "We will have to analyze that. Very interesting. You know, Claire will be most surprised at this. Will she be in today?"

John smiled grimly. "She's preparing for an exam," he said.

The modest brick buildings of Boston University face Commonwealth Avenue, but the best offices are at the back, where the Charles River narrows into a slate-gray, unrippled avenue. On this cloudy winter day the untroubled waters looked to John very much like the asphalt-covered former cow paths Bostonians called streets, as he crossed over the Charles on the BU Bridge.

He found the seminar room at the end of a slick terrazzo corridor and knocked. A portly man opened it, smiled warmly, and said, "You must be Dr. Bishop. I'm Donald Hampton, we spoke on the phone. I was just making some remarks to the committee."

John went through ritual introductions while Hampton seated him at the end of a long table. There were two other archeologists, professors Aiken and McCauley, but Hampton seemed to dominate matters. Hampton explained that Claire had already left at their request; he preferred to get John's version of events before the committee, without her "possibly intimidating presence." John listened to Hampton review the history of Claire's site, both for the sake of the committee and for John, spending a lot of time on how the American School of Classical Studies had reached an agreement with the Greek authorities. Apparently the American School usually handled excavations under Greek direction, but the political situation in the last two years had forced any American expedition to accept a Greek co-director—Kontos. Hampton detailed his own attempts to smooth over this change by "going the extra mile with Dr. Kontos," which apparently meant socializing considerably, letting Kontos pick personnel, and bestowing the usual academic perks.

As Hampton shifted into the history of the main dig—unearthing the town, tracing the life patterns of the time, investigating the tomb—it became apparent that Claire had always rankled Kontos, though there was no documentation of this point. He was surprised to learn that the main thrust of the group was the town itself, and the tomb, once seen to be bare, had been delegated to Claire and George because it seemed less promising. Hampton said little of this directly, and John soon saw this was the style of the others as well: verbose, oblique, with much use of foreign terms thrown like pepper into a bland dish. He remembered Claire's telling him that archeologists were more like humanists than scientists—steeped in history, aware of literary and mythological clues. The field retained the old style of publishing always in one's native language, a habit the physical sciences had lost a century before. It meant an archeologist needed a command of French, English, German and one or two other regional languages such as Greek or Arabic merely to keep up.

The seminar room fitted, too. It had dark wooden floors and polished brass lamps. The chairs were comfortable and stuffed, with heavy wooden arms, a style he had seldom seen outside antique shops. Incongruously, against one wall stood the latest model projector, the glossy screen itself a broad square above the cabinet. He wondered why it was there.

"So you see, Dr. Bishop, we would like your view of the events leading up to your, er, dismissal from the site." Hampton smiled engagingly, pulled out a worn pipe and began stuffing it. He wore a tweed jacket with leather patches on the elbows, a vest and a conservative tie. The other two were similarly dressed, a fact which would have been unremarkable in Boston, except that John's experiences with scientists and mathematicians had led him to expect open collars and baggy sweaters. He coughed and began his story.

It was a fiction, of course, in the strictest sense. He and Claire had constructed it over a lengthy series of martinis. Still, his yarn contained no outright fabrication, only omissions and simplifications. He described performing composition tests on several types of artifact, which he had indeed done, without mentioning that the others were warmups, tests of the equipment, and the cube was his true interest. This intersected, he knew, with Claire's omission of the cube, meanwhile stressing the political differences, sexual harassment, and his fight with Kontos that last night.

Hampton said, "So you contend that when he—er—burst in on you, um, at the tomb site, you . . ."

"We were carrying out last-minute tests and doing some packing. We were sure he was going to throw us off the site the next morning and Claire—she's a stickler for getting things in order, you know—she wanted to be sure—"

"But surely you must have guessed that Dr. Kontos, in a state of agitation over the, er, insults you had—or he *thought* you had—hurled at his nation, his government, would react strongly to the slightest misstep on your part. Surely?"

"I don't think it made any difference," John said mildly. "I figure he was layin' for us."

"Seeking a pretext?" Dr. Aiken asked.

"Damn right. He wanted us out because we were Americans, not because Claire had obstructed the dig."

Two furrows creased Hampton's brow as he puffed meditatively on his pipe, filling the air with blue smoke. "Yet Claire *had* gone far afield—to you—for help, without using the *in situ* facilities available in Athens. That hardly seems, er, cooperative."

"She was back here anyway, reporting to you."

"Her trip was hardly necessary for merely that." He glanced at his watch.

"Well, she thought so. Kontos was comin' on to her, you know."

Hampton waved his pipe, as if to dispel this last comment. He had not reacted well to John's passing mention of Kontos's amorous advances, in their brief telephone conversation, and John guessed that he was trying to soft-pedal the subject. That implied that Claire had probably overplayed her hand earlier in the afternoon, when she appeared here. John was trying to decide whether to press the matter when a buzzer on the viewscreen cabinet rasped harshly in the silent room.

"Ah, that will be our other, er, witness."

Hampton rose and busied himself with the cabinet. He placed an omnidirectional microphone in the center of the desk and switched on lamps which illuminated the table. John noticed that a camera snout pointed at them from the cabinet. The buzzer rasped again before he could ask anything, and Hampton called out, "Can you hear me, Alexandros?"

The screen filled with a good quality view of Kontos, smiling. He was wearing civilian clothes and from the way his eyes tracked John could tell he was surveying their seminar room. Kontos replied, "Hello! I am delighted to see you again, Donald. And Dr. Aiken, Dr. McCauley." Nods of greeting. Then he saw John. "Aha. I hope, Dr. Bishop, you have been telling the truth."

John smiled coldly. "Of course. Not that it will do you much good."

Kontos chuckled. "I think you see, gentlemen, that this man, he is biased against me."

"Getting chopped in the face does that sometimes," John said mildly.

Kontos registered irritation. "I was provoked, as I told Donald," he said, gazing at the committee members.

Hampton raised a palm. "We really should avoid these needless clashes, gentlemen. They merely obfuscate the true issues. Let me pose questions to Dr. Kontos, questions designed to illuminate the *facts*"—he glared at John—"and avoid *ad hominem* arguments."

As Hampton took Kontos through obviously rehearsed testimony John's assurance evaporated. Bringing in Kontos on vision-phone had been unsettling, and now Hampton was undermining Claire's position with leading questions about how well the rest of the team liked her, her notorious impatience with those who disagreed with her, her fatigue at the end of a long, unusually hot summer—all designed to build a case for Kontos. This much he and Claire had expected. The tough areas lay ahead. When Kontos began talking about an "unauthorized excavation" he leaned forward intently.

"And without my knowledge, or of anyone at the site, she and George Schmitt *continued* at this, removing portions of the wall. They consulted with no one about the possible structural dangers."

John said, "You were gone nearly all the time. And when you were on site, you were fretting about your political rallies and palace coups."

Hampton snapped, "Please hold your comments!"

Kontos went on as if nothing had happened. "They found a few items, which I shall report to you later, Donald. Dr. Anderson attempted to conceal this by bringing Dr. Bishop. That much should be obvious to anyone."

John kept his face impassive, but he was worried. Kontos was taking a minimum-risk position, not playing up the artifact at all. Every step of Kontos's argument was either factual or probable. From a committee like this the outcome was certain. The question was, how far would he go?

"Luckily, I discovered this in time. I admit, there came the unfortunate incident with Dr. Bishop. I am a patriotic man, I do not take insults to my country. But that is beside the point. It does not prove that I persecuted Dr. Anderson in any way. All these are *excuses* brought up to hide the fact that she and Bishop *hid from me* a new find."

Here it comes, John thought.

But Kontos's severe expression relaxed. "For us this time, the luck was good. They did not destroy anything with their incompetence. The find is minor but interesting. A few pieces of simple jewelry, a bit of ivory." He shrugged.

John blinked. Why was he covering up?

Hampton nodded. "I am happy to hear that. Still, it does not mitigate the principle here in the slightest." Affirmative nods from the other two.

"The find came, I believe, from an observation you yourself made in August," Kontos went on, relaxed and chatty. "To me, to all the team, you spoke of the markings on the one block in the tomb wall. It was at evening meal, perhaps you remember?"

Hampton puffed on his pipe and seemed to nod.

"That was where the find occurred. They barely had uncovered what truly lies behind there, I tell you now. I myself went further."

Hampton interrupted, "I gather you found a very nice *objet d'art*?"

"Yes." A murmur of interest from the committee. John tried to figure out what path Kontos was following.

Hampton said warmly, "These proceedings aside, I would certainly like to discuss the discovery when your results are prepared. What is it?"

"A cube. Very odd, placed behind the wall. And strangely decorated." Kontos shaped a cone in the air with his hands. "I will provide photographs and notes soon."

John realized suddenly that Kontos had not been back to the site yet. He did not know the artifact was gone. And when he got a chance, he planned to "discover" it and bring it to Athens, along with Claire's photos and notes still in the crates.

Only it wasn't there, and neither were the notes. Kontos

must have some of them, but not enough. Claire had rescued the bulk of them.

"Fascinating." Hampton beamed at the camera. "Why was it hidden, do you suppose?"

"A death ornament, it is difficult to guess immediately. I know with your interests in the religious artifacts particularly, you will find much here, possible connections with your earlier work on the tombs. Maybe you come after Christmas? I can show you."

"Thank you, Alexandros, I would very much like that."

"Perhaps we can join together in the movement to return the rest of the Elgin marbles? I am introducing a new resolution this next spring. With US backing—"

"I certainly understand," Hampton said, "but we should conclude this business."

"Wait a minute," John said, "I wanted to ask him—who gets credit for the discovery of the cube?"

Hampton said, "Why Alexandros. You heard him state clearly that he opened the tomb wall and found it."

"I think Claire should share it."

Kontos said evenly, "You are an amateur in these matters. Your opinion is worth nothing."

"Well, I know how you bullied everyone at the site—"

Hampton said, "Come now!"

"—And I'm damn well going to tell it to anyone who'll listen."

Kontos's jaw muscles clenched. "You would be wise to shut up. Or I will deal with you. Personally."

"Dr. Bishop!" Hampton cried. "No more of this."

"Any time, Kontos."

"Stop! Say no more." Hampton held up a hand to John, waving ineffectually. He turned to professors Aiken and McCauley. "Do you have any further questions?"

They didn't. Kontos signed off and the room seemed suddenly tiny, no longer linked with the other side of the planet.

John said, "I hope you realize Claire had to fight that man every inch for the results she got."

Hampton's smile had little of its previous warmth. The man was an accomplished actor, John realized. No doubt he also thought he was acting from the highest moral principles.

"Thank you, Dr. Bishop, for your time."

As he walked home down Commonwealth it started to snow.

CHAPTER
Three

Claire came into the bay with an air John had noticed before. It was as if she owned the place and was strolling through, seeing what the tenants were up to. It was amusing and eye-catching as she approached, wearing a neatly tailored cinnamon jump suit beneath a black coat, with gray gloves and black boots, twirling a collapsed blue umbrella with a jaunty swing. The rain of last night had turned to half-hearted snow and she was prepared.

She brightened when she spied him among the equipment. He saw she was carefully made up: eye shadow and liner, color in the cheeks, lipstick of a rakish near-purple. Her hair was pinned back in a towering, elaborate manner. Celebratory? He called, "Is champagne in order?"

"Maybe with lunch. I've been in the lions' den and am here to tell the tale."

"This morning? They move fast."

"They pontificated and fretted and stroked their beards and decided to put a letter in my file describing their 'dissatisfaction with my handling of the situation,' was the way they put it." Her smile had something in it, halfway between mischief and outright larceny, that matched the dancing excitement in her eyes. She was light years away from the woman at the Ritz.

"Not bad."

"I was afraid of a lot worse," she said seriously.

"That letter, it'll hurt your tenure?"

"I suppose so. Not nearly so much as when they find out what really went on."

He said as mildly as possible, "You could've come out with it."

"And lose the piece immediately? No thanks," she said fervently.

"So what've you gained?"

"Time."

He gestured at the artifact. "Time to work on this."

"Yes, and to think. How's it going? That x-ray stuff you described on the phone last night—"

"Out of date. Abe's found something more. He was just telling me."

At mention of his name Abe Sprangle stopped fooling with his electronics and came over with an anticipatory grin. Claire gave him a warm, professional greeting, and listened while he summarized his thinking on the problem. "A reasonable deduction, I believe, that pitchblende was the source of the x-rays. Archeologically probable, I mean. Do you agree?" When Claire nodded he went on. "But pitchblende it cannot be. I measured the x-ray spectrum. Pitchblende does not fit. So Fred and I, we dragged out the gamma-ray detectors."

Claire said disbelievingly, "*Gammas*?"

"Indeed. And they are increasing."

John said, "Nothing, *no* isotope gives off a lot of high energy radiation. You must have a wrong calibration."

Abe grinned again, enjoying his story. "So I thought, too. But the x-ray spectrum was suspicious. It was not lines, like uranium or radium. I get *all* energies out—soft x-rays up to hard ones, smooth all the way. There is not the remotest possibility that pitchblende could yield such emission."

"That's no single isotope, then," John put in. "There must be a mixture of different radioactive minerals in there."

Claire shook her head. "Unlikely. Somebody *made* this thing, remember? How would they select radioactive ores when they didn't know such things even existed?"

Abe played his hole card. "You can stop worrying about might have beens. Because I measured the gamma-ray spectrum. It's smooth, too. There are no lines."

Nobody said anything. Claire shook her head again, this time so vigorously that her carefully pinned-back hair shook loose a few strands at the neck. "As much respect as I have for your expertise, Abe, I can't believe that."

"We check it, certainly. Fred is setting up a whole different set of detectors, ones I borrowed from Kemberson's group."

John said, "Suppose the measurement holds up. What's it mean?"

Abe's elation wore off a little. "That is the problem. I know nothing that yields such a high energy spectrum."

Claire said, "It's *got* to be wrong."

But it wasn't.

The second, carefully calibrated measurement gave identical results. The flux of radiation from the cube was still not dangerous, but it had none of the spectral lines that would distinguish natural emission from atoms. Checking and calibrating took two days of tedious care.

Abe said judiciously, "Look how relatively smooth this spectrum is. Perhaps a lot of lines, overlapping each other?"

John said, "This means there are either a lot of radioactive isotopes inside, or . . ." He paused awkwardly.

Abe grinned. "Or else we make some stupid mistake."

"And the radiation," Claire asked earnestly, "it only comes out through the two locations—the cone and the hole on the opposite side?"

"Absolutely. The source, it lies deep in the rock itself." Abe meditated on this fact. "My guess is, they buried something in the middle of the cube."

John nodded. "Buried *what*?"

"Wait," Claire said decisively. "I know we're all curious, but we've got to proceed step by step. We have to have chemical analysis of the rock, of the amber in that cone, of whatever's plugging that hole in the back."

Abe said mildly, "Dunnsen in Chemistry, I have already arranged with him to do some analysis. He's had experience, you know, did the work with Watkins and Hampton on that zinc and tin from Italy."

Claire stiffened. "We have to be sure there's minimum damage to the artifact."

Abe nodded emphatically. "We can do all, all with passive means. No damage."

Claire said earnestly, "Only when we have those results will we be able to say something intelligent."

Intelligence is relative. It has biases and blind spots. John had never entertained the notion that two citadels of intelligence he knew well—Rice University, where he had labored long hours, and MIT, which he hoped to make a major professional stepping stone—might be seen most importantly by society as mills grinding out a special breed of intelligent trolls able to wire the machines, titrate the solutions, program the chips, and speed the wheels of industry.

Similarly, Claire had never encountered a situation where a careful series of intelligent tests did not narrow down possibilities until only one remained, and the mysterious substance plucked from an ancient site was revealed as an odd sort of alloy, a trace of decayed matter, or an unusually shaped amalgam of several substances. Abe was similarly biased. He had never been in a situation where the active, emitting substance was unreachable, so that he could not even get a good look at it.

"This composition analysis doesn't make sense," Abe said, frustrated. Dunnsen had brought his expertise to bear and rendered up a detailed list of what the cone contained. This chemist's-eye view was painted in a graphic display of compounds and elements, all found by various diagnostics which tested the sample's ability to re-emit or absorb light of a definite frequency. "That stuff's damned funny."

"Let me see." Claire studied the sheets, which were covered with curves in scarlet, blue and yellow. The peaks and valleys representing differing amounts of each element resembled jagged, multicolored teeth. "Actinium, boron, calcium— good grief, this is nothing like amber."

John said quietly, "What is amber, actually?"

"Tree sap, fossilized tree sap," Claire replied abstractedly. "The resins from trees accumulate in the soil and gradually the volatile elements leak out. That leaves a solid."

"Amber is mostly hydrogen and carbon, then?" John asked. He had always found chemistry boring and impossible to remember. It all seemed so messy and detailed. He remembered declaring as an undergraduate that the subject was trivial, representing merely the tedious working-out of quantum mechanics—an already understood discipline, elaborately mathematical—in complicated, uninteresting cases. The fact that these cases were of immense practical use could not change the matter to his youthful eyes; the subject was simply a form of smelly engineering.

"Mostly, yes," Abe answered. "You can identify it by the nodules in it, and that cone"—he crouched and peered at the artifact—"sure as hell glistens, like it's got inclusions and irregularities."

Claire smacked the pages with the back of her palm. "But *this* says there are a lot of metals in it."

"Cannot be amber, then," Abe declared.

"Why not?" John asked. "Amber with a lot of impurities."

Abe's brow furrowed as he studied the sheets. "Is that possible?"

Claire put in, "Actually, I studied this once in Turkey. The tree sap would have to mix with a lot of odd minerals.. . .I suppose it could happen." She smoothed her olive skirt with spread palms and sat back in her chair. They had commandeered a small office just off the bay, where they could tap into the campus computer with a portable console. The desk was littered with printouts, coffee cups, lab records and books on mineralogy. The inevitable vacuum pump chugged in the distance. "Everything I know about mineral deposition says don't bet on it, though. Inclusion of something like iron, all right. Sometimes that happens and it changes the color. This material in the cone looks like the usual yellow amber, with nuances of orange and red. Iron, perhaps. But a whole *range* of elements?"

John said slowly, "Maybe we're looking at it the wrong way. I mean, trying to find a way amber could get all this variety of stuff inside it."

"They had to get thoroughly mixed in," Abe pointed out.

"Sure. But the cone has been sitting near that radiation source for thirty-five centuries."

Silence while the words sank in. Then Claire said doubtfully, "The x-rays?"

"No, only the gammas could do that," John declared. "Those could cause transmutation."

Abe smiled deprecatingly. "Now that would require an *im-*

mense radiation flux in the gammas. Far more than is coming out of there now."

John replied, "Whatever's in there, it *had* to have some effect on the cone."

Abe shook his head. "I could calculate it for you, but I can tell right off there won't be enough to break up a lot of iron into calcium and oxygen and so on."

John shrugged. "Just an idea." But the set of his jaw remained. "Still, have you got any better one?"

Abe sighed. "Not right away. Here, I'll do that calculation." He turned to the computer keyboard and started work.

Claire was still gazing at the sheets. "We've been worrying about the cone, but look at this—the analysis for the plug in the back."

The spikes of blue and crimson were difficult to read. John asked, "So? Those peaks don't look like the cone's."

"I'd say it's much closer to ordinary rock. Silicates, with some heavier stuff."

"The same sort of composition as the rest of the cube—the limestone?"

"No. Close, though."

"Maybe they plugged the backside with ordinary rock. Why not?—nobody's going to see it."

Claire smiled. "Who ever saw the front?"

"True enough, we don't know. But if they *did* use ordinary rock, and it spent the last few thousand years sitting next to a radiation source, what would it look like?"

"Well, there are some peaks here...." She grimaced. "Perhaps a few impurities from bombardment by the source inside. But look, the limestone isn't all shot through with these heavier elements. I tested the rock myself. Why is the limestone so ordinary, then?"

John spread his hands, as though his explanation was most natural, inevitable. "It's too thick. Only along the axis, at the cone and the plug, do we get to see through a thin layer at whatever's inside."

Claire shook her head, exasperated. "Look, this is an *artifact*. Remember? It must come out of a culture we already know, which had methods we have studied in detail, with a history we can fit into mythology, records—all *sorts* of ways of checking and cross-checking. This thing has to have some continuity with what we've learned about the Mycenaeans. It can't just be a—a rogue object, with no connections to anything else."

"Unless, of course, we just don't see the connections yet."

Claire said darkly, "This is so—so *complicated*. I. . .don't like it. I wonder if it could be a hoax?"

John was startled. "What? How could it?"

"If, say, Kontos planted that there, knowing we would. . . no, that's crazy."

"Yes," John said judicially, "it is." He studied her frowning, introspective face for a long moment. She was obviously troubled with the cross-currents of loyalties, torn between the code of honesty that science demands and the impulse that had led her into this situation. Now the artifact itself was proving to be a puzzle, the ramifications of it impossible to see clearly.

Abe slapped the desk beside the computer keyboard and announced, "There! The present gamma-ray flux could not possibly cause that much transmutation."

They pondered this for a moment. "Well," John drawled thoughtfully, "the source is probably decaying, right? How much more powerful would it have to have been 3500 years ago?"

Abe punched some commands into the program. The MIT computing system was algebraic-interactive now, which meant it could take a simple question, translate it into an equation, and solve that equation for a given range of possibilities. The answer came back only seconds after Abe finished typing. "That source would have to have been about three *million* times more active. How could a source of various isotopes do that?" Abe turned and grinned, enjoying the riddle.

"A pretty tall order, huh?" John admitted ruefully.

Claire said mildly, "Yes. But does anyone have another idea?"

They looked at each other pensively.

The telephone rang.

Claire picked it up. "What? Oh, ah—all right, I'll hold."

She gave John a frown. "I left this number with the archeology department, but I didn't think—" She broke off and listened. Then nodded, said, "Yes," and hung up.

She looked bleakly at the two men. "It was Hampton's secretary. He wants to see me right away. She said he had just finished a call from Kontos."

CHAPTER
Four

Professor Hampton was barricaded behind a formidable oak desk, which in turn matched the heavy bookshelves behind him. Against the long runs of journals and carefully arranged volumes his tweed suit and silk finish, wide red tie made a colorful contrast. Tucked in among the bookshelves, as if to pointedly show that this office's inhabitant was *au courant*, was one of the new 3D paintings which managed to look simultaneously like a vase of electrically colorful spring flowers, and also resemble a particularly nasty aftermath of an explosion in a glass factory.

After Claire was seated Hampton paused for effect, steepling his fingers and gazing through them with rapt concentration, as if the solution to a vexing problem lay there. Claire wondered if this was a method to insure that she would begin the conversation first. There were so many little games of this kind she was never sure what was casual and what had calculation behind it. She resolved to force him to begin, and unconsciously gripped the padded arms of her chair. After a full minute, just as the lengthening silence had started wearing away her determination, he sighed and spoke.

"I had, less than an hour ago, a profoundly disturbing call from Alexandros. He was most agitated."

"Yes?" Bright, expectant, innocently interested.

"He has lost the large artifact."

Her stomach tightened. "Lost?" she prompted.

"Evidently he was studying it at the site, fearing that transport might damage some of the, er, delicate ornamentation. Apparently it is quite a beautiful piece." Hampton said this slowly, sadly, with a hint of reluctance.

"There was, of course, a guard at the site. Yet when Alexandros returned from his duties in Athens, the piece was gone."

"Thieves?"

"The door was still locked."

"It must be the guard, then."

"Alexandros is of course having the fellow, er, questioned."

"Amazing, how these people think they can sell such an artifact on the black market. They should know any reputable buyer would realize what had happened."

Distracted, Hampton said, "Yes, yes, 'tis ever thus, eh? They never realize." He steepled his fingers again and turned meditatively toward the pale light of the window, through which she could see rowing crews earnestly laboring up the gray Charles beneath facetious, cottonball clouds. "Tsk, tsk."

"A terrible thing," she said, to be saying something.

"Indeed. Alexandros said little of the attempt to recover. I am sure a man with his resources in the police and, er, military will have few problems with that. He did, however, ask about your notes."

"Many of them are in the crates he *seized* and took to Athens," she said sharply.

"Ah. Yes, he said there were some....But the bulk, they—er—seem to be in your possession."

"They are *my* notes. George and I discovered the piece, after all."

"You know that discovery, as a concept, does not apply to cooperative digs," he chided, gazing solemnly at her over his fingers, which he had begun to press together rhythmically.

"Kontos deserves no cooperation. He was going to steal credit from the whole group."

"I assure you, that would not have occurred. The *raison d'être* of our expedition was strengthening Greek-American relations. Alexandros has just as much at stake—"

"He'll take what we offer, sure. Then he'll claim this artifact as his own."

"I have prepared my draft of our report, and when your own results are included it will be a solid piece of work. This object, fascinating as it may be, is not so important. It is the slow piling up of detail, as you well know, which makes our profession a reliable—"

"Doesn't that judgment depend on what the object turns out to be?"

Hampton, his set speech interrupted, seemed flustered. "Well—er—of course. I do not think we will have to reevaluate the entire *logos* of our interpretation, however, simply because of one artifact. It could easily be an anomaly, something brought from Crete or another area."

"All the same, I—"

"Claire, you must turn over your notes on this object to Alexandros," Hampton said forcefully, as if he had abruptly decided to shift tactics. The thoughtful, distant professor was gone. He leaned across his desk. "Now."

"I won't. They're not his."

"He will recover the object, and then write that portion of our paper. He will need your information."

"That's what he called for, wasn't it?"

"Not solely, no. But I assured him of our complete cooperation."

"My answer is still no."

Hampton seemed taken aback. "You cannot refuse."

"Oh yes I can."

"This is contrary to everything we agreed upon when we undertook a joint expedition."

"I need my own notes."

"I doubt that, I doubt that sincerely. You are merely obstructing Alexandros's work. I must ask you again—"

"No."

"You are endangering your entire professional position here, Claire. If you—"

She stood up. "Professional? Ha! My father used to say, you have to be able to tell a tracheotomist from a cutthroat. Well, *I* can."

She swung her umbrella in a wide arc, barely missing a stack of books on the big oak desk, and stamped out, her boots rapping angrily on the creaking wooden floor.

*   *   *

She held up quite well until she reached her apartment. Then she began to get the shakes, a mixture of anger and frustration and I-should've-saids. She had poured herself a sherry, and then another.

Hampton was so mired in academic politics that it never occurred to him that she could have done anything so extravagant, so flamingly irrational as to steal an artifact. That was the only factor delaying the moment of retribution.

Maybe Kontos actually believed the guard had made off with the cube. If so, then clearly Kontos wanted her notes so he could fake his way through a preliminary report, establishing priority, buying time until he could trace the artifact.

There was no way this fiction could hold together for long. She lit a cigarette and thumbed on the radio. A nasal voice whined that her honey baby had gone away, she didn't know what to say, she could only sit down and cry, maybe now she'd have to die die die. Claire grimaced and reflected that Cole Porter was not only dead, he was forgotten.

Her sherry glass was empty, so she refilled it. On the way back from the liquor cabinet she saw she was nearly finished with her cigarette and stubbed it out. As she reached for another she caught herself, recognizing the pattern. Alone, fretting, reviewing the day, getting into an addictive cycle. She did not want to face an evening of neurotic jitters. She reached for the telephone.

"Do you know where Locke Ober's is?" she asked when John answered the third ring at the laboratory. She had known he would be there, though it was after six o'clock.

"Uh, I think so."

"Meet me there at seven. I have to repair myself."

An hour later they sat at a small round table on the first floor, drinking whisky and bitters with a twist. The maitre d' had been persuaded to seat them without reservations, not by John's steady insistence, but rather—to her surprise—by recognizing Claire herself. "Just goes to show that having ancestors who came here steadily for a century or two does have some compensations," she observed.

"Um. Nice place," John admitted.

"I love the creamed spinach here." She glanced around at the room, which was rapidly filling. "Tourists and *untermenschen* are seated upstairs, which is a bit more modern.

They didn't let women in at all until the seventies, I believe. The waiters are courtly, though usually also deaf."

As if on cue, a feeble man shuffled over and took their dinner order. Claire ran a fond eye down the script of the menu. "Lobsters off the Portland boat, that's how I remember it here with my grandfather."

"An old salt?"

"No, a banker. Now he and my grandmother are the oldest couple in Vermont; there was a newspaper article about them last year. My grandfather told the reporter his favorite joke, which is, 'Why do people keep buying shampoo when they can have real poo?' He's become a professional character."

"I've heard worse jokes."

They ordered seafood and a California wine Claire had never heard of. She said, "I love it here, it's so, well, reassuring. The heavy draperies, even the slightly musty smell. My family comes here when everyone's in town. They're all so old, I swear they remember it when hansom cabs brought you to the door."

"Thus, archeology?"

"What? Oh, I see. Preoccupation with the past?" She stared moodily into the candle flame. "Perhaps so . . ."

"Now that we're settled in, tell me the bad news."

She did, concluding, "So Kontos has discovered that it's missing, but he's not sure how it was done."

John said speculatively, "Or by whom. But he's suspicious of li'l ol' us."

"That's the way I read it, too."

"What can he do? Until, of course, Hampton finds out that we have it."

"I thought we'd have more time than this."

"I didn't," he said flatly. "Kontos doesn't hesitate."

"Then we've got to push ahead."

"Abe is working hard, and I'm putting in all my time over there. Not that I'm much use. I'm basically a go-fer."

"Even though I'm on a semester sabbatical, I've got obligations at BU. I stupidly agreed to be a women's advisor even though I'm on leave."

"What kind of advice?"

"Academic, personal, whatever. It's fairly discouraging. Reminds me of another of my grandfather's jokes. What do you call a student advisor at a women's college?"

He shrugged. She said sardonically, "An obstetrician. There's more truth to it than I'd ever have admitted. A lot of them are orbiting around those issues."

"What do you tell them?"

"To be captains of their own fates."

"Profound. Who's going to be the crew?"

She smiled despite herself. "Okay, wrong metaphor. Anyway, I've got that advising to do, and it gets in the way of my archeology. I've got to write my part of our paper. Hampton's been sending me notes about it for a week."

"The artifact's part of that paper, right?" He broke open a short loaf of French bread, which steamed in the air, and began munching thoughtfully.

"No, I'm leaving it out. I mean, what can I say without giving away too much?"

"If you ignore it, you'll alert Hampton to something fishy."

"I will?"

"I think so. He's shrewd, beneath that Ivy League pomposity."

"I can never see how to play these things."

"I think Hampton is suspicious already."

"Can he do something dreadful? Can he accuse me of a crime, have me arrested?" The wine had arrived without her noticing; she drank half her glass.

"For what?"

"Taking a national treasure out of Greece."

"The Greeks have to run you down for that. And they're busy with other things."

"What do you mean?"

"Look at the *Globe* this morning. Greece broke off diplomatic relations with Turkey."

"Oh no. Turkey outnumbers them so much—that's stupid!"

He nodded. "Very. But it also means Kontos can throw a fit back there, chew the rug, anything—it won't matter. His government has bigger fish to fry."

"If Kontos asks the authorities here, they could *arrest* me, couldn't they?"

"Now, there won't be any such ruckus," he said softly,

reaching across to take her hand. She discovered that she had, without noticing it, torn her bread into fragments beside her plate. The sudden rush of blood to her face was even more unsettling.

"I. . .you're sure?"

"Yes."

"I. . .we're both liable in this. If Kontos. . .it. . .doesn't bother you?"

He shrugged elaborately. "Naw."

"Mr. Macho."

"Damn right." He grinned.

She noticed his folded hands, and remembered how they had rested on a tablecloth in Nauplia—broad fingers, pronounced knuckles, thick nails with a smooth glaze to them. Sturdy hands that reminded her of working men's, but with few calluses. Hands that moved casually, calmly to pick up a wine glass, or more bread—no fidgeting, no tremor of inner conflict. In the watery glow of the candlelight they seemed large, moving with natural purpose like independent creatures.

She realized she had been staring at his hands. She felt a warmth spreading through her, and thought it came from the wine and her relaxation after the day. The murmur of arriving parties, the ringing as some of the heavy silver pieces came into play for dining, the clink of dishes served—she let the timeless luxury seep into her. She excused herself before the main course and went to the ladies'. Returning, John's eyes followed the sway of her hips, and she saw that he could tell that beneath the clinging blue fabric she wore a garter belt and hose. Men always thought them erotic, she remembered, far better than utilitarian panty hose. From his expression she knew that he regarded her wearing them as a provocation. She felt an automatic stern tightness come into her own face and something made her banish it, letting a half smile cant the corners of her mouth instead. Her choice of old-fashioned style in hosiery had far more to do with a tendency to yeast infections, but let him think what he liked.

They strolled up Winter Place, down Tremont and eventually to the narrow walk along the Charles. A large-breasted girl jogged past them, wearing a T-shirt with HANDS OFF printed across it. Ordinarily Claire would have curled a lip at such display, but tonight she suppressed a chuckle. Brandy warmed her against the chill wind scooting fitfully off the river and she took John's arm without thinking.

"You're so much surer about this whole thing than I am," she said softly.

"No use fretting."

"But why are you sticking with it? You'd never been very interested in archeology before, you told me that at the beginning."

He arched his eyebrows, peering into the distant dancing lights of MIT. "I got interested. But. . .actually, it was you."

"Really? Me?" She was surprised at the eager lilt in her voice. For an instant she reprimanded herself for such obvious coquetry. But then she mentally shrugged, remembering that she was risking far more with this whole artifact business; surely she could afford a certain impish gamble here. She thought of his hands, now hovering at his sides as he turned. She breathed out a pearly cloud and it was as though something was bursting buoyantly free, something she had until now quite effectively blocked.

He was a looming bulk against the city lights, seeming larger than she remembered. "You're hypnotic, ma'am."

"So I made archeology come alive for you?" she mocked. "Stimulated your frontal lobes?"

"More like a li'l further down."

Without her noticing it, he had taken her in his arms. Something instinctive in her started to pull away, but his hands were firm on her arms, the calm, ample hands, and she peered up at him, trying to read his expression in the fitful dark.

"You're not totally cerebral, then." She kept her voice light. Passing headlights on Storrow Drive threw ivory light across his face and she saw that his mouth held an amused smile, almost sardonic, but his eyes were serious, darkly glittering.

"No. But I know how to fish."

"Fish?"

"Mostly it's just waiting."

"Until you get a nibble?"

"No. Wait for the strong bite."

"And now you're reeling me in?"

He only smiled.

"You arrogant so-and-so!"

"Your words, ma'am."

He kissed her slowly, so that she had plenty of time to think, to accept it, to know what it meant. It lasted a long time and when it was over she felt his hands on her arms, through her coat, though he was not pressing, in fact was scarcely touching her. Looking at his face, she felt that the hands fit him, were an essential part of what he was.

She was afraid to say anything, and wished the moment would last. The wind bit into her with a cold flurry, tossing her carefully prepared hair, and abruptly her teeth chattered.

"We'll have to get you inside."

"I. . .yes."

"Where do you live?"

"I thought you'd never ask."

CHAPTER
Five

Abe Sprangle said defiantly, "It's damn well *right*, I tell you."

John shook his head. "I'm not saying you're making a mistake, understand. But that picture just doesn't make *sense*." He poked a finger at the x-ray image, printed out in hard copy. Abe had hit upon another way to diagnose the cube. He treated the emitted x-rays as if they were ordinary light, and exposed an array of sensors. A few hours' exposure gave a ghostly image, formed from a sprinkling of dots.

"These make a square, see?" Abe traced the diffuse outline.

"You're *sure* you aren't getting these from another source? I mean, a square arrangement of radioactive elements . . ." His voice trailed off doubtfully.

"Not just a square. See how there are dots shading in the inside of the square? None outside it at all."

John nodded. "So it's. . .what?"

"A hollow cube, I'd say. The sides have radioactives in them. We're looking right along the axis of the hollow cube, so we see all the radioactivity from the sides."

"Except. . .what's this?"

Abe frowned. "That, I do not know." There was a dark spot at the exact center of the square, far more intense than the fog of points around it.

"Something at the center of your hollow cube?"

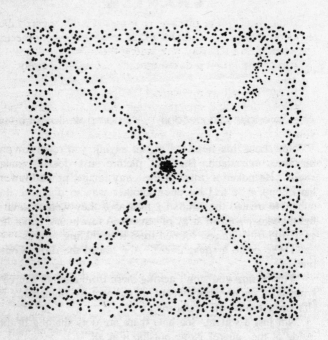

"I suppose so. The image, it washes out from over-exposure."

"A hollow cube *inside* this rock cube?" John's voice carried disbelief.

"That's what the x-rays *say*."

"And the size of this, uh, cube?"

"About two centimeters on a side."

"What? that's—"

"I know, very small. But that is—"

"What the x-rays say, I know."

"There are explanations," Abe said defensively. "Don't

you think? A piece of jewelry buried inside? A handicraft?"

"Well . . ." John stroked his chin.

"We can ask Claire."

"I know what she'll say."

"What?"

"Ridiculous! There must be an error." Claire fingered the photocopy. "The Mycenaeans never made any such objects. The cubic form was very rare among them."

"I have checked it a dozen times," Abe said precisely.

"This can't *be*."

"If you imply that my work—"

"Look," John said smoothly, stepping between them, "nobody's implyin' anything. Still, we've got to understand this thing without going right in, tearing it apart. Correct?"

Claire said impatiently, "Of course. I'm simply saying there must be a systematic error which gives us, well, wrong results. . .somehow." She finished lamely, biting her lower lip.

John saw that she was at the edge of her competence, unable to suggest where Abe had gone wrong but unwilling to accept his findings. Archeologists treated physical diagnostics as newfangled, perhaps deceptive additions to their science. Their instinct was to integrate a newly exposed artifact with the general picture of a society. A single object was often unrepresentative; centuries of owners could have used it strangely, deliberately damaged it, or carried it hundreds of miles from its source. But some facets of it surely had to mesh with the overall pattern of its society; a simple sharpener looked different if it came from a culture of hunter-gatherers, maize agriculturists, or a proto-urban. Such was the faith.

"That dot at the center," John said to deflect attention. "Your first image was washed out, you said."

"Yes, and so I took a shorter exposure. Here."

There was one point at the center of the sheet.

"That's it?"

"Yes. I still have not resolved the central source."

Claire frowned. "What does this correspond to, in size?"

"A third of a millimeter, I estimate," Abe said stiffly, as if bracing for her skepticism.

This time she simply shook her head. Abe said, "In imaging jargon, we are down to one pixel. We cannot see better. I cannot guarantee that the actual source is not still smaller than this. I simply cannot resolve it."

"Impossible," Claire said.

"But true," Abe countered.

The matter rested there for the better part of a week. Abe continued measurements, carefully taking further x-ray images, trying different techniques of isotope analysis, calling in associates from Harvard and Cornell and Brown to puzzle over the findings. The results did not change. Under the steady pressure of confirming data, Claire stopped wrinkling her brow in disbelief at each new finding.

Abe proposed taking a deeper boring of the stone. Claire disliked the idea, but was becoming uneasy at the tenor of the other results. She agreed to a three centimeter boring near the edge of a side face. Abe called in a specialist in the technique from Brown named LeBailly. There was risk in every new person who saw the artifact, for inevitably they would talk. But Claire had invented a plausible story to gain secrecy from these new investigators. It was an artful retelling of what had actually happened, with heavy emphasis on Kontos's mixing of personal, political and scientific motives. The story implied without expressly saying that they had gotten the artifact out of Greece by "pulling strings," and that to not embarrass the principals involved, everyone was keeping quiet, in view of the steadily worsening political situation in Greece. This fable kept silence for the short term, but both John and Claire knew it was bound to bring trouble later, when the guest investigators heard nothing more and began to ask questions.

All this occurred against a backdrop of other ongoing research interests. Claire had her report to finish and a myriad of the minor chores which fall steadily upon faculty. John was meshed in a long program of calculations, many of them occasionally tricky but mostly straightforward, requiring only time and patience and a certain dogged resistance to boredom. Abe, with the greater freedom of movement accorded a full professor, could occupy himself several hours a day with sharpening the diagnostics. Details of troubleshooting the electronics and processing the data he relegated to technicians, moonlighting their time from grants devoted to more sober, practical pursuits.

Not that it was all work. John squired Claire several evenings to top restaurants, demonstrating an ability to pay wildly unreasonable bills without visible effect. This was not easy. His salary was not large and he still lusted to replace his car, now a fondly remembered luxury. Jetting through Boston in Claire's Alfa Romeo only rubbed in the loss. He did not mind her driving for ego reasons, but her unconscious recklessness was unsettling in a city of downright claustrophobic streets.

Then, by unspoken agreement, they progressed to simpler, cheaper amusements—seafood restaurants of Spartan, steamy atmosphere and abrupt waiters; the symphony; walks along the brick sidewalks near Garden and Brattle streets in Cambridge, where gray eighteenth-century Gothic houses brooded like chaperones. He discovered that he disliked the opera. She showed a parallel distaste for country and western music, at least when heard in the single club devoted to it in the greater Boston area; in defense, he maintained that this watered-down version was not at all like the mellow, authentic sounds heard in Houston. But wherever they went, the discussion turned to the cube sitting in the bay of Building 42.

"I don't believe Abe's element abundance measurements," Claire said one evening as they finished coffee in a Hungarian restaurant, the Cafe Budapest. Claire had offered to take him at her expense to the ornate, somewhat stuffy basement spots on Copley Square, arguing that he needed to broaden his gastronomic education. He had murmured not a single objection to her paying. To do so would have invited a lecture on how she made more than he did; BU assistant profs earned marginally better than MIT postdocs. And aside from that, he had never felt that a man had to carry all the social load. He was a man fitted for the new century.

They had both been in the bay when Abe finished a full week of labor on the deep boring. The Brown specialist, LeBailly, had been inordinately interested in the cube. He had reluctantly and somewhat prissily packed away his tools, which looked to John like a jeweler's, plainly wishing he could do more.

Abe had made separate chemical and physical analyses of the elements present in the rock, using samples from the full three centimeter depth, to avoid surface contaminants. The inner sample showed a hundred times the heavy element abundance than the surface rock had.

"That's *highly* unlikely," Claire concluded forcefully.

"Abe had two specialists check him," John said.

"But how could it be? This is *limestone*, laid down in an ocean long ago. How can there be that much difference in the composition of the heavy elements in just three centimeters? That's hardly more than an inch!"

"An unusual specimen."

"I talked to geologists at BU. They've never heard of anything remotely like it."

John swirled his coffee, watching it rotate like a black coin in his cup. He said tentatively, "There's one way you could explain it. . . ."

"How? The cube is intact rock, we know that. No one of that era could have hollowed it out entirely and inserted other rock inside."

"Suppose the heavy elements come from bombardment by the central source?"

Her eyes widened satisfyingly. John sat back and watched; he enjoyed upsetting that Bostonian reserve. He had never seen any good reason to give up his suggestion of weeks before, that the central source of gamma and x-rays might have been ferociously stronger only a few thousand years ago. Certainly the idea was unlikely, on the face of it—but then, everything else about the artifact was unlikely, too. And it did explain why the amber cone had such an anomalous abundance of elements. At one time in the distant past a great deal of radiation had poured out of the center, irradiating the cone, the plug at the back, and all the rock.

"I. . .I'll admit it would explain the analysis of the samples from the boring. . . ." She concentrated prettily, unconsciously, and he admired the play of emotions across her face. A lip turned down in dismay and disbelief. A nostril flared. An eyebrow arched with a partial, provisional acceptance. "And the cone abundances, too." She had seen the connection quickly. "But it would mean such a *burst* of radiation."

"That it would."

She sipped her coffee with a lopsided grin. "This is beginning to sound like that Shroud of Turin business."

To his puzzled look she responded, "A piece of cloth that was supposed to have the image of Christ seared into it somehow. It was a big issue, back in the eighties. The religious types believed it provided substantial evidence for the miracle of Christ's rising. The problem was, to explain how the image got into the cloth, you needed another miracle."

"Occam's Razor wins again."

"Yes. Much better to look for a less complicated explanation. But in our case, what other explanation is there?"

"Archeology seems like a detective story with only physical evidence, and not even a clear idea of what the crime was."

She nodded pensively. "You know what Abe wants, don't you?"

"I can guess."

"But to bore through that plug in the back...that's destroying potentially vital material."

"That stuff is just rock. You saw the analysis."

"I still don't like it. I...never had to make decisions about this kind of question before." A somewhat plaintive note came into her voice. "I shouldn't have the artifact in the first place, and now, to carve it up..."

"You took the thing in order to study it. Now it's turned out to be a real riddle, not just another totem or whatever. No time to back off now, ma'am."

"I...somehow, back here, what we did in Greece seems, well, *crazy*."

He said softly, "Your feeling that way is only natural. Boston is your anchor, m'dear. You're a very traditional woman."

"Yes," she countered, "right down to my stockings."

His lip curved with the merest suggestion of a leer. "Point conceded, and gladly so."

He became solemn, and signaled for more of the thick coffee. "But there are two Claires—the one who is steeped in Bostonian rigor and correctness, who's sitting here now. Second, the secret Claire. The one I knew in Greece, who was free of her relatives and college and friends and the weight of history around here." He gestured expansively, taking in the beamed ceiling, nineteenth century woods and stuffed furniture of the restaurant. "She was willing to stand up to Kontos, elude the police, snatch the artifact. But now, back in the old setting, the doubts come crowding in. Her profession, her chairman, her dear old aging grandparents—they'll all be aghast if they find out." He paused and said gently, "Isn't that it?"

She blinked, and he was astonished to see small, crystalline tears. "Y—yes. Something like that. I ne—never thought of myself. . .as two . . ." She stopped, and gave him a broken smile.

"If I'm wrong . . ."

"No, you're not."

"I've known you only a short—"

"I can see, I *do* look that way from the outside, and . . ."

"I didn't mean to. . .pry."

"No, no, you're not, I *want* you to." She opened her palms to him, as if in mute explanation.

"That Claire Number Two, I'd like to see more of her." He grinned.

An expression of genuine regret crossed her face. "I would, too."

"I reckon you've been dividing your life that way. I can see the difference, when you walk into the lab. The Bostonian girl gets swept away and here's this crisp, bright woman who won't take crap from anybody."

She smiled wanly and reached across the starched white tablecloth to grasp his hand tightly. "I. . .no one ever cared enough to see the two sides."

"You're a master of disguise." He pressed her two hands together between his. She liked holding hands more than any woman he had ever known. He could not decide whether it was a romantic symbol for her, or something deeper. Not that the answer mattered very much.

"Jekyll and Hyde," she said ruefully, her mouth still uncertain, fragile. He thought of what she probably faced at the hands of Hampton and the others. Now that he understood better how the profession of archeology worked, he realized how much she had taken on. His throat tightened. He squeezed her hands.

CHAPTER

Six

"Come on, get up."

"Uh," he groaned. "Have some respect for the dead."

"Give them a little ride, they want to loaf in the hay."

"*Little* ride? I distinctly remember your clock reading 2 A.M. You were on top at the time, as I recall, ma'am."

"A concession to your condition. You didn't have to drink all the rest of that Chablis."

"That's what it was? I *thought* it tasted better than the Boston water."

"Come on, I'll make oatmeal."

"Is that supposed to be tempting?"

She yanked the sheets back, exposing him to the chill. "Ah! All right, I give up, where are my clothes?"

"You *are* a primitive. Shower first."

"Sho' nuff, I remember readin' that in the tour guide to Boston. Don't shower and the natives will know right off you're a monster."

She smiled. "We already have a Jekyll and Hyde, remember."

"Great hip swivel, that Hyde."

The towel hit him on the chin. "Cleanse thyself, defiler."

When she came back with tomato juice he was sitting, nude and showered, looking over a copy of *Vogue*. A cat stropped itself on his ankles. "Clothes are customary before dining," she said with mock primness.

"I was looking for something in my size." He waved the

magazine. "Studying to become a transvestite."

"My mother gave me a subscription when I was fifteen."

"Gee, my mother gave me a governess."

She grimaced. "The johns always want to tell you about their first time."

"Mornin', Miz Hyde." He kissed her. "You dress an order of magnitude better than this." He tossed the *Vogue* aside.

As he sipped the juice she brought him a yellow terrycloth robe. "Fits all sexes," she said, slipping it over his shoulders and rubbing his neck.

"Interesting, isn't it," he said between yawns, "how women's magazines are filled with pictures of women, and men's magazines . . ."

"Yes, more pictures of women. Vast gulf between the sexes. Metaphysics of our oppression." She smiled. "Maybe you should do a thesis on it."

"Too bad there aren't any *Playboys* left over from Mycenae. We could—what're they always asking for in the humanities?—compare and contrast. Probably worth a grant from the National Endowment for Exhausted Ideas."

She blinked and he instantly regretted saying it. It summoned up all the conflicts the night had banished; her face clouded and the luminous eyes turned inward. But then with a visible effort she brightened, leaned forward and kissed him fervently. "How'd you like to earn that oatmeal?"

The array of electronics and sensors around the artifact was deeper, more tangled. John had never fully gotten used to the fact that a working scientist was seldom neat. To his mathematician's sensibility, messy surroundings somehow undercut the necessary orderly scheme of framing an idea, thinking of a way to check it, and carrying out a clear test. Yet, undeniably, physicists brought serene order from such chaos.

Abe Sprangle sat at the center of the tangle, muttering over a new arrangement as John approached.

"What's this?"

"Your tax dollar at work," Abe said sourly.

"Looks to be new gamma-ray detectors," John said, glad that he could by now identify some things.

"They are. I thought maybe something was wrong with the old ones."

"Why?"

"I'm getting more counts from that plug in the back."

"And were the old detectors—"

"No, that's the trouble!" Abe said angrily. "There really *are* more gammas now."

"You're. . .?"

"Sure? Yes, there's no way I could be wrong on this one."

John said diplomatically, "If the gamma flux is increasing . . ."

"Can't be. Any natural source decays, that's obvious."

"Maybe something was in the way? I mean, partly blocked the gammas before? We've rotated the cube—couldn't that have knocked a rock out of the way inside there, or somethin'?"

Abe looked dejected, his ruddy face pinched so that it became jowly. "I suppose. How to check that, eh? If it were dislodged, perhaps we can reverse the movement."

"You watch the readout. I'll turn the cube."

Squatting, putting his shoulder and full weight into the cube, he could move it smoothly. As he touched it a slight, odd sensation came into his hands, an effect he remembered noticing back in the tomb. There he had attributed it to the spooky surroundings, but here the feeling was more obvious, a faint tugging at his fingers as he moved them to get a grip on the rough stone. Grunting, he spun the cube back and forth, stopping whenever the plug faced the sensors. After half an hour of this Abe shook his head. "Still the same, I fear."

"How's the reading from the cone?"

"As before. It has never shown the increase, as does the plug."

John stopped, puffing. "Maybe the plug itself is getting thinner? That would let more gammas through."

"Thinning how?"

"Dunno."

"Maybe is not a theory, you know, it is merely maybe."

John ignored his patronizing tone. "It feels a little funny when you turn it."

"It is heavy," Abe said dismissively and went back to his electronics. A technician worked nearby at a counter strewn with equipment, which gave a 60-cycle hum. The antiquated heaters in the bay could barely take the edge off a chill as unforgiving as the Puritan God. He could hear irritated honking outside on Vassar Street. Something nagged at him and he didn't want to let it go.

"Did you ever measure for ferromagnetism?"

Abe looked up. "No. In limestone, there is none."

"How about from whatever's inside?"

"Unlikely. The source is small."

"How would I do it?"

Abe sighed with exasperation. "Ask in Metallurgical Stores. I think they have some such device. It is for field work."

Like every seemingly minor task, this took much longer than it should. General Stores had a file card on it but the kit was not in its bin. Odd-shaped devices were crammed into any available space, another symptom of a great university which had long ago exceeded its physical bounds. John got a technician to help him rummage among nearby bins, and after an hour found the small, flat case, not much larger than a good manicure set. Figuring out how it worked consumed another half hour, and it was nearly noon before they got a reading on the counter-mounted needle. By checking the reading some distance away from the artifact, he got the right value for the Earth's magnetic field, half a Gauss. The needle wavered significantly as he neared the cube.

"Nearly two Gauss," he proclaimed.

"What?" Abe had not noticed his return.

"The cube has a big magnetic field."

"That I do not believe."

"Five will get you ten."

Abe ignored the challenge and repeated each step of the measurement. "Perhaps something wrong with the battery," he muttered, and did it again. The result would not go away.

Abe was silent for most of the next two hours, while they mapped the strength and direction of the magnetic field. John said nothing. At length Abe remarked casually, "I believe it is a quadrupolar field."

"What? Not a dipole?" A magnetic source in the cube would have given a pattern similar to the Earth's. The field lines would leave one pole and loop around to the other. A quadrupole or four-poled field was a complex set of loops, as though there was a pole at each point of the compass.

"The pattern is unmistakable," Abe said almost sadly.

"If there were two magnetic sources inside, pointed different ways—"

"Yes, that surely could do it. Still, it is strange."

"Maybe there are lodes of iron, separated."

Abe was silent, staring at the sketch he had made of the field pattern. "One more. . .strange feature. I do not like it."

"It just means we've got something important."

"But I do not understand. Why would the Mycenaeans make such a thing? How could they? It must be elaborate inside."

"Well, they did."

Abe shook his head, still disturbed.

Claire was equally upset. She quizzed him intensely about it that afternoon, talked to Abe in his office, and would not let up on the subject even as she drove to a reception that evening in Cambridge. To John their objections were puzzling. They were vexed as each measurement made the artifact more unusual, whereas his interest quickened. Their reaction seemed to come from an archeologists' attitude that the aim of their field was weaving a seamless web. A rogue object with uncertain ties to the conventional picture of Mycenaean society would do little to cement our view of that time. It could be the work of a crank, or an isolated genius, or of course from someplace else entirely. It seemed to John that such objects should be expected, but the others regarded this as simple bad luck.

The reception was at a large brick home tucked down a shadowed lane near Harvard. Mozart soaked into the crowd from speakers that ringed each room. One of the local radio stations was having an Orgy Week, devoting a day apiece to a single musician or group—Wagner, Beatles, Beethoven, Dylan—thus insuring, it seemed to him, that a diligent listener would be terminally saturated.

In his distracted mood, expecting a Harvard party to yield stimulating, original conversation was roughly like hoping that the telephone directory would read like a novel. Claire drifted off into other circles, leaving him; and John somehow got caught in a clique of literary theorists. Feigning polite interest was harder for him than any other social duty except remembering names, so under cover of freshening his drink he found some mathematicians and physicists. He knew several of them and fell into a discussion of one of his side pursuits, the quantum theory of gravity. There was always with the Harvard faculty a slightly lofty attitude, a feeling that MIT was, in the words of a guide published at the turn of the century, "that trade school down the river." In retaliation, MIT scientists regarded Harvard as a quaint liberal arts school trying to play catch-up ball. While it was a long time since an eighteenth century Harvard professor insisted on his contractual right to graze a cow on the Cambridge common, keeping the cow in his living room during bad weather, Harvard still imagined itself more creative, eccentric, and donnish than the grim gray drudges of MIT. They coveted stylish oddness. Sidney Coleman, a famous particle physicist, had such a skewed personal schedule that when he was asked to teach a 10 A.M. class, legend had it that Coleman replied, "Sorry, I can't stay up that late."

Sergio Zaninetti, a leading theoretical physicist, fully shared the assumption of intrinsic Harvard superiority, conveying it nonverbally, with Italian shrugs, lofting eyebrows, twists of his full lips, and eyes which bulged in bemused surprise.

"You have abandoned your earlier work on manifolds?" Zaninetti asked incredulously.

"I got interested in some problems in solid state physics, simultaneous integral equations—"

"But your thesis, it was *important*!"

"So's this," John said defensively.

"You should have remained with the pure, the beautiful work," Zaninetti pronounced, puffing energetically on Nazionale cigarettes, which he had shipped to him from Italy. He was a short, barrel-chested man with large tufts of blond hair escaping around his shirt collar. His thin, sallow face, described as "artistic" in a HighTech Magazine profile, never rested. When John replied that he wished to broaden his area of knowledge, Zaninetti wrenched his mouth around in dismay and barked, "A young man, he must concentrate. Nothing venture, nothing have!"

He then lectured John for five minutes on the duty of mathematicians—the lovers of the pure, the ideal, the eternal—to use their best years in nonapplied pursuits. John shrugged and endured Zaninetti's emphatic, accusing voice. It was true enough that mathematics, like music, was a young man's game. The ability to play with abstracts and find new twists, to see deeply into entities which existed only in the mind—this eroded quickly, leaving a gathering inventory of skills, but less of the sparkling zest that once came effortlessly.

John knew this, every mathematician did, but he also had a pestering curiosity about applied mathematics and, lately, physics itself. There came a time in every young scientist's life when he knew with heavy certainty that he was not the next Einstein, that in fact he would probably not win the Nobel or even one of the lesser prizes, never discover a startling new truth or unveil a fundamental corner of the universe. With that depressing realization there came a compensating freedom. You knew that to follow your nose, to work on what most delighted your mind, would not deprive you of the great opportunity to stand the world on its ear. That was gone. Gone. John had passed that point years before, had gotten thoroughly and systematically drunk for a weekend, and now was becoming irritated at Zaninetti's blandly arrogant lecture.

Answering it would have simply led to more of the same. Instead, he deepened his Southern accent and made a few small jokes, relying on the long, rounded tones to ease the situation. It was a handy maneuver among these people, who inevitably assumed the possessor of such an accent was surely a little thick-headed. He slipped away to get a drink and encountered Claire. "Setting your social pitons higher?" she inquired sardonically.

"You mean him? More of a molehill."

"I saw you talking to him, and decided it was best to keep my distance." To his questioning look she replied, "That's the famous Zaninetti the womanizer, isn't he?"

"To me he's just your everyday brilliant theoretical physicist. I didn't know his repute extended to BU and archeology."

"Oh, he's a wonder. There was a Lampoon piece last year, a parody of final exams. One question was:

" 'Nasty, brutish and short,' Thomas Hobbes's famous words, describe

(a) The life of man in the state of nature;

(b) Sergio Zaninetti;

(c) Sex with Sergio Zaninetti."

John filed the story away for a letter to his parents, and felt a bit better. By this time what he called the Cocktail Party Instability had developed. He had noted that the noise in a room rose as the square of the number of people in it, as each new loud pair forced the others to try to talk over them. It saturated only as people were driven from the room. He anticipated this, shaking off Claire's invitation to meet some archeologists, and stepping out onto a freezing balcony. It looked down on a street that might have come from the early nineteenth century but for the jam of parked cars.

He liked this feeling of slipping effortlessly back into the past. There was nothing like it in Texas, and though Georgia had been one of the original thirteen states, there were few substantial buildings to show it. He felt the torrent of talk behind him as a force, pressing against the glass doors at his back. His mind turned again to the artifact—it was seldom far away now, hovering like a presence—and he let himself realize the suspicions that had been building in him. The thing was not going to fit into the history of Mycenae, ever, unless Abe's measurements were dead wrong. The incident with the magnetic fields had underlined a central fact: they could assume nothing about the piece was commonplace. He would have to persuade Abe to check all sorts of physical properties.

The door clicked open behind him. Claire said, "I thought I saw you duck out."

"Wanted to think." He leaned on the railing. "You could drown in Mozart in there."

"I was talking to a field archeologist who's visiting Harvard this year. He asked me about our artifact."

"Oh?"

"He says he heard it from someone at Brown."

He straightened. "LeBailly is talking."

"Yes." Her face was tight, nervous. Claire Number One.

"How much time until Hampton gets wind of it?"

"Very, very little." She made a crooked smile.

CHAPTER
Seven

The next morning was tense. They all braced for the coming storm and worked quickly, earnestly, to make as many measurements of the cube as possible. John had duties in his office, but promised to return in the afternoon.

Claire puffed on a cigarette with her coffee, thinking of strategies for dealing with Hampton. How she handled the inevitable revelation would be crucial. The Old Boy Network still worked in archeology, and despite the steady progress women had made since the 1980s, the humanistic areas of the university pyramid were notoriously the slowest to change. She had never been skillful at handling the old style men. Professions would be egalitarian only when women like her—comparatively guileless, a bit crusty, unwilling (or, she admitted ruefully, unable) to use sexually tinged strategies for advancement—could pursue a career without becoming neurotic and defensive.

Three years ago, at age twenty-five, she had gone through a protracted soul-searching and had more or less written off her chances at a conventional life. She certainly had no great desire for children, though there were still moments which could touch off a bout of tearful reflection, or even depression. A melancholy song on the radio, or a gushy letter on cream paper from a securely wedded old Radcliffe friend, could do it. Things weren't *fair*, dammit. . . .

It particularly wasn't fair that when she should be rehearsing confrontations with Hampton, she drifted off into fuzzy ruminations about her life. She gave up, stubbed out her cigarette, and went to help Abe.

She had spoken to him earlier in the morning, revealing to him that she had brought the artifact out of Greece without the proper clearance, but he seemed unconcerned. To her surprise, he had brushed such formalities off as mere paperwork, and gone back to his 'scopes.

Abe had thought of a new method to explore the cube's interior. It involved an independent source of gamma-rays, which Abe could project through the plug. His hope was that some of the gammas would be absorbed by the dense parts of the core. The rest would pass through the less dense portions and exit from the amber cone. He could detect those and build up a projected picture of the interior.

It worked. However, the image was mottled and blurred. It showed the same square they had seen before by looking at the emitted gammas. The central dot remained as well. This meant that the source was dense, which was no surprise. The question was, how dense? Abe handled this by turning up the gamma-ray energy. The stronger the rays, the better they could penetrate.

Claire and Abe worked through the morning, with Claire simply following instructions amid the tangle of cables and humming apparatus. The square formation blurred as Abe increased the gamma-ray energy.

They sent out for food from the Italian bar at Albany and Cross Streets. Abe increased the energy again, then again, and finally to the extreme end of the device's range. The central dot remained unchanged.

"That's a hell of a lot of energy we put through there," Abe said, shaking his head. "But the center keeps absorbing it."

"Doesn't that tell us how long it is?" Claire asked.

"If we had a model geometry, most certainly," Abe said. "See how the size of the dot never varies? A sharp profile. That means we're looking at a rod, I'd guess, end on. From the flux of gammas I'm using . . ." He scribbled numbers on a pad.

"Supposing it's made of iron, say," Claire put in. "That would account for John's magnetic field."

"Iron...okay..." Abe shook his head, checked his numbers.

Claire waited next to the screen where the dot swam, a blue cipher on a circle of green. The circle was the image of the cone of gamma-rays coming from beyond the cube, through the plug at the back. The cube rock, which absorbed the gamma emission totally, formed a blue enclosing field around the circle.

She felt again the strangeness of this fusion, an ancient artifact probed by the latest technology. Such devices, far from the techniques still taught by the old style archeologists, were now the primary source of change in the field—more important, in fact, than any of the new theories of ancient immigration patterns or social organization. In Egypt a complex net of acoustic detectors had listened to the echoes of sonic waves and found tombs buried so deeply that even millennia of grave robbers had missed. In China a shredded manuscript had been restored in a weekend by computer analysis of the billions of possible combinations, a job which would once have been an entire five-year thesis.

Abe shook his head again. "Something wrong. This says you'd need a rod of iron over two meters long in there. That's..."

"Impossible," Claire finished for him. "The cube itself is smaller than that."

Abe sighed. "I'll have to go over the whole rig. I've fouled the calibration somewhere."

"Could the center be a lot better at absorbing gammas than iron?"

"I don't see how. You'd need something truly dense."

"Like rock?"

"You cannot make a rod of rock. It will snap."

"What's better?"

"Nothing plausible. This rod, or whatever it is, must be also a gamma-ray emitter. Remember? So strong an emitter that I could not see any detail in that little dot."

"And we've got to explain John's magnetic fields, too."

"With this 'rod'?" Abe laughed sourly. "The Mycenaeans, did they know how to make such a rod?"

Claire shook her head. "I doubt it."

"Then we cannot make sense of this thing. We must go inside."

Claire clenched her teeth. "Not yet."

"This thing is—is *impossible*! We cannot understand—"

John's excited voice called, "Hey there!" He came trotting toward them from across the bay. "Abe! I just saw Hampton down in your office, asking—" He saw Claire. "Looks like you were right."

Claire bit her lip and felt the old sinking sensation, the descent into a cloud of wordless bleak anxiety.

"I suppose you all understand," Donald Hampton said gravely, "the seriousness of this."

He stood with hands judicially clasped behind his back, studying the artifact. His three-piece suit of blue wool was spattered by the rain storm that had settled on Boston like a sodden pall. His face was red from the chill outside and he puffed, the knot of his plaid tie bulging. There had been only a few minutes' wait until he appeared, scowling distrustfully at the messy array of diagnostics.

"This is an in*cred*ible breach of elementary professional standards. I can perhaps understand the motives of Dr. Bishop and Dr. Sprangle, but *you*, Claire, a trained archeologist—!"

John said mildly, "You haven't heard what led to this."

"I needn't know every detail." Hampton scowled at John. "Professor Kontos was right about you, that is all I need to know. And to *think* how you deceived our committee hearing, sitting there and lying—"

"I never lied," John said with sudden sharpness. "It's not my fault if you don't ask the right questions."

Hampton snorted. "So you hold that theft is permissible if undetected?"

"We got it back from where Kontos had hidden it," John said.

"I am sure Professor Kontos had no intention of doing anything—"

"He stuck it back in a hole, to keep it from being shipped with the rest of the gear, to Athens," John said. "He was going to claim it as his own discovery."

"Fantastic," Hampton said dismissively. "How could he? You and Claire had evidence, pictures."

"Only because Claire went back to get her notes and records. It was while we were there, in the tomb, that we saw what Kontos was trying."

"I simply do not believe such a wild, *ad hoc* story. If it was true, why did you not bring it up during our committee hearing?"

Claire said, "You wouldn't have bought it."

Hampton stared at Claire, then John, then Abe. "You should *all* be *ashamed* at such a deception. Your failure to argue your case merely underlines your duplicity. Abe, you in particular should know this undermines all that our joint program stands for."

"I did the research. I didn't ask about the details of getting it here."

Hampton reddened further. "What you call *details* concerns the theft of Greek national treasure."

Abe said calmly, "From what I've heard, there were mitigating circumstances."

"I am afraid you understand *nothing* of the international standards of respect for a nation's past, for its heritage—"

"I am a scientist," Abe said simply. "I have research to do, I do it. This is one fabulous artifact, Donald."

Hampton sniffed. Claire realized that since he had come into the bay he had not taken a close look at the cube. He saw it as a pawn in a larger game. His curiosity as an archeologist had atrophied. "I can see it is unusual," Hampton declared. "A beautiful amber, yes. Fine artwork. But the exact nature of the piece is immaterial; we deal with *principle*."

Claire had deliberately said little since his appearance. Now she murmured, "I want a hearing to make my case."

Hampton chuckled sardonically, "Oh, a hearing you shall get. Rest assured, young lady, rest assured. Meanwhile—" He turned to Abe. "I want this artifact placed in the care of Boston University immediately. We shall prepare it for shipping back to Dr. Kontos."

Abe smiled thinly. "Not until I'm finished with it."

"You have no right—"

"It's a piece that demands close study. It was brought here by one of your own faculty."

"Illegally!"

"My position is that your internal disputes have nothing to

do with the MIT-BU cooperation on archeological physics. *Nothing.*"

"I will get the—the *police.*"

Abe's white eyebrows arched. "Come now. They wish not to get into something like this."

"We shall see."

"No we won't. Our administrations will have to battle it out. You know how much time that takes, Donald."

Abe put his hands in his pockets and beamed at Hampton. Claire had never seen the mild experimentalist in this persona, and she suddenly understood how he ran his department with such studied ease. He simply could not be cowed, particularly not by blustering.

"You are being unreasonable."

"This artifact has properties that simply do not associate with what we know of Mycenae, Donald. I can show you gamma-ray and other data that cry out for explanation."

"You expect me to lend *my* expertise to this?"

"We thought you might—"

"I cannot *believe* you are taking this attitude in defense of a woman who has lied, stolen—"

"You callin' her a liar?" John asked threateningly. He stepped closer to Hampton and squared himself. Claire's eyes widened.

Hampton stared in open disbelief at John. "You are *threatening* me?"

John reached out and gave the knot of Hampton's regimental tie a jab with his index finger. "You bet."

"This is incredible."

Abe stepped forward. "I think you'd better leave, Donald. This will be settled by the administration."

Hampton looked mystified. "But you are in the *wrong.* You have taken a precious—"

"Just *go,* Donald."

Hampton's face clouded. "You are mistaken if you believe you can simply hide behind your university. Your activities cannot withstand scrutiny. This is an international matter."

"Go, Donald."

"All right, I will. But as soon as I reach my office I shall call the proper authorities in Athens. I have not been able to reach Dr. Kontos recently, but I know he will be horrified.

And he will have other, more drastic means, I assure you."

Hampton glared at each of them in turn, as if memorizing their features, and then turned and stalked off.

Claire sat down. Beneath her blue jump suit she was perspiring heavily, yet her brow felt cool. She tried to think.

"It's over," John said quietly in her ear. He bent over and kissed her cheek. "C'mon, don't go into Claire Number One on me."

She managed a broken smile. "I—to have it finally happen, I've thought about it so much. . . ."

"I know."

"He was exactly how I imagined, and he's going to call Kontos. . . ."

"Forget him. Abe handled it just right."

Claire looked up. Abe was staring at the artifact, his face impassive. She said, "You knew just what to do."

Abe smiled. "I figured you out two weeks ago. There was always something a bit odd about the way you handled this, you know. Usually, comes an artifact over from BU, it has a stack of paperwork. This one did not."

John said, "We only had the customs papers. No way to document it six ways from Sunday."

Abe shrugged. "So I have put my defenses in place. Mind you"—his eyes narrowed—"I only do so because of the unusual nature of this find. I do not approve of how you got it."

Claire nodded mutely. Somewhere in her a spurt of joy was struggling to burst forth. The worst had happened and, all told, it wasn't bad. Claire Number One had been wrong.

"You're going to need to use up a lot of your time defending yourself against him," Claire said. "He'll make a lot of noise."

"Not before we get our work done," Abe said happily. He gestured at the cube. "We must bore into it now. That is the only way to answer our questions."

He said it so simply and naturally that Claire did not immediately marshall counter-arguments. And she saw that he had been playing one move ahead of them, arranging this bargain: MIT's protection traded for a chance to break into the artifact. She sighed. It was inevitable.

CHAPTER

Eight

They opened the plug in late afternoon. There was a reasonably good drilling kit in the Materials Science equipment inventory, so Claire proposed using that. The better alternative would be to call LeBailly at Brown, who, despite having a big mouth, was the best in this part of the country. But LeBailly would take time to arrive and Claire firmly ruled him out anyway, because she now saw him as a conduit of news to Hampton.

Abe had an appointment he could not break, and wanted to reach the MIT administration before Hampton could. He reluctantly left the drilling to John, who had by now mastered the basic skills. Abe left definite instructions that as soon as the light pipe showed anything, he wanted to be called.

John began drilling with a four millimeter bit, extracting a fine rock dust for study later. The arrangement allowed easy adjustment of height and angle, and held the drill in a vibration-free mouth supported by a heavy steel frame. He worked with extreme care, avoiding any radiation hazard. Even a four millimeter hole would allow a light pipe to slide through. With that, and a good deal of computer enhancement of the optical feed through the pipe, they could probably get decent images of the interior. The technology was getting better every year, and MIT had the best.

The plug in the rear face gave every superficial appearance of being volcanic basalt. This was curious in itself, since the Mycenaeans usually did not use such rock in their stonework.

The plug was virtually seamless, fitting snugly into its hole as though it has been tapered skillfully. Yet there were no signs of chiseling on it.

John ran the whirring drill minutely deeper into its hole, being sure the runoff in rock dust fell into the catcher which would keep it for chemical analysis. Every half centimeter in he stopped and filed the dust in a plastic bag. It was tedious watching him, and Claire found little beyond storing the bags to keep herself busy. The afternoon hours brought stretching blue shadows into the bay from the big dirty windows high overhead. The drill cut into the rock with a high, jarring rasp, grating on her nerves. The rock was hard, progress slow. John had penetrated nearly six centimeters into the rock and was withdrawing the bit, preparing to change it, when he stopped, cocked his head, and listened.

"Do you hear something?"

"No. Is the bit wearing out?"

John withdrew the drill completely. "Hear that?"

Claire leaned closer. A tiny, high note, almost like the sound a television makes with the volume knob turned down. "What is it?"

John looked around. "Some equipment in the lab?"

Claire drew her head back and then leaned toward the plug again. "No, it's louder near the hole."

Gingerly, John put a piece of paper against the drill hole. "Lord God A'mighty."

"What?"

"It's sucking on the paper."

"What do you mean? How—"

"It's a vacuum in there."

She sat in silence. Then, "Here, let me."

He removed the paper and the faint high whine returned.

"It...it must be some sort of pocket, opened in the limestone," John said quietly. "Pretty damned unusual."

"I didn't know limestone did that. I mean, hot rocks will leave trapped gas, and it condenses later, leaving a vacuum. Igneous formations, yes, but . . ."

Claire felt a slight breeze brush at her hair and suddenly realized that it was blowing toward the artifact, *into* it.

"Cover it!" she cried.

John secured the drill lock and reached for a piece of flat

aluminum nearby. He slid it across the face of the cube and covered the hole. The moaning subsided, but not completely. The aluminum did not fit precisely to the uneven surface of the cube.

"What. . .what in the world . . ." John murmured.

"That's no cavity."

"There'd have to be a *pump* inside to do that."

They stared at each other, speechless. Irrelevantly—her mind darting away from this new impossible fact—Claire noticed the *chugg-chugg-chugg* of a diffusion pump from a far corner of the lab, mingling with the steady spattering of rain against the high windows. Yet another storm was rolling in, and brilliant flashes of lightning threw shadowy images of streaming rivulets down into the lab. Thunder rumbled like an old, caged lion.

"This. . .can't be," she said.

"But it is."

The low howling continued, unnerving her. "Can't we get a better seal on it than—wait, I know. Slide in the light pipe, why don't you?"

He nodded. "Of course."

She helped him set the thin, silvery tube in its clamps and feeder. It was attached to an array of optical readout instruments that crowded the working zone around the cube face. When John pulled the aluminum sheet aside the moaning had a ragged, harsh edge to it and seemed to Claire to swell up, filling the lab with its irrational, impossible cry. John quickly inserted the light tube, properly coated with an inorganic lubricant. This made a firm seal and cut off the dreadful hollow howling.

The light pipe delivered a fogged, blue-white image.

"Is that a side of a square?" John pointed at a blur.

"Control your imagination. All I see is clouds, maybe a little brighter toward the center."

"We should be looking at light that comes through the cone. Why is it blue-white?"

Claire peered at the electronics. "Maybe the color setting is off. It's the vacuum that bothers me. This thing could be dangerous. I wish Abe—oh yes, let's call him."

He arrived a half hour later, visibly excited, but could find nothing wrong with the settings for hue and color. He refused to believe their story until John slid the light pipe back out and the eerie drone filled the lab again.

They sat and stared blankly at the cloudy screen image, discussing the latest development in hushed voices. There was simply no way to make sense of a vacuum inside an ancient artifact, and Abe reluctantly raised the question of a deliberate hoax. Could someone have planted the piece, perhaps to embarrass the joint Greek-BU expedition? Who would gain? Why do so much work? How was it done?

No one believed in the hoax theory. But no one had anything better to offer.

The situation seemed stable; the seal was good. Abe wanted time to review his diagnostics carefully, and the other two were tired, worn down by Hampton and now this. They agreed to meet early the next morning.

As Claire left the lab, she noticed John was unusually silent. They ran through gusty rain under Claire's bulbous yellow umbrella—John had forgotten to bring his—to her Alfa Romeo. He spoke little throughout dinner at a lobster cafe, and gave her a solemn, distracted kiss when she left his apartment later. He was clearly following a thread of thought, but he refused to discuss it.

Abe was bedraggled and sour-faced the next morning. He had worked most of the night and found no errors. The diagnostics were giving valid results.

There were some curious new slants, though. The gamma-ray flux had increased to the danger point.

"It would seem that the plug was absorbing a good deal of the radiation from the core," Abe murmured wanly. "Now we can see it more clearly. It is the same—a square, plus the bright center."

Claire tapped the video screen, where blue-white lines made a square. "This is the gamma-ray picture?"

Abe shook his head. "That's the light pipe image. It cleared up gradually through the night."

"Then it gives the same picture as the gamma-ray!"

"True enough."

"Consistent results."

"Yes," John said, "we're lookin' at an intense source."

Abe said, "For something two centimeters across to put

out that much in the gamma—incredible." He seemed to Claire to have lost his momentum, to be numbed by the inexplicable facts. Not that she felt very much differently, she reminded herself. She had simply had more sleep.

Abe said, "For a bunch of radioactive isotopes to do that, they—"

"Not isotopes," John said. He stood up from a lab stool, stretching. She saw fatigue lines around his eyes and guessed he had stayed up late thinking. "It's not a 'radioactive anomaly' at all. I think we're looking at a structure of very hot, very dense matter."

"Hot?" Claire asked.

"That explains all the x-ray and gamma-ray emission. There's something inside hotter than the surface of the sun."

Abe blinked. "It cannot be. It would melt through."

"I don't know," John said reasonably, "but the radiation isn't enough to heat up the cube much—I calculated that last night. And we don't feel the high temperature because we're insulated from the center."

Claire was puzzled. "How? It's only a few feet away."

John spread his hands. "There's a strong vacuum between us. That's what drew the air in when we opened the plug."

They sat in silence for a long moment. Claire could think of no objection, except the by now familiar one—the idea was impossible, absurd.

"But . . ." she began feebly, "something buried in a Mycenaean artifact, in a tomb . . ."

"That's the real point, I suppose. Nobody knows how to make anything like that, that *whatever* in there. Nobody."

Abe curled his lip. "You are suggesting that we resolve our difficulties by attributing this object to—what? Let me guess. Visitors from outer space, correct?"

Claire said scornfully, "That Von Däniken nonsense? Come now, John, we—"

John smiled. "Yeah, I thought of that, too. Not absolutely crazy, but I don't believe it. Just because we can't explain it doesn't mean it's some roadside trash thrown out by a passing superbeing."

Abe said sharply, "What then?"

"We've got to give up the idea that we're dealing with an

artifact here at all. This isn't archeology anymore, folks.
We're studying physics here."

Claire was mystified. "I never heard of any physics like
this."

John grinned, tired but oddly joyous, his eyes gleaming,
his hands curling and uncurling with compressed energy.
"Me either. But I can make some guesses. I think what we've
got here is a singularity."

PART
FIVE

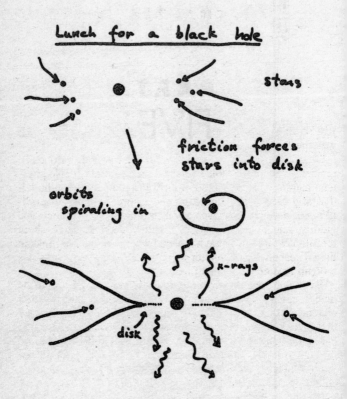

CHAPTER
One

The most important lesson of modern Einsteinian physics was the fact that space could be pathological.

Before Einstein, the world was a place of billiard balls, remorselessly predictable paths and serene certainty. No physicist can now recall without a thrill the moment when he left that arid Newtonian landscape and entered a Lewis Carroll-like world where time was a fourth dimension, space curved giddily, and honest witnesses could blithely disagree about the simplest facts of what happened where and when. Einstein linked space with the matter it contained, returning to physics a depth and mystery it had lost.

By making the universe a partner in the construction of its own geometry, Einstein admitted the possibility that it would contain pitfalls, traps, bizarre spots. As soon as he showed that matter could curve space-time, the possibility arose that curvature could be unbounded, infinite. A particle proceeding through such a region of space-time would find a point beyond which it could not go, a spot where its own existence ended—a singularity.

Claire asked, "Okay, singularity is another word for black hole, right?"

"Almost," John replied. "There might be other forms of singularity, but the one everybody knows is the black hole."

"But black holes are *stars*. Or were."

"Right. I think we've got something here that's *like* a black hole, not identical."

"It gives off radiation. Black holes don't—that's why they're black."

"Not so. A hole attracts matter, which falls in on a kind of spiral path. Suppose there's a cloud of dust or whatever, orbiting near a black hole. Here, I'll sketch it. Some dust gets drawn closer. That makes a disk of stuff coming in, swirling around faster and faster. It gets flattened into a disk by simple friction. That makes it lose some energy and fall in farther. Close to the hole, the matter gets very dense, and starts rubbing against nearby infalling stuff even more. So it gets hotter from more friction. Just before the hole swallows it up, you can see that hot matter radiating heat and x-rays and so on."

"So black holes aren't black," Claire said doubtfully.

"Not if there's stuff to swallow in the neighborhood. The best evidence for that is the center of galaxies, where there are plenty of stars to chew up. This sketch might be what it's like there. Black holes, really big ones, gobble up the stars and give off lots of radiation. They're spectacularly bright. That's prob'ly what makes quasars."

Claire frowned. He could see her wrestling with the introduction of a bizarre idea.

"Okay, I don't know anything about quasars. But this thing we've got, it's *small*."

"Right. There's no limit on the size of a black hole, though. They can be tiny. Small ones don't last long, but it's possible to form one and have it sit around, industriously trying to eat its surroundings."

"And that's what's in the cube?"

"Could be. How else can you explain the radiation?"

Claire grimaced, not liking the conclusion. "But it's. . . *crazy*."

"Sho' nuff," John said, amused.

Abe listened to their conversation with open disbelief. They all had obligations elsewhere and the day was winding down, so John left, pleased to have delivered his bombshell at last. What he hadn't told the others was that he was rusty on the physics of black holes and needed time to do some reading.

He worked through the next night, and appeared at the lab in the morning, ragged and red-eyed.

"You are wanting to measure *what*?" Abe twisted his mouth and did not try to conceal his disdain.

"Local gravity. Is there any equipment. . .?"

They had to get the gravitometer from a geological group across campus. It was used to study faultings and mass displacements, in search of likely oil deposits. Petroleum engineering had developed the technique extensively, so John could do most of the work by himself. Abe was not interested in spending his time on such an unlikely venture, and busied himself with his own equipment. He had no explanation for whatever was in the cube, but he dismissed John's suggestion of yesterday as a pipe dream. The radioactive anomaly notion still appealed to him, but the unrelenting vacuum was a fact he preferred to ignore for the moment. John recognized the pattern. Abe had confronted too many bizarre facts at once. He needed time to digest them.

The device John maneuvered around the lab was a spindly affair of rods and coils, capable of measuring deviations in both strength and direction of the local acceleration of gravity, accurate to one part in a million. John worked slowly with it, sluggish from lack of sleep, but dogged. Claire arrived later in the morning to help. They got their first major result after lunch.

There was a tiny deflection toward the cube at a distance of five meters. Closer, the deflection increased rapidly. Claire could not press the stubby end of the detector closer than two centimeters to the cube, because of a long balancing bar on the frame. There the effect became enormous—nearly one percent of the pull of gravity.

Claire said, "That explains why, when you run your hands over the surface, it feels, well, funny."

"Yes. . .I noticed something like that." John was staring hard at the gravitometer dial. He had moved it to the opposite side of the cube.

"What's wrong?"

"This meter. It reads differently here."

"You mean the acceleration is different from the other side?"

"Seems so. It's about half as strong."

"I thought gravitational force was the same in all directions."

"Yes. Spherically symmetric, we call it."

"But this gravitation from the cube, it isn't?"

"Apparently not. And it's so strong. . . ."

"Only one percent of the Earth's, that's not so much."

"To change local gravity by even one percent, you'd need—let's see." He stood by the tubular array of the gravitometer, careful not to touch the balancing arms, and calculated in his head. "You'd need a cubic *mile* of rock, just about."

"Your idea. . .of a singularity . . ."

"A whole damn mountain! That's pretty close to the mass a black hole would need to survive from the beginning of the universe."

"You think this might be one?"

He shook his head. "Where's the mass? A whole mountain's worth! It'd drop right through the floor with that weight."

"You weighed the cube again?"

"Yep. Assuming there's a pretty big hole in there, then the singularity weighs maybe one, two hundred pounds."

He stood silent for a long while, oblivious. Presently she asked, "Do you want to measure anything else?"

"Huh? Oh, sure. I want to find out what this acceleration looks like at other angles. Make a three-dimensional map of it."

"I'll move this. . . ." She began working the gravitometer between banks of electronics.

"Claire?"

She looked up, biting her lower lip in concentration, perspiring, a lock of hair looped down across her eyes. He smiled and said, "Just because something's crazy, doesn't mean it's wrong."

CHAPTER
Two

The battle between the BU and MIT administrations was short, bitter and conducted at the highest levels. BU had lost none of its contentious edge since the glory days of President Silber, and MIT reflexively protected its own. The president of MIT came to the lab and viewed the artifact. Abe described how its physical properties did not jibe at all with its origin. Claire and John were present, but—on Abe's advice—little heard from. Assorted deans and others came into play, part of a blocking movement organized by Abe, who was calling in all his debts.

Abe took the position that the artifact had ceased to be solely an archeological object and now was primarily interesting for its physical aspects. He told the president that the cube housed a radioactive anomaly, an unusual concentration which defied analysis.

All this was true, but not very forthcoming. Abe held that its appearance in the artifact was surely accidental. The facilities needed for its study were far better at MIT than at BU. The president disliked the appearance of arrogantly withholding the piece from a sister institution, but understood the scientific issues involved. He agreed to propose a brief study period, after which the object would be given to BU, and then returned to Greece.

He communicated this to Hampton and the proper figures at BU. They all agreed the matter was highly embarrassing and did not reflect well on either university. The consequences for Claire were probably rather dire, but that was a matter which could be settled when the artifact was safely back in Greek hands. It would be well if there was a gentlemen's agreement to keep this quiet until some of the more delicate arrangements could be settled.

There the matter rested, until the next morning.

Claire came into John's office without knocking. He was behind on his work for the metallurgy group and was trying to get a solution to a particularly difficult boundary value problem involving integral equations of a knotty kind. If he had something concrete to show for this week he would feel justified in spending the rest of his time on the singularity problem, which was slow work.

"Look at that!" Claire said sharply, as if he were to blame for whatever was in the copy of the Boston *Globe* she tossed on his desk.

"Bad weather coming?" John asked mildly. It was a standard joke between them; to him, there was always appalling weather on the way.

"Hampton's gone public."

"What? But Abe said—"

"Gentlemen's agreement, ha."

"Sonuvabitch!"

"Precisely."

The *Globe* piece was an interview with Hampton, apparently given before the deal had been struck between the universities. In it he described the artifact as "a precious relic of a cloudy time, lost in the mists of antiquity," and deplored MIT's "cooperation with the theft of such a priceless object from its country of origin." He implied that it was all MIT's idea, and that Claire—who was only mentioned once—had been duped into it by "someone over there, working with a postdoctoral fellow, a Dr. Bishop." The Greek government would surely be affronted, Hampton said, and he would not be surprised if this matter even entered into "events at the diplomatic level, especially considering the ongoing issue of the British Museum and the remaining Elgin marbles."

John raised an eyebrow. "Lost in the mists? Florid type, isn't he?"

Claire said decisively, "It could upset the deal." She lit a cigarette and tossed the match out the window.

"Abe can probably patch it up."

"Don't you see?" She puffed furiously. "Hampton did this before the agreement, and then couldn't stop it. Think what else he did."

He frowned. She had cut down on her smoking only last week, but the dark brown cigarette with a gold tip did not look like an impulse buy. Probably she had them stashed away. Her rumpled aquamarine suit showed signs of haste, and she was breathing hard.

"How'd you get here?"

"I walked. I was so mad!"

Walking two miles in the cold was unClaire-like. "Again, I think Abe and the president can handle—"

"But don't you see? Hampton must have called Kontos, and told him everything, before the deal was struck."

"That's what all that jabber about diplomatic level means?"

"I think so."

"Side effects."

"What?"

"As soon as we let this out, I knew we'd get side effects. Abe had to go through the dean, which meant that, plain as the nose on your face, people would start to horn in."

He told her about the half-dozen faculty members who had dropped by the lab, and the others who wanted to know more about the anomaly. Worse, word had spread to Harvard, and Sergio Zaninetti had appeared interested.

"Is that bad?" Claire asked, puzzled.

"Well, better'n a poke in the face with a sharp stick, I suppose."

John was torn between two views of science. On the one hand, spreading of results and ideas resulted in greater productivity and cross-fertilization. Particularly, mathematics and physics often reinforced each other. This was nowhere more true than in gravitation theory. Most of the major results of the last few decades had been obtained by people originally trained as mathematicians.

Opposed to this idealistic model of the way science worked was the simple fact of self-interest. John knew much of the differential geometry of manifolds, and similar techniques, but he did not have the surety of approach that a theorist like

Zaninetti could bring to the subject. The more time he had to work by himself, the better.

"Well, compared with being castigated in the *Globe*, and my probably losing my job, don't you think this rivalry is less important?"

"Sure," John said, but something inside him winced.

Claire's mother had no doubts. They had agreed a week before to have dinner that evening, so despite John's efforts to back out, they called upon Mrs. Anderson in her home at 242 Commonwealth Avenue. It was a thin brownstone townhouse with broad bay windows that let an orange glow out into the shafts of gusty rain.

"Brrrr!" John's teeth chattered as they approached, hunched over against the wind. "This stuff's barely a degree above the ice point."

"Oh, you southern softy types simply don't appreciate the subtle sway of the seasons."

Mrs. Anderson closed the front door quickly after them and led them through the little antechamber where coats were hung. She was a small, smiling woman, well dressed in an old-fashioned way, with a lot of antique jewelry that must have been quite expensive even when new. She spoke with a heavier accent than Claire, vaguely English-sounding to John's ears but with a country undercurrent of flat New Hampshire consonants.

"I hope you can *survive* such weather, Mr. Bishop," she said. "Perhaps you'd like some, ah, restorer?"

This meant not the expected sherry, but a deep, warming brandy. At least Mrs. Anderson was a realist about her climate. She led them from the small, ornate wooden bar through a scalloped archway and into a spacious, carpeted living room with thick oak beams. Vivaldi harpsichord tinkled softly from two wall speakers. Antiques crouched at every turn, the chairs all testifying to their age by being slightly too small for John's frame.

Mrs. Anderson was jovial, almost flighty. Her face was carefully composed and her lined skin had the look of long bracing walks in the open air. Remembering an old adage that a woman's mother is a good guide to how she will age, he noted that she had a pleasant heft to her, muscle tone giving a spring to her movements. Then he felt somewhat ashamed at being so coldly analytical. Still, maybe it was only fair; he deduced that she looked upon him as—the word seemed appropriate here in Boston—a suitor.

"You come from Atlanta, Mr. Bishop?"

"John. No, Athens, Georgia—it's a medium-sized city."

"And how did you come to be in Boston?"

It was all said gracefully, but beneath the high cheekbones her mouth had a concentrated, discerning look. He trotted out the biography. Early interest in math. Decision to avoid going to Georgia Tech, despite his engineer father's wishes. Scholarship to Rice in Houston. No, he didn't work in the space program. Finished his bachelor's degree and kept right on for a speedy doctorate at Rice. Early interest in combinatorial geometries, with later applications to particle physics. A brief year at Berkeley. Current postdoc at MIT, looking into some interesting boundary value problems. He threw in this last part because it forestalled the usual questions. Nothing stopped people cold like indecipherable jargon.

"My, that's most impressive," Mrs. Anderson said warmly. He knew he hadn't given her what she really wanted—a feel for the family that had spawned him—but in truth he didn't know how to. He could tell her about one side of his family, still living in classic old homes in Charleston. There the lawns were immaculate, and sported century-old statues of Negro hitching boys, their faces now painted an egalitarian white, but the hands forgetfully left black. Or he could mention with equal justice the relatives on his mother's side, who, when they were working in the fields with a cold, blew their noses by pinching their upper nostrils and letting fly. He decided to forego that particular bit of local color.

They went into a dinner of roast beef, squash, rice and a decent Bordeaux. Unremarkable, but thoroughly Bostonian. There was much talk of Uncle Alex and the estate in New Hampshire. Only over a wonderful dessert of baked Alaska did Mrs. Anderson say, "I thought the piece in the *Globe* was un*for*tunate," and gazed at him expectantly.

"Maybe Professor Hampton has overstepped," John said diplomatically.

"To bring out such a thing in the *press*, however . . ."

"As we say where I come from, I doubt that Hampton knows grits from granola."

Mrs. Anderson frowned and peered at him suspiciously. "Well, I certainly hope Claire's name can be kept out of it henceforth."

"I'll surely try," he said warmly.

"Mother, you don't have to look out for me."

"I was only in*quir*ing."

"John is not responsible for me."

"I was only asking for another o*pin*ion, dear." She gave her daughter a severe look.

"I'm dealing with Hampton in my own way."

John raised his eyebrows at this, knowing that she in fact had no secret plan.

"All over a piece of stone from someone's *grave*. It seems such a minor thing to engage our name in *pub*lic."

Claire nodded, apparently understanding, but said nothing. It was clear that to Mrs. Anderson appearing in the *Globe* was a disgrace roughly comparable to being shoved into a police line-up.

The moment passed on to the brandy and cigarettes stage, only Claire smoking. Mrs. Anderson voiced opinions on the Boston Symphony and the current president, neither overly favorable. The news of Greek withdrawal from NATO, expulsion of various diplomats from Athens on trumped-up charges, and mysterious Turkish naval maneuvers passed through Mrs. Anderson's attention, received a frown and a tsk-tsk, and passed from the conversation. John played a game of damage limitation, taking no stands until he guessed hers. This proved a winning strategy, but tiring.

When they left the rain had gone and the walk down Commonwealth was lit by the yellow glisten of headlights from every wet surface. The garden island that divides Commonwealth was bleak, the trees denuded and the bushes mere black twigs. A policeman was rousting a bum who slept on one of the benches beneath a plastic sheet, managing to be firm and well mannered at the same time.

"She did a lot of probing," John said neutrally.

"Oh, it's her way."

"I didn't know I'd have to render an o*pin*ion."

Claire laughed. "Sorry about that."

"She'd like you to keep off the front pages, I suppose."

Claire grimaced ruefully. "Typically Bostonian. There's a Faulkner quote, about writing, but it applies here. He said the 'Ode on a Grecian Urn' is worth any number of old ladies."

"Ah yes. So, archeologically speaking, imagine what the urn itself is worth."

"Precisely."

CHAPTER

Three

Sergio Zaninetti said, "*Dio mio!* You are sure?"

John arrived at the tail end of Sergio's visit to the lab. Clearly, Abe was bewitched by the famous theoretician. "Many times I have checked it," Abe said amiably, with muted pride.

"But this is of supreme importance!"

"Thus we going slowly and carefully," Abe said.

They both noticed John picking his way among the cables that now snaked everywhere in the laboratory bay. Sergio shook John's hand and greeted him effusively. "The other night, you did not say to me you had such a thing."

"Well, it's all kind of a big mystery," John said casually.

"*In toto*, an astonishing mystery. You may not know what it is, but this dot at the center—could you show me that again, Abraham?"

Abe happily flicked a few switches and in a moment had the optical image on the biggest screen. "Overnight, it has cleared up a little."

John studied the image, matching it with his memory. The square was slightly sharper and there were wispy traces leading inward from the edges. Mottled and lumpy traces of light, perhaps along the diagonals.

"That peak at the center," Zaninetti said. "You say you cannot resolve it?"

"Smaller than a millimeter. Only so much can I tell."

"Even using the gamma-rays?"

"Yes. I simply cannot resolve better, given the conditions."

"Hard radiation, optical, a picture like this—" Zaninetti gestured broadly at the cube, which was nearly concealed beneath an array of diagnostics. "It is difficult to imagine."

"Don't need to imagine it," John said. "It's there."

A quick orange flash erupted in the upper right hand corner of the screen. In an instant it faded and vanished.

"Eh! What?" Zaninetti asked.

"A gamma-ray decaying inside the light pipe," Abe said. "It leaves a trail of low energy photons when some of the ionized atoms recombine."

John said, "I don't remember seeing one of those before."

Abe shrugged. "They come every few hours. The gamma-ray flux is increasing a little, I believe."

Zaninetti peered at the spot where the light pipe went in, now surrounded by a collar to keep an O-ring pressure seal in place. He turned to John. "I think your idea may be correct."

"What idea?"

"That it is a singularity."

So Abe had let it out of the bag. *Damn.*

Zaninetti smiled thinly. "Abraham here has told me of your gravitometer measurements. You think they are correct?"

John said grudgingly, "Near as I can make out."

"Then I judge you are on the correct course. Is *pazzo*, you agree?" He slugged John playfully in the bicep. "Crazy!"

John had to grin. "Prob'ly."

"I think it deserves serious, *very* serious study."

"There's lots more to be done."

"Something in the rock, you agree? Caught in that stone work. Accidental discovery. Reminds of the quark business in the eighties, remember?"

"Looking for fractionally charged particles?"

"*Sí.* And for monopoles, too. People, they searched in some materials, hoping such particles had gotten trapped in the nuclei there. No success, but an idea worth perhaps investigating. As here."

John peered at the cube. It seemed diminished now, powerless, caught in the vice of a modern laboratory. He remembered how he had felt its presence in the tomb, large and looming in the shadows, full of history, a thing out of ancient lands that now rang only as legends.

He shook himself. Part of that sensation was the one percent change in local gravity, right at the surface, he reminded himself. The hands could sense that when you felt the rock, and the mind played tricks in as spooky a place as that tomb. "Yeah, well, if this thing got into the rock it must've been driven in at enormous energy, a cosmic ray or something, I figure."

"I see, piercing the soil, coming to rest in this block." Zaninetti tapped his full lower lip with a finger. Without his penetrating concentration he would have looked like any shrewd restaurant owner, assessing the tables. The narrowed eyes and askew twist to his mouth betrayed the inner mind. "Then, it chewed a chamber."

"To make the vacuum, right. That's what convinced me."

"To give such radiation, it must be converting something— the rock—into energy, at a high efficiency."

John recalled that black holes were highly efficient that way. They could take the infalling matter, with rest mass energy mc^2, and convert up to a fourth of it into heat and radiation, which eventually escaped from the hole and could be seen from outside. That was the paradigm which explained the quasars' enormously bright emission. Astrophysicists supposed that huge black holes squatted at the center of some young galaxies, drawing in stars and dust and spewing out jets of particles and copious radiation. But that was a long way from saying *any* form of space-time singularity could do that. Abe's data certainly implied that this one did. The theoretical problem was to find solutions which could describe the features of this object and still allow some energy extraction to occur. Zaninetti had already guessed this, he saw. The man was fast.

"You will publish soon?"

John blinked. He gave a little bow to Abe. "That's up to the man with the data," he said courteously.

Abe responded, "I want to be very sure."

Zaninetti said solemnly, "But of course. I respect your caution."

"The interesting question is, *where* to publish?" John added.

Zaninetti and Abe frowned. John went on, "I mean, is this a physics problem now? Or should we deal with the archeological role of the cube itself? Claire's going to want a hand in that."

Abe said, "Well, I know what you're thinking, but this splits into two problems, doesn't it." It was not a question.

"There's an archeological side to this. We can't experiment on the thing willy-nilly," John said.

"We will not destroy the cube, of course," Abe said. He smiled at Zaninetti. "The rock usefully shields us from the gammas, after all."

"Sure, but you've got to deal with BU and the others."

Abe said strongly, "Don't worry about that. Once everybody realizes what we've got here, there won't be any more nonsense from BU. I spoke to the president again this morning, and believe me, he's on our side. Totally."

John nodded. Abe was an able strategist at these bureaucratic levels. Maybe he should simply forget the politics and concentrate on his mathematics. Zaninetti had clearly seen the possibilities immediately.

In fact, John thought suddenly, maybe Sergio had sniffed out the implication in the data that he was working on. He couldn't assume it had clean slipped by Zaninetti.

Things were moving fast. Too damned fast.

He left the lab and went straight to his office, skipping lunch. There were paths to follow in the mathematics, branching and forking possibilities that only patience and intuition could get him through. Sergio had glad-handed him and made some jokes, had in fact been his famous expansive self, charming Abe unmercifully. Sergio's early career had been in elementary particle physics, where he had learned the skills of extracting needed data from tight-lipped experimenters and laconic postdocs. An NSF study had once showed that theoretical physicists were the most verbally deft of all the scientific community, and the assumption had been that this overlapped in some way their mathematical ability. Mathematicians were more apt to be good at music, but—the study argued—theoretical physics was a kind of halfway house, requiring mathematical deftness and physical intuition. Perhaps these correlated with verbal ability, the report wondered. The study had not considered the possibility that good talkers were more successful because they won over opponents and gained needed information more readily.

John knew enough to stay away from talk for a while. He needed time to stare at a blank writing pad and see where the coiling implications of equations led, in search of patterns that lay behind the compressed, deceptively simple notation. The equations of physics were not complicated in form; indeed, they were dauntingly simple, hiding complexity in recondite notation.

The mandarins of physics were those who searched for the basic laws, a hunt which took them inward to the very small—divining how the fundamental particles should work—or outward to the colossal, cosmology. Actually solving the equations in their myriad applications was a problem left for the bulk of mathematicians and physicists. Even though the basic equations describing the sun, for example, had been known for a century—Maxwell's four relations, plus Newtonian mechanics—the magnetic arches, virulent flares and torrential storms on the sun's surface were still only poorly understood.

There were two crucial facts about the cube. First, it weighed only a ton or so. With that little mass, its self-gravitational field was very, very small. But the second fact—the four-poled looping of the gravitational field—seemed to contradict this. How could so little mass make a strong, complicated field nearby?

That was the crucial clue, John thought, scratching his lip absently—those deceptively weak tugs as you ran your hands over the cube.

In human experience, gravity was always simple. Stars and planets were spherical. The solar system and the Milky Way were disks, but that was because their spinning prevented collapse into one big round mass. In all of them, a clean spherical force compressed matter.

The artifact wasn't so well behaved. It proved that a particle could make complicated gravitational fields. In mathematicians' language, that meant there had to be non-spherical solutions lurking in the basic equations.

For the last few days, ever since he discovered the second fact, John had been working on the classical Einstein equations for gravity. Everyone had always assumed solutions to those equations which gave spherical cases—stars, disks. Even the universe as a whole was conveniently assumed to be spherically symmetric.

Convenient was just the point, John saw. If you didn't assume spherical symmetry, the Einstein equations were a mess. He wrote out the more general form, one Einstein had never investigated. He stared at it for a long time, barely hearing the distant voice passing in the corridor outside. There were possibilities here. . . .

To get a contorted field, you had to find solutions which warped space-time like a standing wave. The analogy which led him was to the large, slow-moving pile-ups of water sometimes seen in canals and rivers. He had seen one in a creek near the Gulf once, just before a storm. It was an eerie stack of water, massively crawling inland on the surface of the creek. He had been fourteen and the sight disturbed him, seemed somehow malevolent. He had studied such waves since; they were called solitons. Unlike ordinary water waves, they had only crests, no troughs.

He had found some solitonlike solutions to Einstein's equations, but they had disturbing properties. Staring at them now, he felt again the boyhood uneasiness, a slight rising of the hackles at something utterly contrary to experience.

The solitons required definite mathematical forms to have a stable solution at all. This implied another force had come into play, some field which operated on an extremely small scale. Alone, solitons would look very much like ordinary, tiny black holes. They didn't have to move, like water solitons. They could stand still.

But two black holes together would immediately attract each other, merge, and make a slightly larger hole with a weight at least as great as a mountain's. That clearly wasn't what dwelled at the center of the cube, or else nobody'd have been able to even move it.

Suddenly he glimpsed the way out.

The new force solved this puzzle. Unlike gravity, it was repulsive. It stopped the black holes from forming a deep gravitational pit, by forcing the holes apart, never letting them merge.

It was an odd force. In mathematical jargon, it was a non-

Abelian type, similar to the forces which regulated the sub-nuclear particles called quarks. The only viable solutions were not the point singularities familiar in ordinary field theory. They were something stranger, more like twists in space-time than points.

The style in particle physics was to label solutions with quantum numbers, and give those numbers names, like "color" and "charm." Good terminology was scarce; now there was even "style" and "substance," used to describe obscure mathematical aspects. John decided to label his new force "fashion," just to inject a note of wry doubt. It could be all this was dead wrong.

The particles he had wrestled from Einstein's equations were massive, all right, but the repulsive force between them compensated almost exactly for that mass. Fine. In fact, he might as well take the configuration of two close-together holes and call it one particle, since that was all that could exist. Twists, he decided to call them. Twists in space-time.

He had worked until late afternoon, unmoving, seated in an old-fashioned, cushioned walnut chair. At last he stood up stiffly and surveyed the deepening shadows out his window, hearing for the first time the swish of traffic on Memorial Drive. He had something, but he didn't know what it meant. Or if it described what sat in Abe's lab.

He got up and prowled the room restlessly. He knew he was spent for the day; no one could do intense mathematics unrelentingly. The mind simply lost its edge, its ability to flit through chains of logic and dip into possibility after possibility. He was startled by the knock on his door, but not irritated by the interruption.

Claire came into his office with the same elan she'd had at their first meeting. She was wearing a modish rust-red suit with a frilly off-white blouse showing at the neck. Her nail polish matched her lipstick and she moved as though she was worth a million dollars. He remembered her from that first time with absolute recall, and was surprised to think that it had been only a few months ago. It seemed half a lifetime.

"It's cleared," she remarked brightly.

"Uh, yeah, sun's been out some," he said, his tongue feeling thick.

"No, silly, I meant your desk." She beamed and sat on the edge of it. "It's usually a mare's nest."

"I've been calculating. I always keep papers in order when they might mean something." He leaned against his bookshelves and watched her light one of the dark brown cigarettes with the gold tips. She always dressed well, but he recognized the signs of insecurity; certitude was inversely proportional to the amount of makeup. "What's up?"

She grimaced. "Hampton's building a file on me."

"To deny you tenure?"

"If he can't have me drawn and quartered first."

"Obviously the BU administration will see he's biased."

"So what? They're on his side. An affront to the university, one of them called me today."

"Come here." She did, almost reluctantly. They embraced and John closed his eyes, letting the fatigue of the afternoon seep out of him, inhaling the scent of her hair. It was not the pulse-pounding bits he liked best, but rather moments like these, when she seemed so rich and deep that he could never penetrate to the center of her. Gradually a pliant softness came into her, molding to him. The long moment held, lingered, and then broke smoothly. They kissed and separated. She put out her cigarette.

"If I only knew what to do about this," she said wanly.

"Counter-punch."

"How?"

"Hampton's gone public, blatherin' all over the *Globe*. You do the same."

"Call them up, ask them to interview me?"

"Tsk tsk. Nawthern in'lecshull rigidity. Make them come to you. General Lee used to do that all the time."

"Gettysburg was an oversight?"

"A squeaker that went the wrong way."

"How do I make them come sniffing around?"

"Give a talk. Slides of the artifact."

"At BU? They'd block it."

"Isn't there someplace better? More in the public eye?"

"Let's see.....What about the Museum?"

"Where is it?"

"You've never been to the *Museum*?"

"I'm an illiterate, antihumanistic scientist, remember."

"Oh yes, from Philistine Tech. I forgot." She broke their loose embrace and moved about the office with renewed energy. He was pleased to note that the rust-red suit fit quite snugly. "They *might*, you know.. . .The Museum has occasional public lectures. But how much should I say?"

"The whole truth and nothing but the truth."

"Really?"

"Come as clean as a hound's tooth."

"Abe might object."

"We'll talk to him."

"A lot of it's his to publish."

"Not the archeological aspects."

"I don't know. I've never really played to the gallery like this."

" 'Bout time to learn."

CHAPTER

Four

As Claire left the Boston Museum of Fine Arts she slowed, listening to the sharp echoes of her high-heeled shoes on the stone. Short of the exit she turned on impulse to the left and strolled through the Egyptian exhibit. It was not remarkable, but for the moment she felt the need of its reassurance, its solidity, its silent statement that the past endured, was still present, still meant something.

The meeting with the director had gone remarkably well. He was thin and controlled, and at first spoke so softly that she wondered if his pilot light had gone out. She had sensed within a few minutes that he was attracted to her, and it had been a strain to not use that, to keep everything coolly professional. She had known since she was a teenager that she was not a beautiful woman, so she had worked to be striking. Today's navy suit and red scarf, with matching gloves, had been helpful; she could not deny that. Still, Claire hated Charlotte Brontë's comment that she would have given all her talent to be beautiful. That condemned you always to play somebody else's game—and, when your looks failed, finally to lose.

MODEL PROCESSION OF OFFERING BEARERS, FOUND
WITH THE COFFINS OF DJEHUTY-NEKHT AND HIS WIFE
IN THE BURIAL CHAMBER AT DEIR EL BERSHEH.

245

Wooden figures carrying provisions for the afterlife. There were real supplies and implements in the tomb. Djehutynekht had assumed a direct line from this life to eternity, so they took care to take useful items along. But what modern person, believing utterly, would also take with them objects which were merely beautiful? No, the twentieth century equivalent would store away cartons of canned groceries, rifles, perhaps an electrical generator. This was what never failed to stir her—the unfathomable gulf between today's thinking and the way the ancients thought. They were truly alien, not merely innocent agrarians with a foolish faith. They *lived*, and their response to their world was deep. *And*, she thought wryly, *let us hope they were wrong about the afterlife, for a substantial amount of their belongings ended up, not in the nether world, but uselessly, in museums*.

She wandered into the Greek section, inhaling the faint, persistent scent of her beloved antiquity. Even here, under glass and tastefully lit, the strangeness persisted. The Attic waterjugs from 500 B.C. were marvelous self-referring artworks. Around one, white women in black dresses filled similar jugs from a Doric fountain-house. Water poured from animal heads; the Greeks habitually associated the movements of the natural world with animals. Behind every natural force lurked a personality, a beast. There was a subtle sensuality in the jug's large lip, the curling rear handle, the saucy side handles, the opulent, billowing body.

The jug had lasted over two thousand years in the earth. She moved to the pinnacle of the collection, a Minoan snake goddess. A petite ivory woman with a pensive and distant expression, clutching a snake in each hand. She had lain in the dust of Knossos for 3500 years, and with her disinterment would come her death. Who could believe that she would survive 3500 more years in Boston? Chance would befall her here. A collapsing roof, fire, a war. Claire and others like her were killing the past as they brought it to life, drawing it up from the safe soil and back into the harsh, fatal clangor of life.

She frowned. Such skeptical reflections about her profession were new to her. Certainly the Kontoses and Hamptons of the field inspired cynicism, but they were mercifully few. Or did they merely look that way, viewed by a woman who was at that crucial stage of an academic's career, the final push for tenure? Maybe everyone wilted a bit in that pressure cooker.

Leaving, she passed the famous torso of King Haker— hands clenched at its sides, biceps bulging, wearing only a loincloth, full of power. Headless, she noted sardonically; many of her fantasies featured a faceless man with a similar body. Now, however, she often realized partway through the dream that it was John. He had a quiet, encased force in him. This statue's tight, uncommunicative hands were the opposite of his calm, broad, sure ones.

She shook herself, glanced at the other cases, and left. The director was just John's opposite—insinuating, airy, pencil moustache, as substantial as a butterfly, full of *really! marvelous! but of course!* His eyes had gleamed behind aviator lenses, and Claire could see his mind tripping lightly through the *exciting* possibility of a *first*, with gorgeous press coverage and controversy and maybe a TV tie-in for icing. She had reacted by being even more solemn, stressing the "need" to "air the issues" and, of course, display the artifact itself, an artwork of importance. It had been easy. She was somewhat dismayed to find that even here, one of her favorite institutions, notoriety merged with importance.

She drove slowly away, following the contours of Back Bay along Fenway Drive. John's prediction of the director's reaction had been disturbingly accurate. The director had arranged a public talk Sunday night. No time for much publicity, but then, the size of the audience was immaterial; the *Globe* would be there, and probably WGBH. This was Friday afternoon, and she had to prepare slides, sharpen her arguments. Like most people, she feared public speaking. She wondered if the years of lecturing would give her that impervious manner professors wore like a badge. Then, with a pang of knotting in her stomach, she remembered that she would probably not be lecturing at all. This was the end. She might hope for an appointment elsewhere, but Boston was almost certainly sealed to her. Hampton carried that much weight.

To leave Boston. Maybe John was right about Claires One and Two, that she was constricted here. Yet she loved it. Despite the chill she rolled down her window and leaned an elbow out. Two boys were sliding down the dead grass that bordered the fens, riding on flattened cardboard boxes in the bright, clear air.

Boston. Full of seeming contradictions—the richer you were, the more threadbare your clothes; you always walked to work over the Hill to town, ignoring cabs; symphony attendance was as holy as church, and church felt like a meeting of the state legislature; a man's war record and club membership counted far more than his bank account or advanced degrees. Nothing needed to be expressly stated; everything was known. She wondered what it was like, really, beyond Boston. John's nostalgia for the South hinted that the people there were similar, steeped in the past. Perhaps it would not be so bad to live elsewhere.

Abruptly she saw that the thought had crept unbidden into the flow: John as The Future. She reflexively stepped on the brake, blinking. A horn blared behind her. Brakes screeched. Somebody sped past, swearing.

She had even felt elation when her mother, calling the day after they'd had dinner, had expressed guarded approval of John. Five years ago Claire would have regarded that as a strike against him.

She shook her head. No, she couldn't think of that. Not now.

The cement lab floor seemed to suck heat downward, chilling her legs as she crossed the remaining vacant space in the bay, her clacking footsteps reflected back by bare gray walls.

John was sitting on a lab stool, staring at the artifact. Abe puttered moodily with his electronics. "Who died?" she asked.

"My hypothesis," John replied.

"About it being a singularity?"

"No, not that. I thought the situation was steady, though, and it's not."

She bent over, hands on knees, feet demurely together, and peered at the snaking light tube where it entered the plug. "What's wrong?"

"Abe can see blobs, tiny grains of x-ray emitting stuff. They're falling into the core, along those diagonals."

Alarmed, she straightened. "The cube is falling *in*?"

"No, don't worry, we're talking about a few grams of matter. Stuff that's caught in the singularity's gravitational well and is slowly oozing inward."

"How slowly?" she asked suspiciously.

"That's the interesting part. Abe's resolved those grains for two days now, and they've moved about four millimeters."

"What? That's nothing!"

"True 'nuff," he said lightly. "What do you know that falls in slow motion?"

"Feathers."

"Yup. What else?"

"Uhhh . . ."

"I'll give you a hint." His eyes sparkled. "Relativistic effects."

"What?"

"*Exactly*. This thing's a damned grab-bag of theoretical physics. We're seeing matter, heated up by friction, plunging into the singularity. But it's so deep in the potential well that it looks slowed down to us."

She said guardedly, "You mean, that sort of thought experiment, where one twin goes away in a rocket, and when he comes back, he's younger than the one who stayed on Earth? Because he moved so fast?"

"That's special relativity, and this is general relativity, curvature of space-time—but yes, basically there's an analogy."

Abe shuffled over to them. "How long to fall all the way in?"

John became less easy-going. "Months, if it fell from the inner surface of the cube."

"We could test that, then. Drop something in."

"I suppose so. Sure, why not?"

Claire said, "Haven't we already done that?" The two men looked at her. "When John bored the hole. The vacuum sucked in some of the dust."

Abe snapped his fingers. "Of course! When was that, precisely?"

"Around four in the afternoon." John motioned. "I entered it in your lab book, there."

"Good. However, it does not explain this increase in gamma-ray energy."

Claire asked, "What increase?"

Abe stuffed his hands into the pockets of his lab jacket. "The gamma-ray flux has been rising steadily for days now. At first I thought perhaps an error, perhaps merely a fluctuation. But no, it is real. We're installing shielding."

"That's the gammas coming out through the plug, right?" John asked. When Abe nodded he said, "Couldn't it be due to the rock we took out, from the drilling?"

Abe shook his head. "No, it increases steadily, not just one jump. My idea was, perhaps it is from the dust, falling in, as Claire said. It heats up, emits radiation, we see it."

John said, "But the infall time is long, weeks at least—"

Abe said bluntly, "Perhaps your calculation is wrong."

"Not that wrong," John replied testily.

Claire sensed that the two of them had been going at each other earlier. Probably the uncertainties of their situation were wearing on them. It was not easy living and working with a puzzle that got worse every time you learned more about it. That was what research was like. But never *this* bad, never so long without some sense of the fog clearing.

And she had her own questions. Why had the ancients carved the cube? How did the singularity get inside? Had they simply discovered it that way? And why mount the amber cone? Some ritual value? Or did they look through the murky amber, peer inside?

She shrugged and put in, "Oh, I've got the report on that plug dust, by the way." She fished the papers from her large, ruddy leather handbag. "The BU lab found carbonized vegetable matter in it. Otherwise, it's just rock that's been heated, so the stratified layering is mixed up. The only interesting point is that the vegetable matter is current."

"They dated it with the radio-carbon method?" Abe asked. Claire nodded.

"What does 'recent' mean?" John asked, standing up from the lab stool.

"For archeologists, within the last century or so. Could be yesterday, for all the chemists can tell."

"So someone tampered with the cube," Abe said sourly. "This complicates—"

"Why some*one*?" Claire suddenly brightened. "Couldn't that—that singularity have done it?"

Abe said slowly, "I see no reason to suppose—"

"That would do it," John said rapidly. "Maybe when we, ah, dropped it. Dislodged the singularity a li'l, maybe?"

"Made it eject some hot matter?" Claire asked.

"And absorb some rock, too," John went on. "Which fell in. And took this much time to get close to the core, because of the time dilation."

"Warped space-time," Claire said. Then, ruefully, "Or warped imagination."

"No, it fits," John persisted. "Something shot out—clean out the back of the cube!"

"And melted the cube rock?" Abe frowned.

"Yep. Maybe incinerated some pollen or moss or something in that cave. Mixed it all together. Then the rock cooled. We see the residue as that plug."

"Which is why it's different in composition from the limestone?" Claire wondered.

Abe muttered, "You are asking detailed questions about something of which you know *nothing*."

"It's all we *can* do," Claire said sharply.

"If you ask me, you are pursuing minutae when the real mystery is immense, beyond what we can handle," Abe persisted. "I spoke again with Zaninetti, he thinks we should call in an entire team, get help—"

A loud and instantly recognizable voice said across the bay, "There!"

Claire turned, gulping for a breath in astonishment, her throat tightening, and saw Colonel Alexandros Kontos striding toward them, anger flushing his face a sullen red.

With him there were three men and a woman. All five wore Greek Army uniforms. Claire recognized sergeant's insignia on everyone's sleeve except, of course, Kontos's, who had added some braid across the brow of his high-peaked officer's hat since she had last seen it. The four followed behind him a step, all headed for the artifact. Out of the corner of her eye she saw John move to his right, shielding the cube. Abe stood still, not understanding.

"You have been very busy, you little thieves," Kontos said bitterly as he approached.

John put up a hand. "No more."

Kontos stopped. "You have a Greek national treasure. I demand to take it back."

The four behind him stopped and looked around, as if sizing up the situation. Claire saw with relief that they were not armed.

John said evenly, "Abe, call 4999."

Abe said, "What? Are these, is this—"

"Yeah. Go."

Abe blinked and stepped back into the small office. Claire realized that 4999 must be the campus police.

Kontos stepped forward, back stiffened. "You, get out of the way."

"No."

"You could be hurt."

"I'm terrified."

"You wish another beating?" Kontos asked, icily casual.

"Just a rematch."

"In a laboratory," Kontos said scornfully.

"Don't worry, plenty room for you to fall."

Kontos bristled, his jaw clenching. Claire sensed a crackling tension between them. John seemed to be deliberately taunting him. She understood John was delaying them, but surely they knew that, too, and meanwhile he was provoking them. Maybe his pride demanded that. Claire could not seem to move. She took a half step forward and stopped.

"I see you brought some help," John said. He hooked his thumbs into his belt on each hip, deliberately casual. It seemed a strange strategy, talking tough and giving posture signals of relaxation.

The woman near Kontos stepped forward and said in Greek, "He is swine." She was sinewy and held herself almost like a man, crouched and ready. Her black hair was pulled back in a single coiled braid.

Kontos gestured toward her, watching John. "Sergeant Petrakos likes your attitude even less than I. And she is a forceful woman."

"What's she do for the Ministry of Antiquities, knock down walls?"

"She has less patience than I." Kontos was enjoying this, Claire saw.

"Kontos, we've got possession for at least a few more days. Hampton agreed to that."

"We will see. Do not forget that a government is a great thing and you are a small thing."

"Gee, you're a reg'lar Delphic oracle."

Kontos said angrily, "And you—a boy."

Abe put in, "Your guards here—"

"They are assistants, diplomatic personnel. We have come—"

John said sarcastically, "Diplomats in uniforms?"

"Many of our state functions are under the Army now. But I did not come to explain to a thief." He stepped forward again, studying the cube. John moved to block him. They were still five feet apart.

"Why didn't you report the find to Hampton?"

"What find? It was gone."

"You didn't know that. You hid it."

"You are lying."

"Do you want me to explain it to your Ministry?"

"This is wasting of time." He pointed with a jutting finger. "I want to look at it."

"You want to take it."

"No. My task is to see that it is intact. If you have caused harm."

"We haven't."

"If you have, there come even greater consequences."

"What've you got in mind?"

"We throw you in prison."

"You'll have to extradite us."

"We will!"

"The USA isn't going to deliver up a citizen to your toy-soldier regime."

Claire's throat tightened.

Without warning Kontos stepped forward and struck John in the chest. The blow staggered him and John twisted away, taking Kontos's second punch on the other side, grunting. Kontos shuffled closer, agile, and John blocked another blow with his forearm. Kontos was driving him back.

All the Greeks moved at once. Claire stepped forward and Sergeant Petrakos barred her way, snarling something in guttural Greek.

Kontos sent a fist into John's face, glancing off his cheekbone. John flinched away and then set himself. Kontos came on. John feinted with his left and with sudden speed sank his right fist into Kontos's middle, twisting to put all his weight behind the punch.

Kontos stopped, eyes glittering. The punch did not seem to have damaged him. John was plainly on the defensive.

Kontos struck again and rocked him back, then followed with a chop to the ribs. John gasped. Breathing heavily, John swiped at Kontos and barely caught him on the shoulder.

"Hey! Hey there!"

The campus police.

They swarmed into the lab, brown uniforms separating the two men and warning the Greeks to stay away.

She had ignored the other Greeks during the fight, and they seemed to have watched without any doubt that Kontos would provide an amusing show. Now the campus police tried to straighten out what had happened. Kontos loudly proclaimed diplomatic immunity. Abe accused him of starting things. John stood silent, rubbing his ribs, panting.

Claire said, "Alexandros, we will return the artifact and share all our results."

He turned glittering eyes on her. "It is too late for that. We will have that, yes—and more. From you."

His cold ferocity nearly made her flinch. "But you don't have to—"

"We will have justice!" The sight of her seemed to have brought the rage back, congesting his face, flaring his nostrils. "And no American will work a Greek site again."

"That's too much—"

"*Ever*," he said harshly.

"Look—"

Smoothly, Kontos turned to the police and said, "I lodge a diplomatic complaint. Against this man—this boy—and your university."

John said sourly, "What nonsense."

Kontos's eyes danced and his mouth twisted into a knowing, superior smile. "We are not finished, you and I."

CHAPTER
Five

John's ribs ached. The doctor said they weren't cracked, just bruised. Still, he felt lousy—beaten, frustrated. The next morning was Saturday and he went for a walk before meeting Zaninetti for their work session. The crisp chill helped dissipate his shamefaced irritation.

Kontos was fast. He fought well. He always seemed to catch them off guard. He knew how to make a lot of trouble. John hadn't the slightest idea how to stop the man.

So, as he had so many times before when faced with real-world problems, he buried himself in mathematical physics.

Zaninetti was as quick as a whip. John saw that immediately. He had perceived the importance of the two main facts—the lightness of the cube, and its complicated gravitational field. However, Zaninetti had concentrated on the particle physics aspects, rather than start from classical relativity, as John had.

"Why that?" Zaninetti demanded. His scholarly style was combative, always demanding that people explain themselves, keeping them off balance as they tried to placate his scowling skepticism. "The clue is the quadrupole, yes? Start from there, look for particle symmetries. Pick the right group theory, you have it!" He ended with a grand opera gesture of triumph.

John decided to be distant and casual. Otherwise, he would have to out-shout the man, and that wouldn't be easy. "You sum these diagrams

$$R_s = \frac{G}{mc^2}$$

$$\rightarrow \lambda$$

$$\rightarrow \frac{\hbar}{mc}$$

quark-like bound state?

$M \approx 100$ kg!

lab measurement!

can get the symmetries straight out of the classical gravitational equations."

"You have the particle spectrum calculated, then?" Zaninetti was mock-incredulous.

"Well, I can't get the masses, no, but—"

"Then it is nothing! The mass, we must get a mass that is small."

"Sure, smaller than a mountain. But I think my solutions—"

"That way, you cannot find a crow in a bowl of milk!"

"I got the quadrupolar field out," John said adamantly.

Zaninetti instantly dropped the extravagant manner. "What symmetries? Gravitation, it is not easy to get complicated fields from that."

They began filling the blackboard in John's office with equations. Zaninetti swiftly saw the utility of using soliton solutions. Within an hour they had convinced each other that the other's approach was not wrong, only different. John had started by considering tiny black holes, while Sergio had begun with particles in a flat, uncurved space-time and worked up to larger masses, using the wide range of mathematical techniques he commanded.

In a sense, the merging of these points of view was inevitable. Zaninetti's quantum-mechanical attack rested upon regarding particles as wavelike. The characteristic wavelength of a particle was related to its momentum, and very high energy particles had very small wavelengths.

Taking a different tack, John had begun with the necessary radius of a black hole, the Schwarzschild radius. For a black hole with the mass of a mountain, the Schwarzschild radius was invisibly small. No one would ever directly see such a small object; they could only watch matter fall into it and be heated up, and measure the resulting radiation.

When a particle's wavelength became smaller than the Schwarzschild radius, the disciplines of gravitation and particle physics merged. The minimum mass where this occurred was scarcely a thousandth of a grain of sand. Still, for fundamental particle physics this was incredibly huge, a million million million times the weight of a uranium nucleus.

The crucial point was that approaches developed for gravitation blended into those used to describe tiny particles. John termed his solutions "twists" with an added force, from the "fashion" quantum number. Zaninetti used particle jargon and different mathematics. The two men spoke different languages but came to the same conclusion.

"Is still funny," Sergio said pensively. "Cubic twisting of space-time. Uh!" He grunted aesthetic disapproval.

"Any matter that falls in, it has to travel around the edges of this cubic folding."

Zaninetti scowled. "Sprangle sees that, yes? The cubic structure, it looks like a square to Sprangle, because he is seeing it along a symmetry axis."

"Right. If the twists carry some currents, it also explains that multipolar magnetic field I found."

"Ummm." Zaninetti looked unconvinced.

"So what bothers you?" John put down his chalk and awaited the onslaught. Sergio's style was to speak quietly, then to explode an objection with rapid slashes of the chalk across his opponent's neatly written equations, obscuring them completely.

"I don't like this feature," Zaninetti said bluntly, pointing to an equation describing the force between John's "twists."

"So? There's an attraction between them."

"It is like quarks, see? In the laboratory quarks are always bound together by this force, tight."

"Sure, but this force isn't so strong."

"*Sí*, that is some help. But what keeps these twists, these singularities apart?"

"I don't know."

"I think we have here only part of the solution."

"The thing in the cube fits this one-twist model," John said patiently, sure he was right about that.

"You are crafty, eh?" Sergio's eyes shifted liquidly from the convoluted equations to John. "You ignore the fact that these twists should attract each other, cancel these nice cubic forms you have found."

"Let's say I put it on the back burner for now."

"My mathematics shows they must come along for the ride."

"Oh, right. But I think that's just an alternate choice."

"Something is different about this strange twist of yours. The thing in the cube should not *be*. It should have matched up with another twist and made something different. More stable than this."

"Maybe some other force that intervenes? Keeps the twists apart."

To John's surprise, Sergio did not launch an attack. Instead, he sketched quickly with yellow chalk some abstruse symbols. "Perhaps, perhaps. Only an *idiota* eats every berry that pops off the bushes. You must take from the mathematics carefully. Many solutions, they look good. . .but nature does not want them." He stopped, staring pensively at his drawing. "They should attract, should marry each other. Quarks, they do not exist in isolation. We are missing something here. What? A puzzle."

Zaninetti still followed the habits of his home country, and so left around 1:30 for a large lunch rich in pasta and wine, with a *riposo* afterward to recover. John worked on, nibbling virtuously on nuts and some Castilian oranges, all bought at absurd expense in a fancy, Boston-insiders' market on Newbury that Claire frequented.

The point that troubled him had also struck Zaninetti. Suppose, as the equations said, this new attractive force, operating on truly microscopic scale, did disguise the masses of the small black holes. The system achieved a balance by taking a huge attractive potential energy, and subtracting from it a nearly equally enormous repulsive one.

What if they got out of kilter? How fragile was the balance? A slight mismatch, and the particle could lose its stable cubic space-time formation. If only a little of its mountainous mass was annihilated, it would produce a stupendous explosion. Far worse than a hydrogen bomb.

At the moment the singularity was perched at the center of that stone cube, apparently happy to remain suspended in its vacuum cavity. It floated there, kept aloft by some residual forces, perhaps magnetic in origin. It must have sat there for thousands of years without breaking out. Then the fall down that shaft had upset things.

John suspected that the stability problem was now the most important aspect. He was worried about Abe's steadily higher readings of gamma-ray flux. Did that mean a rise in activity, perhaps enough to destroy the balance of forces inside? Or was the rock being eaten away? It occurred to him that the gamma-rays might be destroying the light pipe. That could break the seal open.

He tired of calculations in late afternoon and decided to go jogging along Storrow Drive despite the chill. He called Abe, told him the worries about the light pipe, and promised to come into the lab before noon tomorrow, Sunday. He put on his running things without any sense of anticipation. Exercise in winter's frigid grip was an effort of will, a building of moral character appropriate for the land of Cotton Mather. Muscles stretched unwillingly and sweat evaporated, leaving a prickly cake. He jogged along the river beneath the unblinking scrutiny of Beacon Street picture windows. The sky was cobalt blue and his breath made great plumes as he ran along the black pathways of the Esplanade, eyes glazed, mathematical notations drifting uselessly in his mind.

Much as he liked working with Sergio, he was wary. A major figure could move into a subject and appropriate it by bringing to bear better mathematical techniques, or simply by publicizing it, talking it up, working out further ramifications. Give an invited talk at an important conference, highlighting your own approach. Edit the first book on the subject; books are always referenced by the editor's name, so you eclipse the actual authors. The early days of black hole theory had seen such maneuverings. Lacer, the American who first proposed electrodynamic methods of extracting energy from black holes, found himself relegated to the sidelines as a competitor took up the subject, using his superior skills at boundary value problems, employing his connections in the astrophysical community, and simply traveling and talking more. Though John liked Sergio, he would have to be careful to keep his work distinct from the prominent Italian's.

He joined Claire for dinner. She was wound up by the preparations for her lecture the next day. She had spent the day working on it at the Hilles Library at Harvard, leary of going to BU. The Hilles was empty except in exam time, when the undergraduates suddenly rediscovered it.

The Museum had insisted that the cube itself be displayed, but Abe ruled that out immediately. This had meant long telephone calls and a final compromise: Claire would show a few slides of the cube in its present state, even though it was mostly covered by Abe's diagnostics.

"I'll shoot some photographs in the morning," Claire said, lounging back in a wicker chair at her apartment. "That'll give the Museum time to make the slides. Go over with me, won't you? I'll need help with the lighting."

"Sure."

"Thanks. God, what a day." She stubbed out her last cigarette and looked longingly at the butt. "There's so *much* to put into the talk. I have no idea what significance the cubic form has. And that metallic stuff at the bottom of the chisel marks—I *think* it's due to paint that was caught in there, and the gamma radiation from inside the cube transformed it, made it glisten. But I'm not sure yet. Should I include it?"

"Might as well. You don't have to nail down every corner of the grand tapestry, y'know."

She nodded and sighed. "Also. I got a call from my mother."

John said diplomatically, "Ummm?"

"She saw a notice about the lecture. She's coming."

"Good. You'll bowl them over, have the city at your feet."

She grimaced. "Or my throat. I'm afraid Kontos will show up."

"Could be. He'll probably take diplomatic action by Monday anyway."

"I'm sure he can get the artifact back."

"We'll face that later." No need to let her dwell on it. "What's it matter if Kontos comes to your talk?"

"He can leap up in the audience and denounce me. Create a scene. That'll make an even better news story, and he knows it."

"Get that Museum director to stop Kontos at the door. Assign a security guard to him."

"Maybe put out a contract? Break his legs?" She smiled wanly, peering into the flames of her living room fire. It snapped energetically. "I guess that bothers me more than Kontos, you know? Looking bad in front of my mother."

"You'll be a smash."

"How'd you like to have *your* mother attending your talks?"

"She'd stop listening after the first ten minutes and take out a romance novel."

Claire chuckled. "That's how those southern girls handle adversity? Lapse into fantasy?"

John said guardedly, "They have their strong points."

"Such as?" There was an edge to her tone.

"Fewer conflicts about—what're they called?—traditional roles."

"Why didn't you bring one along up here to keep you warm?"

"Low boredom threshold."

"I see. Yet I see you at dinner parties talking to women about their children, not a common practice in razor-sharp, competitive Cambridge."

"Aw shucks."

"You prefer stiff-necked northern women?"

He smiled sardonically. "Fire and ice. Flashy combination."

Later, getting ready for bed in her bitterly cold bedroom, Claire said, "Turn out the light."

He picked his way among the fragile antiques which threatened to disintegrate at a heavy, masculine touch. Her study was efficient, Spartan, but the bedroom had frilly blue curtains, flowery wallpaper, ample cushions and even a yellow stuffed giraffe. He switched off the bureau lamp, his skin prickly from the cold, and returned to bed, kneeling momentarily in the darkness to find his way.

She said, "Here's a trick I'll bet those aw-shucks girls don't know," and he felt a warm circle enclose him, tighten, flex deliciously.

"Aw shucks," he said.

CHAPTER

Six

Sunday's silence was oddly unsettling in the streets John knew only during bustling weekdays. They parked in a small lot with chain-link borders and walked three buildings down Vassar Street. Clouds blotted out most of the sun and a cutting breeze gusted up from the Charles. The quiet seemed to hang nearby, a hovering buffer against the hum of the city beyond. They took a shortcut between two anonymous buildings and John let himself into a side corridor of small offices in Building 42, using the key Abe had given him. They walked down a short hallway and turned a corner toward the laboratory bay. John had to unlock the side door. He turned the knob and stepped in ahead of Claire.

Sergeant Petrakos was standing fifteen feet away, looking straight at them. John stopped. Claire, unable to see, butted into him.

Beyond Sergeant Petrakos he instantly took in a frozen scene: Two men in blue jeans maneuvering the cube into its crate, using the ceiling hoist. Kontos, holding the cord for the hoist control, his face startled. Another man at the far end of the bay, where the hoist track ended, working at the lock on the big vertical lift doors there. All wore blue jeans and plain cheap shirts, the jeans tucked into military boots. They were, of course, the team which had been here Friday, sizing up the place.

Kontos swore. Sergeant Petrakos compressed her lips and snapped into a defensive posture like something from the movies—feet at right angles to each other in a kind of T stance, and arms forming another T, left arm high and horizontal, right arm below it and vertical, hand open. John looked at her rigid hands, thick and calloused.

None of the men moved. The cube dangled from its chains, encased in padding, nearly submerged in the wooden case. Into the silence John said, "You could've won it all diplomatically."

Kontos said, "Your system? It would rob us. Like the Elgin marbles."

"Times have changed."

"You stole it yourself—you and the bitch."

"Rescued is more like it."

Sergeant Petrakos made a hissing sound, her breath squeezed out between lips drawn back into a thin, bloodless line.

Claire stepped to the side, speechless. Kontos looked at her. "I believed Americans went to church at this time. Or slept off their drinking."

John opened his mouth to say something and Sergeant Petrakos took two steps forward, moving tightly, and kicked him expertly between the legs.

He had never fought with a woman before, hadn't even been in anything serious since high school, and she took him completely by surprise. A wave of sudden nausea swept up into his belly and the pain following it jolted him into a split-second awareness. He had an irresistible desire to double over, to clutch for the part of him filling now with lurching, sick agony and a bottomless weakness. He had been hit this way three times in football scrimmages. The worst was the stabbing pain and emptiness coming together, the terrible fear like lightning scratched across a black sky, making you curl up, a little boy again.

He doubled halfway over and knew that if he did not do something Sergeant Petrakos would damage him a lot more. He had seen it in her eyes, the set mouth—eager expectation, looking forward to something she was going to enjoy.

He sensed that if he straightened up she would hit him, probably chop him with those hands. His left foot was forward, barely catching his collapse. He slid his right foot out and kept doubled over, head down, until he had his balance and some forward movement. Then he came up from the floor fast. He looked up to see Sergeant Petrakos near, too near, gazing down at him with a look of satisfaction. His left hand came up and caught her on the shoulder, slapping her sideways, surprise coming into her face.

Her right hand struck him a numbing blow on the chin, off target a fraction so that the hard edge of it glanced off, not delivering its full punch. She aimed the heel of her hand at his neck. He shifted heavily to the left, trying to look off balance. His right hook came around and over her guard and landed solidly at the hinge of her jaw. Sergeant Petrakos dropped. She was already off balance but then her legs went out and she fell solidly to the concrete, cracking her head.

John stood up fully and let the blood rush of pain wash over him, trying to put his mind far away from it and not succeeding very well. Sergeant Petrakos was dazed but not out; still, she would not be capering around in the near future. Neither would he. She had used the most devastating opener there is against a man, but then she had watched the effects rather than following them up. On most men it would have worked. Not on a quarterback who had taken a lot of dumpings from 250-pound linebackers, even if he had been only second rate and not worth even a hustle from the college scouts.

There was a lot more to do, he realized dimly, but when he managed to focus Kontos was walking across the lab with an automatic in his right hand. John leaned against the wall and hugged himself, breathing deeply to try and make the spreading pain go away. Claire said something to him and shouted at Kontos.

She lunged, ignoring the pistol. Sudden fear leaped into John's heart. His eyes riveted on the pistol. Kontos stepped wide, dropping the muzzle down, and cuffed her hard across the jaw. Claire yelped angrily and staggered. Kontos swore at her and struck again. She dodged and hit him square on the nose. A man came up behind her and grabbed for her arms. Kontos backed away, one hand cupped to catch the blood dripping from his nose, the other leveling the automatic, his face red.

He swore in Greek. The man's eyes were cold, his mouth twisted. The automatic aimed at Claire's heart.

"Kontos! We quit!" John shouted.

Kontos paused, seemed to think. He brushed at his nose, grimacing, and lowered the automatic.

Claire twisted against the man holding her arms. "You—"

"Claire, leave it be," John said.

They were all panting, staring white-eyed at each other, aware of what had almost happened.

John breathed deeply. His legs trembled. *Well, all right*, he thought. *The play was over, no yardage. Minor injuries, a little shaken up. Just breathe.*

"This is stupid," John said bitterly.

He and Claire were tied to chairs in the small computer terminal room. Kontos had assigned Sergeant Petrakos the job of tying them, and the woman had wrenched the knots tight with evident pleasure.

"Kontos, you can't get away!" Claire called.

Through the glass partition they could see the cube, fully crated now, being lowered onto the bed of a blue quarter ton Ford truck. It had taken the Greeks less than ten minutes to decide what to do about Claire and John, finish the crating, raise the steel doors at the far end and back their truck in. They operated smoothly and with a minimum of talk. John had to admire their professionalism; the entire operation, even with interruption, would take less than an hour.

Kontos came into the office and nodded approvingly at Sergeant Petrakos's handiwork. "You will be discovered soon, I expect," he said. "But not soon enough. We will fly away by then."

"You'll never get it through customs," Claire said.

Kontos sniffed. "A paperwork issue only. I have also taken the laboratory notebooks here. You will apologize to Professor Sprangle for me. He is not to blame for this but he must suffer."

"Listen," John said, "all this cops 'n' robbers is fine, but this isn't about archeology anymore, Kontos, it's more important. That—"

"Our national heritage is the greatest in the world. We will fight to preserve it."

"You're talking like a press release. I—"

"It is you who will be explaining to the press. There will

come unkind questions." Now that he had acted, Kontos was more dignified, though his persistent half smile betrayed his enjoyment.

"Look, that cube is important for physics reasons, too. You should know it could be dangerous."

"Only to people who steal it," Kontos said, amused.

"Like you?"

"We are reclaiming it. Under express orders of our government."

"When we're through with the measurements—"

"That was an obvious tactic, a stupid one. You would wait and explain and find a million reasons for delay."

Claire said quickly, "Donald Hampton must have explained to you—"

"That we must wait, yes. Donald is a trusting man. But there are many reasons for the American government to keep such a beautiful thing. They insult us by keeping it, perhaps, yes?" Kontos's eyes glittered. "But not now."

"Inside it," John said. "there's something we do not understand. I believe it might be a—a new kind of particle, potentially unstable. It's already putting out a lot of x-rays, and it's eaten most of the way through—wait, the light pipe. You pulled it out?"

Kontos was puzzled. "The flexible tubing? Yes."

Claire said, "Then you heard it. The vacuum."

"One of my men removed the tubing. I heard nothing. There is a seal, apparently where you took a sample."

John said quickly, "That's the self-sealing collar Abe put around the light pipe. It'll fill in the hole. But there's dangerous radiation. . . ."

Kontos glanced at his watch and nodded to Sergeant Petrakos. "Obviously, it has not hurt you. We will study this thing in Athens. If it is interesting for physics, is better still. Friday, Hampton remarked to me that this find could make us famous. Better for it to be in Greece, then." He left.

Kontos shut the door after him, to dampen their shouts. They both called after him as he marched across the lab, eyes scanning for anything useful he might have overlooked. Through the glass they watched the truck pull away and the men quickly lower the steel door, letting it bang loudly. In a moment came the distant sound of a revving motor. Then silence.

"Shee-it," John said softly.

"I cannot *believe* he would—"

"Well, he did. Point is, what do *we* do?"

"Remember Friday, the way he was so unpredictable? You two blustered at each other, but all the time his team was figuring out how to come back, break in—"

"I repeat, what do we *do*?"

"Try to work these chairs over to the desk? Knock over the phone? Dial the police with my tongue?" Claire snorted.

"If only Abe comes in early," John said. He worked his hands around but Sergeant Petrakos had secured them well, using nylon rope.

"He might," Claire conceded. "The police could spot that truck."

"Especially since I saw the license plate number," John said. "It was reflected in that stainless steel plating on the spectrometer—see over there?"

"Marvelous! Their flight can't leave immediately. There's a lot of paperwork for shipping something that heavy air freight. A call to Logan—"

"How's your tongue?"

"Good point. I can't even move this damned chair."

John sighed. He was sore between the legs and still feeling nauseous. He couldn't get his feet free enough to lift the chair and move it. All the solutions that movie detectives used didn't seem to apply here. Maybe a university cop would come by on his rounds, but that was probably infrequent on a Sunday. Kontos had undoubtedly had some way to find that out, too. He had channels.

"One good thing," John said.

"What could possibly be good about this?"

"No need for you to be nervous anymore. Kontos won't show up at your talk tonight."

CHAPTER
Seven

Mr. Carmody from Washington was a good dresser. His thick brown hair was cut close and his shoes gleamed with fresh black polish. He sat comfortably at his desk, careful to not blunt the creases in his gray double-knit suit. On his coat rack, Claire noted, a jaunty narrow-brim hat right in line with fashion sat atop a russet topcoat.

They were on the eighth floor of the JFK Federal Building between Cambridge and Congress Streets. The heating didn't seem to be on during weekends. Claire shivered. Mr. Carmody had apparently appropriated the office with a two-minute phone call. As a testament to his power it was impressive. Thick carpeting, maroon drapes to offset the pastel walls, even a couch. He had just finished telling them about how disturbed the State Department was about all this, which was why he had taken the first flight in from Washington.

"This is a small matter, or at least it seemed to me, until Dr. Zaninetti spoke to some figures in the administration," Carmody said. He threaded his hands solemnly. In contrast to his immaculate clothes, his face was pock-marked and rough, a rhinestone in a golden setting.

"He did?" Claire was surprised.

"Must've gotten right on the phone," John said.

"Dr. Zaninetti has a theory that this object, the stolen object, may be dangerous." Carmody looked for confirming nods from them.

Instead, John said forcefully, "It's not his theory, but he may be right. I've done a lot of thinking about the problem, more than Zaninetti, and yes, the singularity at the center of the cube is probably in a precarious equilibrium."

Claire sighed. She knew what came next. Carmody asked the predictable questions about singularities and John replied—how big? (infinitesimal); weight? (a few hundred pounds, no more); binding energy? (megatons of TNT); why did it stay in the cube so long? (trapped in magnetic fields produced by the iron inside the cube).

Carmody asked how the ancients had found it, and Claire said that it must have made some sound or given off light when a piece of stone fell into the singularity. She pointed out that the amber cone was translucent; perhaps they were awed by the occasional bursts of light from inside. There weren't any solid answers yet.

Then discussion returned to binding energies. As John struggled to convey the provisional nature of his calculations, she thought ahead about tonight. The lecture was certainly going to have a dramatic conclusion now—an announcement that the cube was stolen. And strangely, the hubbub of the day had made it impossible to be nervous about giving the speech. She had her slides, and now felt no need of rehearsing. In popularizing a scientific development it was always crucial to sail the narrow strait between the Scylla of professional contempt and the Charybdis of public befuddlement. Perhaps, then, she could err on the side of strait-laced professionalism, relying on the public drama to provide human interest.

Abe had found them about an hour and a half later. The first police to arrive were two bull-necked clichés in a squad car. They studied the steel drop door intently for clues, as though they had never seen one before; and then stood around looking bored. A detective from the Cambridge station appeared, not particularly excited either. He had called the airport quickly enough, but there was no record of anyone shipping a large object to Greece. They were looking into other destinations. Meanwhile the airport police were on the lookout, and so forth.

Beyond that the police were not vastly concerned. Compared to a weekend load of traffic accidents, break-ins with colateral violence, and a sniper incident nearby in Somerville, losing an old piece of rock was not pulse-pounding stuff.

Claire had called Hampton, who was suitably shocked. He professed no knowledge of Kontos's true plans, and emphasized that he, Hampton, had made quite plain the need to let the physics measurements go on at MIT for another week. Hampton had gone on at great length about Kontos's reputation, about how it must be some terrible misunderstanding which had forced the man to do this.

Only Zaninetti had been agitated at the news, and had acted, using the full weight of his contacts in the National Academy and probably elsewhere. Zaninetti was at this moment trying to get more action from the local police.

"Mr. Carmody," Claire interrupted John's carefully phrased explanations of the physics. "You are from the State Department?"

"No, I obtained my information through them. Until today they were handling this as a diplomatic difficulty."

"Then what do you represent?"

Mr. Carmody smiled disarmingly. "Let's say I'm a general kind of troubleshooter. I size up situations when the bigger agencies, well, they might take a little longer to get men in place."

"So somebody thinks this could be dangerous," Claire said flatly.

"If Dr. Zaninetti is correct, and Dr. Bishop, then this, ah, singularity is a potential, well, bomb."

"And the Greeks got out of the country with it."

Carmody shook his head. "Not through any airport near here. A private plane, perhaps—though I do not understand how they could get it through customs."

"Kontos could fake the papers," she said. "I did it once."

Carmody raised his eyebrows at this revelation, but said nothing. Then he pursed his lips and murmured, "The truck, however, we have located."

"Where?" Claire asked.

"On a street leading into Logan."

"They *must* have taken it out by air."

"But the air freight authority says—"

"What about private planes?"

"Those must go through the same procedures. There has

been no sign of the Greeks, or of such cargo."

"Check again," Claire said adamantly.

"Ah. Well, this also indicates they cared little about whether the truck was found quickly. After what Kontos said to you about flying away, he knew we would look at Logan first."

"So you figure," John said, "they thought they'd be far gone by the time you turned up that truck."

"Yes. A mystery. They went into Logan, but they didn't fly out."

"No," Claire said, "the truck ended up there. Where we'd expect it."

Carmody sucked on his teeth. "And they took the artifact elsewhere?"

"Yeah," John said. "Any damn where. Where's the truck from?"

"Hertz."

"Uh." John scowled. "If they transferred the cube to another truck . . ."

"Doesn't that seem like a lot of trouble, when you're trying to get away?" Claire asked.

"These people took pains. They planted bugs all over that lab of yours. My people just found half a dozen."

John said, "What? To eavesdrop?"

"Right. They heard your ideas. Undoubtedly knew you weren't planning on working there Sunday morning."

"Damn!" Claire said. "That fight."

"What?" John looked puzzled. "Oh, I see. While Kontos and I went at it, his people planted the bugs."

"I *thought* there was something odd about the way that happened," Claire said. "He seemed so damned smug."

"So what? He's always that way," John said wanly.

Carmody said, "Depending on how much you said to each other in the lab, Kontos knows some of your ideas about the singularity. That it might be a weapon." He regarded them steadily, as if expecting some reaction.

"Weapon? I never used terms like that," John said.

"Good. It occurred to Professor Zaninetti."

"Look, we don't know enough to even imagine how such a particle could be used that way," John said. "It's all speculation."

"Kontos has real pros with him. Sound intelligence people. Hell, we helped train them, I imagine. Given time, they'll figure this out."

John said, "Even if they do, it's a big leap—"

Carmody tapped the desk. "With the Russian nationalists moving divisions around, the Turks surly, and the depression, this region's a tinderbox."

"But that's just local politics," Claire said.

"We don't want anything as explosive as this getting into the wrong hands. In the eastern Mediterranean, there are plenty of them."

John said with a touch of impatience, "Point is, where's the artifact? Can't your men track Kontos?"

Carmody smiled wanly. "We're stopped cold."

"There must be something simpler," Claire said. "I mean, maybe Kontos changed his plans, after we caught them."

"I'd say 'caught' isn't the right word," John said ruefully. "More like the other way around."

"No, I mean, he couldn't be sure we hadn't seen the license plate of that truck."

"Or that somebody might get it when they drove away," Carmody agreed.

"This is too confusing," Claire said.

Carmody said, "And not our proper function. The police know more about such things, though of course this is not your customary burglary."

"We could look at other ways to get out of the country," John put in.

"Drive across into Canada?" Carmody asked. "The police will routinely—"

"No, by sea. Just sail away with it."

"Ummm. Seems a slow method for someone running from the police."

"Kontos has unusual resources. Greek freighters all over Boston Harbor, for one." John looked at his watch. "Claire, it's getting around to that time."

"What time?"

They told him about the lecture. Carmody scowled. "No, you can't do that."

"Why not?" Claire demanded.

"You're not the only scientists in the world. Kontos may

be a fool, but others won't be. This thing may have enormous implications, and it is *missing*. If it is unstable, and could be in Boston, could be anywhere—you see?"

Claire could, which was unfortunate. She had counted on her talk to get her reputation back, or at least to stem the tide of gossip now running through every archeology department in the country, if not in the world.

She began to explain this, but Carmody shook his head. "You must understand that your interest, and the archeological aspects of this, are secondary." Carmody sucked on his teeth again, a habit which was beginning to annoy her. "National security interests demand that you not speak. In the end, perhaps in a few days, we will probably have it back. *Then*"—he beamed—"then you can tell all. Is that too much to ask?"

Yes, she thought, and ground her own teeth. But there seemed no way out. In one day she had lost her artifact and her chance to speak out.

CHAPTER
Eight

At least his sore ribs were better, John reflected ruefully as he crossed the Charles the next morning, a clear sunny Monday. Everyone had forgotten that particular humiliation, the way Kontos had not only bruised John, but had done it as a cover for planting bugs. It was that last bit that really stung.

He put it out of his mind. His telephone had jangled for an hour this morning with calls from friends who had heard rumors. Abe got through to say that Zaninetti wanted a meeting right away at the lab, to get their story straight. Obviously it was going to be closely scrutinized by Carmody and then, inevitably, the press. Hampton had already agreed. John called Claire and left.

He saw a crowd at the entrance of MIT. They spilled onto Memorial Drive beneath a hard gray sky. TV units paid them the attention and respect now automatically given to any mob with a cause. For a moment he was afraid the news had broken, but as he crossed the Harvard Bridge he could see the placards were filled with the word NUCLEAR, usually written in red with orange outlining to indicate, perhaps, radiation.

As he worked his way through the crowd, which had begun chanting, a woman approached with a large placard and a sheaf of propaganda. The placard said:

NUCLEAR POWER = NUCLEAR WAR =
NUCLEAR MEDICINE

She said, "Will you join us?"

"How do you feel about the nuclear family?" he replied, and walked on.

A few weeks before he had been reading a student senior thesis on the history of science in this century, and had found some of it surprising. In the 1930s people wanted to become radioactive. It was the newest buzz word. Radium could help cancer patients, of course, but that wasn't all. Many thought that a little radioactivity was a healthful stimulant. Spas proudly advertised the natural radioactivity of their waters. You could take radium by capsule, tablet, compress, bath salts, liniment, cream, inhalation, injection or suppository. You could eat mildly radioactive chocolate candies, then brush your teeth with radioactive toothpaste. The manufacturers claimed that their nostrums would give relief from tuberculosis, rickets, tumors, baldness and flagging sexual powers.

Now society was suffering through the backlash. Everything nuclear was tarred with the same brush, uniting Luddites and pacifists and the anti-anythings, Quixotes tilting at satanic mills. John shook his head. It was sad, in a way, because the true stupidities of the age lay elsewhere. To him it was madness to burn precious oil to provide electricity, like making coat hangers out of platinum. What was becoming clear now, only as the oil supply visibly dwindled, was that oil was more valuable as a lubricant, particularly at high temperatures, and there were no good replacements. But this was a subtle argument, unlikely to charm the sign carriers. He sighed. Imagine what this crowd would make of the singularity. He sighed again.

And ran straight into the camera crew at Abe's lab. They were waiting impatiently outside, one leather-jacketed man pounding on the steel doors. They saw him approach and turned to shout questions. John used his key on the side door and slipped in before they reached him.

Donald Hampton came striding forward to greet him, "I want you to know how shocked I am at all this attention."

"*You* brought those TV people?" John asked sharply.

"Well, after Claire's call, I had to notify the president of our university, and he—"

"Great. Do they know anything about the physics aspects?"

"Well, all things considered, I had to account for the fact that the artifact was not returned immediately, and I repeated something of what Abe had said, but—"

"Oh God."

Claire was talking to Abe. John told Hampton to go out and deal with the damned TV crew, since he was the leak, and to talk only about archeology and the regrettable theft. The others were gathered around the forlorn spot where diagnostics waited in an expectant circle for an artifact that wasn't there.

As he approached Claire said, "Ah, you got rid of him. Saves me the trouble of scratching his eyes out."

"Okay, look, he made an error—"

"Impossible. To err is human."

"—And there's nothing we can do but cover it over, not alarm the almighty media."

Claire asked, "How is your jaw? It looks terrible."

John touched it gingerly. "Stiffened up overnight." He spoke with teeth clenched to reduce movement. "Closest I'm going to get to a Harvard accent."

Claire smiled affectionately. Abe's white caterpillar eyebrows arched and he pressed on, "I much agree, no TV. Those bastards have got my data. If I can negotiate its return before this gets onto the idiot tube, perhaps then there comes a chance to get it back. Also, if it is as dangerous as you and Zaninetti say, we should inform the Greek government."

They all agreed. Abe added, "My x-ray and gamma-ray counters, I checked them, too. That is part of the story. They registered a rising flux, steadily going up in time through Saturday night, until it was snatched."

"On all counters?" John asked.

"No, the ones over here show about three times the average count rate." Abe walked to five counters that covered a quadrant. His herringbone jacket bulged with electrical instruments he had absently pocketed and forgotten. "The cone was pointed this way, you remember."

"Yes . . ." Claire said slowly. "We were looking at emission from the plug, and I suppose we neglected the cone side."

John studied the count rates at each detector and frowned. The maximum was along the cone axis, which was unsurprising—less rock to stop the emission. But why was the strongest radiation along the cone, rather than the plug? "The singularity is giving off radiation preferentially in one direction," he said.

"Does that mean it's sucking in more matter from one side than another?"

"I'm afraid so. Maybe it's chewing away at the rock on the inside now."

Abe said, "Despite the fact that the dust from the plug boring came from the opposite side?"

"Right."

"You think it's...getting more unstable?" Claire said quietly.

"Yes." It was only a reasonable hypothesis, not a certainty, but he couldn't think of any other interpretation.

"We should tell our Mr. Carmody," Claire said.

"Yes."

Carmody already knew. He arrived moments later and dealt with the TV crew immediately.

"You sure didn't have to fool with them much," John said as Carmody came back inside the lab.

"No problem. My men took care of it," Carmody said. He wore a trench coat and didn't remove it, as though he wasn't going to stay. A sedate red tie showed at a button-down collar. He didn't even take off his all-weather fedora.

"What'd they tell the crew?"

"Whatever works," Carmody said, clearly closing the topic.

John introduced him to Abe and then Hampton, who stood somewhat apart from the others, looking out of place but unwilling to leave. Hampton plainly saw this was important, but he didn't know what was happening and nobody bothered to tell him.

Abe quickly explained their data and conclusions. He phrased things in the usual scientist's way, using sentences sprinkled with "seems probable" and "working hypothesis" and "perhaps." Carmody was not a man who liked uncertainty. He scowled and asked, "The strongest counts are that way, to the northeast. That mean anything?"

They assured him it did not.

"You believe that thing, that singularity, may be breaking out of the rock?"

"Yes," John said. No point in being overly provisional.

"I talked to Professor Zaninetti this morning. He estimates the minimum mass of the 'free configuration,' he calls it, at an equivalent of a hundred megaton hydrogen warhead. You agree?"

"Yes." That was a reasonable ballpark number. It all depended on how the components separated, and how efficiently they converted their mass-energy into other forms, but Carmody didn't want to hear all that.

"All right," Carmody said, as if making a decision. "Do you have a secure telephone on this campus?"

When John looked blank he said, "Never mind, I'll make a patch through in the car. Come on." He waved at Abe, Claire and John, ignoring Hampton.

"Where?"

"The docks. We have a lead on Kontos down there."

John realized they were not going to the Boston docks only when they stopped to pay the toll at the Callahan tunnel. Carmody was still talking on the telephone in the front of the sedan, sealed off behind a formidable transparent partition. There was an impressive array of communications gear up front, and the Lincoln Continental had a special lumbering solidity about it, as if it weighed more than usual. They could scarcely feel the inevitable potholes on the Boston streets, evidence of extra shock absorbers.

They emerged in East Boston, a mile south of Logan Airport, and immediately turned right onto Maverick Street, past three-storey houses that despite their age were well kept up. They turned south and entered a zone of moldering warehouses and gas stations and seedy diners. Within a few blocks the driver slowed to let the following car, this one's identical twin, catch up. Then he turned left and stopped at a long pier. The air had a salt tang and trucks labored past.

Carmody got out without looking back to see if anyone was following. He strode directly into a brick building with

BRECKENRIDGE DOCKING over the doorway. From the following car came several men in long coats. They stood by the cars and looked around. During the trip over the three academics had been isolated in Carmody's back seat and knew nothing of what was happening. Since no one stopped them, they went inside.

The entrance was dominated by a broad counter littered with papers. An Irishman in overalls stood behind it, looking interested but confused. Carmody was talking to a lean man dressed in a bulky overcoat that didn't fit very well. John wondered if he was carrying a gun under there. Carmody turned, as if noticing them for the first time, and motioned to Claire. "Dr. Anderson, if you'd have a look at this."

The lean man was holding an account book. He spread it on the counter. "Do you recognize this writing?"

Claire peered at it. "Yes, I believe so. Those messy t's and a's, I've seen them. Kontos wrote his entries like that at the site. I had to decipher them for the inventory."

Carmody looked satisfied. Claire said, "This is a receipt for docking charges. They had a boat here?"

The Irishman, leaning across the counter, said, "Yeah, a beat-up old towboat. Nothing much. Greek registry."

"When did they leave?" Carmody asked.

"Look right there in the book. Noon, Sunday."

"They load anything on?" Carmody asked.

"Somethin', a crate, yeah."

"Without clearing the harbormaster?"

"They must've, papers was in order."

"Load it on deck?"

"No, down the hold."

Claire said, "Of course they wanted to keep it out of sight. They unloaded here, then drove the truck to the airport, where we'd expect to find it."

John said, "So they got away."

"No," Carmody said, already walking out of the place. "Their boat went down off Castle Island. That's how we backtracked it to here."

Boston's inner harbor is not lovely, particularly on a chilly winter's day. Castle Island is a stub of land jutting up from the south and defining the mouth of it. South of there is City

Point Beach, where people who cannot bother to travel south toward Quincy go for picnics. Today the bleak stretches of rock and sand that made the crescent beach were deserted except for four scuba divers who had just come ashore. John wondered why anyone would go diving on a day like this until Carmody got out of the front of the Lincoln and marched down toward the four.

Carmody had been on the telephone all during the drive back into Boston and then east on Summer Street. The traffic had eased up on Broadway and they made good time. When Carmody put the phone back into its clip he just stared straight ahead, not attempting to tell the three in the back seat anything. John was beginning to feel like a prisoner being taken to police headquarters.

They followed Carmody again, this time with five men from the other car who didn't look alike but gave the same feel—solid, unperturbed, alert. Offshore, a large motorboat slowly churned north. There were two more divers standing at its stern.

Claire said, "Did you notice yesterday, Carmody didn't actually say where he was from?"

"Sure did," John replied. "He mentioned the State Department, but he didn't say he was one of them."

"Who are these men, the FBI?"

"Not their jurisdiction."

"The CIA?"

"Maybe, but they don't get involved in internal stuff like this much."

"Then who—" But now they approached the divers, who were examining debris. Some of it had obviously washed up on the beach and was wallowing in the swell. The divers were turning over some painted planking. The boards looked scorched at one end.

"Looks like it burned," Carmody was saying to one of the divers.

"There's a big hole in the stern, right below the hatch," the diver said. On his wet suit was stenciled ARDITTI.

"That's what sunk it?" Carmody asked.

"Looks like."

"But there was a fire."

"Not much of one. These pieces burned for sure, but inside the hold there's not much damage."

"The fire opened the hole?"

"I dunno. Funny-looking, not like your typical wreck. I mean, no extensive damage except for this one hole, like I said."

"You can get down to it easily?"

"Sure, it went down in sixty, maybe seventy feet of water. Murky, though." Arditti made a face. From the smell coming off the water John gathered it was more than murky.

"Any trace of the crate?"

"Nossir."

"Any bodies?"

"None so far. Tide'd carry them by now, though."

"Check the vessel thoroughly."

"Yessir."

"Recon the area, looking for the crate. Careful of the radiation. Get more men. I'll have the Harbor Patrol seal this area off."

"Yessir."

Arditti's bearing was military and respectful. He asked no questions, just spoke to his team. They started putting their tanks back on.

Carmody sighed and turned to the academics. "We got a report from the Harbor Patrol. Nobody saw the towboat go down, as nearly as they can tell. It was Sunday, nobody around, but even so, it would've had to go down fast to escape notice. A civilian up by Castle Rock reported it. Harbor Patrol had it in their activity list. One of our men saw it, called me. I sent a diving team out. The Harbor people would've gotten around to it if a craft had turned up missing, but probably not today. The divers identified the Breckenridge receipts on board, still in the captain's log."

"A captain always takes his log with him, doesn't he?" Abe put in.

"Not this one. Probably had to jump for it. If your hull opens you're swimming before you know it."

John said, "Do you think they drowned?"

"No, the wreck's only four hundred yards off shore. They could swim it."

Claire said, "The person who called in the sinking, did they see survivors?"

"No, but their view was impeded, they said. Could be the crew got off earlier."

"Then where are they?"

"Probably where they were going—a Greek freighter, the *Pyramus*, that just happened to be hanging around out past Nantasket."

"But their boat was sunk."

Carmody shrugged. "They could hire another. They have credit cards, a fake ID—Kontos used them on Breckenridge."

"Or they could go somewhere else."

Carmody shook his head, thinking. His pocked face was red in the chilly air, as if he were unusually warm. His eyes were round, excited, but he still spoke in the measured, solid way he had yesterday, unflappable.

"Why not?" Claire asked.

"The *Pyramus* turned out to sea at dusk yesterday. I just got a satellite to take a peep. It's headed out at top speed."

"You can't be sure," John said.

"We're checking boat rentals now. Their credit card names will turn up."

"Can't the Navy stop them?" Abe demanded. "They're *thieves*."

Carmody shrugged. "Board them on the high seas? Contrary to international law."

"Why bother?" Claire asked, turning toward the bay. "They left the artifact out there."

CHAPTER
Nine

Claire stared down at the dirty gray waters of the inner harbor. She remembered how, when a ship went down, planes were always reported to be looking for an oil slick. Well, no problem here—the whole bay seemed to be covered with a thin blue sheen. Plus plastic bottles of Orangeade or laundry bleach, wrappers, dead fish, brown water-logged driftwood—even something like a pale snakeskin that she finally recognized with a shiver of disgust.

She turned away from the sight and leaned against the railing. They were on a large, flat-bottomed barge, its deck stacked with diving and trawling gear. Men worked among the jumbled piles of equipment. The harbor was now sealed off from normal transport and occasionally a news helicopter churned overhead, only to be warned off. For several miles around on the gray waters, motorboats of every type churned in a grid pattern, searching. Divers surfaced, made their reports, and dove again. A slow swell rocked the barge. The afternoon wind cut by her and she hugged the down vest one of Carmody's men had given her. It was adequate, but not by much.

Sergio Zaninetti came staggering along the deck, though it was not rolling. He looked green.

"They find it soon, I hope," he said between clenched teeth.

"You'll get your sea legs," she said.

"Never. I always fly, never by sea."

"They're covering the whole harbor, it will take time."

"When Carmody called I came without thinking. After an hour I am exhausted. What is your saying about this sickness? First you think you will die, then you fear you will not?"

"Yes. What happens when we find it?" Claire asked, bowing her head into the sharp wind.

"Carmody thinks he knows a way. He says, the divers cover the opening with some special *plastique* substance."

"What if it is out of the artifact?"

He shrugged. "Trap it in some fashion."

"You seem blasé about the problem."

"No, only sick." He managed a thin, queasy smile. "These things are beyond my competence. I calculate the field theory, the probable bound states, that is all."

Claire watched the gangs of men preparing a fishing boat for a run. The big winch lowered trawling nets and grapplers down into the boat's stern. A diesel engine surged, moaning. "What's this difficulty you and John are having?"

"A detail, I think, but bothersome. We get solutions that have this cubic funniness to them. That we can do. It only comes when the particle had a kind of concealed mass. The new force we have, it cancels the mass. Good. That agrees with the fact that the cube, it did not have a large weight. You understand?"

"I think so, at the level of—what does John call 'the cartoon approximation.' Gravity attracts them to each other, but this new force, called fashion or whatever, keeps them apart."

"*Sí*, good. That is the picture one gets from a rough calculation. I am faster at some of these mathematical tricks, however, and I have gone ahead with a better field theory, one with not so much hand-waving in it."

"Hand-waving?"

"When we talk, rather than calculate. Italians, they are supposed to be good at this, *sí*?" He gestured dramatically and grinned despite his pallor. Claire saw he was trying to be gallant and entertaining; she gave him a smile in return, to help him forget his nausea.

"Indeed."

"The mathematics gives us pairs of John's 'twists.' But they attract each other and should"—he smacked his palms together—"make a lump. This is the trouble."

"The thing in the cube, it couldn't be the lump?"

He shrugged. "Perhaps, but I do not know what the stable properties are. How do the twists come together? There is energy stored up, so that must be given off."

"You think the singularity in the cube is alone?"

"It is well described by John's first work. So that solution he found, it seems OK. But why is such a particle allowed to be free? It should find its mate."

"Maybe there's something blocking it?"

"Ah, you have gotten that idea from John. *Sí*, it may be that another kind of force is blocking the mating of these. Still, I must say finally, I cannot find any such funny force. Something is wrong."

Claire was alarmed. "Then can it be some kind of potential bomb? You told Carmody that."

"*Sí*, that I believe. It is hard to see how two of these twists could have a stable way to bind together. They must yield energy when they come together."

"But one of them sat safely in that cube for thousands of years."

Sergio pursed his lips. "That I do not understand. There are so many uncertainties here—"

John's voice at her elbow said, "Science isn't certainty, Sergio, it's just probability."

He had come back from his meeting with Carmody in the barge's grimy cabin. He had on a pea jacket from one of the men and she was mildly surprised to see he looked quite natural in it, as though he fit in with all these others. She said, "He says your first solutions are, uh—"

"Misleading," John said jovially. "I still think we've got a handle on the basic properties, though. Hell, I constructed the dynamics so it would agree with that artifact's properties. I *legislated* it."

Sergio revived from his watery look of only moments before. "You cannot argue with the force between your twists, though! *Comprende?* The force is independent of the distance between them, so stupendous energies can be stored. They should come back together with a bang."

"Come on, mathematics can't be done on an open deck," Claire said decisively. "Let's get coffee."

Sergio turned white at this suggestion. Claire noticed that

despite himself John smiled at his colleague's distress. They were friends, but always looking for an edge. A perpetual rivalry machine.

The coffee, dispensed from a hastily assembled kitchen at the bow, was acrid. John dumped three packets of sugar in his and insisted on circumnavigating the deck. Sergio sat on a rickety chair and looked longingly at the solidity of Boston to the west. After a while he closed his eyes.

"A diver just came in with some debris," John said, striding along, left hand stuck into his pea jacket, right cradling a styrofoam cup. "It looks funny—singed."

"Burned under *water*?"

"Right. As if it's been heated up, but didn't catch fire, of course."

"Where was it?"

"Scattered over the bottom. It's old wood, not from Kontos's boat."

"So the cube is moving around down there."

"Carmody figures the artifact burned a hole through its crate and then through the hull. Fast, too."

"Then the currents—"

"No way they could move something that heavy."

"So the cube should be somewhere near the Kontos wreck."

"Sure. Only it's not."

"What makes it move?"

"I dunno." He looked out at the searching motorboats that dragged trawling lines.

"I wonder if it'll even stay in the harbor."

"Sure. For a while."

They came to a group of men laboring with dragging nets. Some were Harbor Patrol; Carmody had been able to muster the entire force within minutes. They were solid-looking and worked steadily. Other than calling instructions or questions, the teams were remarkably quiet and earnest. Claire shielded her eyes against the sun, which had begun breaking through the leaden sky, and squinted at the barge's cabin. More of the other kind of men were there, most of them in three-piece, pin-striped suits and overcoats, shoes well polished and faces blank, watchful.

Arditti, still in diving gear, came up to John and said, "Got a little something to the east."

"What?"

"Funny currents, like you said."

When Claire looked puzzled John turned to her. "Carmody asked me for some kind of signature and I said look for a disturbance in the water flow."

"Why didn't he ask me?" Claire said.

John shrugged. "It's crowded in that cabin. He—"

"Currents? How much water can get through a hole a few inches across?" Claire asked sternly.

"Enough, maybe."

"Wouldn't it be better to look for radioactive substances being carried away?"

Arditti said, "We're doing that too, Doctor."

"And?"

"There's some sign of them, yes."

"Good." Mollified, she went with them amidships, where Carmody was talking to the men in pin-striped suits.

"—Want a team of six divers moving toward it, while we get a grappler into position. Everybody uses a Geiger and sends a reading back every two minutes. I don't want unnecessary exposure. Get going."

The men broke into groups, some returning to a radio setup on the aft platform of the barge. *Their speed and certainty was unnerving*, Claire thought, as though hesitation had been trained out of them.

Abe was with Carmody and when he saw Claire he said, "Did you hear? They turned up Kontos's signature at a fishing rental place down near Columbus Park. Only a mile or so south of the beach."

"So he did get ashore," Claire said.

"Yes, and four others, the rental agent said. The agent's pretty mad. They didn't bring his boat back."

Claire gazed toward shore. Police had isolated the waterfront areas and she could see cruisers with their winking lights blocking every intersection near the water.

Carmody looked older out here under gunmetal-gray clouds, his pocked face like parchment. Claire remembered a quotation from some famous Bostonian, *A man of fifty is re-*

sponsible for his face. Abruptly she asked, "Who *do* you represent, Mr. Carmody?"

He peered dourly at the academics, who were standing together. His hands shoved deep into his overcoat pockets, he sucked on his teeth for a long moment and then said gruffly, "National Security Agency."

"You look after emergencies?"

"Bad ones, yes."

"Who do you report to?" John asked.

"The National Security Adviser."

"And he?"

"To the President."

"I wondered why everybody was jumping around here," Claire said.

"Not just here," Carmody said mildly. "I've been on the phone to Thorne at Caltech and Sherman at Berkeley. They agreed with your results, they said. In principle, anyway."

John said, "How'd they find out?"

"I had Zaninetti write up a summary. We transmitted it last night."

"Checking on us."

"Of course. Unfortunately, the people we wanted to ask weren't all American citizens. I didn't feel I could tell them everything. So we have to go mostly by your estimates."

A helicopter buzzed over the barge, as if to underline the forces Carmody could summon up. "Thorne said something about the total energy requirement for this singularity," Carmody remarked. "He didn't see how it could come out of cosmic rays, the way you said, Dr. Bishop."

"Well, the energy you need to make one of these is large, yes. That's why they're dangerous—when they blow, there's hell to pay. They're not produced often, no."

"How many might be around?"

John shrugged. "This is the first ever. There can't be a whole lot, or we'd have seen one before this. But then some highly energetic particle striking the earth—it would penetrate very far. There might be more of them deep inside the earth. They wouldn't necessarily migrate to the surface."

Carmody twisted his mouth in concern. "You think this might've come up from below?"

Claire put in, "Come on, that's crazy. It was inside an

ancient artifact, remember? The Mycenaeans carved the rock around it."

"But before that?"

John shrugged. "They got it somewhere. Maybe found it in a quarry. Claire thinks the fact that it's a cube is no accident. The optical patterns do look cubic. Maybe the Mycenaeans bored into it, saw something bright inside, and carved the artifact as some sort of container."

Claire saw her chance. "That is why retaining as much of the stone artifact as possible is *essential*. We must understand the history of it. You can't separate that from the physics."

To her surprise, Carmody seemed to accept this. "Dr. Sprangle here thinks it still might be inside the rock."

Abe said, "It was eating its way out slowly, remember. Now, Kontos may have jarred it while he was loading it aboard, disturbed the equilibrium."

John said, "And it burned away that seal of yours?"

"It's a good guess," Abe said.

Carmody looked sourly out at the sea.

"Red buoy!" a man called.

Half a mile away a red ball bobbed. Carmody said, "They've got it."

"To the east," John said. "It must've moved at least two miles from the wreck."

Carmody hurried off. Arditti was leaning over the radio setup nearby, listening with earphones to the divers' comm line. When he was through Claire walked over and said, "Are you sure?"

"Yes, Doctor. It's the crate."

"They can see it?"

"A man got in close. Says it's giving off a lot of blue light."

Claire asked, "The cube?"

Abe said, "That'll be down-graded radiation, probably."

John asked, "From gamma-rays?"

"They'll be stopped in water pretty quickly."

Claire ignored this. "The cube is still in the crate, then?"

Arditti nodded. "Guess it was packed in pretty tight. The thing's dragging the crate with it."

"Like a snail and its shell," Claire said distantly.

"Kind of," Arditti said. He was an angular, direct man

who clearly was enjoying this chase. His team treated him with automatic respect. "They found it by following a rut in the bottom of the bay. A straight line, they said."

"Pointing which way?" John asked quickly.

"They didn't say. Look, I got to go." Arditti moved off. Claire felt the increased tempo around them. She was the only woman on board and there was something fervently masculine about the prickly excitement on deck.

Carmody looked grim. "Is it going to blow up?"

John answered, "No, I see no reason why it should. That's hard radiation they're running into, though. Should be careful."

John began explaining how the in-rushing water probably kept the singularity from leaving through the narrow hole it had opened. It also gave the singularity a powerful new injection of fuel for its central "engine," which would have drastic implications. Claire listened and nodded and hoped he was right about it staying in the cube.

She watched as the barge turned laboriously into the quickening wind and made for the spot where now three red balloons floated. Motorboats ringed the site, bobbing in the choppy waves coming in from beyond Nantasket. Divers jumped from the boats and formed groups. From all directions boats converged and the radio beside them squawked with questions. A team of divers maneuvered a large flat sheet into position on the surface. It was slick but not buoyant. They took it down, releasing the supporting flotation tanks.

"That's the patch they'll try to slap on it," John said.

Sergio, aroused from his torpor, leaned on the railing with them. "They should spend little time near it," he said wearily. "Even the water will not stop all the high energy particles."

Minutes dragged by. Claire breathed in the salt tang and listened to the squawk-squawk of the radio comm across the deck. The divers' talk was unintelligible to her but she could feel the rising tension. There were shouts over the comm as men called to each other down in sixty feet of murky coffee-colored water. The barge turned so its bow pointed away from the scene and everyone moved to the aft deck, peering overboard, straining to understand what the teams of divers were doing. Men surfaced over the site and then dove again but it all seemed chaotic to her.

Then a man on deck cried, "It's holding! They got it!" and a cheer went up all around the site. There was a zest she had not felt since undergraduate football games, when she had gotten carried away and cheered, forgetting for the moment her firm conviction that such events were essentially pointless.

"Up to the bow! Everyone!" Carmody's voice boomed over the ship's comm.

They crowded up toward the cabin and she saw why. The grappling tongs and cables were already lowering into the water aft of the barge, directly over the site. Divers were scattering away from the spot. More indecipherable barking came from the deck radio. The men crowded around it seemed able to follow the overlapping babble of hoarse calls.

The diesel engines below deck began to whine. "Got it! They've got it. It's holding," a man shouted. Answering cheers.

The lines tightened, snapping a spray of water into the air. Motors surged powerfully. Cable drums rotated, drawing up the burden. The deck became silent as everyone stopped to look aft.

Carmody ordered the divers away and without hesitation they scrambled aboard their motorboats. The boats churned away, the divers standing in them, gazing back.

Arditti approached Carmody. "Got a man with a big reading on his exposure badge."

"Bad?"

Arditti nodded. "Got too close. Says he feels woozy."

"Get him treatment right away."

It took several minutes before the leading edge broke the oily surface. Cabling and grapples obscured it, but Claire could see the crate was partly there. One face was completely covered by a creamy patch. The patch lapped onto the other faces and she could see where the crate was broken away. Still, it held together. The crate still sheltered most of the artifact. There might be a great deal of the cube left to study.

Now it was free of the water. The men on deck stood silently. It seemed far less dangerous now, hanging forlornly in air, a bedraggled thing of soaked and muddy wood.

Then John was saying something, shouting, and Claire wondered what could be so dramatic. The crate was simply hanging there—but no, not quite hanging straight. It made an angle with the vertical.

"*O Dio!*" Sergio cried. "I told you! Only we didn't calculate—"

"The separation!" John finished for him. "The two twists don't have to be grouped together. It's a bound state, but what's the binding length, right?"

Claire turned. "What are you talking about?"

"See that? It's not hanging straight because something else is exerting a force on it."

"Pulling it off to the side, you mean?"

John beamed. "Yes! The mathematics is right. There *do* have to be two twists bound together. Only not so close, is all."

"So?"

"There must be another one."

CHAPTER
Ten

The helicopter's rotors went *whunk-whunk-whunk-whunk*, blotting out conversation. With an airy lightness it lifted off the wide foredeck of the barge. Claire looked down at pale upturned faces. Men were bunched up amidships, away from where the crate rested on the aft deck, as Carmody had ordered. A team was covering the muddy brown crate with a tarp and securing cables to the far corners, carefully staying away from the patch the divers had put on.

"I don't like leaving Abe there," Claire shouted.

Carmody shrugged. "He's best qualified to carry on the investigation of the physical properties."

"How long will that physical sciences group take to get here?" she asked.

Carmody glanced at his watch. It was a complicated thing with several simultaneous readouts and a schedule monitoring program, the red dot winking that he was late for some appointment; he ignored it. "They'll be loading at the dock now." He peered out the plexiglass window and pointed. "There."

Claire saw several trucks parked parallel on a long pier beneath them. Police cars blocked the entrance from spectators who clogged the street beyond. Men were offloading large packages from the trucks, using forklifts, and running them onto the deck of a long barge. They moved swiftly, dispersing the packages according to a grid pattern on the barge deck. Also on the pier was a long white house trailer,

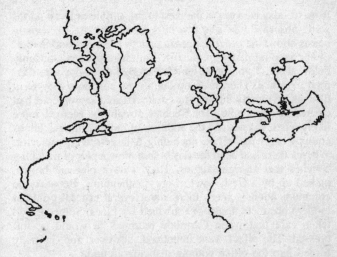

unmarked, without doors or windows along the sides.

"Mobile lab and scientific recon group," Carmody said blandly. *As if he saw one every day*, Claire thought. *And maybe he did.*

"How far off will they take it?" John shouted beside her.

"The crate? Thirty miles, minimum."

"You think that's safe?"

"You tell me, Doctor," Carmody said mildly. "You and Zaninetti calculated that binding energy. That yielded the radius of the fireball, if the thing should go off—right?"

John nodded. Claire felt a sudden chill at this matter-of-fact acknowledgment of what they were dealing with.

"That is assuming the entire mass-energy can be converted," Zaninetti said reassuringly, noting her concerned expression. "Probably is much less than that."

The barge carrying the artifact was already steaming out through the mouth of the harbor. Its bow cut a V across the calm outer waters. As the helicopter turned north Claire could barely make out the pale dot that was the tarp over the crate.

They headed directly into the heart of Boston, over late afternoon traffic jams. New Atlantic Avenue looked like a parking lot, grid-locked. She had never been in a helicopter above Boston, and the chance to survey the entire sprawl,

from woodsy Newton in the west to the jumble of Lynn northward, absorbed her. The few hills seemed to rise like bristly
beasts above the orderly, patient pattern of streets and homes.

The landing pad atop the JFK Building appeared suddenly
below them. Two armed guards escorted them down to Carmody's office. There was no one in the corridors they went
through; evidently this was an exclusive area, or someone had
cleared it of people. The second possibility seemed more
likely when she noticed the addition of more communications
equipment in the office, including a large-screen projector.
Where chairs had been the day before, now a pair of matching
couches met at right angles. They were a pleasant brown,
picked up by a fresh bowl of chrysanthemums. Between the
communications screens there were several tasteful prints of
modern abstracts, mostly in subdued icy blues. Someone had
taken care that when Carmody returned he would be impressed. The effect went unnoticed, however, for Carmody
forged into the office without glancing around.

There were several men in dark suits in the office, sitting
at new consoles, some speaking into hushphones. No one introduced anyone else. People asked Carmody questions and
he answered swiftly, coolly, laconically. The big wall screen
filled with a still photo and it took Claire a moment to realize
the swirls were clouds against the background wrinkled skin
of the sea. In mid-frame, half-obscured by a gray mist, was
an elongated dot: a ship.

"The *Pyramus*," Carmody said. "She turned south several
hours ago." He listened again to an ear plug. "Probably heading for Bermuda. That's the nearest non-US port."

"Why not sail to Greece?" John asked.

"He's following the news. The Turks hit some Greek naval
vessels about six hours ago. There's going to be a war."

"Damn," Claire said.

"Not that it matters." Carmody put the plug down. "Kontos isn't important anymore. Compared to what the artifact
could do, even the Turk thing isn't much."

"The latest round in a five thousand year long grudge
match," Claire said sourly. "A fresh crop of Agamemnons."

"What I want from you two"—Carmody gestured at John
and Sergio—"is a clear description of what this, this second
object is. And *where* it is."

"Is like a quark," Sergio said earnestly. "Only, the binding distance, it can be very, very large."

"How large?" Carmody asked.

Sergio shrugged expressively. "In particle physics, usually we mean an atom, that's already big. But obviously, here we have a different kind of scale."

"So?"

"What he's saying," John put in helpfully, "is that quarks—the particles with fractional electric charges—are in principle independent, only we never see them isolated. That's because they attract each other with a force that's independent of their separation. So if you tried to pull them apart, you'd have to add more and more energy. You can't pull two of them apart by more than an infinitesimal distance. That means they always appear to us as larger particles, two quarks clumped together."

"I'm not following this," Carmody said a trifle impatiently.

"Well, it's all a little bizarre," John admitted. "See, the mathematics said this singularity of ours should have the same kind of force between pairs. A force that doesn't get weaker as you pull them apart."

"Like these quarks."

"Right. What's been bothering Sergio and me is, how come we can see a single singularity. Why doesn't its partner, its—"

"Twin?" Claire asked.

"Okay, call it the twin. We asked ourselves, why isn't the twin attracted to the singularity, and they combine into a new kind of bound state? That could be stable, our mathematics proves that."

Carmody asked, "How come you know the thing in the cube isn't two of these things already?"

"The cubic fields, they are the signature of one singularity," Sergio said. "Two looks different. Might even be spherical."

"Maybe that's the way they were inside the cube before?" Claire asked.

"Before what?" Carmody asked sharply.

"Before we, uh, moved the artifact."

"Packed and shipped it?"

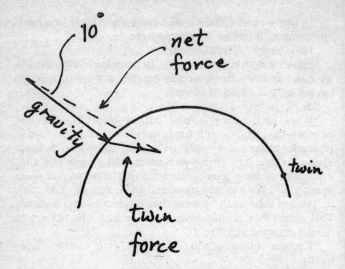

Claire said delicately, "There was an accident. It fell down a shaft in the rock and split open the crate."

Carmody asked, "That could dislodge these twinned singularities?"

Sergio said, "Conceivably, *sí*. The point is, our mathematics shows that the force between the twins is constant. So the angle the artifact makes with the vertical is a direct measurement of the force. Here—" He walked to a blackboard on a side wall, picked up yellow chalk and began to draw diagrams. "Here at Boston, the artifact feels two forces. One is gravity, down. The other is the twin force, off at an angle, pointing to the twin."

"What's the angle?"

"I do not know where the twin is, so this angle, it is unknown," Sergio replied. "If the twin is exactly on the other side of the Earth, then the twin force just pulls down, adds to the gravity. But we know the artifact is swung out about ten degrees or so, correct? So the twin is not below us, in China or something, it is somewhere else."

"Somewhere northeast of here. That's the way the artifact was hanging," John said.

"You noticed? Good! Then I draw the twin here, at some point on a circle that goes around the earth."

"A great circle," Claire said.

"*Sí*. The twin force pulls your artifact like this, to the side. Say the twin is very close, so the pulling, it is nearly parallel to the ground. Horizontal. Then from the fact that the hanging angle is about ten degrees, we know that the pulling to the side, it is about ten times weaker than gravity."

"Not very strong," Carmody said.

"*Sí*, for subatomic particle force it is nothing," Sergio agreed. "The theory says it should be weak, but how weak is hard to tell. All the time, John and myself, we worry about what keeps these twins from finding each other. We thought, perhaps there is some adjustment to the force. Something that screens it. But the right answer is, we were stupid, and there is nothing blocking the force. It is a weak force and the twin, it is simply a long way away."

"How far?" Carmody asked.

Sergio shrugged. "Kilometers, thousands of kilometers, we cannot say. We have only the angle."

A man appeared at Carmody's elbow and whispered something. "Okay," Carmody said, and the big screen across the office instantly filled with a picture from the deck of the barge they had just left. Arditti stood in the foreground.

"I wanted to show you this, sir," Arditti's voice boomed from speakers in the corners of the office. A man adjusted the volume. Arditti held up a map. Claire saw it was a navigator's map of the Boston Harbor. There were a half-dozen big red Xs marked on it, all along a line from Castle Island out toward the mouth of the harbor. "I got some teams to backtrack the path of the crate. It moved straight as you please, see?"

"Any radioactivity in the track?"

"Yeah, it's a kind of groove the thing cut. Gets deeper the farther out you go, too."

"Which direction was it headed?"

Arditti turned the map and looked himself. "Ah, I'd say about thirty degrees north of east."

Carmody nodded decisively.

Arditti added, "Only reason we found the thing was it

started spewing out a lot of radioactivity. Must've slowed down some at the end. It was nearly buried in the mud."

"Heading deeper," John murmured.

"What?" Carmody asked.

"It was burrowing in, moving toward its twin. Look at Sergio's diagram. The force pulls it sideways and down, see?"

Carmody's eyes widened. He turned toward the camera mounted unobtrusively in a bookshelf and asked Arditti, "Can you see that blackboard?"

"Nossir, I got no visual return unit here. I can get one set up in—"

"Never mind. Can your divers tell me what angle the cube was making with the bottom? Measure the depth of the trough it left back at Castle Island and then close to where we picked it up."

"Yessir."

Carmody cut off the image and looked at his watch. "Another hour before the barge nears the safety zone." He shook his head. "Maybe I should've had it flown."

"To where?" Claire asked. "Anyplace they could land would still be in danger."

"Yes, but the barge is taking it east, toward its twin, right?" Carmody said.

The others looked surprised. "Right," Claire said, "but that twin could be a long way—"

"And it could be right below the barge. We don't *know* enough."

"I don't think those depth measurements will tell you a lot," John put in. "The cube was meeting a lot of drag in that mud. It won't make a nice clean angle, the way it does in Sergio's diagram."

Sergio grunted assent. "Too messy down there."

"Look," Carmody said impatiently, "this is all hypothetical, I realize, but why should I care about this twin anyway?"

"Because they are trying to be united," John said. "They'll move around until they find each other."

"Then we should just let the artifact go?" Carmody demanded.

"No, I'd say not," John answered. "It's too dangerous.

Look, now that I understand the theory, I can say that our fears were misplaced. It won't willy-nilly explode, because it's a simple particle, not a conglomerate, the way I first thought it was. But when it meets its twin—well, I don't know."

Sergio said, "I expect the reuniting, it might yield a lot of energy."

"A lot?" Carmody insisted.

Sergio shrugged. "Look at the energy you have stored in it already. The airplane that took the cube away from Greece, every meter it went, it was storing energy, like winding up a spring. Separate the twins, you have to do work against their force."

"But you said the force was small," Carmody objected.

"Yes, small, but the distance! From here to Greece is what?" He looked at Claire.

"Five thousand miles," she said.

"Okay, it is like you took a rock that weighs as much as a man, and you took it five thousand miles out in space, starting from the surface of a planet that has about one tenth of the gravitational pull that Earth does. Then let go. It falls down—five thousand miles—bang!"

"I see," Carmody said. "A lot of energy."

"You misunderstand," Sergio said, shaking his head. "That is nothing compared with the energy which can be released when two of John's 'twists' collide. Then some of their mass can be converted to energy. Gently brought together, OK—they make a bound state. But with one smacking into the other—"

"I see."

Claire got up and went to the bookshelf. There were standard reference works on it, neatly arranged. She found a large Rand McNally Atlas and thumbed through it. There was a projection map of the Atlantic basin and she studied it as the men argued about the energy yield if the twin singularities struck each other at high speed.

Something Arditti had said intrigued her. She fished a pencil from her purse and used the edge of a dictionary as a straight edge. Laying the dictionary at an angle of about thirty degrees, with one corner at Boston, she drew a straight line across the Atlantic basin. It extended up through Newfoundland and across the ocean. Going further, her pencil entered France near Bordeaux and because of the curvature of the Earth then ran southeast. It sliced across the toe of the boot of Italy and plunged into the Aegean south of Athens. She felt an odd chill.

"It all fits," she said.

Carmody, alert, said intently, "What?"

She showed him the atlas. "Even though Mycenae is due east of here, a force acting between two objects doesn't have to follow the curve of the Earth. It slices through, like so. I took Arditti's angle and drew it, that's all."

Carmody finished for her, "And it passes through Greece."

"Yes," she said. It was a minor point of geography, but she was glad to have discovered it when the men were throwing around so much high-powered math. "So my idea was right. The twin is in Greece."

"*Was* in Greece," John said. "It's been moving ever since, I'll bet. Drawn by its twin in the cube."

Carmody asked, "Then where is it?"

"Somewhere along this line," Claire said, tracing it with a polished fingernail. "Inside the Earth."

"It can eat anything," Sergio said. "*Tsssuup!*—It sucks in all. Rock, water. So it makes its way."

"It's boring a hole?" Carmody asked with disbelief.

John said, "It must be. The one in the cube will, too."

"Why's it in the cube at all, then?" Carmody wondered.

"It formed some kind of temporary equilibrium in there, I guess," John said. "Its magnetic fields were strong enough to keep it cradled inside—I calculated that a couple of days ago."

"But it's getting out now," Carmody said.

"Kontos knocked it around, that probably helped," Claire said.

"And the inflow of water kept it pinned in the cube, after the wreck," John added.

"What's holding it in now?" Carmody asked.

Claire saw where he was leading. "The patch. The singularity will *eat* the patch and break loose."

Carmody nodded to an aide. "The barge."

Within seconds Abe's voice, tinny and distant, filled the

room. Claire was amazed how quickly the men in the room sensed what Carmody wanted and arranged the complicated communications. Otherwise they kept silent, watching and listening. She had the uncanny feeling that they had been trained for precisely this event, or else adapted to emergencies with amazing quickness. As Carmody asked Abe for an update on the cube she looked at John. He was drawn and concerned, staring at the pencil line on the map.

"Yes, I am getting more gamma-rays from the patch," Abe confirmed.

"Damn," Carmody said emphatically. "Monitor it. Abandon the ship if—"

"No, wait," John broke in. "Have him turn it."

"What?"

"Turn the cube so the patch is facing southwest. That'll pull the singularity away from the patch, help slow down the damage."

Carmody brightened. "Hear that?" he called to Abe.

"Yes, but I don't under—"

"Just do it," Carmody said briskly. "My men are listening in, give them the directions."

"It'd be even better if they rotated the cube slowly," John added. "That'll make the singularity work on different parts of the inside of the cube. It'll take longer to break out."

Carmody talked to men at the barge, discussing how to move the cube. He gave orders that any crew not working directly on the cube should be as far from it as possible, crowded into the bow. Most of the men had been sent back into Boston by motorboat already and there were fewer than a dozen left.

"That'll buy us some time, if you're right," Carmody said, leaning back in his leather armchair. "But how much?"

"Hard to tell," John admitted.

"I'm beginning to think we might be smarter to simply drop the thing overboard," Carmody said. "Let it tunnel down and find its twin."

Sergio said, "And if it does not?"

"Why wouldn't it?" Carmody asked.

"This is not a strong force we are talking of here. Remember, the mathematics plainly shows it is like the quark force—constant, but weak. Many things are stronger."

Carmody looked less relaxed. "Such as?"

"Volcanic flows," Sergio said. "There are many strong mass currents under the Earth's crust, that is what makes the continents to drift. If a stream of hot rock catches the singularity, it can sweep it along, up, down, anywhere."

"Back to the surface?" Carmody asked.

"There, certainly. Convection cells return deep matter to the surface constantly, on the ocean floors. The singularity may *never* find its twin."

Carmody asked John, "Did you or that guy you were with, George—did you see anything funny? A second singularity?"

"No. It was dark down in that passageway. I saw faint light from a side passage, but it was just another way down to the sea, I thought."

"But you think maybe the second singularity, it got out then—broke out of the cube?"

John shrugged. "Makes sense. The thing made a lot of noise, sure. I thought it was the crate banging around."

"That patch on the back of the cube!" Claire cried. "Recall? There was dirt covering a plug of rock. But when I tested that rock, it was amorphous. That could be *melted* stone that hardened *after* the second twin escaped—out that direction."

John said, "Out along one of the symmetry axes? Sure, that's the easiest route out. So it penetrates the center of that back face—sure, because the crate was falling backwards, wasn't it? Fell on its back, propelled the twin out the back face. Maybe—"

Carmody waved his hands. "Enough of maybe this, maybe that. I want to go back to Professor Zaninetti's remark. You feel these singularities could cause a lot of trouble, tunneling around?"

"*Sí.* Carve open new volcanic vents, for example. If—"

One of the advisors deflected Carmody's attention, whispering. Carmody frowned, nodded.

"I just heard about that fellow in Arditti's team. He got a lethal dose. They've sedated him."

There was a long silence. What had been an abstract discussion suddenly took on a real, human dimension. Carmody let the silence stretch out and then said decisively. "This means we must consider very carefully how to prevent further excursion of these damned things. What are your suggestions?"

Zaninetti puckered his lips, his face drawn and somber. "If we could be sure the twins will come together safely, deep in the Earth, perhaps that is okay. But if a fall down a hole can knock them apart—as Claire tells us—then I would worry. They will stay free, able to move to the surface."

"Okay. What do we do?" Carmody looked as if events were moving too fast, even for him.

Claire said quietly, "Is there any choice? We have to arrange a quiet meeting of the twins."

PART
SIX

CHAPTER
One

Mediterranean night wrapped the ship in fog. John Bishop stood on the strumming steel deck of the tender and stared ahead, seeking some sign of land. The Argolic peninsula lay only a mile or two to the north and they should be passing by the island of Spetsae soon. He remembered tramping around that bleak spot of land with George, to convince the captain of the *Skorpio* that they were merely tourists. Lord, it seemed like years ago, but it was only a little over three months. And then, just as now, he had been preoccupied with what was to come.

A salty pungency filled his nostrils as he leaned on the railing. The throttled growl of the ship's diesels vibrated up through his boots. He was alone on deck; Arditti and Carmody and the others were below, having coffee and monitoring the situation. John felt he was jazzed up enough without adding caffeine to his blood. It was, of course, far too late for second thoughts, but he was having them anyway.

The last nine days had been a confusing rush of ideas, speculations, and steadily narrowing options. Carmody could apparently get any service, command any technical help, right up to the Nobel Prize level, merely by asking. That such men existed in government was news to John, but, once he thought about it, inevitable. Modern crises demanded a broad grasp of many issues. Someone had to know how to slice through interdepartmental jealousies, run down leads, filter self-aggrandizing input and keep everyone focused on the problem.

The crucial breakthrough had come when they calculated the size of a tunnel that would be bored in solid rock by a singularity. The tiny black hole heated the rock nearby, causing it to flow inward, adding to the hole's mass. It ate a small fraction of the heated rock, leaving the rest behind. That heating generated intense pressures, forcing molten rock into nearby cracks and fissures. This left a glass-walled tunnel a few inches wide in the singularity's wake. Even miles down, the weight of rock would not close the tunnel immediately. Wherever the twin singularity was now, it had carved a straight line path from the tomb site.

But where was it? That required not the elegant niceties of mathematical physics, but rather a typically twentieth century welter of grinding tedium.

With the emergence of pseudo-intelligent computers, a new kind of human intellectual had arisen. Carmody called in a team of them to make an estimate of the twin's position. They were not men and women who knew any field in detail, though they were skilled at extracting information from ferret-eyed specialists. Instead, they knew how to integrate knowledge without learning every wrinkle. With huge computer programs at their call, the pivotal decision became precisely how to phrase the question. They translated the jargon, syntax, bias and style of many disciplines, so that computers themselves could carry out the wearying numerical grind of getting a firm answer. These "interactive-correlative" savants swarmed over the problem and came up with bad news.

The twin was probably under France, moving at about three kilometers a day.

The simplest way to mate the two singularities would be simply to drop the cube into a mine in Bordeaux and let them find each other. The savants tried this in a detailed numerical simulation and found that it didn't work. Mass currents in the mantle continually deflected the particles. The twins never found each other. Indeed, it seemed likely that a local lava upwelling near the French coast, added to the attractive force between the twins, would eventually force the lower one to the surface.

What it would do there was uncertain. Surely it would give

off deadly radiation. Perhaps it would find its twin. Perhaps it would wander through subterranean paths, opening fresh vents for lava, disturbing the balance of geological forces, conceivably setting off slippage among the colliding continental plates.

Carmody disliked uncertainty. He particularly disliked leaving problems unsolved. So he had asked for something audacious, something that would bring the twin singularity to the surface in a predictable way, where he could deal with it.

John shivered, despite the black wet suit he wore. The Aegean winter brought biting winds out of the north, curling whitecaps in the ship's wake. The cutting breeze howled out from the land and ruffled his hair with tantalizing, playful fingers. The sea itself would seem a welcome warmth.

He left the flying bridge, picking his way around the signal halyard. Antennae circled endlessly above, probing the horizon.

There were no running lights. The USS *Watson* wallowed in the long rolling swell, heavy laden. She was a specialty ship of the Sixth Fleet, officially part of Task Force 32. Her belowdecks were crammed with electronics listening gear, VHF and radar and TACAN systems. Her job was to reach out for hundreds of miles and tag hostile "elements" before they could engage US craft. There was a helicopter flight deck aft and a nominal ASROC launcher forward of the bridge. Any concerted attack would surely sink her, but things would not normally come to that. The aircraft carrier *Eisenhower* was scarcely a hundred miles east. It had jets standing by in catapults on the flight desk if needed. They could be here in minutes.

In the oppressive dark John carefully retraced his path down side stairs. The weather was perfect, with thick cloud cover and only a thin sliver of moon above that. He hoped it would hold. Before entering the amidships hatch he sniffed the salty, slightly rotten-smelling breeze to see if it had backed into the west, as the weathermen predicted. No, not yet.

The red light above OPERATIONS was the only illumination in the corridor; they were being careful to avoid leaks through momentarily opened hatches. John went through the doors into the semicircle of consoles surrounding the big communications screens. Carmody sat there, studying his clipboard. Around the man technicians murmured into throat mikes and kept their eyes on their console displays, where color-flagged dots moved. They were not scanning east, out to sea, but rather north, above the Argolic peninsula. John paused and studied one overlay map of the area. There were few dots, all blue, indicating light aircraft. Greek military patrols, or perhaps even private craft. The battle front was hundreds of miles away, after all, and civilian life had to go on. Another console showed satellite images in the infrared. He couldn't follow the matted splashes of greens, oranges and apricot. Towns stood out a garish scarlet, but understanding the rest was a matter for experts. He slumped into a bucket seat beside Carmody.

"Any last benediction?" he asked.

"Do your job and get out."

"Don't worry. Just get that boat there on time."

"It's not a boat, it's an inflatable transport."

"Just so it's quiet."

"It will be. Not that it matters. The chopper will be drawing all the attention by then."

John noticed the sketch on Carmody's clipboard. It was the same one he had drawn two days ago in Boston, outlining the plan.

"Still believe it?" he asked.

Carmody shrugged. "Enough to risk some Greek real estate."

"And some lives," John said testily.

"Yeah." Carmody was quite unconcerned. He had done such things before, and probably worse.

The drawing looked innocuous. The twin singularity had carved its tight little tunnel hundreds of miles and now was deep below Europe. Already it had possibly set up minute fractures and shifts that would eventually work their way to the surface, relieving pressure in a quick, snapping jolt of earthquake energy.

It would creep along, sucking in molten rock. An oddity that the interactive computer team had found resolved a crucial issue—why wouldn't it fall steadily downward, to the Earth's core? It was far more dense than rock, so logically it should sink. It was a measure of the team's versatility that they found an explanation before Abe and John had even noticed the problem.

Matter fell into the singularity along the diagonals of its cubic gravitational field. Some was swallowed, and the rest of the molten rock was ejected. Added to this was the uniform downward push of the Earth's gravity. Combining the two gravitational fields led to an uneven ejection of rock downward. This in turn created an oppositely directed pressure upward, cushioning it like a hydrofoil aircraft. This kept the singularity more or less steadily at the same depth. It also contributed greatly to the uncertainty about how two attracting singularities could ever meet.

"I'd feel a lot better if the numerical simulations had come out clean," Carmody said moodily.

"Hell, they only had a couple days."

"And a few odd million dollars. For a tab like that I expect clear answers."

"All their simulation runs showed the twin returning along its own tunnel."

"Yes. But how fast?"

"Some say a day, some say a week."

Carmody shook his head. "Too much latitude."

"If you want certainty—"

"I know, give them another week. Let them include all the mass gradients, and the Earth's spin, and souped-up particle physics—I got the shopping list."

The solution wasn't elegant. The best way to pluck the twin singularity from deep in the Earth was to make it return along its original path. Calculations and simulations showed that if the attractive force was reversed, pulling the twin back along its self-carved tunnel, it would stay on that track, taking the path of least resistance. To coax the subterranean twin into retracing its path demanded that its twin be back in Greece.

Elaborate computer programs examined how the singularity reacted to swerves in the tunnel, to partial closing of the path by collapse of the ceiling, to lava flows nearby—and the solutions all came out with the twin working its way up along its own tube, back to the Mycenaean tomb. They differed in the arrival time, because no one knew how much of the tunnel had filled in.

A majority thought the singularity had reached France. A

minority believed it couldn't have left Greece yet. They differed over fine points of black hole physics, and Carmody
regarded their arguments as Talmudic squabbling.

Still, the minority had a strong, practical point to make.
They thought the singularity would burrow through rock
slowly, and had moved only perhaps a hundred miles. That,
in turn, meant that while the cube was being flown to Greece,
the singularity below would not have a chance to work its
way upward, trying vainly to reach its brother overhead.

The majority had considerable trouble with this point.
While the jet flew, the burrowing twin could be deflected out
of its previous channel. To avoid that, they proposed a complicated flight path flown at top speed, to minimize the excursion of the twin.

Carmody had decided to go with the majority, even though
he was troubled by this difference among experts. He had
said to John. "They're *scientists*, they're supposed to *know*
this stuff!" with a genuine sense of outrage.

The solution was risky. It meant taking the cube back to
the vicinity of the tomb, and using its attraction to draw its
brother back along the previously rock-cut path.

Then they could mate the two singularities. The twin would
probably come barreling out of its tunnel, moving quickly
along the cleared path. If the two met at high velocity there
could be an enormous, many-megaton recombination. To
avoid that, someone had to keep the cube away from the twin.
Surprisingly, this didn't seem to be hard.

John and Sergio had proved—as nearly as jots on paper
could—that the force between the singularities was independent of their separation. That meant that the same steady tenth
of a gravity would be trying to pull the twins together, no
matter where they were. But a tenth of a gravity wouldn't lift
a singularity up into the open air, not when full gravity was
pushing it down. That meant the twin couldn't lift off the
ground. It could crawl like a mole, but not fly like an eagle.

To extract it from the tomb simply demanded that the cube
be kept aloft, tantalizingly close, while its twin circled restlessly below, dissipating whatever energy it had from its journey through the tunnel.

Carmody chuckled. "And here I thought science was exact,
certain. Hell, it's as bad as our goddamn foreign policy."

"Which doesn't work either."

"You can say that again. Y'know, when the President approved this, they had State send a feeler to the Greeks. Asking for a mutual understanding on this thing, cooperation—"

"You *what*?"

"Don't get lathered up now. The cable didn't give away any of our game."

"If they suspect—"

"We kept it vague."

"Still—"

"We just wanted to see what they'd say. Also, of course, to cover our ass diplomatically, once this blows open."

"Will it? If we're careful—"

"Sure. Has to. No such thing as a secret these days."

"What'd the Greeks say?"

"Their customary surly answer. Accused us of economic exploitation, using Turkey against their interests, interference—the usual shopping list."

"Then why bother?"

"State wants to be able to say we went through ordinary channels and were rebuffed. The Europeans will make a big deal about it anyway for two, three days, no matter what. State's worried about Japan and China, though—they're important. That Pan-Pacific trade agreement's about negotiated; they don't want anything screwing it up."

"Did Athens say anything specific about Kontos?"

"No, he didn't sign the Foreign Ministry reply or anything."

"Then maybe—"

"We know he got back home, though. He took a BritAir flight out of Bermuda two hours after the *Pyramus* docked there. Went through Heathrow to Athens."

"If he understands even a fraction of what's going on . . ."

"True, he suspects this thing could be a weapon." Carmody frowned and sucked at his teeth.

"And it could."

"That's what that emergency meeting in the Pentagon decided. All the more reason why, if these things are going to go off, let's do it outside the USA. Symmetric, anyway. Kontos wanted it back, OK, here it is—just like he wanted with the Elgin marbles."

"An international game of hot potato."

Carmody smiled. "But we're the only ones who know it's hot."

"He knows enough to interest the Russians in it."

Carmody shook his head. "His government doesn't have time to listen to him. After all, he's failed. Lost his boat, his prize, the works. And they've got a war on their hands."

Indeed, that was the *Watson*'s cover. It was officially cruising the south Aegean as part of Task Force 32, keeping a wary eye on the fighting to the north. The Greeks were holding their own in the sea battle and doing well in the air. They had stopped the Turks in the Aegean Sea, losing many ships and planes in a big engagement off the island of Chios. Their kill ratio was about three to one, principally because of better pilots, but the Turks outnumbered them.

The crucial issue was who prevailed on the open seas. If the Turks battered the Greek navy to pieces, then they could safely slip amphibious landing craft across the Aegean. They would stage landings in central Greece, near Athens. The war could drag on forever if the Turks could bring their large army across. The Greeks would fight street by street.

There were already land battles far to the north, where the two countries met along a narrow border, but that would not be crucial. The Greeks could hold in that hilly terrain.

Diplomats were struggling to get a cease-fire. Turkey demanded that its NATO allies stand aside.

There were rumors of Russian shipments of a new class of anti-aircraft missiles into Athens. The Greek government was openly calling for support.

Carmody gestured toward a large wall screen which showed a sprinkling of grouped dots over the north Aegean. "The Turks are maneuvering tonight. That'll keep the Greeks occupied."

"Yeah," John said uneasily. "For a while."

CHAPTER
Two

When Claire came into the rec room of the *Watson* after her nap, the TV was showing a Stateside program. Not the news, or even a football game, as she would have expected of the sailors who lounged back, sipping coffee and gazing at the screen.

She had to admit that the clichés she had formerly accepted about the kind of men who would be here had proved significantly in error. They were quick, intelligent, and disciplined without being rigid. Even now, glancing slyly at her out of the corners of their eyes, they had a decorous reserve. She was acutely conscious that they had not seen a woman at close range in over a month. It was like a steady undertone on the ship, a thing of body language and stares held too long, nothing she could object to and perhaps not even conscious on their part. But it was there. Still, they kept it contained, as orderly as their crisp blue uniforms.

They were watching a public television program in which DNA coiled like technicolor dancing bracelets beneath a watchful electron microscope, to an accompanying music-box-like Baroque harpsichord. A voiceover explained how phosphorous and other ions seemed destined for a unique place in our biology, implying an order which the voice quickly traced back to forerunner fifteenth century notions of clock-building and planetary orbits—all intimately connected, in turn, with the development of individual rights in our modern age. The music shifted easily to Beethoven. Darwin made his entrance escorted by the voiceover's praise, then modernist prints illustrating *ennui*, and some further nods in the direction of predestination and Freud.

Science the serene, the clean. Nothing to do with crawling around in a hole in the ground, looking for a mote that spat gamma-rays. Nothing like that, of course. She palmed a cup of awful coffee and left for the deck.

The night chill did not penetrate the thick jacket she wore. She worked her way aft, moving carefully in the heavy boots the Navy had given her. Radar antennae of several shapes and sizes revolved endlessly above, soundless amid the thrumming of the engines and the steady wash at the bows.

George Schmitt was helping the men around the helicopter flight deck. She stopped at the ramp overlooking the broad pad that took up most of the stern. Teams were checking the two helicopters while others secured the big cubic object at the side. She thought of the stone artifact sitting inside all the layers of metal and special plastics and adhesives. The dirty-white crating that now housed it had been put together by materials specialists, hoping to contain the singularity inside for as long as possible. A special crew of four men monitored it constantly. As she watched they made another foray around the cube, pressing instruments against its sides. They listened for acoustic tremors, enhanced radiation, any sign of devouring movement within.

So far there had been no trouble. Still, she was jittery, being this close. The long flight from Boston aboard an Air Force transport had been unsettling for her, until John matter-of-factly mentioned that of course the artifact was not aboard. It was carried separately, in a plane with minimum crew.

She had assumed their party of Carmody and his squads of specialists was all of the operation. Yet more men came aboard when they landed at the base in Italy, and there were escort craft, and slowly it had dawned on her how large this was. And how seriously they all took the calculations of a few physicists and mathematicians. It spoke worlds about how much the security and defense apparatus was linked to the physicists, who had been the mandarins of science ever since 1945.

She remembered sitting in a meeting three days before, listening to a detailed study of what would happen if the two singularities recombined deep in the Earth. The study was necessary because some people advocated letting the two simply meet beneath the Atlantic, where the effects would be minimal. But if just two hundred pounds of the combined mass was converted into energy, it would produce massive quakes all around the globe, and tidal waves that smashed both Atlantic coasts. The patient, reasonable way the men laid out their numbers and equations and graphs had been eerily convincing and chilling. She was struck by the dispassionate, systematic way they reached huge conclusions. In archeology, every nuance of a site was scrutinized for significance. Scholars knew they dealt with human products, shaped by ordinary impulses which, by assumption, had changed little through the millennia. There was a reassuring, humanistic scale. An unexpected turn could not suddenly thrust you above a tortured abyss, staring down into echoing, cold, inhuman perspectives. The difference in tone was so vast that it scarcely seemed the subjects could both be sciences.

"Butterflies?" a voice said at her elbow. George Schmitt leaned lazily against the railing. He always seemed relaxed and uncaring, whether working at the tomb or in Boston or even here. It was a gift, she decided.

"No, just running through possibilities," she answered.

When the full dimensions of the plan became clear, she had proposed bringing George in. Only he and she knew the tomb, and he alone had a good idea of the structural integrity of the walls. No one knew what was going to happen, of course, but there was considerable risk of damage to the site, and Claire took her stand on that principle. At first she demanded to go in and oversee whatever destruction had to occur, to minimize it. Carmody had ruled that out, until Arditti and others had brought up how useful having someone along with knowledge of the tomb would be. The plan demanded a minimum of two helicopters, so she had proposed bringing George in to be in the first one, with her following.

To her surprise, George had readily agreed. Two agents had brought him to Boston. Beneath his casual, cool manner she could tell he was excited by the air of secrecy and power. Carmody's men were lean, efficient, and clearly going about things that were more exciting than cleaning and processing old artifacts at Columbia University on a postdoc.

Claire was set on being there. The major opposition had come from John, who didn't want her in the plan at all. But she would not be pushed aside by anyone. Once that was clear to John he changed to grudging neutrality. Then she had to deal with Carmody. His old-fashioned, solicitous concern was just another tired excuse to keep a woman out; she saw that immediately, and in the end it didn't work. She was going. Not in the first 'copter, no, but once things were calmed down she would go into the tomb to save what was left. She owed that to her profession and to herself.

"Never thought it'd turn into this, did we?" George said eagerly. His hands trembled on the railing.

"Archeology, the field with a future."

"Even though it's about the past."

"That's what I'm puzzling over," she said, watching men attach cables to the the crate that held the artifact. The cables led to a heavy hoist at the underbelly of the first helicopter.

"What the cube means?"

"Yes. Cubic artifact, cubic singularity. Can't be coincidence."

"They carved the rock to look like the thing inside, so?"

"Why? What relation did it have to whoever was buried in the tomb?"

"Maybe he discovered it."

"Where?"

"Dug it up? From a quarry?"

"Ordinary quarrymen don't rate fancy tombs."

"Maybe it was a prize of war. Remember the ivory map."

She blinked, surprised. She had not thought of that in weeks. The crude sketch on ivory, showing Crete and Santorini. Kontos must have found it by now, among the artifacts shipped to Athens.

"Of course. But they must have known the singularity was dangerous. Why—"

Then it struck her. "The chipping on the front of it, the face. Remember? Someone must have been trying to get the singularity out."

"Who?"

"Grave robbers?"

"Doesn't sound like something I'd try to steal."

"Or. . .there was John's idea. That if servants were ritually buried with the dead king, they might try to get out."

"There's very little evidence that any were buried, I thought."

"Correct. But suppose it was so. They couldn't dig their way out of the sand blocking the entrance; they knew that. So they would be desperate. Working in the dark. They had of course heard about whatever was in the cube, knew it gave off light."

"So they tried to get at it?"

"Yes! It can bore through rock, can't it?"

"Come on, Claire."

"It all fits. The servants knew what was in the cube; everyone must have."

"Maybe. They never got behind the first block, though. The mortar was intact."

"Yes. Not enough time. Perhaps they thought they could liberate the singularity from the rock? Bring it to their aid?"

George studied the shadowy figures working under two banana-shaped dark masses. His eyes glittered with a look of alert anticipation as he said, "Look, we can work that out later."

"There won't be much of the tomb left then."

"We'll see. That's what we're for, right? Protect the archeological record."

"And then get out," John said from behind them.

Claire turned and saw he was fully covered by a black wet suit, standing a little awkwardly in incongruous blue Quon tennis shoes. A wordless, jittery excitement passed between them. The sight of the wet suit seemed to sober George, who said, "Wow, gettin' to be about that time."

"I'm due back in five minutes. When the ship slows, that's when we go over."

Claire searched John's face for a reading and failed. He seemed remarkably steady, compared with George. His hands seized the railing firmly and he stretched his legs back, saying, "Got to stay loose."

"You said it," George added.

"You're going in 'copter A, right?" John said, grunting as he stretched.

"Yeah," George replied. "We scout the tomb."

John nodded, tensing his arms behind his head, twisting,

flexing his whole torso. *Like warming up for a football game*, she thought.

She knew exactly what he was thinking. He had gone behind her back and made a deal with Carmody. She rode in 'copter B—not A, which carried the singularity below it. George would go into the tomb first. John was doing as much to protect her as he could. They had had three separate, grade-A fights about what he called her "bull-headed mulishness," an interesting contradictory image. But she had prevailed. She was going, allowing him without comment his minor and rather endearing deception.

"Y'know," John said, "I was thinking of sending a cable back to Zaninetti."

"Carmody has a total transmission blackout," George said.

"It can go out after we're done. Hell, even better that way. Then I can cancel it."

"I'm not following," Claire said.

John grinned. "There was a great mathematician named Hilbert, who telegraphed Berlin saying he had proved the outstanding unsolved problem in mathematics, a thing called Riemann's conjecture. It has to do with the roots of a well known function. He sends this telegram to Berlin, see, where he's going to give a speech. Everybody gets excited. So Hilbert shows up and talks, and says nothing about the problem. Somebody comes up to him after the speech and says, what about Riemann's conjecture, what's the solution? And Hilbert says he hasn't got one. He was taking his first airplane trip to Berlin, and was pretty nervous, so he sent the telegram in case he got killed."

George whooped. "That's one way to get a place in the books."

Claire smiled. "The famous lost Bishop proof of the Riemann conjecture, huh?"

"You got it," John said mirthlessly. He lifted his hands to Claire, palms up, and shrugged.

Together they moved off, leaving George.

"Five minutes?" she asked quietly.

"Yep."

"I still don't see why it's got to be so fast. There've only been a few days to *think*, to—"

"It's this war. It provides a perfect distraction. And if anything goes wrong here, people will write it off as some Turkish scheme that went bad."

"Carmody didn't say that."

"He didn't have to. It's obvious."

"But you'll admit if we had another week—"

"The genie might get out of its bottle over there," he jerked a thumb toward the flight deck, "and we'd have a devil of a time getting it back in."

She gave grudging agreement. "I still don't see why so much sudden attention is paid to a mathematical curiosity." News of an equally important discovery in archeology, she reflected, would have reached a figure like Carmody after a zippy decade or two.

"It's much more than that. The math implies that such energetic, high-mass particles may be useful. Compact energy storage. A versatile radiation source. Hell, you could explore the whole damned interior of the Earth if you could control one."

"How?"

"With two singularities, you could put one exactly on the other side of the Earth. Anchor one twin to something. Then their attraction will draw the second one through the center of the Earth. Time how long it takes, measure its rate of progress. That'd tell you something about densities, maybe the material composition. At a minimum, it'd let you sink really deep shafts, take samples."

"Or make bombs."

He nodded. "That too."

"Which is why Carmody is keeping us isolated from the press."

"Sure. That'll work for a while. But even he knows that can't last long. The science is too interesting. Maybe he could keep you and me quiet, but Zaninetti is too big a figure to shut up."

"Comforting."

"Yeah."

Bow waves splashed below, a slight phosphorescent glow in the foam. The *Watson* rolled slowly, driving forward at half its top speed. Claire leaned against him. "Two minutes," she said. "What'll we talk about?"

"Love and death."

"Whose?"

"Ours."

"Do I get to choose which one?"

He kissed her. "Do me a favor?"

"Sure, sailor. You want it right here on deck? I suppose it's dark enough."

"Don't go in the helicopter."

She looked at him and saw a face vulnerable, open, and she regretted being so flip with him. But it was too late, and they both knew it.

"I. . .you understand, I have an obligation."

"I know. I don't agree, but I know."

"I. . .have to."

"So much for death. Let's stick to love." He put his arms around her.

"Is that what this is?"

"Sure. Done in understated good taste, of course." He kissed her.

"We take things slowly in Boston."

He smiled down at her. "You're just hiding behind that."

She said slowly, reflecting, "That's true."

He kissed her again.

"Hey!" Arditti's voice called from beyond the helicopters. "Bishop! Get your ass down here."

CHAPTER
Three

The *Watson* had deployed a steel side stairway and hoist. At the bottom of it a platform skimmed along two feet above the low churning swell. Spray wetted the steps. John made his way down in the dark, using the handrail, his heart already thumping.

With minimum talk he finished suiting up. The last stage was wrestling on the big cylinder, 72 cubic feet of air compressed at 2250 p.s.i., the stem indicator reading full. A good hour's worth. If everything went right he wouldn't need even half of it.

Arditti handed him the demand valve. He screwed it on and checked it twice. Arditti nodded approval and drawled, "You see the situation report?"

"Carmody said there was nothing significant."

Arditti hesitated a fraction of a second. "Yeah."

John's eyes narrowed, although expression was useless in the pervading gloom. "What's on?"

"Got a report from a survey ship up the coast. Says there're jeeps on the road down from Athens."

"Moving which way?"

"South, looked like."

"How far away?"

"Twenty miles. But the report's an hour old by now."

"They're fighting a war. There must be plenty of troop movements."

"That's right." Arditti shrugged it off. "Plenty."

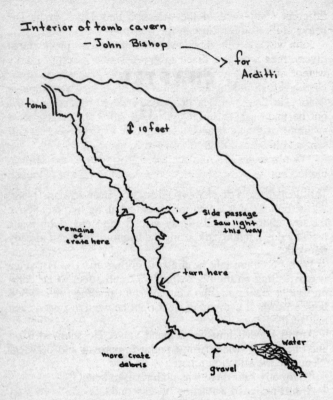

Interior of tomb cavern.
— John Bishop

for Arditti

tomb

↕ 10 feet

remains of crate here

Side passage
- Saw light this way

turn here

more crate debris

gravel

water

There were three of them in the Arditti team, plus John. They were only names to him, lean and rugged men who spent most of their waiting time in the rec room, playing cards and drinking coffee. They seemed utterly uninterested in anything except their mission.

A team member helped John get the straps over his shoulders adjusted. He sat on the platform looking at the water rush by, leaning back against the cylinder. They went through a check-down. Diving knife, depth meter, mask, flashlight, depth gauge, lead-lined belt. Arditti carried several flares as well, for lighting the cavern. Each team member carried a different component of the detection and comm gear. The heavy stuff would follow in the transport.

John was uncomfortably aware that these were professional divers, men who had dived to great depths, through murky waters, at night, everything. He was a weekend sports diver. His biggest thrill had been seeing a shark at fifty yards' range down near Cozumel. The shark had ignored him completely, but he had been close enough to see the face clearly as it swam off with that strange fixed, fanatic expression. That still sent a cold fear through him when he recalled it.

"Two minutes," Arditti called softly. Above, the *Watson* blotted out whatever dull light the sky let through. It looked as though the clouds were thinning; there was a diffuse silvery haze to the east which might be a sliver of moonlight trying to get through. Not good news.

Mask pushed down, John put the regulator in his mouth and cracked the valve. Air hissed and he drew a shallow, metallic breath. Fine.

The *Watson* gradually throttled down its engines, bringing a strumming pulse into the platform beneath him. Spray splashed him.

They would go over the sides of the platform on signal, so they didn't disperse. John struggled over to the edge, the cylinder like a massive parasite on his back. Again he tested the air.

Arditti's party went first. The *Watson* would slow when it drew alongside the tomb site, dropping the team on the port side, where no one ashore could see. The ship would pick up speed again, move several miles farther west, and make its turn. Coming back, it would drop the inflatable transport and a crew of three, also near the tomb site.

The transport would home in on a beacon that Arditti's team had floated at the entrance of the underwater tunnel. The beacon was an infrared emitter, invisible to the unaided eye. When they reached the site the second team would deploy the equipment in the transport, two of them taking it down on air pressure assisted carriers.

John's major job was finding the underwater entrance to the shaft. Arditti had argued that his team could locate it quickly enough, going by John's vague description. Carmody doubted that. Arditti had then argued that they should send in a team in a fishing boat to mark the spot in daytime. Carmody thought that would compromise the mission, quite possibly alerting anyone guarding the site.

So John's bird-dogging was necessary. Arditti was skeptical of his abilities, and had rehearsed him relentlessly in the *Watson*'s belowdecks pool. As long as John had to come, Arditti felt he might as well do a side job, too. They showed him how to deploy the floating antenna, and drilled him without mercy. It was a minor job, and kept John out of the underwater cavern while the others worked their way in. Once he had performed the few simple movements with the antenna, he would wait for the transport to arrive and help unload it.

As soon as the equipment was off the transport, though, he and one man would high-tail it for the *Watson*, which would be slowly returning along its previous track.

John looked at the already loaded transport, a low-slung, flat-bottomed thing with inflated cigar-shaped walls. It took up half the platform space. The second team was already sitting in it. One waved to him.

"On the count!" Arditti called.

John pulled the mask over his face. An hour's air. He wondered what his oxygen consumption per minute was. Somehow he, a mathematician, had never calculated it.

Somebody called down from above, a clipped signal. Arditti counted back from five. John ground his teeth and breathed into the mouthpiece. He was an amateur, these were professionals. He worked with chalk and a blackboard, they—

He realized suddenly that the others were armed, compact submachine guns strapped to their sides. They hadn't given him one.

"Zero!"

He felt a sudden jolt of very real fear. He froze, his legs unwilling to move.

Somebody pushed him from behind. He had just enough time to feel outraged before he hit the water.

He held the mask over his face with both hands, the way the instructors always said. A froth of bubbles enveloped him and he sank, blind and weightless, taking his first breath. In the utter blackness, gravity told him nothing about orientation. He turned, searching.

There, a ruddy light. Abruptly a shadow moved across it. Something flickering—

A figure was waving at him, gesturing. A finger pointing. Follow, yes.

He righted himself and moved toward the dim red beacon. He remembered to let his legs do the work, flexing the flippers.

Arditti's hand light was a subdued red, to avoid detection from ashore. They were all waiting for him, masks regarding him impassively, a cluster of oily shadows. Arditti had somehow gotten himself oriented, and pointed shoreward. They moved off. John had to work to stay up. One man always stayed behind him. Not letting him drop out of sight, John realized.

His heart pounded unnaturally in his water-logged ears. He dragged on the demand valve. Short, shallow breaths, yes. That was the way. Take your time. Hold in the air and get all the oxygen out of it before you set it free.

When he breathed out, the bubbles cascaded upward and were lost in a shrouding mist. Around them, inky nothingness. Below, like a smoldering faint vision of ruby hell, weeds swayed lazily.

Arditti's light was the central sun for this pocket universe. They followed it obediently. Tiny silvery fish hung in an orderly swarm, unbothered by the passing black giants.

He turned his head to watch the fish and ploughed into the man ahead of him, who had stopped. It was only a brushing contact, but it jarred him out of his reverie. Arditti gestured down and cast the reddish beam that way.

Greenish mud gave way to sandy, rolling bottom. They were nearing shore. John tried to remember signs, directions. The pervasive gloom distorted shapes and angles.

The team hovered, looking at him through their panes of glass. *Okay, lead us to it. Do your thing.*

John nodded and looked around. Was that hummock familiar? He couldn't tell. It had been months, after all.

He stopped trying to figure out directions. Better to head shoreward and try to sort it out from the look of things there.

He pointed along a spur of rock and Arditti turned that

way, the red beam casting infernal shadows. They all flippered across the ridge and over a sea of grass. A starfish flattened itself against a stone below. Arditti kept the beam level, letting most of the light diffuse into the gloom, rather than reflecting off the bottom. That reduced the illumination anyone could see from the hill above.

John scanned the dim terrain below. His ears deadened further as he descended for a closer look. Yet the swift hiss of air as he bit the demand valve was loud, reverberating in his head. He thrust thumb and forefinger against his mask, pinching his nose, and blew his ears clear. The burbling rush of bubbles sounded like fitfully exploding popcorn.

They passed over a hummocked region of seaweed and tumbled rocks. The beam brushed by dark cavities and revealed fat yellow fish, mouths puckered as if in alarm. The weed grew denser ahead and John wondered if he had seen anything like this area. Was he even headed toward shore? What if—

A low ridge of rock, nearly straight. And beyond it, another.

They were like ruined stone walls standing a few feet above drifts of sand. Looking left and right, he could barely make them out as they receded into blackness.

The ancient remains of the subterranean stream. He had forgotten it.

The same stream that had carved the seep hole, the tunnel, their destination. John felt a flood of relief.

The team quickly understood his gestures. Their faces seemed impassive behind glass, but their heads followed the lines on the sandy floor below. Arditti's eyes widened. He nodded and gestured for them to go single file.

Arditti turned with an expert movement of his flippers and followed the two stubby, ruined rows of stone. Now that John had the width of the ridges for a comparison, he saw that in the wan glow of Arditti's flashlight their field of view was remarkably constricted, perhaps only thirty feet across. It had been damned lucky to run across the ruined contours. They could have wandered for an hour out here.

He brought his left arm forward in a stroke, the hand looking white and close, the pressure watch enormous on his wrist. Only seven minutes had passed since somebody had pushed him off. Probably Arditti.

He heard cracklings and looked up. High above, thin washes of surf. They were nearing shore.

The bottom tilted up as they flipper-trudged along the lines. More surf. Then there they were ahead, brown buttresses of rock. Far up between them, a cloistered blackness.

He swam beside Arditti up into the narrowing space. Sea anemones spotted the flanks of the big rocks. He gestured upward and Arditti played the flashlight over an upward curving tube. It looked clear, though to John it was nothing like his memory. The red glow distorted perspectives.

Arditti nodded, signaled to the other two and then made a pushing motion toward John. John paddled backwards and the others squeezed past.

He was finished. He had found it. Time to go home. End of the mathematician's duty. All he had to do was ferry the communications cables to the surface.

The last man unlocked an axially mounted drum on his back. He freed the clipped ends of three thin black lines. Then he carefully handed them to John, waved, and turned his back. The cables unreeled from the revolving drum as the man swam away, up the passageway. Bubbles rose to meet the stone ceiling and squashed against it. Arditti's red glow from far up the stone chimney was dimming. Time to go.

John backed out and let himself drift. Arditti had told him to not use the flashlight that was still clipped to his belt, once he was on the surface. Okay. The next step was the hardest and he needed the light, so he had better do it down here. He clicked the light on—red, of course—and let it shine down at the sand. He was far enough under the rocky ledge to avoid detection.

The National Security Agency didn't go second class. The water-sealed, waxy package on his back was superbly engineered. He laboriously unstrapped it, cautiously following each step Arditti had rehearsed with him. His fins rode tip-down on the bottom.

The cable connections slid snugly into their sockets. Good. The five activating and calibrating switches were big and easily turned. He set frequency and power, the numbers well memorized. No transmission yet, he saw from the tiny monitor, a liquid crystal display in bright yellow.

Now the float. He unfolded the plastic underlining and pulled the red tab on it. With a rush it filled with air. He had to snatch at the package to keep it from getting away. The flotation cushion and its stabilizer fins looked like a fat, garish rocketship with an unlikely cargo.

He drifted upward, cradling it, and stroked away from shore. There was a pyramid-shaped anchor, he remembered. He fished it and its coil of plastic line out of the flotation cushion's lower compartment. Everything was marvelously engineered, convenient and sturdy. He dropped the anchor. It fell away below, securing the package against currents.

Only one more step. He clicked off his flashlight as he broke water. Through his mask it was utterly black. By feel he found the rod at the top of the package, which was now floating easily on the slow swell. He pulled. It slid smoothly up and he could feel the small clicks as each set of spindly arms deployed. A crafty little antenna, capable of reaching the *Watson* at a ten mile range.

Atop the floating antenna was an infrared beacon, he knew. If things were going right, the transport's crew would be searching for it now with their scopes. John could barely see the rotating nub above, but it was black, of course, which was reassuring. No emission in the visible spectrum. Nothing to alert a sentry on the hillside above.

He recalled the drill, remembering each step. A wave splashed his mask. Something more . . .

Oh yes. He had forgotten to test the system again. It was harder now, because he was foundering in the lapping surf and the antenna was riding well on the water, reared up. He cautiously grasped the edge of the flotation cushion. Where was the small systems panel? He pushed his mask down, taking long breaths.

There. He could see now, by a diffuse moonglow that seeped through the clouds to the east. The hill loomed behind him, a dark bulk. He could maneuver the antenna better now. If Arditti below had hooked up the cables, the rig should work, should poke a signal through to the *Watson*, should kick off the whole shebang.

He jabbed the REPORT button on its side. It flashed on,

three yellow numbers indicating that transmission was under way. He felt a spurt of elation. He had done it. The endless drilling had paid off.

The guys below were already set up, their comm gear working. That was the signal back at the *Watson* for the helicopters to lift off. They would reconn the tomb site, checking to see if the comm link, cave to *Watson* to airborne, worked in action. Carmody had insisted on that. Systematic, checking each step.

There was a deeper reason, though. The *Watson* was in danger as long as the cube remained on board. Better to get it aloft quickly.

John scanned the darkness. No sign of any craft. He glanced at his watch. At least ten minutes more before he should expect the second team. When they arrived, they could deploy the big radiation and acoustic detectors. With a number of them scattered through the lower reaches of the stone cavern, the helicopter people would have a good idea when the twin singularity approached. By then Arditti's team would be safely out.

John back-paddled away from the antenna. The REPORT display faded out, as it was supposed to. Five feet away he could barely see the vague outline of the antenna jutting against the night sky. Nobody would pick it out from above.

He took a splash in the face and decided to put his mask back on. In fact, wallowing around on the surface was pointless. He could stretch his air supply by treading water up here, but on the other hand the transport might run into him when it arrived. He jackknifed and sank lower, into blackness. The dark was restful in a way. He had been night fishing once at Cozumel and after the first spooky hour had enjoyed it a lot. This wasn't any worse.

He lazily drifted to the bottom. Check his watch. Twenty-seven minutes gone. Less than half his air used. By now Arditti would have finished hooking up the one small Geiger counter he carried, and the rest of his team would be stringing cables up the slope of pebbles and into the stone chimney itself. He wondered if the rope and pulley he and Claire had left there were still in place. If so, a man could haul himself up it. That would let them put some of the later detectors, the ones on the transport, up higher in the chimney.

Anyway, that was somebody else's problem. Turn it over to the specialists. Let them—

A bright orange flash lit the scene. Rocks, pale sand, the bulky brown shore—all leaped into being around him, sudden as lightning.

It was gone in a second, leaving him with a retinal after-image. He turned toward the source.

A flare. Arditti had set off a flare inside the cave, and the glow had come out this far. They must have realized the glare would escape down the water entrance, though, and snuffed it out. He hoped no one on the hillside had been looking.

John waited for the afterimage to fade. Currents swirled in his ears. He breathed slowly with a tinny rush of the intake valve.

On the other hand, maybe it was a signal. They could be in trouble in there, and wanted help.

Impulsively, to be doing something, he swam back up. The anchor line of the antenna rubbed against his arm. He broke surface and paddled. The antenna bobbed within view. He punched for REPORT.

Systems were okay, cables still in place. But there was no transmission under way.

He stared at the blank signal trace, treading water, wishing it said something else.

It could be something ordinary. They had shut off the detectors for a moment. One of the cables had popped out of its socket in the cave. Something like that.

Or trouble. Maybe the goddamn singularity was already in there.

Okay, wait for the transport. Let the specialists take care of it. They were getting paid for it. And drawing a lot more salary than a postdoc at MIT, too.

That was reasonable, but it might take ten, fifteen more minutes.

On the other hand . . .

Arditti wouldn't have violated procedures without a reason. He knew John was out here. It must be a signal for help.

He dove again. Using the red flashlight beam he found the entrance. He would go in, find out what was happening, and report back to the men in the transport. Just that much. No more.

CHAPTER
Four

Claire crouched over the comm console in the helicopter control tower, shivering. She could not seem to get the chill out of her bones, despite standing next to the room's sole heater, which smelled of hot metal. Despite heavy leather gloves, her fingertips were numb.

The control room looked down on the two helicopters, crew already inside the cockpits, engines warmed. They were ready to lift the moment the data link from the first team was complete.

Idly she studied the controller's map table. It showed the coastline, water depths and elevations, all color-coded. She remembered studying a considerably simpler map months ago, and plotting out where John had discovered the remains of the underwater seepage tube. She had sketched it in on such a map—

It struck her at once that in the last few days she had seen something similar. Yes, Arditti. He had come to the JFK Building and marked the path left by the cube in the muddy floor of the Boston Harbor. Amid the meandering contours of water and land it had looked adamantly artificial, straight as a signpost. Yet things were just the reverse—the harbor was man's work, and the cube was following natural law.

She recalled the seepage tube beneath these waters. Matters had come down to two tracks on the sea bed: one from ancient water-hollowing, the other a trail left as the cube dragged vainly after its singular twin.

She wished there were someone to talk to in these last minutes. She missed John acutely, could not stop fretting about him. Sergio would be a good man to talk to at a moment like this; he had a natural sympathy. The joke at that Harvard party couldn't have been more wrong; he was a subtle, gracious man. Sergio had refused to come on this venture, however. Not from lack of interest or bravery, but from seasickness.

George came clumping into the room, face red from the cold. "How long's it s'posed to take?"

"Should be any minute now," the control commander said gruffly. "Keep your pants on." The man clearly did not take to stray civilians in his territory.

"What if they can't find the opening?" George asked.

"We come back tomorrow," the man said, ending conversation.

Claire leaned against a steel bulwark. Everything here was covered with thick gray paint and exuded a faint smell of enamel. The *Watson*'s engines had slowed to a purr and they were nose into the wind, to give predictable conditions for liftoff. The large plexiglass windows still showed only blackness; all exterior lights were extinguished.

The hatch swung open and Hale came through. He was the leader of Claire's 'copter, a wiry man with quick, piercing eyes. His blue overalls fit well and nothing from his cap to his shiny black boots carried any identifying markings. He was from the National Security Agency, Claire gathered.

"I'd like you in your seats, folks," Hale said. He didn't seem under any stress.

"I'm freezing," Claire said.

"We want to get off soon's possible," Hale said patiently.

"Carmody said so?" Claire persisted.

"Sure did. He wants that big thing off the deck right away."

"The twin singularity isn't due for hours," Claire said.

"We want everything in place and checked out. Might have to neutralize the site, you know." Hale grinned serenely.

"Kill the guards, you mean," Claire said dryly.

"Hey, ease off, huh?" George said as though genuinely offended. "Man's just doing his duty."

Hale nodded, still smiling, and said cordially, "Only if they shoot at us, Dr. Anderson. Satellite recon says there was nobody at the site at sundown. This'll probably give us no trouble."

"See?" George said. "And I'd whole lot rather be doing something more important than postdocing, sitting in a one-room utility in Morningside Heights."

"That's not the issue," Claire said primly. The masculine enthusiasm suffusing the *Watson* had put her on edge. Kontos would call all this American imperialism, but to her it reeked of ancient lore and lust.

"Ma'am, this is a nuclear device we got here. Situation like that, Carmody says, we're not going to take chances."

"Is that his usual style? He's certainly acted swiftly."

Hale's grin broadened. "Yeah, ol' Carmody doesn't wimp out on you. He goes straight for the throat. That's why he's where he is."

"I'm sure," Claire said with what she thought was obvious wry sarcasm, but it didn't seem to affect Hale. Probably he'd seen civilians make the same verbal gestures before, and had learned to humor them. And why not? They grumbled, but they went along.

"Hey!" the control commander said. "I'm getting startup data from the first team."

The board showed colored patterns, then a graphic display. "Looks like a normal background count."

"Let's go," Hale said, all business.

Going out the hatchway, Claire said to George, "Good luck down there."

"Sure'll be something to tell them about back at BU, huh?" George asked happily.

Claire thought, *Sure, once NSA clears it for public information. Which might be about the time we draw Social Security.* She stepped out onto the steel deck and made her way down a dark stairway.

The flight deck was suddenly alive with activity, dark shapes rushing by her, the whine of engines sluggishly stirring from their sleep, muffled shouts, the snap of cables popping free. She hurried around her 'copter's tail pylon, head down as Hale had reminded her, then along the fuse-lage and up the steps, past the sliding steel doors and into the cabin. It had an amphibious hull and was surprisingly roomy inside.

Hale was already strapping himself in. The rest of the cabin was filled with electronics gear. Two men in green uniforms sat in drop seats, holding nasty-looking weapons. Long, curved clips jutted out of the stocks, evidently meaning they carried a lot of ammunition. She had seen things like that in movies and until this moment had never wondered how they worked. For that matter, she didn't know what was automatic about automatic weapons. Didn't they all just shoot when you pulled the trigger? The men nodded to Claire and said nothing.

The flight deck lights blazed on. No need for care now; anyone ashore could easily tell something was up, by the revving of the engines.

She watched the first 'copter take off. It lifted with a high whine of effort, taking up the slack on the hoist lines with care. When they stiffened the pilot poured on the power and the crated white mass rose free from the deck, swinging slightly, looking like any other cargo. No melting at the sides, no incandescent sparks.

The physicists on Carmody's team had rigged a containment method. Apparently the singularity's large magnetic fields could be used to insulate it. The physicists used a complicated set of magnets to make a kind of magnetic trap, and that held the singularity back from the walls. Or was supposed to.

Abe Sprangle had suggested that the iron in the cube's rock had made a trap of that sort, and maybe he was right. Something had made the two singularities sit docilely inside the cube for 3500 years or more. *And if no one had dropped it down a 300-foot shaft*, she thought ruefully, *they would've stayed in place.*

Even then, if she and John had left the cube at the bottom of the sea, the escaped twin would probably have found its way back to its brother in the cube. The vagrant "twist" had probably gotten dislodged where the stone chimney took a sudden turn, where the crate first struck, smashing open one side.

It must have plunged down one of the many side crannies. There hadn't been time to seek out its twin before they hauled the cube away. And ever since, the lone singularity had been doggedly following them, chewing blindly through whatever blocked its path.

The fact that she and John and George had seen nothing of the wandering twin suggested that it did not burn and melt its way through rock swiftly. At least not when it had low velocity. But now it might come speeding back along its self-made channel, and no one knew how energetic it would be.

The white crate rose away into the night, dangling from thick cables. Above it, Claire could see George's excited face peering down through the big windows in the sliding doors. The 'copters carried no identification, she saw. The roaring around her rose in pitch and acceleration pressed her into her seat. *Whump whump whump* came vibrating up through her boots and the *Watson* wheeled away below, a gray silver against the inky sea.

The first 'copter was about a mile ahead, flying westward. The running lights were off but she could see the murky speck against the increasing glow from the moon. It drew nearer, moving slower because of the crate it carried. Clouds thinned above. A chill breeze heavy with the crisp scent of land came through the open window. She wanted to close it but Hale had deliberately left it open, apparently for better vision. She tried to make out the coastline but could not recognize any of the low hills. They passed the first 'copter and took the lead, as planned.

Hale studied his board of comm readouts. It was a sophisticated system, mounted to swing out from a slim cabinet. He punched several commands in and watched the shifting patterns. Claire could not understand what they meant.

"Lost it!" Hale called across to her over the engine's roar.

"What?"

"Data link from the cave. It showed normal radioactivity, then—zip—nothing."

"Maybe a mistake? Unplugged it for a minute?"

Hale scowled. "Maybe." He donned a neck mike and called the *Watson*.

She looked out at the dark coastline sweeping by. No lights

showed in the landscape to the north. There were few villages in this area, and none wasted electricity on all-night lighting. She should be able to see Nauplia when they turned north; the angle would be right and they were high enough. She studied the two armed men. They sat impassively, cradling their weapons, only their eyes darting and excited.

They banked, heading north toward the site. They were coming in directly, west of the tomb, to reconn the valley. The first 'copter followed now.

She looked far to the west, where Nauplia's pearly glow silhouetted a crumpled line of hills. Then, directly below, an orange spark burned. She saw it only momentarily through the support struts and undercarriage, so bright it left a retinal image after the turn was finished and her viewing angle blocked. A campfire? Something from the turbine engines? She felt she should report it, and turned to Hale to shout, but he was intently working at his control board.

"No question, it's off the air," he said. "*Watson* confirms."

"Then shouldn't we—"

"We're already committed. Anybody down there, they've heard us."

They passed over the tomb site, she could tell the outline of the hill, but it was impossible to distinguish the tomb itself. They descended for a careful inspection of the area.

"But what use is this if we can't get the readings from the cave? We'll never know when—"

Over the turbine's whine they heard something like pebbles rattling on the roof. A popping sound.

"Can't call it off now," Hale said tersely. "That's small arms fire."

The sounds came through the open window. She realized abstractly that someone was shooting at *her*.

They wrenched to the right. A heavy thumping came from ahead and above and she realized it must be some big weapon of their own firing. Everything took an agonizingly long time. Absurdly, she thought of the assault scene in an old movie, *Apocalypse Now*, and wished she could ride up front where she could see what was going on. She could make out withered trees skimming by in the faint light. They were running down the little valley where she had spent months digging. From the side came flashes of light. She blinked, and saw retinal afterimages.

Things were happening so quickly she did not have time to get scared. More trees rushed by and then a familiar slope rose to the right.

Hale called, "We're clear, but the others, they can't turn so fast. They're taking light machine-gun fire from the camp." As he spoke they veered to the right, banking away and across the valley, toward the sea. The deck vibrated under her feet.

Hale listened intently to his earphones, eyes distant. Then he said reassuringly to Claire, "Small arms stuff won't do much against us. These babies, they're armored. Double-hulled, got that new fiber stuff in between. Not much danger unless—" He fell silent, listening.

Claire twisted to look down the valley and at last saw the first 'copter a half mile behind them. It was moving slowly, swinging the white crate below it like a swollen egg.

Quick flashes from the camp. She was surprised at how loud the clattering, popping noises were. There had to be at least a half dozen people firing now because there was never a silent moment. Some came from over on the hill, at the tomb. There were spikes of light from the 'copter, too, lancing down at the camp. They were returning fire.

Suddenly a loud *rrrrppp* came from the camp. The distant 'copter wobbled visibly, lost altitude, slid off to the left.

"Sunabitch! They took heavy machine-gun fire," Hale called. "Engine's hit."

They turned abruptly, making a circle, heading back the way they had come. She lost sight of the others.

Hale called loudly into his mike, "I don't care, open up on that camp. Suppress that fire!"

The thumping began above. Claire realized that the thumps were rapid bursts so fast she could barely distinguish them as a string of shots.

Hale called, "Try to get over the hills, out of range."

He listened. Claire caught an irregular, grinding noise from behind them. It lifted, turned into a whine.

"They're going in," Hale said quietly.

As he said the last word a white flash came through the window. A *crump* and then a shattering explosion. The white flare dimmed but still lit the cabin with a ghostly light, freezing for an instant the stark, shocked faces.

CHAPTER
Five

John squirmed upward, flashlight thrust ahead, shoulders scraping rock. Exhaled bubbles clouded his vision. The cylinder on his back clanged against the constricting walls.

He didn't remember it being this tight. Could the rock have shifted? No, that was stupid. Before, he had been swimming down, toward the light, not thinking about how narrow the passage was. And he had not carried an air tank.

The sides seemed impossibly close, malevolently red, clasping at him.

He twisted around a knob of rock and in that movement nearly lost it all. His mask scraped against stone. Water blurred his vision and then rushed into his nose. He jerked his head, banging it against rock. Sudden fear and panic filled him. Salt stung his eyes. He forgot that his nose didn't matter, that he was breathing through his mouth. He sucked in and his nostrils filled.

He yanked at the mask, automatically stroked upward for the surface, and slammed painfully into the rock. There was no surface, only rock all around, no way up to air. This was a long tube that led to a tomb, it was all a tomb, a place for the dead.

Stop breathing. Don't draw more in through the nose. Stop. Use your head.

The thought made him go rigid, but he followed the old lesson, waiting for the panic to die. Tombs, death, being buried in stone forever. No, forget that. Take it by steps.

His blurred vision told him nothing. He counted to five and then began an old drill.

Lean backwards. Press the top of the mask against your forehead. Tilt the bottom outward. Breathe in, taking all you want, through the mouth. It felt wonderful. Then let it go out, through the nose.

He emptied his lungs forcefully, wheezing out the last bit. Vision cleared, though fresh contact with air made his eyes sting more.

Bubbles rose and he sank, heavier. He cracked the demand valve, welcoming the filling rush. Incredibly, his mask was clear. He felt a thrill of accomplishment. You could die in a moment, every diver knew that, and he had passed through that without losing control. He wasn't so bad after all.

The glass pane had a rim of fog at the top. The hell with that. He wasn't going to go through the clearing drill for a minor problem. He wasn't going to do anything except get the hell out of here. Have a look, then turn tail. And at this stage, wedged in, it was easier to go forward than to negotiate a turn.

He wriggled past the rock knob and let himself drift slowly upward. He had let himself breathe as he liked, but now it was time to get back to the regular, shallow pulling on the demand valve, holding the half lungful of air as long as felt comfortable, scavenging every molecule of oxygen from it before letting the bubbles trickle out.

The red beam stabbed into consuming, impenetrable dark. The water here was dirty. The beam picked up a haze of suspended particles.

A turn to the left. Yes, he remembered that. The walls yawned, letting him through easily. Up ahead lay the pebbly beach. He probed the beam around, searching.

Then, out of the gloom, he saw someone. The diver was swimming away from him, feet covered in the black warming material divers wore inside their fins, like socks. He had been trained to keep formation while in a group, so the sight of someone ahead automatically made him assume the man was about some task. Silt in the water absorbed the beam, and he could see only the legs. John approached, wondering why one of the men was still working in the water, when suddenly he noticed that the legs were not moving.

He was still concentrating on breathing and that slowed his reactions to outside events. He was even with the man's feet before the truth dawned on him. Now he could see white hands trailing listlessly. Equipment was missing from the diving belt.

He drew alongside. There was no comm gear on the back of the wet suit. Most important, the cylinder was missing. No mask. Arms and legs bent, as though relaxed. And in the chest, a large gaping hole, trickling black filaments into the water.

The hair waved slowly, like seaweed. The body was turned half away and John stared at it for a long moment before he recognized the profile.

It was Arditti.

He bobbed gently, eyes swollen and staring straight forward. John touched the body and it spun, bringing Arditti's gaze directly at him, mouth pursed as though the dead man was going to ask a question.

As John watched the black strands seep out from Arditti's chest and billow away, he realized what made the fine haze in the water. He clamped down on the pad in his mouth, a sour nausea washing over him.

Arditti's quizzical expression bulged and the mouth opened. A bubble oozed forth. It rose like a question, *Why?*, and vanished up the slope, into the mist.

Yes, *why*. Someone had shot Arditti after he got most of his diving gear off. He could not have been far away, because he fell back into the water. Or was thrown . . .

That explained the flare. Someone had lit it as a signal to John, or to light the cavern, give them targets to shoot at.

Whatever the case, it was out of his league. He had no weapon, nothing. Time to get outside, warn the transport team. Let them figure out what to do. Probably it meant the whole mission was scrubbed. The Greeks must be in the cavern, which meant they were surely above, at the camp site—

Claire. The helicopters had already taken off. They would swoop by the camp, listening for the comm signal that wasn't coming, because the gear in the cave was dead.

So they would hang around up there, open to fire from the ground. With Claire riding inside.

He had to get word out. He jackknifed in the narrow space,

bumping against Arditti. The red beam cut through a suspended miasma of clotted blood.

He stroked down, working his flippers. The passage seemed wider than when he came up. The turn came and despite his haste he carefully negotiated it, not risking again the jarred mask and sudden rush of water. It would be miserably hard to evacuate the mask in this position, head down.

The fog of blood thinned as he left it behind. He was nearly clear of the rock walls when suddenly a blue glare burst in upon him. It was ahead, on the sea bottom.

The source moved slowly from left to right, brilliant spokes of light racing from it to fade in the water. For an instant he thought it was the transport team, lighting an underwater flare to find their way, or look for him, but then he saw that there was nothing near the point of light, no figure holding the flare aloft, and he knew what the spitting, roiling fury was.

CHAPTER
Six

The white flare faded. "Their fuel caught," Hale said hollowly. "They're burning."

Claire felt a tightening wave of terror. They completed their turn and she saw a yellow pyre forking up into darkness.

George.

"Signal's gone," Hale said tensely. "Maybe some of 'em got out, though. Let's go see."

They rose above the long, slumped hill, momentarily taking them beyond the spattering rifle fire. Claire saw that the first 'copter had gone down about three hundred yards west of the tomb site, near the base of the hill. It burned fiercely, sending up acrid plumes of smoke.

They passed over the sea, blotting out the view. She glanced down and saw a glimmer of orange. It rippled, became diffuse, and then returned to an intense orange point. She closed her eyes, thinking it was a retinal afterimage, but saw nothing. When she looked again it seemed to have moved. A craft light, perhaps. The transport, bringing John back to the *Watson*? No, they were supposed to run without lights.

Shoreline slipped under them. The pilot had circled, was bringing them around from the west, farthest from the camp.

Loud pounding came from above again. She could see flashes from the camp but there seemed to be fewer of them. The gunner above must have hit the heavy machine gun, because she didn't hear it anymore.

Noise, confusion. Hale was suddenly shouting into his mike again. Men in the cabin gripped their weapons. The 'copter swooped down, coming in fast. A heavy rattling from the gun above.

They landed hard. "Stay here!" Hale ordered her. As if she needed to be told.

Hale slid the big steel doors open with a rattling bang. The men leaped out. They were facing up the hill, so the 'copter itself shielded against fire from the camp. A gust of heat swept across her face. Claire watched as they ran toward the burning wreckage, its skeleton revealed as black struts among the fire. A few crumpled forms sprawled near it. Hale reached the first one, turned it over, shook his head.

One of them, she realized, must be George. And as the men pulled the charred lumps away from the flames she saw that no one had survived the crash.

The sounds seemed to drop away, becoming unimportant. She thought of cocksure George only minutes ago, on the *Watson*, eager to take off on his big adventure. What had he thought when the shooting started? she wondered.

Above the *whump whump whump* of the rotors she heard snapping rifle fire. They would have to get out of here now, forget—

The cube. She leaped up and stood in the doorway, searching the firelit terrain. There, fifty yards away. The crating looked intact, a pearly block lying nearly in the valley, wrapped in cables.

She shouted to Hale, but he didn't hear. The men were still pulling the bodies clear. The fire was sputtering now, running out of fuel. Hale shouted something to them and then ran toward her, crouched over.

"No chance," he said, bounding up into the cabin. "They died on impact."

He slipped the comm headset on and spoke rapidly into it, describing the situation. Claire felt numb, disconnected. She tried to shake it off, but it was tempting to ignore the hammering from the gunner above, the crackling acrid pyre up on the hillside.

Carmody and the National Security Council had been so sure. They had counted on the Turkish war to divert Kontos, on stealth, on speed and—not the least—on a theory. On calculations that, if she understood what she saw out there in the sea, were seriously wrong.

Hubris. They disliked questions unless there were clear answers. They believed so much in their method that they conjured up certainty out of undeniable risk.

"Hey!" Hale called to her. "Get away from that door."

She realized she was standing in it, looking dumbly out at the flickering scene. Hale finished talking and yanked off the headset.

"Navy's sending in two jets," he said.

"The crate," she said. "We have to get it in the air again."

"Yeah, yeah, I'm thinking. Look, soon's that fire's died down and the jets knock out that camp—they're using napalm—we'll get to it. I figure to pull the mooring block for those cables off the wreck, then hook it to our hoist rig."

"Can you do that quickly?"

"Easy. Ten, maybe twenty minutes."

"Then you should know what I think I saw." She told him.

His eyes narrowed. "Maybe we can't wait for those jets to suppress fire."

"Until they do, let's stay away from the crate."

"Okay. We're out of good rifle range, but there's nothing stopping them coming after us."

The heavy gun above rattled again. "Except that," Claire said. "Do you think there are a lot of Greeks?" One of the arguments she had made to justify coming along had been her command of Greek. She realized that her glib debating point might now turn out to be valid, in a most unpleasant way.

He spat carefully on the floor. "Could be."

"We've got to get that thing in the *air*."

"Yeah. Look, I'll report what you said—"

The headset halfway on, he stopped dead. A *rrrrtttt* came from the distance.

"Damn! That heavy sucker again. They musta got it back in action."

Three slugs smacked into the body of the 'copter, each one like hammer blows on wood. Claire cringed. Another burst from above. Hale looked confused. She was glad to know matters were coming a bit too quickly for him as well.

Two more slugs slammed into the body of the 'copter, this time bringing a clang from the tail.

"Jesus, they can come right through the side," Hale said wonderingly. "High caliber stuff. We're just a big target."

"Then let's get out," she said.

More slugs smacked into the 'copter, making it rock slightly. The men nearby set up a cracking din of return fire.

Hale said something into his mike—it was covered by the noise—and nodded. "Right. We'll do that." He signed off.

"Do what?"

"Get up on the ridgeline, see if that thing's out there."

"You don't believe me?"

"Not me, it's Carmody. We got to know what's going on."

"Well—"

"Another thing. Carmody wants you away from this 'copter. Brush fire's dying down, Greek infantry might come up on us any minute. Carmody says I'm to get you away, safe, over the ridge line, before that singularity thing gets here. Check on what you saw. I'll leave you there, hidden. Then we'll get that crate strung right."

"I just run off in the darkness?" she asked.

"I'm going with you."

Another burst rocked the helicopter. The clatter of the shooting was making it hard to hear. "We got the backup chopper coming in, it'll find you, pick you up. We'll have these guys finished off by then."

Claire stared at him. In the midst of all this, he was still sure they could bring it off.

Hale smiled. "It's better than taking incoming fire, believe me."

"But I don't—"

"Carmody's orders, see?" Hale asked sharply. "Look, lady, I got things to do."

She nodded mutely. The gun above rattled off a burst. She noticed that the other men had come back to the helicopter and were crouched around the fuselage. She climbed down after Hale and inched along to the shelter of the undercarriage. A high whine came down from the clouds and then a low, hollow roaring.

"Here's Navy," Hale called. He grinned. "Get set, hey? I'll go with you, these guys'll give covering fire. We'll go up the hill, along that li'l ravine, see? Where it's dark."

"All right."

The whine climbed and she realized the jets must be diving. Suddenly she saw one come down out of a low cloud several miles away, a black mote against the gray cloud bank. It swept down swiftly, like a bird in a flat glide. She lost sight of it as it passed behind the helicopter and then a yellow sun burst beyond, sheets raking the ground. Rumbling, a burned-golden ball rose in the night. It transfixed her, blinded her.

"Hey! C'mon." Hale grabbed her arm. She stumbled after him, in shock.

They went straight up the hillside, scrambling in the loose stones, running hard at first and then grabbing at bushes to pull themselves up. All the time she wanted to look back at the yellow sheets of flame but she did not dare; the footing was difficult even in boots and she had to struggle to keep up with Hale. Their shadows stretched ahead, distorted arms swinging in huge arcs. He led the way into a narrow ravine, running lightly despite being bent over in a crouch. Then the light faded into orange. The napalm was giving out.

She couldn't hear any of the popping noises now, no rifle fire. Panting, she followed Hale's murky form ahead. A pebble-rolled under her boot and she fell hard, rolling, scraping her face. The dry, clean smell of Greece swarmed in her nostrils, and then she smelled something else, like lighter fluid. Napalm fumes, she guessed, struggling upward.

The ravine sloped steeply, narrowing into a rough gully. She glanced back and saw men in the guttered remains of the first 'copter. They were trying to get the cables free already. Beyond, the camp was aflame. Brush crackled and a pall of smoke hung over a growing orange circle.

"Okay, right here," Hale called. He had stopped in a hollow just below the brow of the hill. They were perhaps three hundred yards from the helicopter, she guessed. Only fitful flames lit the valley.

She was amazed to find, as she climbed the rest of the way up, that he was scarcely breathing hard. They scrambled over a rock ledge and looked down at the shoreline.

A dim blue glow spread like a fan from the base of the steep cliff, illuminating the choppy water from below. The inky sea lapped at its edges but could not smother the deep luminescence. *Like a living thing down there*, she thought. *Like an ancient god*.

She surveyed the horizon. Where was the *Watson*? *Miles away*, she thought, *and running with no lights*.

"I guess you were right," Hale whispered.

"And John's down there."

"Huh?"

"Has communication resumed with the men in the cave?"

"Uh, no."

"Then something. . .has . . ." She couldn't finish. The ghostly radiance glided eerily, as if seeking a way into the cliffside.

Then it struck her. The luminescence was moving far too slowly.

The calculations were wrong somehow. The singularity had returned early. Instead of barreling back at high speed, then slamming into the cliffs below, the thing was crawling over the ocean floor.

How long had it been here? Did it return along its previous tunnel?

Everything they had assumed might be wrong.

Hale was talking into his headset rig, reporting to Carmody. He broke off and gestured to her. "You just stay put right here. Navy's taken out those bastards, so pretty soon we'll have the crate hooked up. Fifteen minutes, max, I figure. Then I'll send a man for you, or the backup chopper will be here. Carmody says you're not to go back where you could get hit."

"Great."

"Come back a way, you're too easy to see up here."

They slid down and walked into the gully. Fifty yards down it. Hale held up a hand. "This's okay. Stay put."

He started back down, cradling his weapon, studying the way. He was about halfway down when a quick *brrrrrpp* sliced through the night and Hale fell face forward. The body rolled and then tumbled head over heels before it disappeared in some bushes.

Claire shrank back into the shadows. The awful sound had come from her left, to the west. She peered at the bush where Hale lay but nothing moved. Perhaps he was working his way downhill, crawling. The men at the helicopter had heard, she could see them dispersing. They started shooting. Sharp spatting reports came from the undergrowth near the smoldering ruins. There was no answer from the darkness.

She crouched, trying to get control of her thoughts. Hale wounded, possibly dead. The team below, expecting an attack. Probably some were still trying to free the cables, and the rest were keeping up covering fire. She listened to a steady peppering of shots. Yes.

What should she do? Stay here, certainly. If things calmed down, and no one came for her, she could work her way over the ridgeline, down to the sea.

From the left, a faint snap.

She peered over a clump of brush. From this angle she could make out areas the men below could not, and she thought she caught a shadowy movement. It was so hard to tell in the pervading gloom, but there, yes, another dark patch changed slightly.

Crack. This time closer.

She got the impression of steady movement along the face of the hill. Two figures, perhaps three. Not firing, only maneuvering, coming this way.

Of course. Hale had brought her up this gully because it gave shelter. Anyone descending would seek the same concealed approach when they were going down.

They would come this way, and find her. And Hale, if he was still alive.

What was intended as a safe haven for her was now a trap. She had to act. They were coming. They would probably pass through here. She had to move. Yet all her instincts were to hide, go to ground. And she could not shake the feeling of incongruity, that she shouldn't *be* in something like this, that the world had suddenly spun away into madness.

Coldly, she told herself that this was a time to think and act and let nothing else get in the way. That was the way a man would be, just do what had to be done and leave the rest for later. Analytical. Careful. Mind focused on each problem as it came up. *And*, she thought wryly, *try not to tremble*.

She scrambled up the gully, looking for a break in the scrub brush. Another snapping sound came to her across the chilly air, closer this time.

She found a passage, a narrow lane between two tall stands

of brush and knobby trees. Gratefully she inched up the steep side of the gully, holding to tufts of grass, avoiding outcroppings of loose dirt that might crumble, sending rattling pebbles down. She was panting so strongly it seemed the sound itself might give her away.

She got on hands and knees and crawled into the lane. The enclosing shadows seemed welcoming after the exposed gully. Twigs raked her face but she kept steadily on, following the twists, working her way uphill and away from the gully. Sharp stones cut her hands. The brittle tang of the brush covered the lingering sharp napalm stink.

Once she had started it was automatic to keep on. Her knees rubbed raw, nettles ripped at her face, but she kept the stinging pain suppressed, devoting all her attention to listening.

The staccato shots from below, had stopped. A soft wind brought a mumble of conversation, perhaps the men discussing the cables. Above that, of course, the helicopter kept up its dogged ratcheting. Nothing more.

She stopped and quickly bobbed up to see. The camp was still aflame, oily smoke engulfing the fires. She was amazed to see how far she had crawled—at least two hundred yards. She could barely make out the murky outline of the helicopter.

And at any moment, she knew, the singularity might rip to the surface, burning and irradiating them all. Or worse, a nuclear explosion.

It was attracted by the cube, by its twin trapped in the carefully sculpted magnetic fields in the crate. If what John and Sergio and the others said was right, the strange glow would not remain down there in the sea. Inevitably, their forces would draw the twin "twists" together.

The shadowy figures were moving. She sensed them melting in and out of the rumpled terrain, still angling this way, apparently trying to encircle the helicopter. There were only a few. But if one of them came upon her . . .

She turned, thinking to make her way back over the ridgeline—and was surprised to find the rising scarp of the pathway only thirty feet away. Above it loomed the entrance to the tomb.

The fires from the camp were smothered now in smoky

clouds. She could not see the helicopter but she could acutely sense the men on the hillside, still maneuvering.

She worked her way up to the pathway, crawling over broken ground. The entrance of the tomb reared above her, almost a welcoming, familiar sight. She swung her cramped legs over a boulder and crouched on level ground. No unusual sound, only the rustle of the wind, the helicopter engine idling, and the distant crackling of the fires. She duckwalked around a final outcropping and into the shelter of the limestone entrance. It was so dim she made her way along by touching the limestone wall with her right hand. She panted, still in shock, anxious to get to shelter. The wall ended and she felt her way to the great rectangular door. Her fingers found the corner. She stepped through, pressing against the comforting massive stones, and only then thought that she had not found the iron gate, and the wooden door must be swung open, on the opposite side. She would not need her key. The tomb was open.

A beam of white light shone in her face. She gasped.

"So it *is* you," a voice said. The voice of Colonel Alexandros Kontos.

CHAPTER
Seven

John stared for a long moment at the tiny, virulent blue spark. It rolled on the sea floor, perhaps forty yards away. Yellow tendrils forked from it like lightning, ending in cloudy bursts of violet. A blue aura lit rocks and crevices, casting an eerie radiance on the brown track it left in its wake.

Bubbles popped into existence all around it, sparkling with blue light, then wobbled and cascaded upward like flights of silvery birds.

The twin singularity. It had come back already, traveled over a thousand miles, arrived hours too early.

But how did it get into the sea? It should have come back into the cavern. Its tunnel led there.

As he watched it veered sharply. It struck a rock and yellow sparks shot out, blooming like sulphurous flowers. The rock split in two.

No sound. Ghostly, silently, it rolled and cut, vaporizing seaweed into brown smoke. Ivory bubbles burst across the sea bed, steam trails of high energy particles. The singularity was taking in water and adding some to its mass, ejecting the rest as live steam.

Water stirred in his ear. Seaweed unfurled with slow green majesty before a fresh current. Pushed by it, the singularity abruptly lumbered toward him, spitting forked lightning of purple and gold.

John jackknifed, turning. *Move.* The water stopped most of the radiation, even the gammas, but he was still getting a dose of a respectable level. He had to find shielding.

There was no escape out this way. Not when it was moving. It could catch up to him and fry him in an instant.

He wriggled around and worked his way back over the same course, faster this time. All he wanted was *out*, away. The transport would come and if he could reach it—

No, it wouldn't. The team could see the singularity as they approached. They'd turn tail and go back to the *Watson*.

Leaving him here, with somebody up above who had already killed Arditti and maybe the others.

He stopped at the narrow turn and clicked off his flashlight. Save the batteries. Also, someone above might be able to see it.

Hang in the dark and think. He couldn't go back, he couldn't go forward. And he couldn't stay here, not for long—his gauge showed only twenty minutes of air left.

He shouldn't let the air dwindle down to nothing. If he did, he would have only one way out of the cavern—up, through the tomb. Unless he wanted to swim back through the throat in the dark, with his flashlight, hoping the singularity was not out there.

He gritted his teeth. Be a mathematical physicist, young man. See the world, have adventures, meet interesting singularities. See your equations come alive.

They had all drastically miscalculated the time when the damned thing would arrive back at the site. Some mathematician he was. What else had they gotten wrong?

Still, in an odd way it was satisfying to see the spitting, virulent twin singularity, to know that their deductions from a rarefied field theory had the heft and tang of reality. He smiled. His imaginary dragon in a mathematical garden bore claws that truly slashed, snorted with a breath of real fire. He might not get out of this stupid trap, but he had seen the truth, his basic calculations were right. That was something.

He shrugged. Something, sure. But not nearly enough.

Water sloshed in his ears. Time to decide.

From behind him the burnt-orange glow ebbed, casting shadows. He hissed air in, taking a deep breath, hoping it would resolve his mind. The damned singularity might be leaving. That would be the break he needed. He didn't want to go back into the cavern.

He turned to study the weakening illumination. But no, it

wasn't weaker. The orange aura waxed as he watched, sliding into green. It must be approaching the foot of the cavern, drawn to the shoreline. Why?

There wasn't time to figure that out. He watched the glow getting stronger as he peered down, between his flippered feet. No choice. He had to go up.

He wriggled and worked his way around the neck. The glow was getting stronger. He swam quickly away, pulling at the water, navigating by the light from behind.

There were Arditti's feet. John slipped past the body, avoiding looking at the face. The water was thick with the cloaking haze and he imagined he could taste it. His stomach churned.

Now there was barely enough light to see. He tentatively drifted up and broke the surface. No light above. He let the demand valve drop from his mouth and groped for the side.

Gravel ground under his flippers. He raised his mask and crawled up, trying not to make noise. Every ripple of the water sounded impossibly loud. He floundered up, pebbles sliding beneath his feet, the cylinder lurching to the side. He caught it just before it struck the stone lip where the water ended. Carefully he eased it off his shoulders and rolled it quietly onto the ledge, panting. He crawled farther up, into near total darkness. The ledge was thick with slime. He slipped and nearly ended up back in the luminous water. He crawled upward again. Then came some pebbles and he got the leverage to roll over and pull off his flippers.

Still no movement anywhere. No sound. He had half expected to be met with a hail of fire.

Where were the two others? His hands ran across wires in the dark and he grasped them. The cables for the antenna. They led forward.

He got to his feet and stepped cautiously, careful on the slimy slope.

Get to shelter. He followed a slightly darker set of shadows and found they were a line of boulders. He slipped behind them. The pool of water seemed magically lit from below, eerily like a fish pond in someone's fancy backyard. He could see little by it. He waited. Silence. No, a creaking. Very faint, off to the right, but coming as if from above, too. There, again.

He had to know the situation. Anyone who really wanted to kill him would've shot at the first sound.

Unless they thought he was one of them, of course.

One of the Greeks. Kontos. He'd somehow guessed the tomb was important.

He fetched the flashlight up from its tether at his belt and pointed it upward. Best to get an all-round view, and it also wouldn't pinpoint his location quite so strongly.

He clicked it on. The gallery leaped into stark nearness, a red cavern. No response. He recognized the long slope of pebbles, the arched roof about ten feet above, the scattered rocks and sand.

And there, two bodies. He knew them without even turning them over. They lay among the comm gear. Both had large red stains across their black wet suits. The gear was damaged, too, torn apart as if by an explosion.

Neither was holding his weapon. Their submachine guns were neatly leaned against a boulder ten feet away.

Still no movement. Maybe the attackers had gone away, back up. He snapped off the flashlight and worked his way around the rocks until he judged he was about fifteen feet from the bodies. He would have to come out into the open to fetch one of the guns. He duckwalked his way across, keeping low. Then he scrambled quickly forward, to another group of rocks that provided some shelter from above.

He clicked the flashlight back on. Wet rock reflected the beam back. From here he could see the hole in the roof above. A rope hung forlornly there, and from the end of it, in a harness, swung a body.

The person wore the same Greek army fatigues he had seen in Boston. The body swung slowly, making the rope creak. As it came around fully into his beam he recognized the face. It was Sergeant Petrakos.

She was limp, hands hanging free. Below her lay a light machine gun and at her belt were spherical black hand grenades. One of those had probably gotten the two men, and then she had shot Arditti, who was farther back.

John stood and walked toward the body, pebbles grinding under his feet, careful to stay out of view of anyone farther up the shaft. He was at a bad angle here but there was something about the body that he didn't understand.

The fatigues were blackened over her back and shoulders. And her hair—there wasn't any. He remembered she had long black hair, but this stuff was a stubble.

Then he caught the smell. An acrid, sour stench. The sharp bite of it made him wrinkle his nose and step back. Her face was red on the side he could see, and as she turned the movement brought around stretched, blackened skin, cracked and pitted.

One eye oozed a clear fluid. It ran down her nose and dripped from the end. He stepped back again, horrified, not wanting it to spatter his feet.

Her face was cut in several places. At the neck were several deep gouges. Blood still trickled from them. Below, her uniform was sopping with it.

About four feet above the body, the rope was burned partway through. His eyes traveled to the side of the shaft and there he saw a small circular pattern, brown at the outside and black at the center. Opposite it, on the other wall about ten feet away, was a similar bull's-eye.

The flare. Not set off by Arditti, no. Arditti had been dead by then.

The brilliant flare must have been the passing of the singularity. It had come right through the rock side and across, frying Sergeant Petrakos with radiation, singeing the rope.

It must have struck the rock with terrible force, spraying shards. That would explain the cuts on the body.

He studied the two circular holes. One was about half a foot below the other. As soon as the thing left the wall, gravity would pull it downward. To drop half a foot, while it flew across about ten feet of open air. . .He calculated swiftly. The thing had been moving about sixty miles an hour.

All right. That disproved the minority theory, which held that the singularity would not return along its earlier channel, and therefore would meet more resistance. They had calculated an exit velocity of about twenty miles per hour. Clearly wrong.

On the other hand, the singularity had returned earlier than the majority thought it would. Maybe it had been moving even faster than the seventy or so miles per hour they had predicted.

That meant it had spent a lot of the return taking the easy

route, along the evacuated channel. Okay. John felt better if the numbers matched up, more or less, with their expectations. Except that the crucial prediction—when the thing would return—had been off by enough to kill them all.

Arditti and the others hadn't died from that, though. Politics had killed them.

So when the singularity came roaring through here, it caught only Sergeant Petrakos. And why had she been here? Kontos must have guessed there was something important left in the tomb site, and come to look.

Which meant Kontos was probably up there in the tomb Kontos hadn't heard the shooting, or else he'd be down here now.

Behind him, the cave brightened. He whirled, sending gravel rattling against the walls.

The black water glowed. It cast a diffuse orange on the worn, wet rock walls.

The singularity was being drawn upward. Coming for him.

Of course. The helicopters were above now, and the initial momentum of the singularity had been spent. Now it was eating its way toward its brother. With him in the middle.

Abruptly the orange light dimmed. He stood stock still, hoping it was going away. It was possible that some of his deductions were wrong, after all. Kontos wasn't necessarily up in the tomb. The sound of helicopters had probably drawn the man away. The way might be clear.

Then he heard humming, faint at first. A vibration in the rock. It grew and added an overtone of something he remembered, a strange combination of liquid sounds and a memory. . . .

A dentist's drill. That high, shrill whine.

Suddenly a hammer-blow of light and noise burst into the cave. John crouched, scrambled behind a rock. He saw it for only an instant, before the yellow flare blinded him. The singularity emerged from the rock a few feet below the water line, jetting steam. It made an eerie sucking sound. Then it began to fall, casting long shadows with its watery light, and struck the far wall in a shower of blue and yellow sparks.

He blinked. It was gone. His eyes slowly grew accustomed to the flashlight beam.

Close, too damned close, and he had probably gotten another dose of gamma radiation. The water had stopped most of the other stuff, the x-rays and ultraviolet that had seared Sergeant Petrakos.

The singularity must be following the 'copter, and he had no way of knowing which direction that was. But why was it bobbing in and out of this cavern?

The 'copter must be moving erratically, over land and sea.

Added into the attraction between the singularities was the force from sea currents carrying it to and fro down there, acting as a drag, occasionally letting it cut through the shore-line.

And he was trapped down here with it.

CHAPTER
Eight

Claire struck at Kontos. The heel of her hand smacked his cheek. The flashlight veered away, throwing splashes of light high into the dome of the tomb.

Kontos had an automatic weapon in the other hand. She snatched at it. He chopped it down across her wrist. Sudden flaring pain cut through her, forcing a startled cry.

Kontos backed away. His face flushed and he shouted between clenched teeth, "Stop! I will use this!"

He leveled the weapon. It had a long, curving clip and the muzzle seemed huge when it pointed at her. She suddenly knew without doubt that he would fire if she made a threatening move.

"Back! Back outside."

"But there are—it's dangerous—napalm—I—"

"Out!"

She turned and Kontos shoved her from behind, making her stumble through the doorway. His flashlight had robbed her of her night vision and she stepped gingerly forward, nearly tripped, and he shoved her again.

"To the end! I wish your helicopter to see what I have caught."

"Look, there is something coming, it's dangerous—"

"We make it very dangerous for you, yes." Kontos chuckled. "You thought the war would make me forget. I heard of your ship movements, that told me."

"Something's coming—"

Kontos prodded her with his gun and she edged forward. The helicopter engine revved up in the distance. She reached the end of the limestone blocks and could see it lift off, its engine roaring.

"They leave you!" Kontos cried angrily. He braced his gun on a ledge and fired a burst at the helicopter. Quick, rattling reports came from the brush down the valley.

Claire ducked behind stone shelter. Kontos shouted in Greek. "Bastards!"

The 'copter soared, the crate below swinging wildly. She saw that the ground fire could hit the crate, damage the magnetic traps. "Kontos, don't shoot at the—"

Her words were drowned out by the thundering of the 'copter's heavy machine gun. A horrible, anguished scream came from the brush. Kontos heard it and fired a long burst at the 'copter, with no visible effect. Each loud report sent a bright burnt-orange streamer leaping into the night.

Claire crept backward, away from Kontos. She felt the stones behind her and her wrist turned painfully against them. If the 'copter located him by his muzzle flash—

Kontos whirled and pointed the gun at her. "Stay! Your friends do not want you, but I will take you to Athens, show the world what—"

The 'copter swooped toward them and they both ducked. It gained speed and its machine gun hammered at targets down the valley. More screams.

Kontos ripped off a long burst again—a loud, metallic chattering. It jerked in his hands so much she wondered how he could hit anything.

There was less rattling gunfire from the brush now. The 'copter turned and passed noisily over them again. It was cruising back and forth along the ridgeline of the hill, where it could command a good field of fire both down the valley and to seaward.

Claire crouched down against the limestone. Kontos fired a clip and reloaded, swearing. She could scarcely make out his silhouette.

"Colonel, we've got to get away," she said carefully. "That helicopter is carrying something that is very dangerous right now."

"My artifact, that is what it is, yes?" His voice was excited, tense as he slipped rounds into the clip.

"Yes, and there is something inside it, a nuclear—"

"I know, a valuable something. I read the notes of the man Sprangle. The cube contained it all the time, eh?"

"Listen, there's another. It—"

"I want no other. Only want mine, my country's."

"Country doesn't matter in this, Colonel. That thing—"

"You always have a higher motive when you come in your helicopters."

"But we do . . ."

The 'copter roared overhead, firing incessantly into the valley. There were few answering spurts of gunfire. The screaming had stopped, too, and she was glad of that.

"Your men down there, not many are shooting," she said.

"There have been losses," Kontos said automatically. "But we will hold here."

"For how long? Look, all we want to do—"

"I could get only two squads but there will be more from the towns nearby, soon. Do not think you will get away."

"You called them?"

He grunted. His transmission would be easily picked up by the *Watson*, she realized, and help sent from the Sixth Fleet. Soon.

The helicopter pounded away at something nearby. She could hear heavy thuds as rounds smacked into rock, and the *spang* of a ricochet. Kontos jammed the clip back into the breech of his weapon and braced to fire at the 'copter.

"Wait! They're armored, you can't get through the sides of it with that gun of yours."

"They cannot be armored everywhere."

"They'll see the flash, you're practically the only one left firing."

"Silence!" He fired once at the 'copter, which was hovering over a flat area to the south. He took aim again and abruptly the 'copter surged up into the air and banked, heading back toward the tomb.

"Let's get inside!" Claire shouted. "Please!"

The roar of the engines and the sudden menacing turn seemed to have daunted Kontos. She tugged at his sleeve. "Come on!"

He stared at the approaching craft, stepped back in hesitation, and then turned to stride rapidly back into the tomb. The heavy machine gun barked and rounds slammed into the limestone blocks lining the passage.

They ran to the back of the tomb. The 'copter passed overhead, paused for a long moment, and then banked, pursuing some target to the west. Its distant drone was now the only sound from outside. No more stuttering barks came from the brush.

Kontos swore to himself in Greek. Claire wondered if she could slip away in the inky darkness, find a place to hide. She breathed in the cold tomb's dank smell shallowly, desperately, as she heard Kontos shuffle impatiently near the entranceway. Somehow she had to get away.

CHAPTER
Nine

John had had a bellyful. He cast his flashlight beam upward, where the cord stretched amid shadows. It had regular knots in it to aid climbing. Thick and rough, it seemed suddenly enormously inviting. If he could get past the burned spot.

But would he be safer up there? The singularity was sinking now, sure—but the helicopter would eventually draw it to the surface. It had been quite fatal when it was moving fast—Petrakos's bloody uniform implied that she died from the rock cuts. Now that it was slowed, radiation was the main threat.

He could hear it coming through the rock. On the rope he at least had some vertical freedom of movement.

Right. Climb, then.

He picked up one of the automatic weapons. It was heavy but cradled easily in his arms. He imagined his father saying in his thick drawl, "Situation like this, man ought to have a piece."

He slung it over his shoulder and grabbed the rope where it coiled on the pebble beach. He should tie the end around his waist, in case he slipped. But then, there was the Sergeant to get past, caught in her harness. No, better he stayed free.

Off to the side, he noticed, lay shards of the old crate, the one he had pursued down here at the beginning of all this, months ago. The crate had smashed here, he remembered, and tumbled across the pebble beach, down to the water.

He gripped the rope and boosted himself up, trapping the lowest knot with overlapped feet. The rope groaned with the added weight. He did not relish the idea of working around Petrakos. Her body swung as counterweight to his, making her arms wave, giving her hands a weird animation. He climbed to just below her and tried to reach around. He grabbed the harness line and went up it hand over hand. It was awkward but he got his arms by without touching her upper body. As he wormed past he had to place his feet against her for a moment, and the contact gave him shivers. His distaste drove him upward, upward.

He remembered doing this in football workout on rainy days back in Georgia, exercising in the gym, wearing cotton sweat pants to keep the chill from tightening up his muscles. It had been easier then. He hadn't had to do it in a wet suit after swimming hundreds of yards. And, yes, he was a decade younger then. Already he felt a seeping weakness in his arms, and in the gut muscles which had to pull up the legs as they pawed the air, searching for purchase. The rope stung his water-softened hands.

He went perhaps fifty feet before he saw the second set of holes in the cave walls. They were blackened and, hovering a few feet away, he caught an acrid stench. So the singularity had shot through here more than once. This time he could not see any difference in elevation of the holes. The thing had been moving even faster when it made this wound. So he had been wrong about the lower two holes. They had come later. The singularity was wandering, sometimes rising in response to the upward attraction, usually falling under gravity.

He pulled upward, letting his legs do most of the work. The flickering beam of his flashlight at his belt cast deceptive shadows on the damp stone.

He reached the big rock ledge. His arms trembled and the gun over his shoulder banged against stone, echoing. He hauled himself up a last few feet and hooked a foot over onto the ledge. Slithering off, onto the slick wet shelf, was a tremendous relief. He lay there for a moment, letting the shakes seep out of his muscles. He cast a flashlight beam across the narrow cavern and saw the side passage, remembering the blue light he had seen there months ago. The walls were glassy now, not at all the way he remembered. He knew immediately that the singularity had been this way.

He rolled over and shone the red beam behind him. There was a small blackened hole in the rock, and around it a glassy brown stain. Fragments of chipped rock littered the ledge beneath.

The singularity had come through at high speed here, shattering the rock with shock waves even as it chewed its way through. This must have been where it returned, heading back from somewhere under Europe, just as Carmody had hoped. But too soon. Perhaps an hour ago, or more. It had made a blistering track through here. . .and probably attracted the attention of Sergeant Petrakos.

Then it kept right straight on, heading for the *Watson* and its twin. Only the helicopters lifted off about then, and so the singularity turned about and shot back to the cavern, killing Petrakos, and finally emerged onto the sea bed. The difference in height of the two holes was where it had *risen*, following the helicopter, before falling into the sea when the helicopter turned out to sea. It had been wandering around since then, buffeted by water currents, passing into the hill and criss-crossing through this cavern.

That explained something he recalled from last autumn— the blue light he had seen down a side cranny. He had thought it was the radiance of dawn, refracted through the blue Mediterranean waters. It must have been the aura of the second twist as it digested some tidbit of shale or limestone, far down below. The blue glow he had followed *was* dawn. . .but not the other one.

He smiled. That seemed so long ago. Such a simple observation had brought forth a simple, ordinary explanation.

Wearily he searched the ledge. There were the shattered bits of the old crate, lying as he remembered them. Apparently Sergeant Petrakos had left everything undisturbed.

A faint strumming sounded up the cavern. John rolled back from the edge, seeking shelter.

The humming came. He backed against the wall of the ledge. A shrill, greedy whine, much worse now than a dentist's drill. The sucking sound was like a rising wind, a consuming voracious firestorm. He felt a pulse of heat in the air. A brilliant flash. Not pure orange now, there was a blue cast to it—and then it was gone, the shrill angry sound diminishing as the thing found its way into rock.

He breathed deeply, his heart thumping, waiting for the red retinal image to fade. Limestone, falling into the singularity, gave off a blue spectrum. Sea water had produced orange. The twin had been ingesting a varied diet of rock for these past months, while its brother was isolated in the magnetic trap of the cube; this gave them different emission signatures. He would be intrigued, ordinarily. In these circumstances, though, the point seemed less than fascinating.

The singularity was rising up through the Earth, drawn by its twin above. So the twin must be nearby.

He had to get out. Since the thing was rising, odds were that each time it passed through this area it would be higher. It might never return this way, but if it did, an instant's close exposure would kill him.

He grabbed the rope and pulled himself up rapidly. A panic seized him, but he knew how to use it, let the fear sing through his blood and give more power to the work. He struggled up, ignoring the rope biting into his palms, the sharp pains in his thighs, concentrating on making each grip secure, each knot reached a small victory. Only a bit more to go. He peered upward and saw the edge only twenty feet above.

The last few knots were difficult. The adrenaline surge ebbed away and his muscles stung with pain. The automatic rifle butt swung painfully against his leg as he struggled over the lip, onto sticky mud.

For a moment he panted, thinking of nothing. He felt chilled, exhausted. His arms and legs trembled, remembering the ascent. The slimy mud reeked in his nostrils. Then he heard the voices.

Faint whispers, impossible to distinguish the words. Greeks, they must be Greeks guarding the tomb, waiting for Sergeant Petrakos to come back.

He sat up and slipped the weapon free of his shoulder. Now that he looked at the automatic rifle, he realized that he had never fired anything remotely like it. Here was the breech, with the cartridge clip inserted. It had a green plastic pistol grip, a carrying handle with the rear sight sunk into it, and a conical flash suppressor at the muzzle. In movies people just picked up guns and fired them, never having any trouble loading them or having the breech jam in a misfire. He worked the bolt and saw the brass gleam of a round in the chamber. Good.

He wondered what he should do. Could he really shoot the men outside? Without warning?

They must have seen the helicopters, must know that something was up. In fact, he thought he could hear the *brrrrr* of a chopper in the distance. Would they be jumpy? Maybe he should try to take them prisoner.

Cautiously he got to his feet in the slippery mud. He was covered with the clammy, smelly stuff. He clicked off his flashlight and inched through the hole into the tomb. There was no light. He felt a soft pressure on his face and realized the sheet was still hanging over the pipes, still hiding the hole where the cube had been.

Inky blackness lay beyond. He sensed the high entrance, a slightly lighter patch. The voices came from over there.

He could not make them out. Greek? Maybe.

He stepped silently into the tomb itself, straightened, and realized he would have to turn on the flashlight and hold the gun at the same time. He grasped the pistol grip and leveled the rifle.

The red beam clicked on, showing two startled faces: Claire and Kontos.

CHAPTER
Ten

Kontos held a submachine gun cradled in his left arm, muzzle pointing at the ground.

John dropped the flashlight, letting the cord at his belt catch it, and stepped forward quickly. He chopped down with the automatic rifle. It struck Kontos on the arm, loosening his hold on his weapon. Kontos grunted with pain, coming out of his surprise, turning. John raised the muzzle and slammed it into Kontos. He caught the man on the arm and across the chest. The submachine gun thumped into the dirt.

"Move and I shoot," John said, backing away so that Kontos could not grab the muzzle. "Claire, come away from him."

Kontos swore angrily in Greek. The flashlight swung, making their shadows veer crazily.

Claire said, "Thank God! Everything's gone wrong up here."

"It hasn't been a day at the beach down below, either," John said.

Kontos began, "Sergeant Petrakos—"

"Dead."

"Your Marines—"

"No Marines, Kontos. The guys who came with me are dead, though—Petrakos did her job."

Kontos asked incredulously, "Then you—?"

"Nope. A li'l piece of theoretical physics killed her."

"You—"

"Shut up."

John edged toward the tomb door, peering out. It was impossible to see anything.

They stood unmoving in the dim red circle cast by John's flashlight. Equipment and tools from the archeological work still littered the floor. The crates which John had seen here months ago were gone, shipped to Athens.

Kontos rubbed his arm and said with steely menace, "I advise you to give yourselves up."

John laughed.

"You cannot hold this position forever, even with aircraft. I guessed you would come, that there was something here you needed."

"But you know about the singularity."

Kontos's face became cautious. "I could not understand the tapes—it is a particle? Something in the cube?"

"Forget it—no time."

"Soon more troops will come—"

"Shut *up*." John turned to Claire. "Tell me what it's like out there. Will somebody shoot at us? How come you're here?"

Claire rapidly filled him in, concluding, "After the napalm, I think the 'copter killed most of the rest of Kontos's men."

"God, what a mess."

"The 'copter is up there now. Kontos was figuring out some way to use me, when you showed up. Beautiful timing." She grinned crookedly. Her voice quavered and he saw she was on the verge of breaking down. She was a mass of bruises, her clothes torn and muddied. Her eyes brimmed, damp and wild.

"Here," he said, handing her the flashlight and unhooking it from his belt. "Keep it on him."

Kontos swore at them both, his body tensing. He wore fatigues, but without the usual pistol at the belt which designated officers. Instead he had a big knife sheathed on his hip. John eyed the man, wondering if Kontos was agitated enough to jump him unarmed.

"Where's the 'copter headed?"

"It's overhead now."

"Damn!"

"Why, what—"

"What if we use the flashlight to signal the 'copter?"

"That might work."

"Any Greeks left alive out there to shoot at us?"

"I don't think so."

"Good. Let's get out of here."

He gestured at Kontos with the gun. The man was staring intently at the rifle itself. Was he watching for the clenching of John's hand, a sign that he was going to pull the trigger? The man looked like a glowering lunatic in the red glow. Kontos cast a giant shadow, amplifying his movements. He shifted, setting his feet wider apart, and his shadow raked across the ancient limestone blocks.

"Come on, Kontos."

Still the fixed look, the eyes showing white.

"Move."

Kontos sprang at him.

Like many people, John had always wondered if he had the resolve to shoot in the split second when hesitation meant death, and now the doubts were resolved. He had been through too much; the last hour had worn away his civilized reservations.

He pulled the trigger. Nothing happened. The trigger was stiff and would not give. John realized that he had never checked the safety on the weapon, and now it was locked in the off position.

Braced to fire, he reached up with his thumb to click the safety over—and Kontos hit him sideways across the chest, sending the rifle flying.

They struck the floor with Kontos on top. Kontos tried to slam his knee into John's stomach but he rolled aside. John chopped at Kontos ineffectually with his left hand. They both twisted away and struggled to their knees. Before either could rise Kontos swung, a right cross that landed on John's cheek, splitting the skin, bringing sharp, shooting pain.

John slipped the next punch, a wide swing with the left, and jabbed Kontos in the neck. Kontos aimed a hook, missed, lost his balance and rolled away. John got up, trying to see where the rifle had gone. He glanced quickly around the tomb but could not spot it. If he could reach it, get the damned safety off—

Kontos was scrabbling at his belt. The knife. John backed

away, nearly stumbling over some gear. Claire was transfixed, holding the flashlight near the rear of the tomb. Why hadn't she gotten the rifle? He frantically searched the cluttered mud floor, stepping away from Kontos. *Where was it*? But there was something else, too, something warning him—

Kontos got the knife out. The man's eyes jerked from Claire to John and he went into a low crouch, saying nothing. John saw suddenly that the rifle lay behind Kontos, hidden from him by the man's shadow. No chance of reaching it.

John watched Kontos's fevered eyes, trying to guess what he would do next. Kontos had combat training, knew how to use a knife. He was in a practiced crouch, feet shuffling forward.

As John watched, holding his breath, there came at the edge of his perception a sound, a humming that he knew was important.

Kontos came in with the knife held low, pointing up, its thick blade honed to a gleaming razor edge.

John backed away farther. No chance of reaching the doorway; though he was ten yards away, Kontos was set, ready to spring in pursuit.

"Claire!" John took two quick steps and snatched the flashlight from her. Kontos edged closer on the balls of his feet, readying himself.

John deliberately took aim and smashed the flashlight against the tomb wall, bringing sudden darkness.

"Through the hole!" he whispered to Claire. "Get through, go down the rope."

He reached out and gave her a shove in the right direction. He could feel her hesitate and then crouch down to make her way.

He threw the flashlight toward Kontos. It crashed into the wall. The man shouted something but John paid no attention. They were equally blind now and that might delay Kontos. Kontos would come for him slowly in the complete blackness, listening, careful to avoid getting jumped.

Kontos could have escaped then. For a single stretched instant he could have made for the hole. Instead, he swung wildly, hoping to hit John. Revenge came first. He lunged, but in the wrong direction. Toward a spreading glow.

A diffuse luminosity spread like an ominous stain across the other side of the tomb.

The far wall behind Kontos glowed, an ivory radiance. John fumbled after Claire. He bent to slip through the hole and saw that there was enough light now to actually make out Kontos silhouetted. A pearly pattern came from the stones themselves. Sparkling facets of yellow and green played patterns, dancing.

A humming. A bass vibration coming up through his feet.

Kontos whirled and faced the tomb wall now, his quarry forgotten, not understanding. John opened his mouth to call out. Abruptly the noise rose, shrill and menacing.

An orange dot shot out from the tomb wall, dropping, spitting streamers of violet. Shifting blades of prickly light, a cutting wail.

It struck Kontos in the chest. John felt a wave of heat on his face and ducked, slipping behind the stone blocks of the tomb wall, into the passageway beyond.

He staggered forward in slippery mud. Blue-white glare streamed through the hole behind him and the awful sucking whine reverberated. Claire was already on the rope, two knots down. She stared upward at him in amazement.

"Keep going!" He scrambled for the rope, caught it. He slid down, barely holding on, letting the rope burn his hands. The blue brilliance grew. Massive crashes came from above.

"Go for the bottom! All the way!" he shouted over the gathering roar of collapsing stone.

They slid quickly, Claire catching herself on the knots at each interval. They reached the first major turn and John looked upward. Still the hot blue glare, but fainter now. A series of heavy, dull booms signaled more of the tomb falling in. The singularity must have dislodged blocks, destroying the precarious balance of the beehive vault.

His arms stretched, aching with pain. As his feet struck each knot he let them buckle, carrying him down, until he caught the rope again with searing hands and momentarily caught his weight on his arms. Descending seemed to take forever. Streamers of blue and green played on the slick wet walls. He looked down in the fading light. Claire's feet found the large ledge and she staggered onto it. John landed beside her, and gestured across the tunnel, at the side passage with glassy walls. "Over there! It's out of the way."

She hesitated. He grabbed the rope and swung across, barely catching onto the slippery ledge. "Come on!" He pushed the rope back across and she caught it. She looked doubtful but came a moment later, backing up and taking a running start. He caught her clumsily and lunged away from the edge. They fell heavily onto a level area. A massive lip sheltered them from above.

"What. . .I . . ." Claire gasped for breath.

Three rattling concussions shook their ledge. A large mass hurtled past them, cracking into the side, shattering into fragments. They cowered back. Another huge chunk of rock fell past, bouncing from the walls in hammer blows.

The blue-white glare from above ebbed. Another crash, more massive thumps from far up the shaft. Small stones rattled down. Green fingers of light. Another distant smashing. This time nothing fell past, and darkness closed in.

"Kontos . . ."

"Forget him," he said tersely. "Forget the son of a bitch."

They worked their way farther back from the edge in the last faint light.

He did not tell her what he had seen only in an instant's glimpse, before fear drove him forward through the hole and to safety. The blue point of light had slammed into Kontos, splitting his chest. The body staggered with the impact but remained erect, arms half-raised, knife still gripped tightly.

The rest lived in his memory in slow motion. The singularity paused then, tugged by its twin.

Instantly a swirl of rainbow colors broke out over the body, as if Kontos was being illuminated from within. The arms went limp, the head flew back as the thing ate him. A fluorescent effect sent waves of brilliant red shooting through Kontos's arms.

The man began to crumple. For an instant John saw deep into the body—the skeleton, its bones outlined by the scattered radiation. Arms flailing, knees in the act of buckling. Ribs turning, attracted inward, being visibly bent and sucked down toward the source of unbearably intense light.

And at the center of the chest, a rigid frame rotated slowly. A cube, sparkling and vibrating with a cascade of colors— burnt-orange, electric blue, red, smoky orange.

The singularity was bloated, gut full with its eating. It spun. Streamers of yellow licked from it, breaking off a rib. The piercing, ruddy glow lit up the entire rib cage. The chest was a lattice of glowing orange bones. Along them danced forking red tongues of licking flame.

Just as Kontos started to fall, his back swelled and bulged, a blister alive with sulphurous radiance. The singularity was carrying through Kontos, ceaselessly gnawing, ripping apart sinew and bone in its thirst for matter. For a frozen instant in John's memory he could see the swollen mound of flesh rip open the green fatigues, making Kontos into a grotesque hunchback. Then the festering bulge erupted like a volcano, spraying gobbets of flesh into the air with a sound of liquid explosion.

John closed his eyes, panting, and saw it again, and knew he would never be able to forget it.

CHAPTER
Eleven

Claire pressed back into the wet stone as the bluegreen shafts on the wall ebbed. Reverberating crashes died away. A silent darkness descended and she could hear her heart hammering in her chest.

She lay like that for a long while, gasping, unable to think of anything other than the wondrous fact that she was alive. Slowly then the pains in her hands, arms and legs diffused, swelling into a general ache that came from every part of her.

"I don't think. . .we got much radiation," John gasped.

"Good," was all she could think to reply.

"The whole damned tomb. . .collapsed, sounded like. Prob'ly. . .sealed us off."

"Yes."

"No light coming in that I can see."

"No."

"Here, scrunch over this way."

She felt in the clammy blackness and found him. He drew her into an embrace, entwining their legs. His wet suit was chilly but she pressed against him, glad of the contact. For a while they said nothing; she simply let the fevered impulses of her nervous system flicker away, bringing a deep fatigue.

A long time later she asked, "How about. . .down there?"

"We might go down by rope."

"Do you suppose the cave-in blocked this shaft?"

"Could be."

"Shouldn't we explore?"

"Rest. . .a minute."

They stayed that way for a while. The chill of the stone began to seep into her legs. Claire waited and when he did not respond to her efforts to press closer to him she thought he had gone to sleep.

She shook him and felt the welcome quickening of his breath. "Shouldn't we do something?"

"Okay. I'll see. . .if I can reach the rope."

She could feel him get slowly to his hands and knees. He moved to the lip of the ledge and she reached out to steady him.

"Nothing here," he said. "I'm stretched out into the shaft, feeling around. No rope."

"Perhaps it's hanging farther away."

"I don't think so. It was just about in the middle of the shaft. I should be able to touch it."

"Do you have anything to probe with? A stick or something?"

"Nope. Do you?"

"No."

He moved carefully back and put his arms around her.

"I'll try," she said.

"Your arms aren't any longer than mine."

"Well, it's got to be there."

"No it doesn't. I think the cave-in ripped it away."

"Oh."

A long silence.

"Is there any way to get down without it?"

"No. It's 'way too steep. You'd fall and break your neck."

"Then. . .what *can* we do?"

"Nothing. Not every problem has a solution."

"We'll—we'll *freeze* in here."

"Or run out of air."

"Carmody will find us."

"Prob'ly. But who knows we're here?"

"They'll search."

"I don't know if they have the time or the equipment to pull away those limestone blocks up there."

"Time?"

"The Greeks'll be back."

"Oh."

"Could be the second underwater team will come up from below. Unless that way's blocked by the cave-in. I'd guess it is. Those were big chunks."

"We've got to *do* something."

"Stay warm."

"You sound like Marcus Aurelius."

"Who?"

"A Stoic."

"Huh. Just stay warm."

Another long silence. She was unnerved by his acceptance of their situation. She thought furiously.

"Does this side passage go anywhere?"

"Sure. Straight down to somewhere below France. It's the tunnel the singularity bored."

"Oh." She reached out and felt along the cold, slick surface.

In the utter blackness her sense of touch was amplified, exaggerating every crevice and slope into valleys and mountains. She thought wistfully that if the shaft and this side opening had any archeological significance, it was lost now; such damage had surely erased any record of the past.

She asked him what had happened to Arditti and the others. He told her sketchily, plainly not wanting to remember. His voice was deep and gravelly and she concentrated on it in the absolute blackness, using it as an anchor. The words came slowly to him and his voice trembled when he told how he had found the bodies. She was horrified by the repeated passings of the singularity. She wanted to ask how much radiation he had gotten but saw it would do no good, that he could not judge and was trying not to think of it.

He slowed, his words dropping into the silence like pebbles into a deep well. He stopped. Then, as if from a long way off, he said drowsily, "C'mon, rest, cuddle up. We prob'ly got a long wait."

She wrapped herself around him, feeling protective. He was exhausted and probably had mild shock. She had been banged up, but nothing like the strain of swimming and climbing for so long, not to mention the terror he must have felt in this awful place.

She held him, trying to ignore her numb feet. The cold spread gradually, her muscles tightening, fingers of dull pain working up through her legs. She could not sleep. The excitement had abated, leaving a residue of darting attention, unable to subside. It would be better if she were played out, like John. Then she could sleep and save her energy for later. She could not keep her thoughts from skittering over the grim future. They were trapped in the cold and dark, no one knowing their location, perhaps even believing them killed in the cave-in. As much as she went over the facts she could see nothing to do, no real hope of ever escaping this silent grave. Much the way others might have faced death in the ancient tomb above, if in fact servants had been buried with their masters. John had spoken of that long ago, felt it there in the tomb, the horror of burial.

Gradually she shifted away from their prospects and thought of the tomb. She smiled to herself, recognizing that even when she lay in what would probably be her own tomb, she still regretted the destruction of such a fine site. The artifact had opened up many possible interpretations of the burial site, ideas which could be tested, leads which would reward a careful combing through the record.

It was obvious that the singularity had been magnetically trapped in the stone before the cube came to the tomb. Possibly the amber cone was a way to view the singularity's awesome light without leaving a howling hole in the cube.

But why bury it? Because it belonged to a ruler, a great man? Perhaps. But the Mycenaeans gave their dead implements which would be useful during the passage to the land of the afterlife. The implements were left near the body. Why bury the cube behind the tomb wall?

Because it was dangerous? Not to the dead, but to the living who finished preparing the tomb.

If the crude marks on the outer block were in fact from servants buried with their master, then those servants wanted to get the artifact itself. Perhaps they knew that it contained something which could cut rock, make an opening in the tomb walls. They certainly knew that they could not escape through the sealed doorway and the tons of sand beyond.

They had tried for something they might have been able to reach. But whoever made the gouges never got beyond the outer block, and perished.

Suppose everyone knew the artifact contained something

terribly dangerous. Something was trapped inside, or else the great man wouldn't have kept it with him. But if it got loose after the man's death, his mourners did not want it around, on the surface, where it could kill and destroy.

Pride. All this suggested a certain hubris, the boasting of a man after some feat, some victory now vanished in the dust. He might have prized the artifact, had the stone-trapped singularity chiseled out of rock and fashioned into a cube.

That way he could return in grandeur, bringing the captive monster back to his people, he could boast, *Here, gaze upon my prey.* And watch the stay-at-homes cower, fearful and awed, before the rough-cut cube. *See*, he could say, *look at the amber. It glows with the inner demon.* To show how unconcerned he was, he could have the cube ornamented, carved further with a Linear A inscription, and an ivory map attached.

The map. What would be more natural than to attach to the cube a record of his travels, his triumphs?

A sign of where the cube came from. Santorini.

The ivory rectangle was the first map of any kind found from Mycenaean Greece, from the old times when the legends were born, before Homer had spun the central images of his culture into his rich tales. Almost certainly map-making arose from navigation, so maps would be drawn on useful, cheap parchment or other writing material. Something a fisherman or trader could afford to carry around. Not an ornament, laboriously inscribed on precious ivory. That fragile rectangle was clearly a gesture of opulence and great glory.

So for some reason the great man, the King, had gone to Santorini and brought back the thing in stone. He must have pursued it beneath the Earth and found it embedded. A bit of luck, which he turned into a grand tale.

She tried to remember what John and Sergio had said about the twinned singularities. Together they might be much more benign. Once they paired up, buried in rock, the accidental magnetic trap into which they had blundered could hold them. Perhaps that was how they had come together—one becoming caught in the accidental magnetic cup, and then the other seeking it out.

Unless the pair were jarred, as she and John had jarred them. So perhaps the King had found the twins reunited, trapped in the rock, had commanded his men to carve out a stone vessel around it, brought it across the sea. . . .

No, that was unreasonable. Maneuvering tons of rock onto a sailing vessel, bringing it hundreds of miles—somewhere it would have slipped, jounced, separated the singularities.

What if the King found only *one* singularity? A sole singularity could remain relatively quiet in such a trap for at least months; theirs had, sitting in Boston. Then the King would bring it home. . . .

. . .And its twin would follow.

Suppose the King thought he had found the monster, caught it. But in fact he had only gotten one of the monsters. The second twin was probably nearby, perhaps on Santorini itself. They would seek each other, trying to reunite, but continually deflected by the ocean, by volcanic currents deep beneath the rock.

Suddenly she remembered the ruined outline of the shaft in the sea, the trench they had supposed was a seepage channel. . .which led to the shaft where they were trapped now. A singularity, cutting through limestone, would open a small passage. Rainwater would preferentially flow there, eroding the limestone easily, enlarging the bore of it. In time it would look the same as the millions of seepage shafts that wove through the soft limestone beds of Greece.

There would be no way to tell that something had cut the seed passage, searching for its twin.

The twin twist had found its brother in the tomb, bored the hole in the back of the cube along the precise line bisecting the cube face—and reunited, forming a bound state. And no one had seen it because it tunneled under the Aegean, slowly working its way through rock, from far Santorini. It had never broken onto the open soil of Greece. It hid itself in a tomb, waiting silent and content, till it was unearthed.

Claire felt a welling certainty. She thought of that ancient prince, a man who knew well the sharp glint of sunlight on olive trees, the many rich smells of newly turned earth, the wind's whisper of storms coming. Picture a clever man, close to the rub and clamor of the natural world, and then confront him with a tiny point of virulent light that ate everything, that dwelled in the Earth, that sliced through rock itself.

The King must have found it by its piercing, grating whine.

The sound of it feeding. Perhaps the natives of Santorini had seen the thing before, or its twin—watched it break free of fiery rock and rip and burn through their fields, their homes. Would they have called for help, and drawn to them a King who craved danger, loved the hunt, believed that monsters were as natural as rain and sun?

So he had ventured below, into caverns, and come upon the shrill thing that called through massive rock. And when it did not move or emerge, he guessed that it was caught. He did not have to fight it. He could simply chip away at its cage, and take it with him.

But a brave man would want to know what he had. He would look through the small hole, through which the first singularity had entered. From which howling and light emerged.

And would never feel the killing sleet of radiation that flowed out, dooming him to a hideous end months or years from that moment. His end had been sealed then, fating his burial in a corbelled limestone tomb, interred with the glowering ageless beast who killed him.

She turned restlessly, deeply chilled, her mind flooded with ideas, possibilities. John stirred against her, seeking warmth. The blackness pressed in.

What would the King make of it? What tale would he spin from such glory, while his artisans labored to decorate the cubical trap? She tried to imagine the King's death, wasting from the radiation, spinning tales in his delirium, perhaps finally guessing that the growling thing in the stone had given him the sweaty, hot fever dreams, the wrenching nausea, the listless failing death.

She shook John awake. He groaned, fitfully struggling up from some deep place. "Ah?"

"The amber cone, I know what it means."

"What? I dunno . . ."

"It's golden, don't you see? The bull's head in Crete, remember it in the museum?"

He reached up and felt her face in the darkness with icy hands. "Take it easy.. . .Lie back down—"

"No, I'm OK, I only want to tell you this. Listen! The golden horns are ceremonial in Mycenaean civilization, and that's what the King, that dead King up in the tomb, that's

what he had put on his prey. A horn. So the legend was built
around that image, a horned thing in the Earth—"

"I don't—"

"—That the King hunted and killed. Brought back with
him. You see? You and Sergio, you're always talking about
this like it was a new piece of particle physics. But people
saw the singularities then, too, some must have broken onto
the surface, burning and terrorizing and—it was important, it
was *history*."

"Look. . .I'm tired, I—"

"History we know! Only it's gotten all twisted up. What
can you expect of farmers who're trying to describe something as horrible as *that* thing on the loose? The King, he
really was a great King, because he killed the beast. Or captured it, anyway."

"Uh?" He was groggy. "Beast?"

"The beast or god or demon *we* let loose again. We
dropped it down the shaft, so it shot out through that natural
exit—the 'symmetry axis,' you said. Just the way it had come
in, shortly after the King was buried. *Both* singularities lived
in the caves of Santorini and burned people. Maybe the volcanic currents brought them there in the first place. And the
King heard, he came and caught one—heard it humming,
already trapped in the rock! A great quest! He didn't know
there was a twin. They were searching for each other, and
they'd break onto the surface sometimes. How could the
Greeks tell them apart? They thought there was only one."

"So'd. . .we. . . ."

"Yes! And when the King caught it they made up a legend
about the beast. A garbled version of the truth. It was in the
Earth and when the King died, it went back into the Earth.
With its horn! The amber horn!"

"Uh huh."

"The horn is the key." She laughed. "The singularity was
the Minotaur."

CHAPTER
Twelve

Cold that cut bone deep, robbing the body of its will to move, its urge to pump blood into the numbed limbs, even its lust to breathe. He had been cold so long he had lost track of the gathering ache and now it was a separate thing, an aura of pain, a presence that lived in his body with him and fed upon him and would never leave.

He opened his eyes to the consuming dark. From Claire came a mild diffuse warmth, a wan sun about which he orbited in eternal hard blackness. He held her to him and felt her heart thud slowly, almost reluctantly.

She had chattered on for a time and he had half understood what she was driving at, but it all seemed so far away, history and ideas, abstractions as distant as the chilling stars. He had tried to listen but the tiredness pulled the strength out of him and he could barely stay awake. Then she had run down, talked less, her voice happy in a way, a liquid sound in the endless total dark, and finally the sleep had claimed her, too.

He had slept, he was sure of that. How long the two of them had been here he didn't know. He didn't have the will to lift his watch to his eyes. That movement would have let precious heat escape, and anyway time did not matter anymore. Time was simply enduring, and when you stopped doing that there would be no more time, no matter what the watch said.

But now he had woken up and he wished he had not. Asleep, the grasping, leaden pain did not sit on your chest and breathe into your face and send ice knives forking up through your legs into your gut. Asleep was better. Awake was to live and to know what came next.

He blinked, and saw luminescent retinal patterns. Drifting stabs of light, coming and going like drifting clouds, silent and unknowing. The clouds, he had never really looked up into the sky and studied them, never tried to find out what those cottonball ships meant. He had spent his life staring at pieces of paper or endlessly talking or crawling around in the goddamned smelly dirt, when he should have been watching the clouds, lying in the warm sun and sopping up the plentiful eternal heat that came streaming down from the burnt-gold sun, warmth without end. Streaming . . .

Yellow, rippling streamers. Long stabs of light. On the walls.

He moved his hand and could see fingers knotted into a tight fist constricted by cold, a slightly darker outline among the shadows.

He opened his mouth and nothing came out. The tightness in his chest robbed him of air.

"Hey! Arditti! Anderson! Anybody down there?" An echoing call.

"Ah!" he croaked. He shook Claire. "Ah!"

Dimly: "Hear that?"

Even fainter: "No."

"Ah! We, we're here!"

"Damn! Hear that? There's somebody down there."

When John stumbled from the ruin of the tomb he refused to wait for the stretcher they offered. His first few steps had brought savage lancing pinpricks into his legs and he knew abstractly that the circulation would have to hurt anyway, so he walked, just to be in the open. His legs were wooden, chunky logs of blood. The weight on his chest was gone. The exercise of getting into the harness, of dumbly holding onto the rope as they hauled him up, had brought him out of his aching stupor.

He stumbled beyond the tumbled blocks of the tomb and walked slowly out the long entranceway, one hand on the wall. Hale was with Claire, making her lean against him, just ahead. So Hale had come through after all. Good.

A man kept telling John that he should get on the stretcher but he ignored the voice and made his way. There were humming white lamps every five yards or so and the whole area was lit brilliantly. Helicopters clacked overhead and jets roared, cruising above the clouds. The Sixth Fleet was present in force. Carmody had dropped the mask.

John reached the end of the entranceway and sagged against the last rough limestone blocks. The fire in the camp had died out and a ceiling of murky smoke hung over the valley. Helicopters rested on a flat space to the east. The men who rescued them had come in them, obviously; the stretcher bearers were approaching from that direction. Crimson dawn rimmed distant hills.

But his attention turned immediately to the blue spark that drifted in the west, at the far end of the valley. Above it hung Claire's helicopter, the bulky crate suspended like an egg sac below. The helicopter drifted north and below it by sympathetic magic the hot blue point followed, echoing each turn. It was as though the singularity was on a leash, obediently following the pilot's unspoken orders.

They had drawn it away from the tomb and into an area where they could maneuver it, test out its response. Now as John watched the helicopter lowered and the underside of the crate flexed open.

The engineers had designed this with simple failsafe devices, but in fact no one knew whether it would work. Decades of research on extracting fusion energy had advanced enormously the art of magnetically confining plasmas. Physicists knew how to trap and hold hot ionized matter in magnetic pouches shaped like donuts or figure eights or links of sausage. But this thing was not a plasma, and the physicists' experience might not apply. Experience yielded only crude rules of thumb, approximations.

Men had gathered near him but they let him be. He tucked numb hands into the folds of the down jacket they'd given him. Claire and Hale sat on the hillside. There was no talk. The helicopter slowly lowered the crate, rotors slapping. The crate's underside was a complex contraption of magnets and conducting surfaces. Heavy steel plates shielded the helicopter from the singularity's spitting gamma radiation.

The blue-white sun rolled on its own fire, scorching the

land, scratching a path of orange flames, leaving smoking plumes in its wake. A faint keening came from it, and when it bit deeply into soil the high notes drowned and a long, low bass note sounded down the valley as it ate.

Perhaps the ancients of Santorini had seen it like this. John reflected that he could easily believe this thing was a monster of the scalding volcanic depths, bellowing its rage, bringing scorching death as vengeance for man's failure to send it sacrifices, failure to come and seek and appease it in its vast, sulphurous labyrinth.

The crate came closer, lowering, its white now a dusky blue as it reflected the fire below. Nearer, nearer—a brilliant flash, a thundering clap. Suddenly the whole scene was plunged into darkness.

The shock of disappearance was frightening and everyone gasped. But then John saw that the helicopter's running lights still shone. The twin singularity had been drawn into the trap and found its brother, and now they slumbered together. The binding energy of recombination was very minor compared with the megatons he and Zaninetti had calculated. But they had assumed the worse case, when the two met with high velocities. Slowed, the twinned twists recombined softly. The flame was snuffed.

A ragged cheer from the crowd. The helicopter rose, its engines revving triumphantly.

So at low speeds the energy lost from binding the twins was quite little. He should have known that, if he had had time or wit enough to think through Claire's theory. If the two singularities had reunited while inside the cube, 3500 years ago, then obviously they couldn't have released much energy—otherwise the cube itself would've been blown apart. He and Claire and poor dead George would never have discovered more than fragments. He chuckled to himself. If he and Zaninetti had paid more attention to the archeology, maybe they'd have been spared some of this.

Now, as long as they kept the two twins united, they could experiment with them, open up a whole new field of physics. Keeping them confined, that was the problem. There was lots to be done. He tried to concentrate on the possibilities but found his head was a smoky, blurry place where ideas darted away into the murk.

Hale and Claire were standing beside him, he saw. The stretcher bearers came at a trot. He decided that indeed, the broad white expanse of the stretcher, and the luxuriant blankets, did beckon.

"Are you. . .OK?" Claire asked.

"C minus, as we say in the teaching trade," John said wanly.

"Sonuvabitch," Hale said wonderingly, pointing at the helicopter. "It works."

"Yeah," John said. "Until somebody drops it."

EPILOGUE

She was going to be late.

Claire hurriedly assembled the xeroxed pages, tucked them in the envelope addressed to *Science*, and licked the flap. Done.

She had set herself the quite probably neurotic goal of finishing the review paper by this date, and now "Ethnohistoric Connections Between the Minotaur Myth and an Unusual Mycenaean Burial Artifact" was ready for the sanctified precision of print. She had planned a somewhat more circumscribed piece—just the facts, ma'am, as John described it— to be followed by a full book, which would try to link the separate pieces of the puzzle in a lengthy format, copiously annotated with reservations, maybes, on-the-other-hands and however-ifs.

But as word leaked out through February and March, she saw that piecemeal publishing would only bring the academic predators more quickly. Someone would see the connections and publish a short note in *Ethnoarcheology* or somewhere, nailing down the general idea. To protect herself she had to make a big splash on the first go. A few phone calls to major figures in the field had established that *Science* would welcome a paper touching on the mysterious events in the Peloponnese. John was slated to give a review talk on his theory in New York next week, and the two would dovetail nicely.

Claire gathered her things and left her office without bothering to straighten the mess on the desk. Time enough for that later, much later, somewhere in the rest of her life. She fidgeted her key into the lock, unfamiliar with the ancient warp of the door. The department had grandly offered her a new office, about three times larger than her former claustrophobic cubbyhole, and with a commanding view of the Charles. There had not been enough time to sort her files. She left a note to the cleaning man to leave everything where it was for the weeks she would be away.

Commonwealth Avenue shimmered in late spring green. Bedraggled students passed, self-absorbed as finals approached. She drew in the damp air, its weight promising a humid summer. The welcome press in her lungs reminded her of smoking, which she had given up months ago and still missed, a fidgety lust. She found a mailbox. The solid thump as it received the manuscript neatly punctuated her life. Done and done and done.

She found her Alfa Romeo, threw away the parking ticket under the wiper, and pulled out into traffic with a screech. She had deliberately left her briefcase behind in the office; while preparing the paper, it had come to symbolize the weight of the past year.

A horn blared at her as she darted onto Storrow Drive. She glanced at her watch. Probably the best bet was to shoot up to Cambridge Street and loop into town. Early afternoon on a May Saturday, the baseball crowds were headed the opposite way, toward Fenway Park. She made good time, overtaking Volkswagens with her customary contempt.

The swelling, time-consuming labor of putting together the paper had come when she tried to nail down corroborating evidence. Time enough later for experts on Minoan ethnohistory and the archeologeology of Santorini to come forward with their suspected connections and compatible ideas, all based on fragments of pots and scattered bits of metal and wood. That was all fine and good. But the clincher would have to come from new research.

She had persuaded Carmody to map the ruined outlines of the shaft that lay in the sea near the tomb. The Sixth Fleet had taken up a shore-hugging formation for a week following the incident, covering a scientific team that explored the effects of the singularity on the terrain in detail. There had been plenty of time for divers to verify that the shaft made a straight line which, drawn on a larger map, neatly sliced through Santorini. What's more, the line passed through the giant caldera of the exploded volcano, not through the remaining crescent of the present island. That implied that the singularity left Santorini, searching for its twin, before the final eruption.

Was it coincidence that the movements of the singularities, the dead King's quest for one of them, and the eruption of 1426 B.C., all occurred at about the same time? Or had the King gone to Santorini to find the mythic beast, to quell it, because the natives saw with foredoomed intuition a connection between the sun-bright, scorching things and the restless massive tremors beneath their feet? Did the singularities *cause* the eruption?

So perhaps the Minotaur legend had come from man's futile effort to control the world, block the uncaring shrug of the Earth that would send down into dust all his creations. Then all the wondrous myths of the Minotaur became a tale of pride, of hard-won temporary success, transmuted by tribal talk into a story about a thing half man and half beast.

Still, as John said, maybe wasn't a theory, maybe was just plain maybe. So she had searched for something firmer, something with the hard glint of physics behind it. The King's bones and scattered tools were in some of the crates brought back early by Hampton, so she had worked on those. A radiological analysis of the bones showed a clear excess of several isotopes. The King had suffered a lethal dose of radiation. Other bones from the tomb floor, from other bodies, showed no excess. To her this was the capping argument. The singularity had slain him even in his moment of great victory.

Archeology was a quiet, methodical field. Like all sciences, it rewarded caution. She was advancing a theory from which later evidence might force her to retreat, speculating broadly in order to explain seemingly isolated facts. This was always dangerous, and she knew it. But audacity was in her blood now and she liked the zest of challenge.

Cambridge Street was unusually jammed. She kept looking at her watch. There was still time to get ready, but just barely.

She passed the JFK Building, turned onto Tremont Street, pulled over to the right and parked the car in an illegal zone. She spotted her Uncle Alexander standing at the intersection of Tremont and School Street, talking with two Irish policemen. She hugged him, pointed to her car, and from the way the policemen touched their caps and nodded she saw that Uncle Alexander had already tipped them. The No Parking sign was temporary, flimsy, she saw now; this block was clear and there were plenty of spaces. Uncle Alexander made a joke and she laughed, feeling her chest expand, the cramped anxiety lofting away.

King's Chapel crouched like an indomitable bulldog of the past, square and gray and blockish among the mindless high-rises of School Street, monotonous in their endlessly repeated windows. Claire hurried across Tremont on the light. In front of King's Chapel, Uncle Charlie was talking to Aunt Edna, so rapt in gossip that they missed her as she slipped between the formidable solemn columns and into the central portal.

A small sign warned PRIVATE CEREMONY. Good; no tourists. Their shuffling, blank attentiveness had always muted the tone of churches for her, given them an air as public as railway stations. King's was an historical site, its granite towed on barges from open pits in Quincy in 1749. Its gravid solemnity enveloped her and she stood for a moment, unnoticed by the early arrivals in the forward pews. The stony Episcopal values that King's first introduced into the New World had faded into that stoic Bostonian compromise with the future, Unitarianism. The church still lacked its white Protestant spire, though hard-pressed building committees still occasionally brought out the centuries-old plans for one. The past inevitably seemed melancholy here, as if the hushed and graceful spaces remembered when they were the pivot of a theocratic Boston. Yet in the narthex were signs of persistent purpose: the chaotic bulletin board and hopeful pamphlet rack announcing the inner life.

She turned and ascended the stairs, steep enough to win Cotton Mather's no-nonsense stern approval. Here were the others—jittery, nervous, knowing she was late. She made the usual excuses and surrendered herself to them: mother, assorted aunts, cousins, all in tasteful mauve or muted yellow or puce. Most had come down from Vermont or New Hampshire, where so many of the old families had retreated; travel time had dictated an afternoon wedding. They had the old dress, passed down from Great-grandmother, still a trim and brilliant white. Her own dress evaporated and the ancient cloth enveloped her, carried on impatient hands. The air up here was close, with that cloying smell of varnish and trapped heat. Claire had invested three hours yesterday in having her hair done, and was relieved to find, in the mirror, a well-sculpted cap of faintly blondish brown. Her mother hovered, adjusting the hem, minutely tugging the shoulders so Claire's slip straps did not show. The elaborate, embroidered mantilla seemed almost excessive, but calmed her with its comforting drape about the shoulders. She turned before the mirror, inspecting, critical, and was pleased to find its folds conformed elegantly to the slopes of her body; Great-grandmother must have felt the same sly satisfaction.

Talk swirled around her, approving, remembering, tremulous with an ordained excitement. These women called out their assent in coos of admiration and she saw them affectionately in their pastel gowns, immersed in their element. She had always thought them admirably bright in the minutia of living and strangely passive in the larger curve of their lives. Now she was not so sure. Perhaps it was possible to gather from so many petals a bouquet of fresh meaning.

Slow swells from the organ loft. Below, dutiful cousins were escorting relatives to the box pews. The air of anticipation rose; other boxes yawned, beckoning, yielding jewelry; she chose a pearl ring but rejected any necklace, as too great a contrast with the ivory excellence of the mantilla.

Time. She descended the steep steps, shoeless upon the advice of her hovering mother, afraid she would stumble. At the stone floor she paused and a cousin slipped on her white satin pumps. The box pews were nearly filled, their red cushions a rich display beneath the upward swoop of the white Corinthian columns. The organ stopped on signal. She glanced up and saw the organist nod to her, smiling, and begin with gusto, *Here comes the bride*, and she thought with a shock that, incredibly, it was she.

Down the aisle, on the arm of her red-cheeked grandfather. Past the pulpit, paneled and pilastered, its sounding board hanging above, a symbol of authority all unused for this ceremony. The minister smiled at her and the music swarmed up and there was John, coming forward in white tux to claim her. She recited the archaic vows, suitably altered to omit promises of obeying, all in a husky tone that seemed tentative and inaudible in the open spaces encasing her.

As they left to a Vivaldi trumpet voluntary, she glanced back at the scene, the crowd, to remember it. Then, without noticeable pause, she was at the reception at Eliot House, 6 Mount Vernon Place. She and John arrived first, chauffeured, to the welcoming salute of the caterer, who pressed lobster salad rolls and brimming glasses of champagne upon them. The reception line formed before she had finished admiring the flowers, and John's father, resplendent in his tux, asked the first kiss of the reception. Uncle Alex gave her a burly hug and repeated his old joke about an archeologist being a person whose future lay in ruins.

They were all there, the seldom seen denizens of distant farms and villages, and John moved among them, smiling, genuinely engrossed in whatever they had to tell him, no matter what lore of regional delirium they summoned up. Aged uncles asked him if it really was true that atoms were little solar systems, the electrons whirring around like planets. Aunts moved about the room, unsteady, carefully navigating past the treacherous unpadded furniture. She realized that he was genuinely interested, and that he still carried the automatic Southern faith that families were intrinsically fascinating.

Sergio approached, beaming. "*Esquisito.* I did not think the Bostonians, they knew how to do these things."

"We've had many Italians to teach us."

"So you have indeed. I hope you will come to supper when you return. And in the fall, John will be in the department."

"Of course." By "the department" he meant, obviously, Harvard.

The offer had come to John out of the blue, six weeks ago. A discovery of this magnitude carried perks, fame, security. She had been so involved, so fretful over her breach of ethics, that she had quite missed the true import of it all. John had gotten a dozen offers in a single month, with Harvard coming as the crowning touch. He would be an assistant professor; tenure seemed automatic.

Sergio congratulated John effusively and Abe Sprangle joined him. Abe and Claire were to collaborate on a detailed paper about the artifact once she returned. Already it was Abe's best-known work, and it had not even been written, much less published. The rumor mill made more reputations than the journals.

The crowd noise rose and the band began. She waltzed with abandon, not consciously remembering the steps but falling into them with ease, her head high, the chandelier lights whirling like constellations. In a momentary giddiness she leaned her forehead forward onto John's white tux, seeing it as a clean expanse to rest upon, as welcoming as the stretcher had been that distant morning.

Her mother gathered the principals around for the obligatory photographs. A ferret-faced man arranged lights and people, then maneuvered them through the ordained configurations of immediate family, stiff group shots, static-smile closeups. Though this was the least natural event of all Claire felt uplifted by it, encased in unfurling eggshell light, oddly able to see them all as though they were fixed forever, not she. Her mother toasted the new couple, holding high a cup of mysteriously potent punch: "Cheers, dears." A dribble of spilled punch fell, turned into amber drops, and the photographer snapped them up, froze them—wobbly globes hanging in slanting yellow sunlight, to her mother's genteel yet slack-jawed surprise.

Professor Hampton appeared, grinning, face flushed with the heat of champagne. "I certainly am looking forward to having you in the department," he said with forced jollity. "This has all been the *pièce de resistance* to a truly in*cred*ible year."

She smiled and said something meaninglessly polite. She might stay at BU another year, but she was damned if she'd remain under Hampton's tutelage. Either he went or she would. But that was another battle, she reminded herself, another day.

"I believe you should change for your plane," her mother said. The party was swirling about her, voices shifting up in timber, a ripe fullness in the air. She did not want to leave. She wished to cling to this afternoon and savor it, a moment she had thought would never come, that she had halfway feared anyway. But it had all come out, she had found the distant shore, and time did not need to stand still.

"It's time," John said at her elbow.

*　　*　　*

Summer had shouldered its way through the gossamer Manhattan spring, bringing a swarming, leaden heat to the afternoons. They made lunch an ample center of the day and retired to their room at the Astor for the hottest hours, lazing away the time in an erotic haze. A week went by without a feeling of time spent, but rather of a river's movement, the current endlessly streaming and yet the river never changing.

They had told no one their destination. John's father had driven them to Logan, in a car besmirched with shaving lotion and JUST MARRIED signs. At the Callahan Tunnel the driver ahead of them paid their toll, honking and waving in salute. John's father had helped them with the luggage and then given John a solid, man-to-man handshake of goodbye. On the plane they both agreed that the reception had been wonderful, and in fact they regretted having to leave before it dissolved.

The ample, almost wasteful busyness of New York enveloped them. They steeped themselves in art, ate well, saw the season's hit play, *I Would If I Could But I Can't So I Won't*. John liked it, Claire didn't. They spent a morning at the new amusement park between 130th and 142nd Streets. It was artfully done, a technicolor carnival planted like a Bradbury fantasy in the middle of a block's-wide greensward. The rolling hills reminded her of a golf course, and indeed their foundations were heaps of bricks from the tenements that had squatted here. Two phony skyscrapers towered above the rides and booths, serving as props for a frightening ride known inevitably as The Beast With Two Backs. Claire took it once and emerged trembling.

The sensation came back that night and she wrestled up from sleep, gasping.

"John, I—I—"

He woke and saw instantly. He held her for a long time, stroking her, and listened to the disconnected images pour from her. Falling on the roller-coaster blended with the swinging, terrifying descent down the shaft. And her panicky, whistling plunge ended at a mouth, the gaping hole with gleaming horns above and snorting scalding breath—bellowing, teeth sharp and rasping, eyes flared and white-hot with devouring rage.

"They'll come for a while longer," he said quietly.

"They'll go away, though. I've had them, too."

"Really?"

"Of course."

"You never said."

"We're not supposed to. It's the price of owning a penis." She laughed. "Idiot."

"Only where you're concerned."

The next day the chairman of the New York meeting of the American Physical Society took them to lunch at a new vegetarian restaurant, the decor in opulent contrast to the stern, sparing menu. Claire gathered that the place allowed businessmen an opportunity to chasten themselves with a morally uplifting lunch. Each vegetable was brought with a flourish, as if it was a new course. Over the entree—a chicken-shaped thing of mashed nuts—the chairman asked John if he would consent to a press conference after his invited talk.

"Nope."

"It wouldn't have to be very long," the thin-faced man said anxiously.

"Good. Let's take that to the asymptotic limit of none at all," John replied cheerily.

That afternoon, waiting while John prepared his viewgraphs in a side room, Claire roved among the physicists. In several large rooms standing panels formed corridors, and each long board had papers and graphs pinned to it. Men and women stood in front of them, framed by the papers they had authored, answering questions, handing out preprints, defending their ideas. It seemed very far from the meetings of archeologists, who tended to hold forth in lengthy verbal talks illustrated by slides in darkened rooms, answering questions only briefly at the very end. That bull-moose-like pattern, trumpeting one's position from a lordly lectern, had always irritated her. The physicists, with their unassuming posters, flatly displayed to lure an audience by snagging their curiosity, seemed more honest and democratic than the humanists.

John's talk went well. He spoke with a perceptible Southern drawl, underlining highlights in viewgraphs already crammed with equations. He had formalized his approach to the singularity problem, using mathematical entities of his own invention, their dizzying complexity belied by a simple, subscripted notation. She had seen a poster paper on these compacted symbols, described as "Bishop functions," in the hall outside; here, too, word of mouth had attracted science's necessary army of detail-worriers.

The reunited singularity pair had been carefully carried back to the United States, insulated from any shocks and cupped in overlapping traps. A few months of study at MIT had clarified some of their properties, but the question of the stability of the configuration remained. John's mathematical model was a simplified approximation, leaving out several local distortions, such as the Earth's gravity itself. John and Sergio had labored to improve the model, with limited results.

The nettlesome problem of stability eventually got booted up to the National Security Agency. No one knew precisely how good the magnetic trap was. John and Sergio were reasonably certain that the twinned singularities were no danger because they no longer had any binding energy to yield up. "They're as safe as two ordinary rocks," John had said when he appeared before a secret session in Washington.

The National Security Agency preferred caution. They ordered that the magnetic traps be improved by encasing them in an added layer of close-knit magnetic bottles of greater strength. This done, they decreed that further research would be carried out in the High Orbit Laboratory only recently assembled. Of the particle physicists consulted, most thought this an unnecessary and cumbersome precaution. There was no evidence that the pair would break out, and having them handy would surely speed research. None of these arguments convinced the NSA. The shuttle launch had gone off easily the previous week, and the high orbit tug was slowly towing the multi-layered package up to the laboratory dock now.

Carmody had urged this precaution. He had enjoyed a certain notoriety, for the first time in his career, because of the Greek incident. Overall, Claire was surprised at how little initial furor the raid caused. NSA reflexively said little, and the Greeks showed no desire to trumpet a defeat. They were busy with the uneasy truce struck with Turkey, under U.S.-Italian auspices. War still threatened fitfully, but both parties were content for the moment to lick their wounds and fire salvos of words. Most of their energy was spent acquiring more advanced weapons from whomever would supply them, in preparation for what many parties predicted would be merely Round Two.

The hall was packed for John's talk, and the applause afterward kept up for what seemed to Claire an unusually long time for an academic audience. She and John left soon afterward. Three reporters were near the entrance, one with a videocam team shooting over his shoulder. John waved them away. The video team man called, "Dr. Bishop! Dr. Anderson! May I ask you just one question?"

"You just did," Claire replied. Chuckling, John ushered her out into Manhattan's bristly heat.

That night she was restless and awoke quickly to the retching sounds coming from the bathroom. The strangled gurgle echoed from the tiles, amplified, and she swam up from sleep in sudden fear. John was on his knees, his face compressed and red, eyes glazed.

"My God! Are you . . ."

He shook his head weakly and threw up again. He had been this way for a week after Greece. The specialists at the hospital in Wiesbaden said they could not easily estimate how much radiation he had received; unlike Arditti and the others, he had not been carrying a dose badge. The vomiting and drop in corpuscle count indicated a moderate exposure, but these things were not certain; they swam in a gray margin of unknowns.

"I. . .lost it all." He gasped, tears sliding down his nose, mouth yawning for air.

"Do you. . .think . . ." She hovered on the word, not knowing how to express the swelling knot in her.

"That damned phony chicken at lunch. Rotten stuff. Knew it'd get me."

These words threw open a window upon sunlight; she sighed, realizing that she had been holding her breath. "You're. . .sure?"

He got to his feet unsteadily. His skin, pallid from a northern winter, was given an ivory grain by the fluorescent radiance reflected from the tiles. "Science isn't certainty, y'know." He made a broken grin. "It's just probabilities."

The doctors had given him a host of tests, taken samples, fretted over the unknown spectrum of radiation from the singularity. Their fractional uncertainties, stacked atop one another, mounted to a tottering edifice of prediction. His effects might be short term, easily flushed from the body. Longer term damage was difficult to assess. Certainly there was increased cancer risk. If certain symptoms recurred, the prognosis was not good.

She bit her lip and decided to hide nothing, to let her own fear come out. "How long ago did you have one of those blood tests?"

"Just last week." He bent and threw cold water into his face, snorting. "The count was normal. Agh! I can still taste that damned chicken."

"That's. . .good." It seemed suspiciously late to be getting sick from lunch. "I mean . . ."

He smiled. "I know. Always ask me, Claire. Always unload your feelings onto me. That's what I want."

"I . . ." She blinked back tears. "Thank you." She put her arms around his shoulders.

"Let me brush my teeth first," he said gently. "Or you'll love me less in the morning."

She grinned. "Come to bed and I'll give you a present."

"Gee, I always liked presents when I was a kid. Tell me what it is. Can I ride it?"

"As much as you want."

Two hours later the telephone rang. When Claire drifted up from a contented warm place, John was talking.

"I see. What kind of motions?"

She propped herself up against the pillow. It was 4 A.M.

"So the paired singularities act together? This isn't driving them apart?"

He bit his lip, concentrating.

"Good, at least whatever's happening isn't disturbing the stability of the pair. But what could make them do that? I mean, they should drift around the cabin, same's any ordinary matter."

She gathered they were talking about the pair up in the high orbital satellite. The tug craft must have reached the big laboratory.

"No, I don't understand it. Can't they control them? Keep them from slamming into the wall?"

He listened, shaking his head. "Well, I can't think of anything right away. Hell, you know what *time* it is?"

John listened for a long time. "No, I can think about it, sure, but I'm not going anywhere."

More talk. Finally, "No, Sergio, 'fraid not." He hung up.

"Sergio? What was his news?" Claire asked.

"The team got the singularities into the lab, or rather they tried to. As soon as they were free to move, the contraption they're in started hugging the walls of the lab."

"What? Moving around?"

"As nearly as I can tell from what he said, the whole rig—singularities, magnetic traps, insulation, the works—has pinned itself against the interior wall."

"One wall? It's not moving?"

"It's settled down, he says. It got stuck against the wall closest to down—I mean, the side closest to Earth."

"Why?"

"I don't know. Sergio says Carmody called him. Didn't know where to reach us, so wondered if Sergio would know where we'd gone."

Claire frowned. "Sergio must've called my mother."

"Right. Carmody wants me to hustle down to Florida. The next shuttle flight is three days away."

"What?" Claire sat up straight, alarmed. "They want you to go into orbit?"

"All the way out to the High Orbital Lab."

"To supervise experiments. To figure it out for them."

"Right. Only I'm not going."

"I don't want you to."

"On my honeymoon? Not likely."

They talked further, drowsy, and John fell asleep before Claire did. Still, two hours later the telephone rang again John answered it again. As she revived, she saw he must have been already awake, because he held a yellow lined pad in his lap and had covered it with squiggles of equations.

"Yes ma'am, I know that ma'am, but—"

A pause.

"I'd reached much the same conclusion myself, just now. Both the singularities must be attracted by a very long range force. They're being drawn to something on Earth. Or in the Earth, it doesn't matter."

Another pause.

"Of course, it does imply some further interaction, something we don't understand yet. They're being pulled back toward Earth, that's right, so they preferentially get pinned on the inner wall, and—"

The voice on the other end became louder.

"Yes, I agree it's potentially very important. No, I don't see the implications immediately, not fully—"

More argument from the other end.

"But I'm on my honeymoon, for Chrissake—"

Claire snuggled close to him. Tension came into his voice.

"I'm afraid not, ma'am. I won't."

His lips compressed as he listened and a set, adamant look came into the bunched muscles of his jaw.

"I've been here before. No thanks."

He listened only a short time and then said loudly, "I said *no* and I meant it," slamming the phone down. He puffed dramatically with exasperation.

"Who was it this time?"

"The President."

"The president of MIT? Why would—"

"No, of the US."

"*What*?"

"I *told* 'em I wouldn't go."

"John. . .you. . .*hung up* on the President of the United States?"

"Yeah." He thought a moment, staring into the distance. "I really did, didn't I?" He chuckled with pleasure. "She just plain wouldn't take no for an answer. Strong-minded lady. But I figured I had no more to say."

Though they talked about it for another half hour, John saw no reason to reconsider. He peered moodily into space, thinking.

"You know," he finally said, "those twins must not be the basic unit, the fundamental bound system. Our equations say they are, but this attraction to Earth means we've been too simplistic, assumed too much."

"Your theory is wrong, then?"

He grinned. "The tragedy of science is the heartless murder of beautiful theories by ugly facts."

"How wrong?"

"Too early to tell. Ever since Greece, I've been running around like a chicken with its head chopped off. No time to think. But I have been mulling over one thing, an over-simplification. Sergio and I did a theory of singularities in flat space, with no overall gravitational curvature of space-time. Thing is, over distances as big as the space station orbit, that's not a good approximation. The change in the gravitational curvature due to the Earth is substantial. We should include that."

"How hard is that?"

"It shouldn't be so all-fired difficult. Maybe that'll change the basic equations enough, and some new force term will pop out."

"What's attracting the pair to the Earth?"

"Other pairs. Or maybe singles, unmatched singularities. I bet this is the first time there've been a pair off the surface of Earth for a very long time. If there is some attractive force between all singularities of this type, an aspect of the whole force law we've missed—then the ones on Earth are going to be drawn up to the surface, trying to reach that satellite."

"From below?"

"If there are any down there, burrowing their way around. And there must be. It takes an enormously high energy collision to make these things, granted. But Sergio integrated the rate equations for cosmic ray events that could yield massive singularities like ours, and he calculated there should be at least a few hundred produced inside the Earth's volume, since the planet formed. Cosmic rays come booming in, smack into nuclei in the Earth, and you get a singularity."

"Deep in the Earth?"

"Well, except for your dead King, nobody's found any on the surface. The rest must be wandering around down there."

"Then. . .they might pop out at any time. Pairs . . ."

"Right. Or singles."

"That would be terrible."

"Sure would."

"What can we do?"

"I'm not sure. I hadn't considered possibilities like long range forces. The equations . . ."

"Do you think you could find some way of, well, pacifying

them? Some more complex configuration, a new bound state?"

John smiled. She recognized the look now, a turning inward. He was remembering the way the howling thing had devoured Kontos, and the legacy it had left him in his own blood and body, leaving him with an uncertainty, a precarious hold on life itself. For them both, that night had been the end of the long summer of youth, an end of bright assurance— all lost without real regret, for they now sensed a new need that could be met only in each other. From the comfortable small compass of their academic lives they had been sucked into the raw world, a window thrown open on the whistling abyss. Yet in that fact there was a curious maturing freedom, a restful bittersweet glade. Their lives were now touched by freshening unknowns, like science itself, provisional and personal and evolving.

"Sure," he said. "For a while."

A TECHNICAL AFTERWORD

Our relations as experimentalists with theoretical physicists should be like those with a beautiful woman. We should accept with gratitude any favors she offers, but we should not expect too much or believe all that is said.

—Lev Artsimovich

In fiction about science, it is difficult to loft into the realms of high theory without risking a nosebleed. My mood in constructing this book has been playful, as if to say, see how *odd* the world could be? I include this afterword to answer, for the reader who wants to know a bit more, the salient question: just how imaginary *is* this dragon I have introduced into a relatively real garden?

A crucial property of the artifact is that the force between it and its twin is *constant*, independent of distance. It is just as strong when they are 5000 kilometers apart as it is when they are mere centimeters away. This is odd, indeed, for everyday objects, but not at all in the world of particle physicists.

In 1964, hundreds of new particles were being discovered. They were all subject to the "strong interaction," the force that holds protons together in a nucleus. Murray Gell-Mann and George Zweig suggested that this zoo of particles could all be made up of more fundamental building blocks, called quarks. Only three quarks, suitably combined, would account for the hundreds of apparently different particles. This was aesthetically pleasing, and everyone liked the notion.

Better, it was successful. The theory predicted particles which hadn't been seen before, and experimenters duly found them, with all the right properties. There was a serious problem, though, hinging upon what is called Pauli's Exclusion Principle.

Simply said, the Principle commands that no two particles with spins of ½ (say, electrons) can be identical. All that identifies a particle is a set of quantum numbers which describe energy, momentum, spin and other properties. This means that no two electrons in the world can have exactly the same numbers. To differ by at least one quantum number, they can be located in different atoms; that takes care of Pauli's requirement for nearly all electrons. For electrons in the same atom, though, the Principle introduces a very important bit of new physics.

A helium atom, for example, has two electrons. The Principle, which has been well verified, says that since they have many properties in common (mass, energy, charge, orbital angular momentum), they *must* differ in spin. And indeed, they do.

If you look one level higher in the periodic table, at lithium, you find that its three electrons have two precisely like a helium atom's, but the third must occupy a higher energy state; it cannot ape either of the others.

One can build up all the elements this way, requiring that each added electron be different. That explains the difference in chemistry between atoms, and therefore, the whole periodic table. This was the revolutionary understanding that quantum mechanics brought.

Quarks run afoul of Pauli's Principle because you cannot pack apparently identical quarks into a larger particle. Yet there were particles that demanded such an explanation. To explain completely the confusing swarms of observed particles, and still obey the Pauli Principle, physicists had to invoke a new quantum number, which described an added property, called *color*. An unfortunate choice of words, perhaps, because this facet of quarks has nothing to do with what you and I call color.

This lets quarks crowd into a larger particle, determining its properties, because the quarks could always happily differ in their color quantum number. At first the three choices of color were red, white and blue. Some Europeans correctly pointed out that white was not a color, and suggested a change to yellow. I always wondered if they secretly objected because these were the colors in the US flag (and the British), but I suppose that is an unprofessional suspicion. Even yellow wasn't used by everybody, though, for the prosaic reason that green shows up better during talks using an overhead projector.

This color-coded theory worked well, successfully predicting particles. Interestingly, all observed particles are "colorless"—the three colors add together to yield no color at all. Now, all this seemed like a bookkeeping device, and many physicists regarded color and even quarks themselves as mathematical conveniences, mere recipes. Successful predictions, though, in a variety of detailed experiments, have convinced most physicists. But an annoying question kept popping up: Why don't we see individual, naked quarks?

Here again, color saved the day. It turns out that color is as basic a facet of particles as their charge. We all know that charge permits particles to experience the electric and magnetic forces, which we see acting daily in everything from pop-up toasters to lightning. Color is more subtle, though. It regulates the "strong" force, which holds together tiny, subnuclear particles. It is the underpinning of our whole world, and we obliviously rely on it to hold matter itself together for our convenience.

The difference is that electric forces don't have to exchange charge, even though they use them. When a radio signal travels from a commercial station to your receiver, it doesn't convey charge. Instead, it wiggles the electrons in your antenna, and your receiver amplifies this wiggling, to draw out the message. There is no net charge transmission.

Color is more demanding than charge. It has to flow from one spot to another before the strong force will work. This simple difference makes it impossible to see free quarks.

Electrons, which have charge, make simple fields. We can draw these field lines from the electron, spreading out spherically.

The strength of the electric force is proportional to how many of these lines cross a given area. Far away from the electron, there are fewer lines in a given neighborhood, so the force is weaker. Gravitation works the same way. That's why the Earth, which is nearby, attracts us more powerfully than does the Sun, even though the Sun has much more mass.

Two electrons nearby have field lines that link them, running from one to the other:

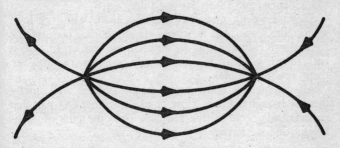

Again, the strength of the force is determined by the number of field lines which cross a given area.

Now take two quarks, Q and Q, which have color, not charge. The color must flow steadily between the quarks, like a current. We can make an analogy by saying this color flow is like electrical charge flow (currents), which produce magnetic fields. We can imagine wires between the two quarks, which carry electrical currents. These cause magnetic fields, and the fields squeeze the wires closer together (called the "pinch effect"). The wires crowd together, making a tight group of field lines:

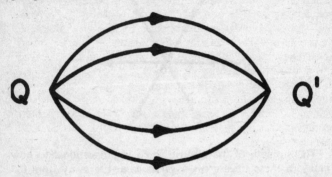

Now the number of lines crossing a given area is larger than in the electrical case. In fact, the number is constant, since they squeeze together along the cramped axis between the quarks. Since the number of field lines lancing through an area is constant, the force between the quarks is constant, too, independent of how far apart they are.

Suppose we try to pull two quarks apart. We work hard against the force, and it never gets any easier, because the force doesn't diminish as we separate the quarks. In fact, it isn't merely difficult to separate two quarks so we can see them, it's impossible.

All this pulling adds energy to the system, until finally there is enough to create more quarks—another QQ' pair that appears, *poof!*, out of the vacuum. Then the tube of wires breaks, and we have:

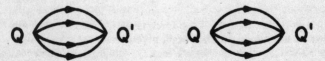

Two sets of closely bound quarks again! Trying to separate a QQ' pair—which are really a pair made up of a quark and an anti-quark, to be technical—is like trying to isolate one pole of a magnet. Chop a bar magnet in half and you don't get a "north" end and a "south" end—you just end up with two smaller magnets, each with two poles.

Similarly, pulling quarks apart—say, by ramming an electron and an anti-electron together and watching the wreckage—gives you quark-antiquark pairs. In such an experiment, we see narrow jets of particles flying apart in opposite directions. They started as a single QQ' pair that in turn decayed into a lot of other debris.

You can think of the electric field as a swarm of "photons" surrounding a charge. Similarly, around a quark there is a "gluon" swarm. ("Gluon" because they glue strongly interacting objects together; the terminology of physics isn't all that high-falutin', after all.) But gluons don't let quarks get free, where we can see them.

Or rather, they're not free on a scale that humans can see. The strong force is so powerful that quarks can't get more than an infinitesimal distance away from each other.

So I began to think.. . .What if there was a force regulating very, very heavy particles? If it was weak enough, it would allow the heavy particles to separate quite a bit. Was this possible?

Square Forces in a Round World

The first trouble crops up immediately. For a weak, though quarklike force, the mass of the particle must be large—say, a ton or so. Yet it is *one particle*—and quantum mechanics tells us that particles can also be considered as wavelike. The wavelength of a particle is smaller, the larger the mass. A one-ton particle would have a wavelength so small that its mass would be compressed into an unimaginably small volume. Its density would be so high that its gravitational attraction would be enormous at its surface—so strong that light itself could not escape. That is, it would be a mini-black hole.

This means things are getting very exotic, indeed. On the other hand, this links up with our ideas about quarks. There are theories of gravity which may apply when the quantum nature of matter acts on the same dimensions as does gravity. These "supergravity" theories have quantum numbers similar to color.

Suppose supergravity is right. Then in the future, characters like John Bishop and Sergio Zaninetti could determine the quantum numbers by known methods of calculation. Instead of the boring old gravitational force law, out pops an attractive force which is quarklike.

At first, John and Sergio know only that the particle is awfully massive. They then realize that it warps the spacetime around it in a cubic way—another exotic property! Everything in our ordinary experience is dominated by spherical forces, like gravity. But this object doesn't pull with equal force in all directions. How to reconcile these facets?

John remembers his boyhood experience with a strange, moving water wave. It was a soliton, and in fact seeing one move down a canal was how they were discovered in the 1830s. These "solitary waves" are concentrations of energy which stay confined and do not dissipate.

It is easy to miss soliton-type solutions in the equations of mathematical physics. Solutions revealing wavelike motions are technically easier to extract, so historically they have been favored. Only lately have we begun to find the harder solutions, and many suspect that such exotic animals lurk in the Einstein equations for gravitation.

So far, few soliton solutions have been pursued in gravitation. Although the compressed notations of Einstein's equations are elegant, they conceal a bewildering complexity—a set of ten coupled, nonlinear differential equations. To make these manageable, mathematicians nearly always assume spherical symmetry. After all, stars and planets are spherical, and perhaps the universe is too, in a more generalized sense.

The equations don't tell you how to solve them. So far they have rewarded simple assumptions, like spherical symmetry in the resulting objects. But it is quite plausible that cubic symmetry is also "natural," and is allowed by the equations. No one has yet looked for it. There is no evidence either way for these types of solutions, so I imagined that they were there. It fitted nicely into the "fact" that the artifact itself was cubic, and not merely by whim of the artisan who made it.

John proceeds from this assumption. The cubic forms he finds allow a mass of a ton or so. Mathematically, the force arises from a conserved quantity John terms "fashion," which plays a similar role to "color" in the strong force. His conversations with Sergio further reveal the quarklike nature of the force he has discovered, but neither takes the hint. After all, they see a single particle. Nobody sees naked quarks, though. They both think this is a flaw, a puzzle.

Seeing the artifact hanging by a cable, pulled toward the northeast, they both see the solution. The force *is* quarklike, but it's so weak that the "quarks" can be separated enough for humans to see them. In fact, they can wander around as they like, attracted to each other.

From the angle of the cable, they estimate the force is about a tenth of Earth's gravity. The energy required to separate two of them is then the product of this constant acceleration (0.1G) times their separation. To make a new pair of these singularities (mathematically indivisible points) requires 2Mc of energy. Dividing this by the energy of separation, they find that to make a new pair takes a separation of *ten light years*.

This means they'll never see a new pair pop out of nothingness. But the two singularities *can* recombine, yielding a lot of energy—perhaps hundreds of megatons.

Indeed, as John and Sergio study matters further, this new force doesn't seem so crazy after all. The singularity mass is about a ton, which means the force between them is roughly one percent of the force between quarks. So considering the force alone makes the two theories not so wildly different; they differ primarily in the masses involved. This allows the particles to be seen on a human scale of distances.

Another crucial clue for John was the fact that passing a hand over the artifact gave a peculiar, rippling sensation. The rippling of the gravitational field near the singularity caused this, and was direct evidence that the strength of the cubic gravitational potential far exceeded that of the *net* mass of the singularity.

Put technically, the octopole term in the potential (i.e., that which describes forces which have poles, like the magnetic force) exceeded the monopole term (that which describes spherical forces, like gravity) by orders of magnitude. This could only be true of a distorted, soliton-type solution.

To sum up, the physics surrounding this narrative requires only a few assumptions, none of which we know to be false:

1. A soliton solution to the gravitational equations, with cubic symmetry, exists.

2. The force involved has a quantum number similar to quark-style color.

3. It yields a large mass (a ton).

4. The force is about a tenth of gravity.

I have played as fairly as I know how—all the rest of the story follows from these conditions.

Yet see what a richness of circumstance can flow from so seemingly abstract a set of assumptions! Human history is based on assuming a rather humdrum world in which we know all the rules. Change one aspect, and—presto! We are perched on a precarious world view.

I have played rather more circumspectly with the archeology in the story. My only major deception lies in my implication that servants were buried with their masters in Mycenaean tombs. There is no evidence for or against this practice. Indeed, this assumption is not really necessary for my narrative, though it does add a bit of spice.

In all this I am much indebted to Dr. Marc Sher for numerous discussions of the physics involved, and his contribution to this Afterword in particular. Professor Hara Georgiou, a Greek archeologist, caught my errors in an early draft of the manuscript. They have my thanks, though of course they are not responsible for any mistakes which made it through to the final version.

Gregory Benford
Athens-Laguna Beach-Cairo

COSM

Gregory Benford

This is a world in which intellect, passion and politics collide.
This is the real world of science.

On an otherwise ordinary day not long from now, inside a
massive installation of ultra-high-energy scientific equipment,
something goes wrong with a brilliant young physicist's most
ambitious experiment. But this apparent setback will soon
be regarded as one of the most significant breakthroughs
in the history of mankind.

For the explosion has left something behind: a perfect sphere
the size of a basketball, made of nothing known to science.

And when the physicist discovers the secret it holds,
she names it 'cosm'.

'Fascinating . . . this novel's strength lies in its portrayal
of scientists as real people and the explication of the poetry
of sub-atomic physics'
TIME OUT

'Benford is a scientist who writes with verve and insight
not only about black holes and cosmic strings
but about human desires and fears'
NEW YORK TIMES BOOK REVIEW

THE MARTIAN RACE

Gregory Benford

March, 2015. NASA's first manned voyage to Mars
is about to launch.

But disaster strikes. The rocket explodes, killing the
entire crew, and the US government abandons the project.
What they come up with in its place will change
the nature of space exploration for ever.

Businessman John Axelrod and his consortium have every
intention of winning the $30 billion Mars Prize for the first
successful mission to the red planet. He knows that it will
involve far higher risks than the one NASA had planned.
But he has no choice. He has to win.

The Martian Race has begun.

The Martian Race is the extraordinary new science fiction
thriller from the author of the Sunday Times bestseller
Timescape, *Cosm* and *Foundation's Fear*.

'Benford is a scientist who writes with verve and insight
not only about black holes and cosmic strings but
about human desires and fears'
NEW YORK TIMES BOOK REVIEW

EATER

Gregory Benford

When a distinguished astrophysicist is presented with evidence of a new artefact approaching the solar system, his initial reaction is that figures must be wrong. But they are not.

The mysterious object is not only real, it is heading towards us at an incredible velocity.

Then the data indicates that the visitor is a black hole.
A black hole that can change direction.
A black hole that is sending us a message . . .

I DESIRE CONVERSE

EATER is a fast-paced thriller from an author who is both a great storyteller and a highly respected scientist.
It is a combination that makes for classic SF.

FOUNDATION'S FEAR

The Second Foundation Trilogy

Gregory Benford

Isaac Asimov himself suggested that there were areas in his
monumental Foundation series that needed further exploration.
In *Foundations' Fear*, Gregory Benford rises magnificently
to that challenge and the classic series continues . . .

Hari Seldon, close to perfecting his theory of Psychohistory,
is now a reluctant candidate for First Minister. But dangerous
enemies force him to flee Trantor. However, the difficulties
he faces only serve to hone Hari's political skills
for the confrontaion to come.

Benford's superb storytelling, grand vision and firm grasp
of hard science combine to produce an important and
compelling work and take Asimov's Foundation into
new, unexpected and disturbing territory.

EARTH

David Brin

It's forty years from tomorrow, and a black hole has accidentally fallen into the Earth's core. A team of scientists frantically searches for a way to prevent the mishap from causing harm, only to discover another black hole already feeding relentlessly at the core – one that could destroy the entire planet within two years.

But some even argue that the only way to save the Earth is to let its human inhabitants become extinct: to let the million-year evolutionary clock rewind and start all over again.

From an underground lab in New Zealand to a space station in Low Earth Orbit, from an endangered species conservation ark in Africa to a home in New Orleans, EARTH is a gripping novel peopled with extraordinary characters and abundant with challenging new ideas. It is a towering achievement from one of science fiction's most compelling writers.

MARROW

Robert Reed

The Ship is home to a thousand alien races and a near-immortal crew who have no knowledge of its origins or purpose. At its core lies a secret as ancient as the universe.

It is about to be unleashed.

'Robert Reed is the new century's most compelling SF voice . . . *Marrow* is one of the most original visions in a long while'
STEPHEN BAXTER

'It's an exhilarating ride, in the hands of an author whose aspiration literally knows no bounds'
THE NEW YORK TIMES

Orbit titles available by post:

☐ Cosm	Gregory Benford	£6.99
☐ The Martian Race	Gregory Benford	£6.99
☐ Eater	Gregory Benford	£6.99
☐ Foundation's Fear	Gregory Benford	£6.99
☐ Earth	David Brin	£7.99
☐ Marrow	Robert Reed	£6.99

The prices shown above are correct at time of going to press. However, the publishers reserve the right to increase prices on covers from those previously advertised, without further notice.

ORBIT BOOKS
Cash Sales Department, P.O. Box 11, Falmouth, Cornwall, TR10 9EN
Tel: +44 (0) 1326 569777, Fax: +44 (0) 1326 569555
Email: books@barni.avel.co.uk

POST AND PACKING:
Payments can be made as follows: cheque, postal order (payable to Orbit Books) or by credit cards. Do not send cash or currency.

U.K. Orders under £10	£1.50
U.K. Orders over £10	**FREE OF CHARGE**
E.C. & Overseas	25% of order value

Name (Block letters) . . . .

Address . . . .

. . . .

Post/zip code: . . . .

☐ Please keep me in touch with future Orbit publications

☐ I enclose my remittance £ .

☐ I wish to pay by Visa/Access/Mastercard/Eurocard

Card Expiry Date